WANT FREE BOOKS?

Go to http://subscribepage.com/alphastemp to sign up for Renee Rose's newsletter and receive a free books. In addition to the free stories, you will also get special pricing, exclusive previews and news of new releases.

ACKNOWLEDGMENTS

I wrote the first Zandian Masters book in 2016 and I'm grateful fans are still asking for more. I'm so grateful to Alta Hensley who suggested the project that spawned the first book, and to Rebel West who now partners with me on the spin-off series Zandian Brides.

And of course, thank you, readers for indulging my master/slave fantasies!

HIS HUMAN SLAVE

CHAPTER ONE

Zandian Breeding season.

That was the last consideration in his mind before liberating his planet from the Finn.

Breeding season.

Zander sat at the round platform, studying the faces of the elders he respected most, the ones who had risked their lives to save him when the Finn invaded Zandia and wiped out the rest of their species solar cycles before.

"You can't be serious."

"Dead serious," Daneth, the only Zandian physician left in the galaxy said, tapping his wrist band. "You are the best male representative of the Zandian species, the only one left of the royal bloodline, and, more importantly, the only one young enough to produce healthy offspring. If you go to battle without first procreating, our species will die with us." He gestured around the room at the other members of his parents' generation.

He leaned back in his chair and closed his eyes in exasperation. "And exactly which female do you think I will produce these offspring with? Last I heard, there is no Zandian female under the age of sixty left alive."

"You will have to cross-breed. I purchased a program and entered your genetic makeup. It uses all the known gene files in the galaxy to predict the best possible mate for breeding."

He raised his eyebrows. "So have you already run this program?"

Daneth nodded.

He glanced around the table, his gaze resting on Seke, his arms master and war strategist. "Did you know about this?"

Seke nodded once.

"And you approve? This is foolish. My time should be spent training with the new battleships we bought and recruiting an army, not…" He spluttered to a stop.

"The continuation of the species is paramount. What is the point of winning back Zandia if there are no Zandians left to populate it?"

He sighed, blowing out a breath. "All right, I'll bite. Who is she? What species?"

Daneth projected an image from his wrist band. The image of a slight, tawny-haired young female appeared. "Human. Lamira Taniaka. She's an Ocretion slave working in agrifarming."

A human breeder. A slave.

Veck.

Zander didn't have time for this excrement. "There's been a miscalculation." He waved his hand at the hologram.

"No, no mistake. I ran the program several times. This female bested every other candidate by at least a thousand metapoints. This female will produce the most suitable offspring for you."

"Impossible. Not a human. No." Humans were the lowest of the social strata on Ocretia, the planet where his palatial pod had been granted airspace.

"I realize it seems an unlikely match, my lord, but there must be some reason her genes mix best with yours. The program is flawless."

"I thought you might suggest someone worthy of formal mating—an arranged marriage with royalty of another species. Not a breeder. Not a *pet.*" Humans were not mates, they were slaves to the Ocretions. An inferior species. He hadn't had much to do with them, but from what he understood, they were weak, fragile. Their lifespan was short; they did not recover easily from injuries. They spread disease and died quickly. They lacked honor and fortitude. They lied.

Zandians—his species—never lied.

"I was not seeking a lifemate for you—I found the best female for producing your offspring. If you wish to find a mate, after you have bred, I will search the databases for the female most compatible to your personality and lifestyle preferences. But this is the one you must breed. And now, during the traditional Zandian breeding season."

He closed his eyes and shook his head. The breeding season didn't matter. For one thing, they weren't on Zandia—weren't affected by her moons or her atmosphere. For another, he wouldn't be breeding with a Zandian female coming into cycle.

But Daneth was like a sharkhound on a hunt—he wouldn't stop until the stated goal had been reached. He'd been his father's physician and had served on Zander's council as a trusted advisor since the day they'd evacuated Zandia during the Finn's takeover. Zander had been only fourteen sun-cycles then. He'd spent the last fifteen sun-cycles working every day on his plan to retake his planet. He'd settled in Ocretia, where he'd amassed a small fortune through business and trade, making connections and preparing resources, training for war.

"I will take care of everything. I will purchase her and bring her here until you impregnate her. Once it's done, you can send her away. I'm certain you'll be satisfied with the results. The program is never wrong."

"She's human. And a slave. You know I don't believe in keeping slaves."

"So set her free when she's served you." Lium, his tactical engineer spoke.

"A slave will have to be imprisoned. Guarded. Disciplined."

"She's beautiful. Would it be such a hardship to have this woman chained in your bedroom?" This from Erick, his trade and business advisor.

Beautiful? He looked again at the holograph. Dirt covered her hands and cheeks, her unkempt hair pulled back and secured at her nape. But, upon closer inspection, it seemed Erick was right. She was pretty—for a human. Her tangled hair was an unusual copper color and wide-set green eyes blinked at the imager that had captured her likeness. A smattering of light freckles dusted her golden skin. She wore drab, shapeless work garments, but when Daneth hit a command to remove the clothing and predict the shape of her naked body, it appeared to be in perfect proportion—round, firm breasts, wide hips, long, muscular legs. His horns and cock stiffened in unison.

Veck.

He hadn't had that reaction to a female of another species before. He'd only grown hard watching old holograms of naked or scantily clad Zandian females from the archives.

For the love of Zandia.

He didn't want a human. He wanted the impossible—one of his own species, or, if not, then a female of a species that was on the same level as his own, not inferior.

"Why do you suppose her genes are best? What else do you know about her?"

"Well, there's this." Daneth flashed up a holograph of a human man, dressed in combat gear, a light ray gun in his hand, blood dripping from his forehead. "He was her father, a rebel warrior who fought in the last human uprising before her birth. He may even have led it."

"Hmm." He made a noncommittal sound. His species were warriors. Why would he need the human genome for that? "What about her mother?"

"Not much to be found. She's still alive—they're together now, working on Earth-based plant and food growth production. Keeping their heads down, is my guess. The data about her father isn't in the Ocretion database file. My program gene-matched to give me that information. I'm surprised the Ocretions don't do more gene study."

"I'll probably split her in two the first time I use her. Humans aren't built for Zandian cocks."

"The program can't be wrong."

He sighed. "Is she even for sale?"

"No, but you are highly esteemed royalty and the unofficial ambassador from Zandia. I'm sure she can be purchased for the right price." Daneth referred to his position on the United Galaxies. Since the Finns were not recognized by the UG due to their genocidal practices, Zander served as the Zandian ambassador. Not that it did much good. No one on the UG was willing to put their resources behind him to overthrow the Finns.

He made a grumbling sound in his throat. "Fine. But don't spend too much. Our resources are needed for recruiting soldiers."

"Your offspring are top priority. Even over the war plans," Seke said. The male didn't speak often, and when he did, it always had a definitive ring to it, as if his was the last and only word.

"As you wish. I'll breed her. But if she doesn't survive the first coupling, her death is on all of you."

Daneth chuckled. "Humans aren't that weak."

~·~

Lamira crouched beside the row of tomato plants and flicked a bug off the leaf before anyone saw it. The Ocretion foremen always wanted to spray the plants with their chemicals at the first sign of any bugs, even though it had been proven to harm the plants.

Her stomach rumbled. She longed to pluck just one juicy tomato and pop it into her mouth, but she'd never get away with it. She'd be publicly flogged or worse—shocked. The fresh Earth-based fruits and vegetables they cultivated were for Ocretions. Human slaves had to live on packaged food not fit for a dog.

Still, her life was far better than it might be in another sector, as her mother always reminded her. They lived in their own tent and had little contact with their owners after working hours.

It might be worse. She could be a sex slave like the sister she'd never met, her body used and abused by men every day. After the Ocretions took her sister, her father had led a human uprising, which had resulted in his death. Her mother, pregnant with Lamira, had been picked up by slave smugglers and sold to the agrifarm. Her mother had been careful to hide her beauty and taught her to do the same, keeping mud on her face and hair and wearing clothes too big. They hunched when they walked, ducked their heads when addressed, and kept their eyes lowered. Only in their own ragged tent did they relax.

"You, there—Lamira." A guard called her name.

She hunched her shoulders and lifted her head.

"The director wants to see you."

Her heart thudded. What had she done? She was careful, always careful. By the age of seven her mother had taught her to distinguish what was real—what others knew—and what was claircognizance. She'd learned to keep her mouth shut for fear she'd slip up and say something she knew about someone without having been told. Had she made a mistake? If she had, it would mean certain death. Humans with special traits—anything abnormal or special—were exterminated. The Ocretions wanted a population they could easily control.

She dropped the bushel of tomatoes and walked up to the main building, showing the barcode on her wrist to the scanner to gain admittance. She'd never been in the administration building before. An unimpressive concrete slab, it felt as cold and dreary inside as it appeared from the outside. One of the guards jerked his head. "Director's office is that way."

The gray concrete floors chilled her dirty bare feet. The director was a fat, pasty Ocretion female with ears that stuck straight out to the sides and cheeks as paunchy as her belly. Beside her sat a male of a species she didn't recognize.

"Lamira." The director said her name, but didn't follow with any instructions.

She stood there, not sure what to do. She tried for a curtsy.

The humanoid male stood up and circled her. He stood a head taller than a human, but unlike the doughy Ocretions, he was all lean muscle. Tiny lines around the outsides of his eyes and mouth told her he might be middle-aged—whatever that meant for his species. Two small horns or antennae protruded from his head. "She's in good health?"

The director shrugged. "I wouldn't know."

The male lifted her hair to peer under her ponytail. He lifted her arms and palpated her armpits. His skin was purplish-peach, a nice hue—an almost human color. His interest in her seemed clinical, not sexual, more like a doctor or scientist.

"What is this about?" she asked.

The male raised an eyebrow, as if surprised she'd spoken.

The director touched the fingertips of her four-fingered hands together. "They are not house-trained, the humans we keep here. They're mainly used for outdoor agricultural work."

House-trained. What in the stars does that mean?

He cupped her breasts and squeezed them.

She jerked back in shock.

"Stand still, human," the director barked, picking up her shock-stick and sauntering over.

Lamira froze and held her breath. She hated the shock-stick more than any other punishment. She'd heard if you got shocked enough, permanent paralysis or even death may result. In her case, she feared she might say something she shouldn't while coming out of the daze from it.

"I'll take her. We'll require a full examination to ensure her good health, of course, but if everything seems in order, I will pay for her."

The director folded her arms across her chest. "Well, we weren't planning to sell her. I understand Prince Zander has a lot of influence with the United Galaxies, but—"

"Two hundred steins."

Her breath caught. Surely they weren't negotiating for *her*—for her life? What about her mother? Her plants? She couldn't leave.

"Three hundred fifty."

Her head swam and she swayed on her feet. No. This couldn't be happening. Her claircognizance should have warned her about this, but it never worked in her favor— only told her meaningless things about other people. A true curse.

"Done." The male punched something into his wristband and a beep sounded on the director's handheld communication device.

The director glanced at it and smiled. "When do you want her?"

The male gripped her upper arm. "I'll take her now." He bowed. "It was nice doing business with you."

She swung around to meet him, terror screaming in her chest. "I can't— wait—"

The male ignored her, pressing a device to the back of her neck.

She felt a sting before everything went black.

CHAPTER TWO

She awoke on her back, naked in a well-lit clinic of some kind. The same male bent over her, taking blood from her arm.

"Ow." She attempted to move her limb but found her wrists and ankles strapped to the table. "Where am I? What are you doing?" Her tongue felt too thick in her mouth.

As before, he ignored her. He injected her blood into a test tube and shook it with a solution then inserted it into a machine and watched the readouts.

When he returned, he put on a pair of protective gloves. He had five fingers, like a human. He wore a lab coat with a name tag that read *DANETH*.

She licked her dry mouth. "Daneth?"

He gazed directly at her for the first time. "It is not your place to address me, slave."

It wasn't her *place*. Right. This must be the "house training" the director had referred to. Though she'd been a slave all her life, other than suffering hard work and poor conditions, she'd escaped the subtleties of groveling indoor slaves were taught. "Are you my master?" She needed to get clear on what was going on.

"No. Your master is Lord Zander, Prince of the Zandians."

Prince of the Zandians. But Zandia had been taken over by the Finn solar cycles ago. So if this man was a ruler, he was king of nothing. Just another wealthy statesman living in exile in Ocrea territory.

"His name is Lord Zander. What, was he named after his planet?"

Daneth brought the pads of his fingers to her right breast, massaging in small circles around the nipple then squeezing it, hard.

She gasped and jerked.

He repeated the action on the other side, checking the readout on his armband, as if following a protocol. With two fingers in her mouth, he pried open her jaws, adjusting the light from his wrist cuff to shine inside.

"Lift your tongue."

It was stupid, but she refused to obey. She'd inherited her father's rebellious mind, she supposed. Knowing he died trying to free his daughters from this exact situation obligated her to resist.

He nudged her tongue up with his finger. She attempted to snap her teeth closed, but he was far too strong, and she only succeeded in straining the muscles of her jaw and throat. Her rebellion did not seem to bother him.

He traveled down the length of her body, palpating every inch. Her nudity felt shocking after a lifetime of baggy clothes. Someone had washed her and even applied a shimmery powder over her skin. Her hair sprawled in soft waves around her head. It, too, had been cleaned and smelled sweet, like citrus blossoms. Violation at being touched so intimately—especially when she'd been unconscious—coursed through her. She had to get out of here. To escape and—

Veck. She didn't even know where "here" was.

She thought they were finished when he unclipped her ankle cuffs, but he only readjusted them, placing her feet in stirrups to lift and spread her legs.

Her bare sex lay open to him for his examination. Her belly quivered, every muscle in her body tense.

"This shouldn't hurt." His tone was matter-of-fact. With his thumbs, he pried open the outer lips of her sex and spread them wide. He prodded her anatomy with a light touch, pulling back the hood of her clitoris as if to make sure it was there.

She whimpered when he shoved two fingers inside her and used his other hand on the outside to massage her inner wall.

"Does it hurt?" He sounded curious, rather than concerned.

"It's not pleasant," she growled through gritted teeth.

He raised his eyebrows, as if the news surprised him. "Hmm." He removed his fingers from her channel and spread her ass cheeks with his thumb and forefinger.

She lifted her bottom in the air, squeezing her back hole against his examination.

He pushed her pelvis back down and pinned it in place with one hand, wiggling a finger into her anus with the other.

She pinched her lips closed on a moan and held her breath, squeezing her eyes closed and willing it to be over. She could get through this. It was a physical examination.

As long as they didn't find out her real secret, she would survive.

~.~

. . .

Zander exited the battleship, unbuckling his helmet. Training for war had been a part-time job for him since he was fifteen solar cycles old. The rest of his time was a nightmare of campaigning for support to wage war on the Finn, and keeping up with business to fund the war.

A crowd of servants and advisors stood on the landing deck, waiting to brief him on various aspects of business or the household.

"I have her," Daneth said, dropping in to walk beside him as he strode into the pod.

Veck. The breeder. His new slave.

"Where? Here?"

"In my lab."

"Fine. Bring her to my chamber." *Ugh.* The thought of breeding with another species turned his stomach, but he'd do what he had to do. He entered his chamber and washed up.

When he emerged from the washroom, Daneth had brought the slave. She stood fully nude, except for the wrist, ankle, and neck cuffs he would use to keep her chained up. She crossed her cuffed wrists in front of her sex. Daneth led her by a chain attached to the ring on her collar.

Her jaw was thrust forward, mouth set in an angry slash.

Excrement. No, Daneth couldn't have chosen a meek, submissive human, trained to serve males as a human slave should. This one would be a pain in his ass.

He scanned her body. Fragile. Small. Weak.

How could this human's genes be the perfect mix with his own?

But the sight of her bare nipples, jutted out in stiff points, her flat belly and long, shapely legs did stir his cock and stiffen his horns. Daneth had been right; without the dirt and grime, she was beautiful. Exquisite, even.

But what need did he have for beautiful children? He wasn't bad-looking himself. He needed cunning warriors.

He folded his arms across his chest. "She appears stubborn."

Daneth looked at the data readout on his armband. "Actually, elevated pulse would indicate she's afraid."

She darted a glance at Daneth, as if frightened to hear he was monitoring her vital statistics.

"Then why doesn't she look afraid?"

"Perhaps she wishes to hide it, my lord. Humans often attempt to mask their emotions."

Humans. He had no time for their deceptive ways. "They lie, yes. But it doesn't make sense. If she showed me fear, I would take pity on her. Insolence, I will beat out of her."

The stubborn mask fell away for a moment. *Ah.* There was the fear. So she *had* tried to hide it. Why? It made no sense. And she continued, even after he'd said how he would deal with her attitude.

He reached for her, and she shrank back, attempted to dodge his touch. Daneth yanked her chain forward too harshly, and she stumbled against Zander, her fragile form soft against his body, her skin baby smooth under his hands.

He gripped her upper arms to immobilize her and studied her face. Her eyes were moss-green with yellow starbursts around the pupils. He'd never seen eyes like them before. All of his people's eyes were the same color—brown, rimmed in violet, a complement to their purple-hued skin.

"Are you afraid, slave?"

Her little tongue darted out to moisten her lips, which had cracked. "Yes, my lord."

Finally, the truth. "Good. Learn to please me and we will get along well enough."

"Why am I here?" she croaked.

He glanced at Daneth. "You told her nothing?"

Daneth shrugged. "I thought it best to minimize my interaction with her, as she will be yours to mold and shape."

Stars, he didn't have any interest in molding or shaping any being, much less a human slave. But he supposed Daneth's caution made sense. He would be her master; he would have to be the one to train her to his liking.

He heaved an exasperated sigh. "You're here for breeding."

Her eyes flew wide and she stopped breathing for a moment. Real alarm flitted across her face. Her throat worked to swallow. "I'm not a breeder."

Her lack of deference when she spoke annoyed him. He was used to being treated with the utmost respect by all those around him. "The choice is not yours," he snapped.

Daneth picked up his irritation. "She may require some correction, my lord, but I'm certain she will learn quickly. She was not house-trained by the Ocretions, so her manners require refinement." Of course he wanted this to work, since it was his idea.

Zander released her and crossed his arms once more. "What makes you so certain?"

"Her brain activity is very high for a human. She's intelligent. We already know she has excellent genes."

"I'm not a breeder," she repeated. "I wasn't trained for sex. I'm a virgin."

A virgin. *Veck.* That was the last thing he needed. He already had concerns about his cock fitting into a being so small.

He waved an impatient hand. "Cease the prattle. Do not speak unless you are invited to do so."

She shifted in agitation. "There's been some kind of mistake."

He definitely didn't have time for this. He jerked his horns toward the cage

Daneth had installed in his room for her. "Put her in the cage. I'll breed her later."

At the mention of a cage, she spun and tried to make a dash for the door. He didn't know where she thought she'd go, considering he had guards at every door in the pod, and the only exit was in an airship.

He caught her around the waist and yanked her back against his body. "Enough," he growled in her ear. Looking to Daneth, he asked, "How do they recommend punishing her?"

"A beating with the flat of your hand on her buttocks should suffice for minor infractions, my lord."

He sat on his sleepdisk and flipped her face down across his thighs, bringing his hand down on her bare bottom.

She inhaled sharply and tightened her cheeks.

He didn't use his full strength, even though it was just his open hand. She was female, and human—he didn't want to cause her real harm, only to quell the rebellion in her. He slapped her upturned backside over and over again, watching as her pale skin turned an enchanting shade of pink.

She squirmed and kicked her legs until he caught her ankles and fastened the cuff clips together. That impeded the kicking.

He resumed the steady beating, wondering how much it would take until she broke. She held her breath then let it out in little gasps and cries. Each time they came out, they sounded more plaintive, but she hadn't yet begun to weep. Humans were emotional creatures, or so he'd heard. Far more emotional than his species. They cried when wounded.

He stopped paddling her and wrapped a fist in her hair to lift her head. Her face was red, but her eyes were dry.

"She's not crying," he said to Daneth. It came out like an accusation. Well, this whole scheme was Daneth's doing, so he should prevent it from being so difficult. "Don't they cry when they're in pain?"

"Yes, well, her vitals indicate stress."

"It is not sufficient. She should be crying."

"There are harsher methods of punishment, but they may cause permanent damage or excessive stress. We want her healthy for breeding."

"Research it further. This isn't working."

"Note the color of her buttocks."

His cock stirred at the mention of her rather attractive posterior. As if he hadn't noticed it already. Her skin had turned a mottled red where he'd disciplined her, and the flesh had already swollen.

"It worked, my lord. She is just stubborn."

He pulled her roughly to stand, out of patience with her deceit, which made no logical sense. Why wouldn't she simply cry and concede to him if the punishment had worked? "Put her in the cage."

Daneth stepped back, as if too squeamish to lift her. He supposed there was some reluctance on his advisor's part to get intimate with the human, if she belonged to Zander.

"Never mind," he muttered. "I'll do it." He scooped her up. She was lighter than he expected. And softer. She smelled sweet, like some kind of flower, but not in an overpowering way. His horns stiffened and turned. His blood warmed. All right, apparently he *could* be attracted to a human.

The truth was, he had little experience with females of any species. He'd been evacuated from his planet when he was a youth, and most of his species had been destroyed in the takeover. He'd experimented a bit with other species as he came into manhood, but Seke had advised him he scattered his energy in doing so—he should keep it for his training. He'd put off breeding until now.

But his slave needed reminding of her place. He'd have time enough to breed her later, if his irritation with her faded. He hefted her through the door of the cage, slamming the door shut behind her.

Unable to move much with both her wrists and ankles bound, she curled up on her side, with her back to him. He saw trembling in her buttocks and thighs. Yes, Daneth was right. The punishment must have had its effect. Too bad she hadn't learned from it.

"I'll leave you, my lord, unless you require anything else?"

"More information on discipline. That is all."

Daneth bowed and left the room.

He flicked on his hologram and checked the daily reports on his trades.

A sniff sounded from the cage.

⁓.⁓

Her bottom was on fire. The Zandian prince's hand had fallen like a paddle—stinging her flesh as well as leaving a deeper hurt below the surface—the kind that would leave lasting soreness. She'd kept her emotions at bay during the punishment, but now that it was over, tears leaked down her nose, dripped onto the finely woven carpet in her cage.

Yes, her *cage* had the nicest rug she'd ever seen. Well, apart from the one on Zander's floor. The cage itself was polished hardwood—light in color. Not a wood from Earth—she was familiar with all of those from her work in agriculture. No, this was a very hard wood, sanded and polished until it gleamed. Zander's entire space pod spoke of wealth and opulence. She'd never seen such finery—not even in the holograms she'd glimpsed over the guards' shoulders back on the agrifarm. The rooms and corridors were shaped by domed walls, which were textured and colored in rich, happy shades of yellow, red, and purple. Prince Zander's egg-shaped bed, draped in rich-hued silks, hovered a foot off the floor without any visible means of support. So did her cage. A skylight in the ceiling had a fist-sized crystal embedded in it, which seemed to provide all the natural light the chamber needed. Zander may have lost his planet—or, rather, his father had, if she knew her history—but he still lived like a king.

"*Lamira.*"

It was the first time anyone had called her by her name since she'd been taken from the agrifarm.

The prince's voice was deep and resonant. Commanding. As masculine as a voice got. It reached inside her and made something flutter in her belly.

She ignored the sensation and him.

He spun the cage so she faced him.

She attempted to roll to her back to change sides, but not before he'd seen her face.

"*Now* you're crying."

His powers of observation were overwhelming.

"Why?"

She completed her roll to the other side, away from him.

He spun the cage back so she faced him once more. "Open cage," he commanded, and the voice-activated lock clicked. To her, he said, "Come out."

She didn't move.

His tone went sharp. "Do not anger me a second time, Lamira."

Well, apparently he'd already cowed her completely because his words went straight to her chest, creating a sudden tightening and sending her instantly into motion. She hated how easily he'd mastered her. One stupid spanking and she rushed to please him.

She sniffed back the tears and attempted to push up to her hands and knees—no easy feat with her wrists and ankles bound.

"Release wrist cuffs. Release ankle cuffs," he commanded. They sprang apart but not off.

She backed out of the cage, toward the door, not sure how she would get out until his large hands grasped her waist and lifted her easily to the floor.

Where to look... Certainly not at the prince—her master—although his presence was more than commanding. He stood almost seven feet tall with thick, corded muscles across his chest and arms.

Moisture gathered between her legs.

He looked more warrior than prince. No, he was all king. A warrior king. Earlier, she'd stared at him boldly. Now she kept her eyes lowered, trained at his bare feet. They were no different from hers, except larger and with the brown-purple skin tone of the Zandians. She glanced at her own toes. They were cleaner than they'd ever been before. Even her toenails had been buffed to a glossy shine. How long had she been out?

The prince cupped her chin and lifted her face. His touch was gentler than she expected. She still couldn't meet his gaze, choosing instead to stare at his thick neck and the part of his bare chest visible beneath his loose, finely woven white shirt. Her fingers itched to touch his skin, to find out if it was as smooth as it appeared. What a strange idea. She'd never thought about touching a male in her life. In fact, she'd avoided males as best she could. This one had her completely discombobulated.

Was his chest hairless? Did he have hair anywhere other than his head? Zander, Daneth, and the guards she'd seen outside all wore their hair shorn close to their skulls. Perhaps their horns got too hot otherwise.

When she'd first seen Daneth, she'd thought the horns ugly, but Zander's suited him, somehow making him even more handsome.

He leaned forward and opened his mouth. She tried to pull out of his grasp, but he held her fast, his gleaming teeth aimed straight for her cheek. For a moment, she thought he planned to bite her face, but his tongue flicked out, and he licked one of her tears. She caught his scent, a clean, masculine aroma with a slightly exotic spice.

Her nipples tightened; her pussy pulsed. No—she definitely was not thinking about licking him back to see how he tasted.

He made a sound, almost as if he found the taste of her tears pleasant. "Why are you crying?"

She tried once more to pull away. Not succeeding, she averted her gaze. "I'm not."

Zander switched his hand from her chin to her nape and yanked her up to her tiptoes, until her nose came within inches of his bent head. "Why do you lie?" he snapped. "I can see your tears with my own eyes."

Her eyes filled and spilled again, her lips trembled. She hated crying like this. She shouldn't act so weak. Her father was a revered revolutionary. She and her mother passed messages for the insurgents along a secret human network. But, now—naked, bottom still pulsing with heat, face inches from his, she'd lost all dignity.

She lifted her bound wrists and rubbed them across her eyes. "It's what I wish were true."

He cocked his head. "You wish you were not crying?"

"Right."

"Can you not stop?"

She blew air through her lips. "I thought you were supposed to be the superior species here. Is it so hard to understand?" She immediately wished she hadn't spoken, because his face hardened and his fingers tightened on her neck.

"You will speak with respect." His tone sliced through the air, ice-cold.

She flinched. For once, she swallowed back her pride and said the right thing. "Forgive me."

He blinked as if he was considering whether to believe her. His grip on her nape eased, and he lowered her to her feet. Snapping his fingers, he pointed at the floor. "Kneel at my feet. I work here in my chamber. When I am here, that is the position you will assume."

Everything about her rebelled at the dictate, but she managed to keep her mouth shut and hide her reaction. She dropped to the floor to assume the required pose. The cuffs on her ankles dug into the already raw flesh of her bottom. Her stomach rumbled. She hadn't eaten since the morning she left the agrifarm. She didn't know how long ago that was—how long she'd been unconscious—but her stomach said it had been a long time.

Prince Zander settled in a hover chair beside her and opened a hologram. She watched as he scrolled through numbers and opened messages. A light flashed in the upper right quadrant of the projection. "Connect Daneth."

Daneth's hologram projected into the room "My lord, my monitors indicate the human may require food already. Would you like me to take her to the kitchen? Or have something sent to your room?"

Zander's gaze flicked down at her with impatience. "Is that why your stomach grumbles?"

She nodded. "Yes, my lord." It cost her to speak to him with respect, but she even managed not to sound mocking. If those were the rules of this new life, she would follow them. It was the way her mother had kept them safe and together so long. Head down, feign compliance. Plan a revolution. Besides, she had bigger battles to pick—like avoiding the intended taking of her virginity.

He snatched up the leash and clipped it to her collar, jaw tight, disgust painted across his handsome face. "I'll take her to the kitchen. How often does she require food?"

Daneth winced. "Two to three times a day. And they recommend she have liquids at all times. The lack of fluids may explain why her lips have cracked. I thought it might be our atmosphere, but that's all compatible."

He lifted her to her feet, using the leash, which caused her to choke.

"Ouch," she protested, glaring.

He frowned and shook his head. "Fragile human," he muttered, but her sixth sense registered guilt behind his frustration. He hadn't meant to hurt her.

"How often do you eat?" she asked. There was accusation in her voice, or maybe it was defensiveness. Whatever it was, it offended the prince.

He popped the leash toward him.

She flew forward onto her knees, pain flashing up her neck and into the base of her skull. Lights danced before her eyes.

Veck and excrement. He bent and picked up the weak human female from where she'd fallen to her knees. Dropping her back on her feet, he rubbed her nape to ease her pain.

He hadn't meant to yank her so hard, had forgotten how little she weighed. Anger at himself quickly morphed into general irritation with the whole *vecking* situation. What was he doing with a *vecking* slave? He hadn't the slightest idea how to train her or care for her well-being. He hadn't even wanted offspring. He didn't want any of this mess.

He unclipped the leash and threw it on the floor. "I don't need this damn leash. You will follow a step behind me or you'll be beaten. Is that clear?" He shouldn't yell at her. It wasn't her fault he'd hurt her.

Her eyes swam with tears, and guilt stabbed at his consciousness.

"Why are you crying?"

"I'm not."

For the love of his species, were they really playing this game again?

He ran his fingers around her collar, checking for wounds. "I hurt you?" Rug burns reddened her knees, but nothing terrible.

She shook her head. "I'm hungry, that's all." Her voice choked with tears.

The sound of it grated on him—made his chest tighten. She affected him in far too many ways. He wasn't an emotional creature by nature. Not like a human. But, in the course of an hour, she'd inspired anger, frustration, and guilt. And yes, lust. Because the sight of her naked body had him itching to *veck* her senseless.

"And you don't wish to cry, but still you do." He growled with impatience and snapped her wrist cuffs together in front of her. "Follow." He marched out of the room. He didn't look back but her light footsteps padded right behind him.

His guards stole surreptitious glances as they passed. For some reason, it made his fists clench. They were lucky none of them openly gawked or he'd have their heads. He glanced over his shoulder and caught Gunt, the guard who stood at his chamber door, staring at Lamira's naked buttocks, which, of course, still glowed, painted red with his handprints. Gunt caught his glower and immediately shifted his gaze to the wall.

He grasped Lamira's elbow and pulled her up to his side.

"You said to walk behind you, my lord," she protested.

"Do not ever argue with me, slave. Your duty is to follow my lead at all times. I may change my mind or directions at a moment's notice. You will adjust."

When she didn't answer, he halted and spun her around to face him, raising his eyebrows.

"Yes, my lord." She sounded sullen, but her eyes remained lowered. It was a small step forward. He waited a moment longer for her to lift her eyes so he could give her a fierce glower of warning.

She blanched.

Good. She would learn. Hopefully sooner than later. He walked her to the kitchen.

Daneth, being the ever-capable advisor, had called ahead, and his servants there had already prepared several possibilities to feed her.

"Will this do, my lord?" Barr, the chef, asked, placing several plates piled with food on the counter. "Master Daneth was not certain what she would eat, but he suggested a few possibilities." The chef's eyes flicked to Lamira's peach-tipped breasts and Zander's horns twitched.

He wanted to throw the plates of food at the male. "She'll eat what we feed her," he growled, but he pushed her in front of the plates and allowed her to choose for herself.

He didn't know what to expect, but she picked the same one he would have picked, had it been his day to eat—a meal of delicate birdflesh with fruit compote over a serving of grain.

She gazed up at him with a question in her eyes. Or was it a supplication? His horns leaned in her direction and his cock stiffened. He enjoyed that look on her. He imagined her on her knees, pleading for his mercy, or for him to grant her a boon. He wasn't sure what it was she wanted now, though.

She dropped her eyes back to her plate and grasped the curved utensil.

He suddenly understood. She wanted her wrists freed to eat.

"Release cuffs."

Oh Zandian sun, she was beautiful. Her smile of gratitude sent a wave of something unfamiliar through the center of his chest. He didn't like it. She was trouble. A pain in his backside. She lied. She deceived. She couldn't control her wild human emotions. She would distract him from his work to no end. The last thing he needed was to feel pity or...anything else for this female.

He did not often visit the kitchen, but there were far more servants crowding into the space than belonged. All of them stole curious glances at Lamira and her naked body.

She ate quickly, as if afraid someone might take the food away from her. She *had* been hungry.

No, he wouldn't feel guilty about that, either.

She finished one quarter of the food on the plate and set the utensil down, pushing the plate away. She flashed a brilliant smile at Barr, the only being who remained in the kitchen now. "Thank you. This is the most delicious meal I've ever had."

He wanted to throat-punch the chef. Which wasn't fair. His entire staff— every being in the pod—was made up of Zandians. Many of them were highly skilled professionals, but they'd chosen to take serving positions to be near him, or perhaps to be near the Zandian crystals in his possession. His species needed them to survive, so, when they'd evacuated Zandia, they'd taken a load of crystal as well.

"Please, my lady...er—" Barr's eyes darted to Zander.

No, definitely not *my lady*. She was far from his mate. But he suddenly didn't want his staff thinking of her as beneath them, either.

"Lamira," he corrected.

Barr bowed. "Lamira, please eat as much as you like..." he trailed off again, once more realizing he'd overstepped his bounds.

Zander gave him a cold stare. "She will require sustenance two to three times a day. She obviously eats very little at a time, however."

Barr bobbed his head. "We will provide her with whatever she wishes."

What emotions twisted around in his chest now? Some odd mixture of jealousy combined with satisfaction. He wanted Barr to care appropriately for his slave, but he didn't like the way she smiled at him.

Stars. Having this *vecking* female created a starstorm of issues in his pod. She was not an honored guest here. She was a slave. Except only for him. "Treat her like a fellow staff member. No higher, no lower. She serves me like you do," he snapped. He swept his gaze around the room, making sure they'd all heard it.

Everyone nodded their assent.

And stared at her breasts.

Excrement. She would not be allowed out of his chamber unclothed again.

~.~

She almost had to jog to keep up with Zander's long strides back to his chamber. He refused to look at her, a muscle flexing in his temple. She couldn't figure out why he'd be angry. She didn't mind hurrying, though. Parading through the halls naked with her freshly spanked ass hanging out for all to see was not her idea of fun. It was utterly humiliating. It also had her sex wet again. Now that most of the pain had faded, the memory of the spanking strangely excited her. She imagined him doing it again, then forcing her to breed.

But no. She didn't want that. She wasn't supposed to want the attention of any male. Which might prove difficult here. From what she'd gathered, there were only males in Zander's pod. And, yeah, the Zandian males were...very masculine. Something about being around so many huge, ripped bodies, giant cocks stuffed in tight pants, and horns pointed right at her while the beings stared at her body had her nipples hard and her pussy damp. It had her skin flushing and tingling. It had her wondering how big and long the Zandian prince's cock might be.

The guard who stood outside Zander's door grabbed her ass when she passed him on her way into the room. No, he didn't grab it. It was more of a grope. A fleeting touch—his fingers brushing her inflamed flesh, questing along her curves.

She turned and glared at him but, he stood staring straight ahead, as if nothing had happened. Should she tell Zander? But, no, he didn't want her speaking unless spoken to.

"Door shut." The door slid closed at Zander's command. "In this chamber, you will always be naked. When you leave this room, you will cover yourself."

She lifted her arms and made a show of searching around her body. "With what?" It was the wrong thing to do—she certainly ought to know better.

But her claircognizance told her Zander wasn't cruel. He wasn't dangerous—not like the Ocretion foremen with their shocking devices. Maybe she sensed that underneath the arrogance and superiority, he was an honorable being. Maybe part of her thought it was fun to goad the prince who thought so little of her species. Or maybe she was just a stupid, crazy female who couldn't suppress her macabre curiosity in receiving punishment at the prince's hand. Because the pain and humiliation of the first spanking he'd given her had left her changed.

His expression hardened. He sat down on the hovering disk that served as his chair, snapped his fingers, and pointed at his feet.

She didn't miss his meaning and didn't have the nerve to pretend she didn't understand. She lowered herself to her knees near his feet.

"Look at me."

She craned her neck to meet his gaze.

"Lamira, you have tried my patience too many times already today. If I am to believe Daneth, you are not unintelligent. If you speak to me in a disrespectful tone again, I will make your earlier punishment seem like a caress. Do you understand?"

She swallowed. "I'm sorry, my lord."

He stared at her for a beat. She gazed into his chocolate brown eyes and realized the outer ring and the pattern within the iris was pure violet. Incredible.

"Humans lie."

"I'm not lying." Was she pushing him too far again? Why couldn't she stop herself?

He slapped her face.

It stung and brought tears to her eyes, even though she knew he might have struck her far harder.

"Why do you continue to fight me?"

"I don't know," she whispered, staring at the finely woven rug as hot tears slid down her burning face.

She wondered about her mother—if she even knew what had happened to her only daughter. If she'd ever see her again. How all this would turn out? Did she truly belong to Zander now? His sex slave? His breeder?

Her father had revolted and given his life over his first daughter becoming a sex slave. It would kill him to know his younger daughter also ended up with that fate, to be a breeder.

She hated the quivering place inside her that found the idea half-arousing. She should not be thinking of how it would feel to be strapped down and taken against her will by a giant Zandian male.

Zander cupped her chin. His touch was surprisingly gentle but still strong and sure. He brushed her tears with his thumb then rubbed it together with his forefingers, as if mystified by the substance. "I don't like when you cry."

She didn't know what he meant by that. Was it an order to stop crying? She swiped at her tears with the back of her hand. Thankfully, he hadn't reattached her cuffs after she'd eaten. She gulped in her breath and held it, trying to stop the tears from flowing. "I'm sorry, my lord."

His fingers wove into her hair. "We eat once a week in Zandian time, which on Ocretia is about ten planet rotations."

She stilled, surprised to hear him answer the question he had scolded her for asking.

"The rest of the time, we get our energy from light. The solar rays are different here on Ocretia than they were on Zandia, so we use a crystal amplifier for light baths once a week or more."

She didn't often have visions. Usually the curse came as claircognition, not clairvoyance. But, in that moment, she had a flash of the most beautiful rainbow light bathing her skin, making ecstatic ripples of joy shimmer all around her. Gooseflesh stood on her skin.

She swallowed. "Thank you," she whispered hoarsely.

"You're still thirsty," he said. "There's a fluid tube in your cage. You may go and drink from it."

A fluid tube. In her cage.

She wasn't sure she would ever warm up to being kept in a cage like an animal, but there was something oddly comforting about having her own space within this terrifying new reality. When she started to stand, he lifted her with a hand under one arm.

His superior strength made her knees weak. He could hurt her. Far worse than he had. He certainly had shown restraint. Why did that turn her on?

She crawled into her cage and located the tube. The liquid inside tasted sweet and fruity. Delicious. She drank her fill and then crawled back out, settling once more at her master's feet. He didn't acknowledge her, but the tension between them had eased.

She watched him work, listened to his conversations, watched his messages. His large hands moved with elegant grace as he traced holograms, stretching them, shrinking them, sliding to the next one. The same large hands that had paddled her raw.

She longed for him to touch her. There. There it was. The unacceptable truth. He had slapped her face and spanked her ass. He had cupped her chin and gripped her nape. He'd held her arms. But she was his sex slave. His breeder. Shouldn't he be interested in touching her breasts? Her pussy? When would he do so?

A tap sounded at the door.

"Enter."

Daneth came in, followed by two servants carrying various objects. The first one brought a piece of furniture—some kind of bench. The second one carried...oh *veck*. They were instruments of torture. Things to beat her with. Frightening, cone-shaped objects. Various tubes of gels and ointments.

Daneth began explaining them all to Zander, who watched her face as she absorbed it. She tried to keep it blank, but probably didn't succeed. Her ears burned. Her bottom, which had stopped throbbing, tingled. A loud rushing sound in her ears made their voices sound far away.

"Slave, come here," Daneth said.

Zander spoke. "Lamira." It sounded like a correction—to Daneth—and it made something in her chest flutter. Not *slave*. Lamira.

She rewarded the consideration with obedience, stepping forward, even though she knew what would happen. The doctor, or scientist, or whatever he was, pushed her down over the bench, snapping her wrists and ankles to the legs. She lay naked, with her ass lifted and spread, offered up for punishment.

"It can also be used for the breeding, you see," Daneth explained, tapping her sex with two fingers.

She wriggled away.

"Oh, this should also be useful during penetration. It may prevent tearing from your larger size." Daneth roughly smeared something cold and liquid across her folds.

She tightened both holes, straining against her bonds.

"Leave us." Zander's voice sounded even deeper than usual.

"Yes, my lord." She imagined Daneth bowing and backing toward the door.

Her legs trembled on the bench. This was it. He was going to shove his enormous Zandian cock in her virgin hole now. Her hands turned cold and clammy. She gripped the legs of the padded bench so hard her knuckles turned white.

It occurred to her to beg—to plead with the prince, who might not be such a terrible being, to postpone their copulation. But her lips wouldn't work, tongue didn't move. She remained silent in the horrible position, offered up to him like the slave she was.

Zander probed her entrance with his finger, rubbing the slick substance around her entrance. He pushed his finger inside.

Her foot jerked, and she sucked in her breath across bared teeth.

"Does that hurt?"

She didn't answer him. No. It didn't hurt, but she didn't want to tell him that. She wanted him to stop, to put her back in the odious cage and leave her alone.

He slapped the back of her thigh, and she yelped. "I asked you a question."

"I don't like it," she said sullenly.

A long silence stretched while he screwed his huge finger inside her. It met her virginal resistance and he paused, going slowly, investigating her interior walls. Her belly fluttered. Heat flooded her sex, flushed out across her skin. Her pussy swelled under his touch, the lubricant spreading with a more pleasing sensation now.

"Your genes, of all those recorded in the Ocreatic galaxy, are predicted to mesh best with mine. I don't know why—it doesn't make sense to me how a human could bear the best offspring for me, but that's what the program says. So neither of us has to like it...but we *are* going to do it." There was a steely dominance to the dictate.

It made something pulse deep inside her. She experienced an opening, a yawning of her sexual organs, as if they accepted his words at face value and wanted to oblige.

She didn't want to oblige, however. This shouldn't be happening to her. She wasn't meant for breeding.

"I know you're small and I'm large. I will do my best not to hurt you."

"No." It sounded stronger than she felt. In her mind, it was a whimper. She knew the inevitability of her fate, here.

He slapped one cheek, hard. "You don't tell me no." He shifted behind her, the rustle of clothing signaling his disrobing. He rubbed the head of his cock against her entrance.

She twisted to catch a glimpse of it, but, from her position, saw nothing but the chiseled muscles of his bare torso, his strength and power almost shocking. No, it was his sex that shocked her. He pushed it in, wedging the huge organ into her tight channel.

"Oh, oh! No, no no," she moaned, her teeth clenched.

"Hush, human."

"Lamira. My name is Lamira, you overgrown alien ape. You think you can —*uhn*—" she broke off as he bumped her ass with his loins, driving deeper, right up against her resistance. "You think you're so superior, you can afford to buy any slave you want—oh, oh *veck*!" He broke her hymen. A brief pain flashed when it tore and then he was deep, filling her with his enormous cock. "No, no, no more."

He reached around and covered her mouth with his hand, moving in and out of her. His breath rasped behind her, rough and labored.

She bit his finger as hard as she could—hard enough to draw blood.

"*Veck*!" He yanked out of her.

She thought she'd feel relief, but her body experienced his loss as a disappointment, even though it had been far too much.

He cursed again and then she had a split second of warning from the whistle through the air before something hard and thin struck her across the ass—across both cheeks.

She screamed and looked over her shoulder. He held a wooden stick of some kind, about a half-meter long and five centimeters wide. The whapping sound it made when striking her flesh sounded nearly as loud as her screams. He beat her with it—ten times in rapid succession.

She wailed as if he were killing her. *Veck*, he might kill her. There was anger and force behind his strokes. Not that she blamed him. She'd certainly inflicted her own damage.

Fortunately, the wooden implement wasn't that thick. It didn't pack a wallop like a heavy wooden paddle. She'd been beaten with one of those once at the agrifarm and didn't want to repeat the experience.

He went still behind her.

She continued to wail, with no semblance of pride now.

"Stop the noise."

She tensed, waiting to see what happened next. Her ass throbbed, the welts he'd laid stinging like a million pinpricks. Her bottom twitched of its own accord. Her sex pulsed, hot and swollen. Moisture seeped from her slit. It must be his fluids—had he finished?

Vaguely, she was disappointed.

No, flesh slapped audibly behind her, but he wasn't touching her. Was he...servicing himself?

~.~

It couldn't have gone worse. He was going to ream Daneth for this idiotic plan. He pumped his cock in his fist, but he'd lost all interest in copulation after the human's ridiculous wails. Daneth must have made a mistake—Zandians and humans were not sexually compatible. He may have been initially aroused at the sight of her bound and presented for his taking, but not anymore.

He closed his eyes and willed himself to a finish. He would reach the point of climax then enter her one more time to deposit his seed. He didn't want to endure any more of her cries than necessary to get this finished.

There. Almost there. He gripped her hips and pushed back inside. She grew even wetter than before, more welcoming. Her muscles gripped his cock.

Stars...*yes*. He shot his load, finishing deep inside her. As soon as it was over, he pulled out and released her from the bonds. The wailing had quieted down to a mewling, panting cacophony.

"Get in your cage." He was utterly disgusted with her. With himself, too. He should have researched this himself, instead of relying on Daneth's knowledge. Perhaps there was something he could have done to prepare the delicate human for a Zandian intrusion.

He turned his back on her, listening as she pushed herself to her feet and crawled into the elevated cage.

"Lock cage," he murmured. "Lights off." With a sigh, he climbed onto his sleep disk and lay on his back with his fingers interlaced behind his head.

Her breathing still sounded ragged, long terraced inhales she held and then let out with a burst. The scent of her tears hit him. Were they fresh? Or from the spanking he'd given her?

He didn't think he'd paddled her too hard. The slender wooden implement had packed more of a wallop than his hand, but it was too light to have left anything more than surface bruising.

She sniffed. Yes, she was crying.

He hated the way her tears made him feel—agitated. Cranky.

Veck, he hated all the feelings the foolish little human invoked. He preferred not to feel, in general. Zandians weren't emotional like humans. He couldn't have her disrupting his life so much.

Another sniff.

Veckety veck veck.

He climbed out of bed and padded over the hand-woven Ostrion rug to her cage. "Unlock cage." She flinched when he touched her ankle, but he laid his hands on her anyway, pulling her out of the enclosure and carrying her to his sleep disk.

"Lights on." He stared down at her.

She blinked, her large green eyes wide and wary. He grasped her wrists and attached the ring on the cuffs over her head to a fastener Daneth had installed.

"No," she wailed, fresh tears starting up again.

"Hush. I'm checking you for injuries. What hurts?" He parted her legs and peered at her sex.

Most of his seed had spilled out of her, coating her inner thighs with the rainbow-hued semen.

That wasn't right. Another sign they were incompatible.

"Call Daneth." He spoke to his processor on the wall.

A hologram of Daneth's face illuminated, hovering before him. Daneth blinked in his dark room. "My lord?"

"I think I inflicted internal damage. She won't stop crying."

Daneth flew out of his sleeping platform. "I'll be right there." A few moments later, he knocked and entered.

Lamira shrank from his physician.

"Why is she afraid of you?" he snapped, his agitation not diminishing.

Daneth arched his brows. It wasn't like Zander to be out of sorts. "I imagine she's tired of being poked and prodded."

The scientist clipped her ankles wide and examined her.

Zander gritted his teeth when Daneth probed her sex, although he wasn't sure if it was because he didn't like it, or her obvious displeasure. "All your seed spilled out of her."

"I saw that," he snapped.

Daneth tapped his lips with a forefinger. "I will research it."

"You'd better. If things don't improve drastically—" he broke off, not wanting to speak about Lamira's future in front of her. She might try to thwart his attempts to breed her if she knew how close he was to writing off the whole project.

Daneth completed the exam and flashed images of her vital statistics and internal organs up for him to see the holograms himself. "There's nothing seriously wrong with her. She shows signs of stress and likely is experiencing some discomfort from punishment and copulation. Nothing serious."

"Then why is she still crying?"

Daneth shrugged. "It could be emotional pain."

"Emotional?"

"Yes. Human females are quite sensitive."

Veck. "So what do we do about that? Nothing?"

He couldn't read Daneth's expression. It had better not be amusement. "I will research now, my lord. I will bring you my recommendations in the morning."

He blew out his breath. "Fine." He knew he sounded peevish. He was often curt, but not usually so irritable. He was becoming as prickly as his little slave.

"Do you wish me to give her an analgesic for pain?"

He hesitated. If her only pain was from punishment, she deserved to feel that. On the other hand, if it was from losing her human maidenhead, he ought to soothe that wound. "Yes."

Daneth produced a needle gun and filled it.

"No." The terror in her voice struck straight through his chest. She rolled against him, cowering.

It shouldn't anger him to see her afraid of Daneth. He hadn't hurt her, at least Zander didn't believe he had. She was foolish—the needle wouldn't hurt, and the drug was only meant to ease her pain. But she didn't trust Daneth. Didn't trust him, either.

"Never mind. She doesn't want it. You may go, Daneth."

"I can take her to sleep in the clinic so the crying doesn't bother you."

The offer was tempting. She'd already taken up so much of his day, and now she threatened to ruin his sleep, too. But she'd tensed beside him as if the idea frightened her.

"No. I believe she's finished. If she continues, I will call you." He gave her a warning glance and swore he saw answering submission in the lowering of her chin.

Daneth left.

"Lights off." Zander rolled on his side to face the human.

"Thank you," she whispered in the dark.

Her human eyes couldn't see him—she blinked in his general direction, but with an unfocused gaze. His eyes worked fine in the dark. It gave him a chance to study her. She looked sweet. Not like the kind of rebellious human who would take a hunk out of his thumb with her teeth.

"Release my wrists…please, my lord?"

He liked her begging. More than he ought to. His horns roughened. "No."

She'd be likely to attempt murder during the night.

She must have expected that answer because she didn't protest. "I need to relieve myself," she said.

"What does that mean?"

Embarrassment colored her skin. "Empty my bladder."

It might be a trick to get her hands free. But then again, she had eaten and drunk not long ago. He commanded her wrists cuffs to release and turned on the light. "The washroom is there, the door in the corner. You have thirty seconds."

She scrambled out of bed and ran to the bathroom door, throwing it open. She didn't bother turning on the light or shutting the door. He heard the sound of her relieving herself and the flush of the waste. She washed and returned, surprising him by holding her wrists back out. He reattached her cuffs to the head of his bed and brushed a lock of her copper hair from her eyes.

She drew in a ragged breath.

Emotional hurt. What in the galactic kingdom did that mean?

"Was the life I took you from so preferable to this one?" His words sounded bitter to his own ears, as if he'd expected her to thank him for buying her and forcing sex until she bore his offspring.

Her green eyes blinked. She had beautiful, long lashes—black as night. "You took me from my mother—the only person in this galaxy who loves me. The only person I love."

Love. The word grated on him. Love was a foolish human construct. Or, if it existed, it mattered far less than humans believed. Had he ever loved? He cast his mind back to his parents. He didn't remember loving them or being loved. All he remembered was the pain of losing them, and the majority of his species, on that horrible day the Finn invaded. He had grieved for them for solar cycles. Was that love?

He fingered one of her curls. It was impossibly soft and silky. He wanted to smell it but not while she watched him with those big green eyes.

Had he given her the same grief he'd felt when he escaped the genocide of the Finn and ended up in Ocretia alone? Not alone—he had the whole pod of devoted Zandians, but no family.

His chest tightened in sympathy for her pain. "Do you want me to return you there?" He didn't know if he would—he couldn't, really, not until he'd bred her. Still, he held his breath for her answer.

She gazed up at him with those lovely eyes, caught in indecision. Her hesitation was enough. He relaxed.

Her eyes filled with tears.

"Why?" he asked, thumbing up the tear that leaked from the corner of her eye and licking it. He loved the taste of her tears almost as much as he disliked her crying. It was a strange paradox.

She closed her eyes and shook her head.

"No, you don't want me to return you there, or, no, you won't tell me why you cry?"

"I...I don't know," she rasped.

He shook his head. *Humans.* If he was smart, he'd get rid of this girl as quickly as possible, before she disrupted his entire pod. He sighed. "How long do humans sleep at one time?"

"They only allowed us five hours at the agrifarm. How long do you sleep? My lord?" She tacked the *my lord* onto the end. The question was still disrespectful, but at least she was starting to learn to speak with deference.

"I sleep four hours. You may rest as long as you like here." The longer, the better—she interrupted too much of his work time as it was.

The corners of her lips lifted in a faint smile. "Thank you, my lord." Her eyes were already drifting closed. He watched her breathing deepen and her muscles relax. She tugged at her wrists in her sleep, her brow furrowing when they didn't move. She rolled into him, tossing one leg across his hips and making a little cooing sound, like a faint hum.

He smelled his scent on her, her warmth and softness more luxurious than his fine sheets and blankets. His cock hardened again from the contact with her flesh. He ran his fingertip from her bound wrists down her arm and around her small but perky breasts. He traced her nipple. It stiffened and stood up, much like his horns' reaction to her closeness. He had to rub his horns on her. Careful not to disturb her rest, he leaned up on one elbow and dragged one horn down the length of her torso.

She hummed again, her expression blissful. He loved that tiny smile on her. She was far more pleasant when asleep. He rubbed the other horn around her breast, shuddering at the pleasure of it. He wanted to *veck* her again. The first time should have been like this—with her lying face up so he could explore her body and watch her expression.

No, she probably still would've yelled and bitten him. Hopefully, she'd get used to it soon. When she wasn't testing his temper with her constant sass, he found her intriguing. Far more fascinating than he'd imagined a human female might be. Complex, yes, and deceitful, not unappealing.

He thought about taking her again. It was his right, after all. She was his slave, chained to his bed. But, no, she'd had enough for one day. He didn't want to make her cry again. He'd probably have to do plenty of that again in the next planet rotation.

CHAPTER THREE

She woke alone on Zander's sleeping platform. She opened her eyes without moving, not wanting to call attention to herself. The fabrics touching her skin were silky soft, finely woven with incredibly intricate patterns in beautiful colors—some she'd never seen before.

Zander sat shirtless on his platform in front of his holograms. His back was to her. He worked quickly, fingers flying as he opened holograms and sent them. He had the volume turned low—was that for her? He truly had allowed her to sleep in, as he'd promised. Something warm and syrupy slithered through her chest and belly.

With her gaze, she traced the lines of his rigid muscles from his wide shoulders and down his corded arms, tapering to a narrow waist. Her body heated as she remembered the way he'd taken her the night before, strapped down to the bench with her ass in the air. Something jumped and fluttered in her belly. Her pussy clenched. She squeezed her bottom, testing. It didn't hurt anymore, even though she'd thought she'd die at the time. So the punishment had not been so awful after all. Her pussy still stung, but not in a bad way. It was the initial stretching that had hurt. When he'd entered her the second time, she'd almost enjoyed the feel of him surging inside her. It was like scratching an itch—both satisfying and uncomfortable at the same time. But it had ended sooner than she wanted.

She honestly didn't know why she'd cried afterward. It wasn't because she hurt, although she had. It was more the buildup and shock of the entire day. Being away from familiar surroundings, having to adjust to new rules. Grieving for her mother.

When he'd asked her if she wanted to return to her old life, she hadn't been sure how to answer. She missed her mother, yes. And she'd loved her plants. But her life there had been full of hard work, with little rest or sustenance. Beatings there were brutal—life-threatening. There'd been no beauty.

The punishments here had been painful and humiliating but had caused her no lasting harm. And all she had to do to avoid them was grovel—something she hated, but that only damaged her pride. In Zander's pod, she was surrounded by opulence and beauty. The food and drink practically exploded with flavor. Color and light and fine quality materials glittered at every turn. So far, the worst she had to suffer here was kneeling at Zander's feet, showing him respect, and letting him use her body as often as he pleased. She wondered how often he would please. Daily? More than once a day? That thought should not excite her so much, and she felt guilty for enjoying things here when her mother remained on the agrifarm.

Zander opened a new communication hologram and spoke rapidly in another language to the male whose image appeared in the chamber.

The being raked his eyes over her with a leer and said something.

Zander whipped his head around to look at her and scowled. He waved his hand and disconnected the transmission with a sharp command.

"Cover yourself."

Was he jealous about other males looking at her? The thought shouldn't please her half as much as it did.

"It's a little hard to do with my wrists bound."

His lips tightened.

"Master," she added.

He stood up and walked over, towering over her as he gazed down with a speculative look. "You continue to sass me."

She caught her breath at his glower. Her pussy leaked moisture. Why did his dominance excite her traitorous body?

"I'm sorry." She truly was. She didn't want to start the day off with punishment, not when her dreams had been filled with scenes of the Zandian tracing his fingertips across her breasts and stroking her torso with his horns as if it gave him some kind erotic pleasure.

He shook his head. "I can't believe anything you say, little human. Your deceit is the only constant."

She didn't know how to answer, so she kept still, making her posture and expression subservient, hoping he'd release her wrists so she could use the washroom again.

"Release cuffs."

Blood rushed to her hands and arms. She winced, shaking them out.

Zander still stood above her, staring down. His eyes shone more purple than before, and his hungry expression sent a zing of electricity shooting up her inner thighs, straight to her pussy. She shivered.

His lips twitched and he leaned down and grasped her hips roughly, flipping her over to her belly. She squeezed her eyes closed, thinking he meant to punish her, but he only stroked his large palm over her buttocks.

"Minimal marks. Your buttocks do, indeed, make a good target for punishment."

"How is your thumb?" She didn't dare show her face when she spoke, and it came out in such a tiny voice she thought he didn't hear.

"It's healed." He flipped her back over and held his palm up. "Zandians repair quickly, unlike humans."

She fought the urge to roll her eyes. "May I please use the washroom?"

He stood back. "Go."

And, he dismissed her, turning his back and returning to his work.

She climbed out of bed and jogged to the washroom. It took her a moment to figure out how to illuminate the room and how to shut the door. She used the commode and washed her hands in the sink of polished gray gemstone. The liquid soap smelled of exotic complex spices, earthy and vaguely sweet. She recognized it as part of what made Zander smell so sinful. In the corner stood a cylinder of the same gemstone. Was that where he took the light baths? Remembering the vision she'd had of herself enjoying it, she traced her fingertips along the opening, searching for a spring to open it. Finding the latch, she triggered it, jumping back and gasping when the door lifted vertically rather than in.

Inside shone the same as the outside, a smooth polished stone cylinder.

"You may wash, if you like," Zander called from the other room.

Wash. Was this for washing? She stepped inside and examined the small enclosure. The door slid shut and suddenly water shot out from nozzles all around her.

She yelped. The temperature was warm but the spray hit hard. After she grew accustomed to it, she enjoyed it, but the entire tube filled up fast. Water had reached her waist already, then her chest. She spun in a circle, looking for an off switch. She saw nothing of the kind. Liquid rose to her chin.

"Um...Zander?" Panic pitched her voice higher than usual.

She couldn't hear over the spray of water whether he answered or not.

Oh galaxies, oh suns, oh *veck, veck, veck.* The level reached her nose. She tipped her head back to lift her mouth out of the water and screamed, "Help!"

Water filled the entire cylinder. She held her breath as it rushed in swirls around her, like a mini hurricane. Just when she thought she might die from holding her breath, it began to drain. The tube emptied as quickly as it had filled. She gasped, her heart hammering against her ribs. The door slid open to reveal Zander leaning against the doorframe, amusement playing on his face. And *veeeeck.* The sight of his muscled bare chest sent fresh spirals of arousal straight to her core. Or maybe it was his heavy-lidded gaze.

"Have you never washed in a quick-wash tube before?"

She shook her head, sending droplets flying from the ends of her hair. "No...master."

His lips kicked up another notch. He liked being called that.

Her pussy moistened again.

Zander slid his eyes down the length of her dripping body and back up again, and his irises turned deep violet once more. His horns tilted in her direction.

She craned her neck to peer around the little chamber. "Is there, um, a towel?"

He smirked and hit a control on the side of the cylinder. The door slid shut once more.

"No, wait!" She banged against it. "Please! I don't want another bath."

His deep chuckle echoed against the gemstone walls of the tube.

But, this time, the tube did not fill with water, it filled with warm air, blowing from every direction, drying her body. After a few moments, when her skin had dried, it stopped. Her hair still hung in wet ringlets, but it no longer dripped. The door slid open again.

Zander had gone. Disappointment flickered through her. Wait...was that true? That she missed Zander's mocking presence? Or even his stern one?

She found a large stone comb on the counter. It hadn't been there before, so Zander must've put it there for her. He certainly didn't need a comb with his short hair. She pulled it through her hair and, after investigating the hidden controls on the outer wall, reentered the "quick-wash tube" for a second dry, this time for her hair. She discovered there were also controls for "oil," which sprayed a fine mist of oil over her body. She managed to pull her hair up off her back just in time to avoid getting it sprayed. "Shine" lightly dusted her with the glimmering powder she'd worn on her first day there. Thank the one true star—she'd been afraid Daneth or some other being had washed her before she awoke at Zander's pod, but more likely they'd put her in some form of washtube. Although how did she not drown? She discovered different scents were available—the spicy scent of Zander, and also the lighter, citrusy fragrance she'd smelled on her hair the first day.

She emerged with her long hair dry, a glow on her skin, and smelling fresh and clean. She'd feel incredible if the cuffs on her neck, wrists and ankles didn't rub now that they were wet.

Zander swiveled in his seat when she emerged. Remembering his edict from the day before, she went and knelt at his feet. His usually stern gaze softened and he dropped a hand on the back of her head, stroking her hair. "Yes, if you stay at my feet, you will not be seen while I conduct business." He tweaked a nipple between his thumb and forefinger. "And then you may remain naked, the way I like you."

A shiver of excitement ran through her.

"Forgive me, master." Obviously, it hadn't been her fault she'd been seen— she'd been bound to his bed—but she wanted to experiment with acting slave-like. She liked his amused smile far better than his glower. If winning his approval was truly as easy as feigning subservience, it was worth playing his game.

Or did she actually wish to please him? Surely not.

She did like the way his glittering eyes roved over her.

He hooked a finger through the ring at her collar. His thumb touched the leather. "You washed with these on."

"I cannot remove them, my lord." *Because you hold the controls.*

"Next time, ask me to take them off first. Release wrist cuffs. Release ankle cuffs. Release collar." All five dropped to the floor.

She rubbed the raw skin at her neck.

He wrapped his huge hand around her throat. She caught her breath. One squeeze from that powerful fist would end her life.

"Delicate human skin," he muttered.

Her stomach rumbled, and he released her neck and frowned. "Again?"

She bowed her head, biting back the reminder it had been half a planet's rotation already since she'd eaten. She would be a good slave today. Avoid getting spanked. Learn her way around here.

"Clothe yourself." He jerked his head toward the sleeping platform. While she'd been in the washroom, some being had straightened the covers and left a neat pile of clothing on the end.

She started to stand but saw censure in his expression. She froze. What did he want? Oh. "Yes, my lord." She spoke with her head lowered.

He turned back to his holograms, effectively dismissing her.

Arrogant male.

She stood, her knees cracking from kneeling, and made her way to the sleeping platform. A fluffy pink sweater, knit of the finest natural material she'd ever seen sat on the top of the pile. She picked it up. Downy soft. She rubbed it on her cheeks. She'd never felt anything so soft—not even the fuzzy little seed pods from the *rheebush* she loved so well. It had the same slightly citrus smell as the soap from the washtube. She pulled it over her head. It touched her skin like a caress, hugged her body. For the bottom, there were panties, leggings, and a skirt that was really more like a cape—open in the front and covering the back to mid-thigh. They were also constructed of finely woven fabrics.

Zander's seating platform rotated and he examined her with a critical eye. A frown appeared between his brows.

It shouldn't bother her so much.

"Come here."

She stepped forward to stand before him.

He brushed his thumbs over her nipples, which stood out under the fabric. His touch hardened them, pushing them forward even more. One of them poked through the open weave.

"No." His voice was harsh. "This is not acceptable."

She covered her breasts with her hands, a flush of heat climbing her neck to her face.

He flicked open a hologram and barked something in his own language to a servant. She hadn't considered the Zandians spoke another language. Every being had been speaking Ocretion, the language of the planet they were on. The galaxy superpower who had overtaken Earth and stripped all her resources, including humans, one thousand solar cycles before.

He pointed once more at his feet. "Kneel."

She dropped to her knees, and he went back to work. A few moments later, an older Zandian came in carrying a stack of clothing. He set it on the bed and fished a tiny undershirt out of the pile. "Will this do, my lord?"

Zander spared a glance over his shoulder. "Yes."

"Will that be all, my lord?"

"Yes. You are dismissed."

"Thank you, my lord."

The elderly Zandian bowed and backed out of the room.

She started to move but realized she should wait for his direction. She raised her eyes, expectantly.

He glanced down, his mouth open like he was about to bark something. He halted and stared. "I like that look on you."

She glanced down at the clothing.

"Not the clothing. Your face."

A flush of heat warmed her cheeks and ears. What expression had she worn—supplication? Of course the arrogant bastard liked that. Her annoyance didn't travel to her sex, however, which clenched at the thought. Holy star, why? Her pussy liked subservience? Or liked that he liked it? Or was it the way his eyes bore into her, shining a deep, hungry amethyst?

Maybe she was crazy or perhaps it was some strange survival instinct finally kicking in, but she *wanted* his desire. Not only because it was better than his cold, impatient indifference.

He reached down and grasped the hem of her sweater, pulling it over her head and staring at her breasts like she hadn't already been naked for him for the entire past planet rotation. His nostrils flared.

Something on his hologram flashed and he blinked several times, shaking out of it. He jerked his head toward the clothing on the bed. "Dress yourself. No nipples showing. Gunt will take you to the kitchen to dine." Dismissed, like the elderly servant.

She stood and he handed her the pink sweater. The undershirt was constructed of the finest material—some kind of spider silk. It slid along her skin in glorious sensations—a creation of true beauty and function. The pink sweater fit back over the top. She wished Zander had a mirror or self-imager in his chamber. She felt so beautiful.

"Gunt," Zander called out.

The door to his chamber slid open and the guard who stood there stepped in. "Yes, my lord?"

"Escort Lamira to the kitchen."

"Yes, my lord."

Zander didn't spare a glance for her, which shouldn't have been so disappointing.

When the door shut, Gunt took her elbow. An unpleasant jolt ran through her. It settled in the pit of her stomach. "So, he let you wear clothes today?" His lips curled in a sneer.

Her chest tightened. "Yes."

Obviously. What else did he want her to say? He was drawing her into a complaint against Zander, she supposed. She'd have to watch out for him.

He led her down the colorful hallway. Expensive rugs caressed her bare feet. "What's it like being the prince's sex slave?"

Two disparate things happened. One, her pussy moistened and clenched at hearing herself called Zander's sex slave. Two, her fingers curled into a fist because she wanted to punch the sleazy Zandian guard.

She chose not to answer.

"That bad, huh? I figured when I saw your bare ass shredded yesterday. He's a harsh master. Where'd you come from?"

Was this considered polite conversation? She didn't care for the guard or his questions.

She paused to show she wasn't interested in the conversation, but not long enough to imply she had completely snubbed him. "I worked on an agrifarm." She didn't know if Zander's guards were allowed to beat her, too, but she didn't want to take the chance. Thankfully, they'd arrived at the kitchen.

The chef, Barr, laid out three dishes of food on the counter.

"Good morning, Master Barr," she said brightly. If she was going to be staying here, it was time she started cultivating some friends. Especially the ones who fed her.

Gunt, her guard, scowled.

Barr's skin turned more violet, and his horns twisted. His eyes traveled down to her breasts, even though she wore clothing today. "Lovely sweater, my lady, er, Lamira."

"Thank you." Her stomach rumbled. "Is this food for me?"

"Yes, my l—" He stopped himself short. "Yes. Either a citrus-flavored breakfast pudding, shredded leg of maca, or—"

"The pudding sounds amazing." She didn't think her stomach could handle the meat plates first thing in the morning.

Barr pushed the bowl to her.

She picked up the gleaming spoon, which must be made of some precious metal because it felt smooth and heavy in her hand. She took a bite.

And nearly convulsed with pleasure. Her eyes might have rolled back in her head.

"Mmm," she rumbled, swirling the creamy, rich treat around in her mouth. "This is incredible, Master Barr."

"Just Barr. We're equals, remember?" His eyes crinkled and he bobbed his head.

"Thank you, this is so delicious." She took another bite and once more rolled her eyes heavenward as she turned it around in her mouth.

"I could send the food to the prince's chambers for you next time. If you wish."

She flashed him a smile. "Thank you, that's very kind of you. It's nice for me to get out, though. And I have a feeling Prince Zander was happy to be rid of me for a short time, as well."

"Oh, I doubt that," Barr said.

Gunt's upper lip curled.

"No, I think he's a busy being, and my presence has disrupted his routine. He gets annoyed with me."

Barr reached out as if to pat her hand then withdrew his to his side. "I'm sure you'll settle in soon. We are all happy he has chosen...er, to breed." Barr's skin turned a pinky-purple.

She suspected he was right about her settling in soon and she wasn't sure how she felt about it. Part of her wanted to keep rebelling, to fight her new role here, to reject this "sex slave/breeder" identity. But her body had accepted it from the moment he took her virginity. Her spirit may be softening to it, too. Here she was, making friends in the kitchen. She would learn her way around the pod. Things were beautiful here. The food was worth killing for. And Zander...

Her pussy clenched again at the memory of her huge, muscle-bound master, his thick cock stretching her wide while he pounded into her. She might get used to that. Her tummy fluttered. She might learn to please him and avoid his punishments.

She finished the pudding and stood, giving her spoon one last lick. "Thank you so much, Barr. If I only had that to eat for the rest of my life, I would die a happy woman."

He chuckled and took the bowl away, his skin flushing violet again.

Gunt gripped her elbow. "Let's go, slave."

Barr frowned. "The prince said to call her *Lamira*. That she serves him like we do."

Gunt shrugged. "Let's go, Lamira."

She flashed Barr a grateful smile over her shoulder. At least there was one being in this pod who liked her.

Once in the hallway, Gunt stopped. "Do you want a tour? Of the whole pod?"

It was too good an offer to turn down, even if she disliked Gunt. "Yes, please."

He led her down the hall in the opposite direction from Zander's chamber. Like her first day, she noticed how beautiful even the corridors were. The walls were plastered in beautiful hues and natural light— she stopped and looked up. How did they get so much natural light in there? Ocretia's atmosphere was covered in smog. Normally, the three suns did not offer so much light.

A giant crystal was embedded in a skylight in the ceiling above. Its crystalline structure magnified the light coming in. Was this what he meant when he spoke of light baths?

"Whoa."

"The crystals are all from Zandia. They provide our species with energy. They're also used in laser weaponry, which is why the Finn invaded our planet—to control the supply."

Gunt pilfered crystals from Zander and sold them on the black market.

The knowing dropped into her head from nowhere. Things she shouldn't know arrived in her head without any deductive reasoning. Without being told.

She hadn't liked the male, but she couldn't tell Zander. Not without revealing the trait that would equate to certain death. Humans with gifts like hers were executed. Zander would be required to turn her over to the Ocretion law for disposal.

He opened a door into a huge open room with vaulted ceilings and even more light. The longest table she'd ever seen took up much of the floor. Embedded like skylights glittered five giant crystals—each twice the size of her head. The light pouring in wasn't only magnified sunrays—the crystals cast rainbows around the room. She gasped.

She could grow things in here. Wonderful food and flowers.

"The formal dining room." He pulled her back and shut the door, continuing down the corridor. "The great hall." Another enormous room, with a domed ceiling and a giant crystal beaming light down. A large, stone chair sat upon a dais. "This is where Prince Zander hears the complaints, requests, and cases of our species."

"How many Zandians are there?" From what she'd heard, the majority had been wiped out by the Finns when they invaded the planet.

"Very few. Two hundred. Maybe three. They're scattered about, but many come to visit this pod for the crystal light baths. They are open to any Zandian, one planet rotation a week. The same day Prince Zander hears cases and pleas from our species."

He tugged her elbow, pulling her from the beautiful room, and led her down a narrow hall with lower ceilings. "This is the staff quarters." Even though they were not as magnificent as the rest of the pod, they were still beautiful to her.

"This is my chamber." He stopped and opened the door, pushing her forward, as if to guide her in.

She froze, catching his intent. "I should get back to Prince Zander."

He swiveled his dark-violet gaze to her. "You're the only female we've had around here in a long time. We've never had one live here."

She tried to back up. "Well, I'm just a human—hardly pleasing to your species, if Lord Zander can be believed."

Gunt's eyes glittered. "Oh, I think every male in the pod finds you pleasing." He pushed her against the doorframe, pressing his large body against her, mashing her back into the hard wood frame.

She threw her hands up to push him back, but he was too solid.

"I could help you around here. Protect you from the rest of them." He leaned forward, his horns pulsing, his breath foul in her face. "Maybe even help you escape."

"Oh sure. And all I have to do is what? Suck your cock?"

Zandians didn't understand sarcasm. Gunt's eyes turned dark-purple. "Not *all*. But, yes. That's a start."

She turned her cheek away from him. "No thanks."

Gunt's expression changed in slow motion, developing from lust to rage. His hand shot out and closed around her throat. "What?"

She gurgled, trying to suck air through her closed windpipe.

"You think you're too good for me, *vecking* human?"

She shook her head, and he dropped her. A door whisked open down the hall. Before he had the opportunity to do or say anything more, she took off running. The expensive rugs slipped under her bare feet. She didn't hear Gunt's footsteps behind her. Chancing a look back, she saw him walking purposefully but not running. Perfecting his cover, she supposed, in case anyone saw them.

She slowed her steps as well. No reason she should act guilty either. By the time she reached Zander's door, she'd caught her breath and held her head high. She didn't know how to open it, though. She stared at the door, waiting for Gunt.

He arrived behind her. "Let me know when you change your mind," he said as he reached past her, pressed his palm to the security screen, and opened the door. "If you tell the prince, I'll say you offered yourself to me. He won't believe a human over his own species."

CHAPTER FOUR

"She'll be back from her feeding soon," Zander told Daneth, who had arrived full of information on human reproduction. "You can take her for the implants then."

Daneth believed a "natural conception" was important for Zander's child. He said they would only resort to harvesting her eggs and breeding offspring in the lab if natural conception failed after 200 planet rotations. Zander had grumbled about having to breed the human for two hundred days and nights. If things went as badly as they had the night before, he would insist on a lab breeding by the third moon passing.

Lamira burst into his chamber, a spot of high color on her cheeks. Red blotches marred the slender column of her neck, too. It must be from the wet collar.

Humans and their weak constitution.

"What took you so long?"

She lifted a shaky hand to her hair and smoothed it away from her face. "Oh...um, Gunt gave me a tour of the pod." She pulled her shoulders back and drew a breath. "My lord, the crystals provide excellent light here. I could grow plants for the pod—food you could eat, or flowers."

"I have no need for—"

Daneth lifted a finger. "My lord, this could be useful knowledge for rebuilding an over-mined planet."

He was right. But surely that wasn't the only reason this human had been selected as his best mate. Knowledge of agriculture could be found or bought. "All right," he grumbled. "You may grow things, Lamira. Later, you can tell me what supplies you'll need."

Her face lit up so bright, it almost made the hassle worth it. Almost.

"You may take her now."

Daneth planned to insert sensors in her female canal and womb which would send constant feedback of her physical state directly to Zander's armband.

Lamira's eyes went wide, the beautiful green of her irises growing as her pupils shrank. He didn't have to be an expert on humans to recognize fear. *Veck*, he could smell it on her. Why was she so afraid of Daneth?

Before he could explain what would happen to her, Daneth had touched his wand to the back of her neck, and she crumpled. His physician swung her up over his shoulder.

"Not like that," he snapped.

Daneth put her down, supporting her upright, and stared at him.

"Don't carry her like that. It's disrespectful to the mother of my future children."

Daneth bowed. "Yes, of course, my lord. You're quite right." He picked her up in two arms, cradled like a baby, instead.

Zander scowled, not liking the intimacy of it. "I will carry her." He waved an impatient hand to dismantle the hologram he'd been working on and surged to his feet, snatching his bride—no. Not his bride—his slave—from Daneth's grasp. "Let's go," he growled.

"The procedure will only take a few moments, my lord. It would be useful if you stayed, and I could show you what I learned about her anatomy and arousal."

His guard Gunt followed them with an overly-interested gaze. Zander turned back to give a disapproving glare.

To Daneth, he said, "If you insist."

"I would not presume to do so, my lord."

That wasn't true. Daneth presumed to insist on a great many things, but he let it go.

In the lab, he laid Lamira on Daneth's table and helped the physician strip off her clothing. Daneth attached new ankle and wrist cuffs to her. He clipped her two wrists together over her head and attached her ankles to a pair of stirrups that lifted and spread her knees wide. With an imagescope, he implanted several miniscule sensors inside her vaginal and uterine walls.

He requested Zander's armband and programmed the sensors to transmit directly to it.

"Now, my lord, let me show you what I learned. The human female's climax is important for breeding. The contraction of her vaginal and uterine muscles help propel your seed up into her cervix. Deep penetration would be important if she were breeding with another human, but, considering your size, it should not be an issue."

His little human stirred, the effects of the stunning wearing off.

"Ah, good timing. As soon as all her faculties return, we can test it out. In the meantime, let's examine her anatomy." He peeled back Lamira's labia, exposing the heart of her vagina. With one thumb, he lifted a hood of flesh, revealing a delicate pink button.

Zander gritted his teeth, not liking Daneth touching her.

"This is called the clitoris. Touching it gives her pleasure. See?"

The little nub had thickened as Daneth brushed his thumb over it.

It took all his control not to shove the male aside. "I'll do it," he clipped.

"Of course, my lord."

Lamira's lids fluttered open and she stared at him with those spectacular green eyes. Green with gold starbursts.

He took Daneth's place between her legs, fumbling to find the secret nubbin.

Lamira cried out when he touched it, yanking against her cuffs and giving him an accusatory look—half panicked, half something else.

He hesitated. Had he been too rough?

"She likes it. Look at her responses." Daneth kept his voice low, as if Lamira might not hear him. He wasn't sure what responses the male meant until Daneth pointed at the projection from his wristband.

Thirty percent aroused.

Interesting. So that was what aroused looked like. Angry and panicked.

He slid his thumb over the nubbin in a slow circle.

Her face flushed and her breath shortened. She swallowed. Her inner thighs began to quiver.

"Now, inside her channel is another cluster of nerve endings that give her pleasure. It can be found with your finger on the front wall if you reach in and make this motion." Daneth curled two fingers as if beckoning someone. "You will find a place where the tissue tightens when touched, the same way her nipples do." Daneth reached out to tweak one of her nipples but stopped shy of it, probably catching Zander's murderous glare.

Lamira thrashed against the bonds holding her wrists, trying to move away from the physician.

"Ahem." Daneth cleared his throat and took a step back. "Why don't you attempt to inseminate her now, my lord, and we can monitor her arousal rate?"

His cock had no arguments with that plan, already straining against his pants, painfully thick. Zandian moons, he'd been ready to mount her again since the moment he woke up that morning.

He released his cock.

"No." Lamira thrashed her head from side to side. "No, you are *not* going to breed me here like this."

Veck. Her resistance again. It took some of the eagerness right out of his spear. But the breeding had to be done. The sooner she conceived, the sooner he could stop torturing the poor girl. Although that plan didn't ring true on several levels.

The table was the wrong height for him to enter her. Plus, he preferred the sight of her ass, so lush, soft and feminine. He unbuckled one of her ankles from the stirrup. The moment her foot came free, she kicked him in the nose, hard.

"Ack!" Stars flashed before his eyes. "Enough, human," he roared. "I am tired of your resistance."

When his vision cleared, he found her cowering, as best as someone with three limbs cuffed can cower. Her one free leg was tucked up and she'd twisted in a protective manner. Mostly it was the terror on her face that inspired his sympathy and calmed his ire.

~.~

She hadn't meant to kick him in the face. She'd only wanted to get free of the bonds. The last thing she wanted was to have sex with Zander while his scientist or physician or whatever Daneth was watched.

But she'd hit Zander square in the nose, and a trickle of red-violet blood ran from his nostril n.

"I'm sorry, I didn't mean to—"

Zander swiped at the blood with the back of his hand. With verbal command, he released the cuff on her other ankle and both wrists.

She tried to draw up into a ball, but he grabbed both ankles and pulled her off the table.

He flipped her around and shoved her upper body over the examination table, pulling her wrists behind her back and clipping them together.

She tensed, knowing what was sure to come next.

"I'm sorry," she moaned, knowing it wouldn't do any good.

"I believe you're sorry." To her surprise, it sounded like Zander had recovered his temper. It didn't stop him from clapping his huge hand down across her buttocks.

She lurched forward, as if she might somehow get away, but he continued to spank her, his large, paddle-like hand crashing down on her upturned buttocks again and again.

"Ow, please," she moaned. She'd given up on defiance, at least for the moment. A little sympathy wouldn't hurt right now.

Zander continued to light a fire on her behind, his huge hand clapping down on one cheek then the other then right in the middle.

"Look at her arousal rate," Daneth murmured.

Arousal rate?

She must've heard wrong. Her ass was on fire. She was completely humiliated, being punished in front of Daneth and now—

Zander ran a finger across her already engorged clit. It pulsed and her pussy clenched.

Okay, her pussy might be a little wet. Actually, dripping wet. But that didn't mean she was aroused, did it? Aroused by the spanking? Or what had happened before?

It didn't matter because Zander's malehood prodded her entrance and, for some reason, she pushed back at him, as if she wanted his entry.

The head of his cock stretched her wide, and he eased into her.

She caught her breath, but it didn't hurt this time. Not at all. In fact, it felt...

Delicious.

A wanton sort of sound escaped her lips.

Zander gripped her elbows, using the bound circle of her arms to brace her each time he shoved deep inside.

"Zander," she gasped.

A growling sound came from his throat.

She arched back for him, spread her legs wider as he stroked in and out, his giant cock filling her with each plunge.

"Zander," she cried again, sounding a bit more desperate.

"Nearing orgasm," Daneth's cool manicured voice didn't take her out of the moment. She heard it, as if in the distance, far away from the only beings that mattered—Zander and her.

Zander released her arms and gripped her pelvis with one hand, reaching around the front of it with the other. He rubbed his finger over her clitoris, and she shrieked.

"Oh please, oh—"

"Zandian moons, yes." Zander shoved deep inside her, his hot seed filling her.

Flickering lights danced before her eyes, and she let go. Her muscles spasmed around his cock, squeezing around his thick girth. They continued clenching, ripples of release that went on and on, even after Zander started to pull out.

"Wait—do you feel how her orgasm milks your seed up higher in her channel?"

Zander pushed back inside her.

"It serves an important purpose for conception."

She shivered. Hearing her physical processes discussed made them all the more intense. Her internal muscles continued contracting strongly around his cock.

"Now, we want to invert her so she doesn't lose any of your seed."

Zander flipped her up into his arms, cradled like a baby, but with her ass-end slightly higher than her head.

She ducked her face into his shoulder, not wanting to show it after—well, after any of it.

"She should rest like that for at least a half hour. I can chain her up here or—"

"No."

She was relieved at how quickly Zander cut in.

"I'll take her back to my chamber. Give me something with which to cover her."

Daneth produced a thin blanket, which Zander wrapped around her.

She felt oddly like a baby. It wasn't an unpleasant sensation.

Zander carried her out of the examination room and back to his chamber.

Gunt, the odious guard, watched with his lip curled as they passed him at the door. It made her stomach tighten. She wondered if she ought to tell Zander—not about what Gunt had done to her, but about the crystals he was stealing. No—what was she thinking? She couldn't. How would she explain her knowledge?

Zander carried her into his chamber. She expected him to lay her on the bed, perhaps with orders to keep her butt in the air, but instead he sat upon his sleep disk and continued to hold her, cradled in his arms. He tossed the blanket off and studied her, his violet eyes sweeping the length of her body, lingering on her breasts then her face.

She gazed up at him. Like with the bite mark, his nose had already healed. "I truly didn't mean to kick you in the face."

"Hush." He picked up one of her curls and twirled it around a finger.

For once, she did as he asked and stopped speaking. After all the shock of the past few days, being held by him eased the strain. No, it more than eased the strain—it felt incredible. She didn't want to say or do anything to bring it to a close.

Zander seemed softened by sex, his features relaxed, his touch gentle. He traced one of her eyebrows with the pad of his finger, measured the size of her ear with his digits, and compared it to his own, as if fascinated by her. He slid her upper body off onto the bed, keeping her pelvis in his lap with her legs in the air, and explored the intimate folds of her sex. His horns thickened, and they leaned toward her.

This time, she didn't mind the scientific curiosity, as Zander parted her lips and, once more, found her clit. He didn't seem intent on arousing her. Instead, his touch was exploratory. He brushed her clit with a feather-like touch, fingered her labia.

It brought her pleasure, but not in a needy way, like before. This time, she found it profoundly relaxing. Her eyes drifted closed and she floated away as Zander continued his light caresses and explored every part of her.

Being his slave might have some perks. No, she shouldn't think this way. Guilt stabbed her conscience. She couldn't be happy here with her mother all alone at the agrifarm.

· · ·

Zander couldn't believe how delicate her parts were compared to his. Sweet little ears, a button nose, the light dusting of coppery freckles across her glowing skin. Her flesh was so soft, and he loved the way she smelled—like fresh, delicious female mixed with his own scent.

He rubbed his horns along her inner thighs and her flat belly, nudged them against her clitoris. He held her for far longer than he should—he had twenty other things to do—but the more relaxed and contented she appeared to grow in his arms, the less he wanted to put her down. But Daneth had said thirty minutes and it had already been forty-five. He eased her down onto the bed and extricated himself.

"I have work to do. You are free to rest."

She gave him a slow blink, as if she'd drifted far away, and it took her a moment to understand him. Then she sat up, propped on one hand, and watched him as he resumed his position at his work wall. He flipped on the latest charts from his trades that day.

"My lord?"

He gritted his teeth at the interruption. "What?"

"May I use the washroom?"

"You don't have to ask me things like that," he snapped, but instantly regretted it, because the peace slid away from her expression, replaced with that familiar look of stubborn pride.

She lifted her chin. "Forgive me for trying to learn my place."

Another lie. Humans called it something. That's right, *sarcasm*. He turned back to his work again and she went to the washroom.

It occurred to him that she might be rinsing out his seed. Was that possible? He certainly wouldn't put it past the deceitful little human.

When she returned, he beckoned her to him. "Come, Lamira."

She hesitated but pleased him by obeying.

He'd intended to be stern and stand her before him for questioning, but his hands reached of their own accord and pulled her onto his lap.

Well.

He did like the feel of her on his thighs. So light and soft in his arms. So easy to control. He enjoyed the weight of her, small and helpless, yielding, for now. His.

It gave him a good vantage point for studying her face while reminding her who she belonged to.

"Lamira, you will not be permitted to wash out my seed."

She blinked at him. He didn't know her well enough yet to know if it was faked, or not. "You think I washed out your seed?" Her lip curled a little and he saw the flash of anger in her face.

Her bare breasts were so close to him, he forgot himself and palmed one.

He expected her to fight him—to wince and twist away, but confusion flitted across her face and, to his surprise, she rocked on his lap, arching her breast into his hand, as if she liked his touch.

"I would punish you if you did." His voice sounded deeper than usual. His wristband flashed something at him—her readouts.

Forty percent arousal.

In truth? From what? The breast squeeze?

He slid his hand between her knees, stroking up her inner thigh.

Her breath quickened.

He reached her pussy, still swollen from their breeding. With his middle finger, he stroked along her slit, prodding at the opening.

Sixty percent aroused.

"Did you?" His voice definitely sounded hoarse.

She flinched when he entered her, but the mewl from her lips sounded wanton.

"Are you sore?"

"Yes...a little. But I...don't mind it."

The shock of her admission flamed his passion, which had already renewed in full force. But he couldn't breed with the little human again. She'd just told him she was sore.

"You don't mind? But why did you kick me in the face, then?"

She stiffened, and he wished he hadn't brought it up, although he probably did owe her a more substantial punishment for it. Her full arousal during the spanking had redirected his attention at the time.

She clenched her teeth. "I don't wish to be inspected and bred like an animal. It's humiliating to have Daneth watching while you—" Her eyes swam with tears.

"I see."

For once, he believed her. She may be a slave, but she still had pride. He should not underestimate it. She'd found Daneth's presence humiliating. Perhaps that was why she hated to go with him—not because he'd hurt her, but because he embarrassed her.

He slid his finger inside her, not to be certain she hadn't washed—he believed she hadn't—but because he wanted to feel her wet heat all over again. It had only been an hour since he'd had her, but he wanted her again.

She gasped and clutched at his shirt with her bound hands.

Eighty-three percent aroused.

"You are my breeder," he said, pushing his finger all the way inside her, pumping it a few times. "If my physician needs to be present to monitor things, you will have to adjust."

He added a second finger.

Eighty-nine percent aroused.

"Or you'll be punished."

Ninety-four percent aroused.

Had the threat of punishment bumped up her arousal rate? She'd become 100 percent aroused during her spanking earlier.

"Why does punishment arouse you?"

Her tissues literally plumped against his fingers, growing more swollen and slick,

One hundred percent aroused.

She rocked her pelvis to meet his thrusting fingers. Her head fell back and to the side, her lovely copper hair falling across her bare shoulder and breast.

"It doesn't."

Another lie.

He picked her up by the waist and spun her around to face away from him, her legs wide and hooked outside his knees. He delivered a sharp slap to her pussy.

The *fully aroused* message blinked in red in his left peripheral vision.

He slapped her again. "I've lost all patience with your lies."

"Oh because you were *full* of patience before."

Her words gave him pause, because they were not true, and then he recognized them as the annoying human communication habit—*sarcasm*.

He slapped harder.

She cried out and covered her mons with both bound hands.

He picked up her wrists and clipped them together behind his head, which had the pleasing effect of lifting her breasts. He squeezed both her nipples at the same time, pinching hard enough to make her squirm.

He shouldn't enjoy hurting her. Except it excited her, too. Her nipples were hard as little pebbles; the scent of her fresh arousal filled the room. With the fingers of one hand, he continued pinching and rolling her nipple, while the digits of the other once more sought her hot core.

This time, when they penetrated her, there was no mistaking the wanton tone in her moan.

"Do I need to breed you again to teach you who you belong to?"

She bowed up, arching her pelvis and rocking his fingers into her tight channel.

Fully aroused kept blinking.

Veck it. She deserved a little more pain.

He deserved a little more pleasure for putting up with such a naughty slave.

He reached between their bodies to free his length, lifted her hips, and speared her with his malehood.

"Oh." Just one syllable, but the little cry nearly drove him wild.

He mastered her easily, lifting and lowering her onto his shaft, marveling at the way her perky breasts bobbed up and down with the movement.

"Is this what you need, my naughty little slave?"

"Ohh..."

Her hands were still trapped behind his head and she used them now, gripping his head and leveraging her hips over his cock.

She felt so good, her tight wet pussy squeezing his cock like a glove. He didn't want it ever to end. But his little human was sore. Plus, the need to drive into her more deeply gripped him. He lifted her from his lap and carried her to the sleep disk, tossing her onto her back.

He shoved his pants off. To his surprise, when he crawled over her, she brought her bound hands to the hem of his shirt, tugging it up over his abs. He helped her, flinging his shirt off.

She spread her knees for him when he crawled up, and her surrender nearly took his breath away. Her long coppery waves fanned out around her face, the striking green eyes flashed dark with desire.

Desire? Truly? From his little human?

His own lust spiked even higher and he had to hold back to keep from tearing her apart.

Fragile human.

He forced his breath to slow, somehow kept from shoving into her with all the force he wanted to unleash.

She winced and he almost stopped, but her legs wrapped around his back and she pulled him in closer.

She wanted it this time.

His beautiful little human slave.

He pumped into her with measured strokes, holding back with great effort.

Her eyes rolled back, she arched underneath him. "My lord..." she moaned.

All moons of Zander, she shattered his control. He drove deep, angling for the pleasure place Daneth had described. Her channel practically gushed moisture, the slickness allowing him to plow even deeper, stretching her wide to take his girth.

She moaned and rolled her head, her bound hands reaching for him.

He forced them over her head and pinned them there as he rode her. Rational thought left him. A primitive, driving force took over. He found a hard, pounding rhythm, and she matched it, lifting her hips to receive him on each instroke.

Little cries left her lips. He'd never seen anything so beautiful. He bent his head and bit her shoulder, her neck, her ear, all the while sawing in and out of her with vicious thrusts.

"Zander..."

The sound of his name on her lips made him bury himself deep inside her and come—hot ribbons of his seed filling her channel a second time.

Too late, he remembered to watch and wait for her orgasm, but it didn't matter because the squeezing of her muscles told him she'd reached it before his eyes found the readouts.

Her climax was *vecking* glorious. Her mouth opened into a perfect O, her breasts thrust up as she arched, lifting her bottom to meet him, pushing back with more strength than he'd thought she possessed. When it passed, she collapsed, suddenly limp. Her cheeks were flushed a charming shade of pink, her eyes bright and glassy. She panted to regain her breath.

Yes, he could see the appeal of a human slave. He hadn't understood it before, but now, with one glistening underneath him, he saw what he'd been missing. He would have to be careful she didn't become too big a distraction. And stay on his toes, because he couldn't trust anything that came out of her mouth.

⁓.⁓

For the second time, Zander settled on the sleeping platform. He scooted the lower half of her over his lap, to raise her hips, her legs lifted up along his torso. She hadn't expected him to breed her again. Hadn't expected her own reaction to it. Her body had responded to the Zandian prince as if it belonged to someone else's brain. From the moment he pulled her onto his lap, flames of desire had licked her into a frenzy.

And *veck*, yes. He had delivered. He'd found all her pleasure zones. He'd been rough—too rough. She'd be sore in more than one place, but she didn't mind one bit. The euphoria flowing through her now made her wonder what her objection to being Zander's sex slave had been in the first place. Apart from missing her mother, her life had improved five hundred times over.

Zander stroked his large palm down her thigh, his touch light as a caress. He bent his head and rubbed her calf with one of his horns. It tickled.

"You *are* lovely."

He put the emphasis on *are,* as if someone—like himself—had argued she wasn't.

She decided staying silent was best, since there was no good answer to a backwards compliment like that.

"You were a good little slave, taking my cock again so soon."

His words should not affect her the way they did, but as if he'd spoken some tremendous endearment, warmth swirled in her chest, turning her insides gooey with a desire to please. To please? That wasn't her. That had never been her.

Of course, she'd never had sex before—particularly not with a hot Zandian.

He brought his thumb to her slit and stroked straight up to her clitoris again, rubbing lightly. "A good little slave to orgasm as soon as I finish."

Frissons of heat traveled down her inner thighs, incited by his touch. Her belly quivered. "Please no more," she whimpered, not because it hurt, but because she didn't think she could take any more orgasms. It was all too intense.

"I won't," he murmured.

He thought she meant no more breeding. He continued to stroke her.

Her heart rate, which had finally slowed after her climax, now climbed in speed again. "Zander," she choked.

His eyes flicked to his cuff and something he saw there explained her predicament. "Ah." His lips curled into a satisfied smile. "I see. My touch has excited you again." His thumb stopped moving but remained on her stiffened bud.

"How many times can a human female orgasm?" It sounded more like rhetorical musing than a real question.

"No." She shook her head. "No more, please."

He flashed a wicked grin. "No more breeding. Just another orgasm. To pull my seed up higher."

She struggled to comprehend his meaning. Before she arrived at any possible conclusion, he palmed her ass with both hands and lifted, bringing her pussy right to his mouth.

She shrieked when his tongue licked into her—more from the shock of pleasure than from any real resistance.

He sucked her pleasure center, licked along the insides of her labia, penetrated her with his tongue.

Her face grew hot, her breath short. She clamped her knees around his ears. When one of her calves brushed his horn, he groaned.

Were they sensitive?

She deliberately rubbed both horns with her lower legs.

His fingers dug into her ass; his tongue lashed her pussy, He pulled her up and down over his mouth.

A scream rose in her throat.

She kicked and thrashed with her legs—not to push him away, only desperate for relief.

He shifted one of his hands under her ass, bringing his thumb to her anus.

She came, hard, bucking in his hands, as he wrung a third orgasm out of her.

"Good girl," he murmured.

Once more, the praise warmed her.

He eased her back down to his lap and pushed her knees open like butterfly wings. "Show me this little pussy of yours. I'm beginning to grow quite fond of it."

Her head swam. No, those were not words to swoon over.

He pulled the cheeks of her ass apart and inspected her anus. "I'm going to take you there, too. It will hurt, I suppose, because you're so tiny. I'll reserve it for punishment."

Her pussy clenched and he noticed.

"You like when I talk about punishment."

She shook her head. "No, I don't."

He flashed the cuff in her direction. "I have proof. And that's another lie. I'm going to start punishing you for lies. Perhaps your first punishment will be me taking your ass."

Her mouth went dry. She attempted to squeeze her bottom together, but it was impossible with him holding her cheeks spread wide. "No, my lord, Please."

His lips curved into a smile; his eyes grew heavy-lidded. "Not this time. But you've been warned."

Her pussy clenched again.

Mother Earth, her core should not be a quivering, bundle of heated nerves right now. Why did his threats affect her that way?

He sighed. "All right, little slave. You've taken me from my work all day. Now it's time for me to put you to work."

"I thought this was my work."

His mouth stretched into a toothy smile. "You're right, it is. But now you're going to make me your list of supplies for the plants you want to grow here. I'll have them delivered tomorrow."

He lifted her from his lap and crawled off the platform, pulling his clothes back on.

Hooking a finger in the ring in her collar, he tugged gently, forcing her to crawl to the edge. "Come." He lifted her off the sleeping platform and onto her feet. Using the collar once more, he led her to his work station and pointed at his feet. "Kneel."

A 3D hologram popped up with a picture of a memo pad and a pen.

She'd never used the technology before—communications and information systems were forbidden to slaves. The very fact she could read was a secret she kept as hidden as her claircognizance. But Zander didn't seem to know it was forbidden, and her pride kept her from playing dumb. She reached for the virtual pen and twirled it in the air, watching as the letters scrawled on the pad.

As she built her list, her spirits rose. But she shouldn't be happy about being an alien's sex slave. Her father would roll over in his grave. He didn't die trying to liberate humans to have his daughter drop to her knees and happily serve the first master who gave her an orgasm.

CHAPTER FIVE

Zander rubbed his horns against Lamira's bare back. She lay naked in bed beside him, her wrists cuffed to the bed, one knee drawn up in sleep.

"Mmm." She stirred, rolling toward him as much as the cuffs allowed.

"Disconnect cuffs."

Her wrists came free, and she turned to face him, blinking her beautiful wide-set eyes.

He loved having her in his sleepdisk. Loved waking with her soft, naked form ready and willing beside him. Today was the day he made himself available to his people, but there was probably still time to enjoy his slave's lush body.

"Do you need to use the washroom?" He'd begun to understand her physical needs.

"Yes, please." She rolled off the bed and darted to take care of her needs.

He stretched onto his back and stroked his throbbing cock.

When Lamira emerged, she eyed his cock. "If I were trained as a sex slave, what would I know how to do?"

He smirked. "Are you asking me to train you?"

He expected her to scowl, but she shrugged, the corners of her mouth turning up. "I guess I'm wondering why they would need any training at all if they're bound and used at will." There was a new quality to her voice he didn't recognize. Was it teasing?

"Come here and I'll give you your first lesson, slave girl."

He'd guessed right, because she smiled in reply and crawled up over him her lids lowered seductively.

Lust kicked through him, making his cock surge in his fist. "Put your arms behind your back." When she did, he ordered, "Connect cuffs."

She gave an exaggerated scowl. More teasing, he suspected. Or playing of some sort. Another form of human dishonesty. Funny how it didn't bother him so much this morning. Maybe he was getting used to her.

He angled his cock toward her face. "Put your mouth over it."

Her jaw went slack and eyes widened.

"Be a good slave or you'll go over my knee for a spanking."

That excited her. He no longer needed to watch the flash of her arousal rate from his cuff—he was learning her physical signs. The way her pupils dilated, her breath quickened. Sometimes she blushed—he loved that.

She licked her lips and bent at the waist. "Like this?" she whispered when her lips reached his cock.

A drop of opalescent pre-cum shimmered. Her tongue darted out and she tasted it.

He bit back a groan. He couldn't imagine any scene sexier than the one unfolding now. "Take it," he growled.

She obediently parted her lips and lowered her head over his cock, enveloping it in the hot, moist recess of her mouth.

"Lamira," he rasped and wrapped a fist in her hair, pushing her down.

"Mmph." The little surprised sound she made reverberated around his cock.

"Do that again."

She lifted her eyes in question, her mouth still full of his malehood.

"Make that sound again." He guided her head up and down over his cock as a shudder ran up his inner thighs. He wouldn't last ten more seconds at this rate. And he shouldn't waste his seed in her mouth—not when he needed her to conceive.

She hummed while her head bobbed up and down.

He thrust up to meet her, balls tight, his eyes rolling back in his head. In and out he pumped, wanting it to last forever, knowing he should stop before he came. "Enough," he barked.

She jerked off him, her hair mussed, a confusion on her face. Her pretty peach-tipped breasts shifted as she moved.

"Good girl." He forced some control, reached out and caressed her cheek with his thumb. "Lie down on your belly, legs spread wide."

He helped her into position because her bound wrists made it awkward to lower herself. After he climbed over her, he brushed her hair away from her shoulder and nipped her ear. "You are so *vecking* beautiful like that."

She moaned and lifted her ass in the air, offering her dripping pussy to him.

He fit his cock between her parted thighs and shoved in.

Another moan from his slave. Her arousal rate already flashed at ninety percent.

Yes, they were sexually compatible. More than he'd ever dreamed.

He rocked his pelvis, gliding in and out of her, savoring the tight fit and the perfect sight of her pinned beneath him, her wrists bound behind her back, her shimmering hair fanned out beside her.

"So *vecking* beautiful."

He shoved in deep and came, only remembering to reach around and diddle her clit at the last minute. It didn't matter—her muscles squeezed the moment he orgasmed, timed in perfect harmony to his rhythm.

She fit him.

~.~

Zander released her wrist cuffs and kissed the back of her neck before he got up and went to the washtube. A gooey warmth swam through her, not only from the orgasm, but from Zander's show of affection—the kiss, the muttered words about her beauty.

It made her want to be the best slave possible, to earn more of his approval. If it made her life here easier, was it so wrong to give him what he wanted? A submissive, obedient servant, willing to part her legs any time he demanded it?

Zander emerged, dressed in a finely woven white tunic and pants, with a rainbow-hued mantle over his shoulders.

She leaned up on her elbows and opened her mouth to ask him where he was going, but then closed it again. He would find that too forward.

He hadn't missed it, though. His understanding of her personality seemed to improve daily. "You may speak."

A shiver of desire went through her at the words. Why did she like it when he treated her so far beneath him? Did it make her admire him more for his elevated power?

"I was wondering if you're going somewhere special today?"

"It is visiting day. You will not be permitted from my chamber today because the pod will be full of outsiders."

She remembered Gunt's explanation. This was the day Zandians could recharge with the crystal light or visit with Prince Zander. When he left her alone in the room, he locked her in the cage. Her stomach tightened.

"Must I stay in the cage?"

"You must. Go and wash up if you wish first. If you're a good girl and you go in without protest, I will let you attend the weekly meal with me tonight."

The promise of any variety to break up her day had her scrambling to be his "good girl." She jumped into the washtube, dressed, and went into the cage without protest.

"I'll have your first two meals sent in and the servants will let you out to stretch." He turned the cage so his face was inches from hers through the bars. He touched her nose. "You please me."

Three simple words—they filled her with such joy. *Veck,* she was totally losing it. Wasn't there an ancient Earth term for this? Oh yes, Stockholm syndrome. She supposed it was a natural human instinct to bond with the person responsible for her survival. But what would her father think? He must be rolling over in his grave right now.

She noticed Zander's multi-colored mantle shimmered with thousands of tiny crystals woven into the fabric. A gasp left her lips and she propped herself up on one elbow to see better.

Zander fingered the mantle with an apologetic, almost embarrassed expression. "What? The crystals? They are from Zandia." He lifted the edge and fed it through the cage bars for her to examine. "This was my father's. Personally, I'd like to forego the throne and royalty thing—skip the adjudication, but my advisors believe it brings our species hope. The elders weep and reach out to touch it. I'm like a relic of what's been lost."

She caught her breath, stunned at how much of the real Zander she'd just glimpsed. "It's beautiful."

"I think...when my species see the crystals and the colors, it affirms who they remember themselves to be."

When she brushed the pad of her index finger across a crystal, a wave of power rolled over her. If she had not been lying down, it might have knocked her off her feet. It felt like traveling at time warp speed. Her teeth buzzed and thousands of images fell into her head at once.

Although the sensations were not unpleasant, she jerked her finger away from the soft fabric and glowing crystals.

"What do you feel when you touch them?" she asked, forcing her voice to sound steady.

He frowned and she realized she'd done it again—her reaction had been paranormal, out of range. "I did not choose to rule over any other being. It was a position forced upon me when the Finn killed off the rest of my species."

"Of course," she said quickly to soothe his defensiveness. She hadn't meant to touch a nerve.

He plucked a crystal from the mantle, tearing the threads. Reaching through the bars of her cage, he pressed it to her forehead, between her brows.

A shock of energy rang through her like an electric charge.

"Zandian females decorated themselves in crystals. They pierced their nipples and navels, their faces and anywhere else they wanted decoration."

Her entire body trembled—both from the crystal he'd stuck to her forehead and the idea of wearing more. Something about it excited her on a cellular level, thrills spiraling out in waves from all the places he'd suggested.

Something buzzed on his cuff, and he drew back from the cage. "Be good, little slave. I'll come for you later."

The heat burned into her forehead and traveled down her body to her pulsing pussy, which had grown moist just at his admonishment to be good.

It took effort to make herself speak, but she managed to croak. "Yes, master."

The moment the door slid shut behind him, the images rushed in again. Far too many to follow—too fast. Her vision blurred and nausea forced her to shove herself more upright—as much as she could in the small space.

A fierce Zandian warrior flashed before her eyes. He was older than Zander—perhaps by ten solar cycles. Flanking him, she saw armies of ships and warriors of a variety of species.

With a flick of her fingers, she removed the crystal from her forehead and drew a measured breath to slow her heart rate.

She didn't know what all this meant, but it was far too dangerous, no matter how sweet the energy of the crystal felt. The last thing she needed was to get confused about what she should and should not know about.

~.~

Zander found himself oddly excited about the prospect of bringing Lamira to the weekly meal. It was probably a terrible idea. She wasn't trained well enough yet. She still tested him, still sassed. But she had improved over the past several days.

But if he was honest, he'd admit wanting her near him wasn't a rational decision. She'd become an addiction. When he spent the day away from her, he felt itchy. On edge. He burned to have her writhing naked under his hands, to hear the little cries she made when he took her, to examine every inch of her glorious body.

The *vecking* human was becoming a huge distraction. And, like any addiction, he couldn't pull himself back.

His guard Gunt pressed his palm to the screen outside his door, so it was open when he arrived. He nodded at the male as he passed him, his eyes already on the cage.

"Have you been a good slave, Lamira?"

She shook the bars of her cage impatiently but wisely held her tongue. She was learning.

He opened the door and caught her waist as she launched herself out.

"Washroom," she murmured, twisting out of his grasp.

He let her go, watching her ass sway as she scampered to the washroom.

When she re-emerged, she held up the dress he'd sent a servant to buy today for her to wear. A simple Zandian traditional dress, it was constructed of white linen with a halter-style neckline and long, slim skirt. "Is this for me to wear?" Color had risen to her cheeks.

Was she excited?

"Yes. Try it on to see if it fits."

She started to go back into the washroom then blushed, as if realizing she had nothing to hide from him, and stripped out of what he called her "cage clothes"—clothing he permitted her to wear in the cage on days he had to have servants sent in to care for her. The dress slithered over her head and down her lovely curves, fitting perfectly. Her skin looked pale compared to a Zandian's, but she looked no less beautiful than any Zandian female he'd seen —live or in a hologram.

She must have seen the appreciation in his eyes because she blushed and dropped her eyes. "Does it look nice?" She spread her fingers at her sides, as if presenting herself.

He held his hand out. "Almost perfect. Come here."

She crossed the room and stood before him.

"Release wrist cuffs. Release ankle cuffs. Release collar." The soft leather pieces dropped to the floor. He wound a bit of the ceremonial rainbow fabric around her neck. "This will show you're mine, without screaming slave." He cupped her chin and lifted her face. "Now, listen to me. You will not speak unless spoken to. Keep your eyes lowered and speak respectfully. Any transgressions and I will bare your ass and lay you over my lap for punishment in front of every being at my table. Understand?"

Her lower jaw thrust forward at a defiant angle. She didn't like that.

"Or do we need to get that spanking out of the way before we go?"

He saw the flash of arousal projected from his cuff at the same time he picked up her physical cues.

She shook her head. "No, master."

"Hold your skirt up."

She blinked, her breath quickening. Her fingertips dragged up the hem of her skirt until it rose above her waist. "Like this?"

He sauntered around behind her and hooked his thumbs in the waistband of her panties, dragging them down to her ankles. "Step out."

She obeyed.

"Spread your legs wide."

She widened her stance.

"Don't move." He spanked her buttocks with the flat of his hand, first the right side, then the left.

To his delight, Lamira stayed perfectly still, not trying to get away or dodge the blows. Her little gasps made music with the sound of his palm striking her flesh.

After a dozen slaps, he ignored the projected readout, showing she was eighty-five percent aroused, and swiped two fingers between her legs to test for himself. "Lamira, you're soaking wet."

He wanted to make her bend over and grab her ankles so he could *veck* her raw right there, but a wicked idea occurred to him. "Don't move," he ordered again, and gave her ass a slap as he walked to the box of implements and retrieved two bullet vibrators. When he returned to stand behind her, he gripped her hips and tilted her pelvis so her ass lifted and her back arched. "Show me what's mine," he said, his voice thick.

She hollowed her back, arching even more.

He rubbed the first bullet in her moisture and slid it inside her, *vecking* her with it until she whimpered with need. With her lubricant providing ample coating, he switched it to her anus, pushing it against her little rosette.

She jerked and tucked her tail like a *sharkhound*, pulling her cheeks together and forward.

He slapped each cheek. "Bad girl. Open up or you'll get a punishment spanking with the wooden paddle."

She whimpered, but her arousal rate had reached almost 100 percent.

"Are you scared?" he murmured, his lips close to her ear. With his left hand cradling her throat, he used the right to push the tip of the bullet vibrator against her sphincter muscles. "Or merely ashamed to have me touch you in a place so personal?"

Her chest rose and fell, the fine fabric of the dress shifting over her breasts with the movement. She moistened her lips with the tip of her tongue. "A little of both."

"I'm not going to hurt you. I'm just torturing you because I know you like it, no matter how much you lie." He eased the plug into her ass and pumped it a few times before pushing it all the way in. After delivering another sharp slap to her pink backside, he plunged the second vibrator into her pussy and turned them both on.

Lamira whirled to face him, shock streaking her face. She fell against his chest, her little hands fisting in the fabric of his tunic. Her eyes pleaded, desperation simmering just below the surface. "Zander!"

He deactivated both vibrators. "Who do you belong to?"

"You, my lord." Her legs wobbled, so he took her elbow and guided her toward the door.

"Good. Remember the rules and I won't have to punish you publicly."

He saw a retort in her expression, but she clamped her lips closed, too smart to test him.

~.~

She stopped as he opened the door. She'd never put her panties back on.

Gunt stood at his post, his cold stare boring a hole in her head. He didn't like seeing her happy with Zander—or so it seemed.

She tugged Zander's arm, trying to get him to come back into the chamber.

He turned, lips thinning.

"My...um..." She jerked her head toward the panties on the floor.

Zander followed her gaze and his lips turned up in a sexy smirk. "Leave them. Let's go."

Oh Mother Earth, what a trial. Her pussy practically gushed with moisture from all the attention he'd just given her. Her entire body must be at least fifty degrees hotter than usual. After the disquieting visions produced by the crystal that morning, Zander had brought her firmly back into her body.

She walked on shaky legs beside Zander, who kept one hand around her back. It was an oddly tender gesture, which only served to further discombobulate her.

Zander led her to the Great Hall, which had been transformed with a long table that took up the entire length of the hall, beautifully dressed in colorful fabrics and crystal centerpieces.

She drew in a breath at the magnificence of it.

Zander glanced at her and smiled.

The table was crowded with Zandians, who all stood when they entered, facing them like they were royalty. Which, of course, one of them was.

Zander inclined his head, and his fellow Zandians bowed back. He drew back a chair next to the head of the table and indicated it was for her. Once she sat, he took the place at the head. She realized that everyone was gazing, not at their prince, but at her. Well, yes, she was the only human present.

"Drop your eyes," Zander said in an undertone.

Of course, her immediate reaction to his order was to swivel a defiant gaze on him.

He raised a brow and activated both vibrators inside her.

She caught the edge of the table, eyes glued on her plate in an effort to control her reaction. Heat washed over her skin; her pussy leaked moisture onto the skirt of her dress. Knuckles turning white, she ground her molars, trying to block out the intense sensations. She wanted to crawl under the table to hump her hand until she climaxed by the time Zander turned it off.

"Lamira, this is Lium, my tactical engineer. He's responsible for purchasing and handling our airships."

She looked across the table at the grizzled Zandian the prince indicated. His face was lined and short hair had turned white, but he looked every inch a warrior, with massive shoulders and a thick neck.

Lium looked at her but didn't acknowledge the introduction, so she followed his lead and said nothing.

"Beside him is Erick, my trade and business advisor."

Erick did not appear as old as Lium, but, still, like everyone in the pod but her, had to be at least twice Zander's age. He actually smiled at her and inclined his head. "How do you find your new life?"

She glanced at Zander as a thousand answers clogged in her throat. The question shouldn't come as such a surprise. How did she answer such a question? *Other than being kept in a cage and tortured with two vibrating devices at once, fine.* Or how about, *I love it when your hot Zandian prince spanks my bare ass and shoves his huge purple cock into me, but I'm not so crazy about subservience.* Because he seemed kind and genuinely friendly, she gave the most gracious reply her mind conjured. "It's beautiful here."

Zander seemed to doubt her reply, because his eyes narrowed.

Fearing he would turn on the vibrating devices again, she adopted a pleading expression.

One corner of his lips lifted.

"You already know Daneth. Next to him is Seke, my master at arms."

Another massive warrior, this one a bit younger than Lium, but still much older than Zander. Scars decorated his middle-aged face. She saw pain etched into the lines there, too. A flash of claircognizance told her he'd lost his wife and infant in the massacre. The weight of his tragedy punched her in the chest. She realized everyone at this table bore similar losses. They may live in a beautiful pod, but they had suffered—perhaps no less than she and her mother had suffered.

Now she understood the importance of Zander breeding. If the prince was the youngest of his species, he'd be the only chance for it to survive. It also explained why he'd chosen a human—clearly there were no females of breeding age. Only three females sat at the table, and they were all ancient.

He introduced her to the other half-dozen Zandians who sat near them. From what she gathered, the table was organized by status, with the prince and his most powerful advisors beside him and the lowest servants who weren't responsible for bringing the food at the far end.

Zander's hand idly tangled in her hair as he listened to a report from Erick on a business deal.

Barr himself arrived to serve Zander's food, and his face broke into a broad smile when he saw her seated beside the prince. "Good evening, my lord," he said with a bow as he set a steaming bowl of soup in front of Zander. "Good evening, Lamira."

She straightened and beamed back at the old chef. "Good evening, Barr. That smells delicious."

Servants arrived and placed matching bowls in front of the rest of the diners, including her. "I didn't know you were eating here, or I would have served you a smaller portion. Save room for the rest of the meal, little human." Barr liked to tease her about how small her stomach was.

Zander glared at the chef, whose skin colored darker purple as he bowed and backed hastily away. Every being took a sudden interest in their soup, so she did the same. Was her prince actually jealous? Or had she shamed him in some way? She hoped not.

After that, she did keep her eyes lowered, though she listened in on the conversations with interest. Despite the dwindling numbers of the species, the Zandians must be excellent in business, with trade in a variety of sectors. That must be how the pod came to be so opulently decorated and how Zander planned to launch a campaign against the vast population of the Finn.

After the soup came huge platters of ostrich meat, wild bluegrain, and Relo sea vegetables. She realized now why Barr thought she ate so little. The Zandians piled their plates high and emptied them several times while she only finished a half a plate of the rich, exquisitely-prepared dishes. Barr served a blueberry wine that made her head swim. It loosened the Zandians tongues, and soon they were all talking in louder voices, laughing and gesturing like old friends.

A pang of remorse for something she'd never known stabbed her heart—this sense of family, of community they all shared. She wanted to belong with them, wanted to be a part of it all.

When she had finished eating and Zander filled his third plate, he tugged her onto his lap, holding her on one knee while he ate and talked. He stroked his hand up her inner thigh.

She jerked and held her breath, her arousal so close to the edge as it was.

He shoved her knees apart, angling his fingers straight over her clit.

She bit her lips, closing her mouth on a cry.

Zander hadn't looked at her once, intent on some conversation with Erick about the price of sand rocks. That didn't stop him from turning on the vibrator in her pussy.

"No," she whispered. Her thighs pressed closed around his fingers. "Please, Zander."

The vibrator in her anus zoomed to life.

Please, no. Mother Earth, no.

"Please," she whimpered in his ear. "Please, I'll be good. I'll be a good slave."

Zander still didn't take his eyes from Erick, but his lips curved into a smug smile. He slapped her thighs open and smacked her pussy twice.

She bit her lip so hard she drew blood. Zander's sense of smell must be better than a human's because he sniffed and turned, his brows drawn together with concern.

He frowned and cupped her chin, taking her lip into his mouth and sucking.

She came.

Yes, right there, sitting on his lap in front of his entire household, she climaxed.

Zander laughed and turned the vibrators off. "Go back to my chamber little human. Take off your clothes and wait for me on the sleepdisk. I'll be in soon." He murmured the words, but she feared everyone at the great, long table knew exactly what had happened and what was going on. Her cheeks burned with embarrassment.

She stood on trembling legs and affected a sort of curtsy.

Sweet Mother Earth, what was happening to her? This alien had a terrifying effect on her. She needed to get a grip. Fast.

CHAPTER SIX

Three days later, Zander fingered the laser gun hidden beneath his robe. He had four other weapons also hidden within quick reach. Seke and Lium flanked him as they faced Joan-Angeline, the Ocretion smuggler.

"Your ships are on the way. I require the remaining payment now."

He shook his head. "Payment will come when I have the ships in my possession, as we agreed on."

She smiled an ugly smile. Half her teeth were blackened or missing. "I'm changing the arrangement."

He turned, daring to give her his back. Seke and Lium would cover him, and the feigned nonchalance was more important than his personal safety now. "Deal's off." He walked away, not turning to look back as he spoke.

"Wait a moment, Zander the Zandian."

He didn't stop.

"The ships are here," she called out.

He paused, but didn't turn.

She gave a deep laugh. "In the hangar. Come, I'll show you."

He pivoted slowly and folded his arms across his chest. "Stop playing games with me, Joan-Angeline."

Again, the toothy smile. "No games. I have your ships. Let's go. You'll be satisfied, I assure you."

He snorted. He didn't believe her assurances for a millisecond, but if she had the fighting ships he'd been seeking, she'd be the first of many who promised to actually deliver. And he needed these ships. Without them, the liberation of Zandia would be impossible.

He, Seke, and Lium followed her down a metal walkway to a large hangar. There, nine beat-up fighting ships stood parked.

"I paid you for a dozen."

"You paid *half* the cost of a dozen. And I require the remaining half now. They were difficult to acquire. The price has gone up."

Once more, he called her bluff. "No deal. These ships may not even be airworthy. I'll take them for the money I already paid, no more."

"Ah, sorry, Prince Zander, but I have another buyer. If you don't take them, he will."

Zander hesitated. This might be true. He'd been attempting to acquire an air fleet for the past sixteen lunar cycles and these were the first he'd seen. He couldn't be the only being in the galaxy who wanted to buy ships on the black market. Joan-Angeline had maybe fifteen beings standing around with guns. None of them looked particularly smart. The three Zandians could probably take them all in a fight. They were all well-trained warriors. But he had honor. He wouldn't steal what he had pledged to buy, even if Joan-Angeline didn't deserve it. "The ships are mine. I financed their purchase. Because Zandians have honor, I will pay the price we agreed upon, but only for the ships that are here."

Joan-Evangeline puffed her fat cheeks and stared at him, her bug eyes never blinking.

He kept his knees soft, his hand on his weapon, ready if she struck.

"Load the ships into their carrier," she snapped at her underlings, whirling and walking away.

Lium and Seke didn't relax, still as alert as he to any danger.

The smugglers loaded the fighting ships onto his carrier, though, while Joan-Evangeline stood guard at the door to make sure he didn't leave without paying. He counted out the steins and placed them in a burlap sack, which he tossed to her when the transfer of the ships was complete. She gave him another toothy grin. "Nice doing business with you Zander of Zandia."

He inclined his head. Zandians didn't lie, and he'd be lying if he said the same about her. They boarded the craft carrier, and he took the controls to fly them out of Joan-Evangeline's docking station and back to his pod. Only when they had flown several miles without a tail did he begin to relax.

He finally had fighter ships. Now all he needed was an army.

CHAPTER SEVEN

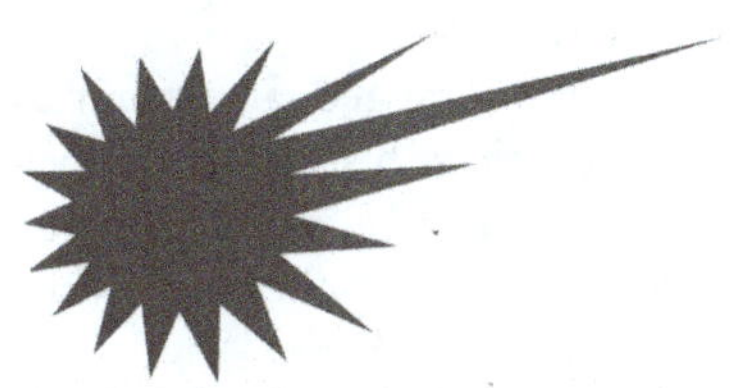

Lamira touched the first sprout of a watermelon plant from her row of starts. Her pussy was raw and sore from fresh use and her limbs wobbled like they were made of rubber. It must be the recent orgasm that made her spirits soar now. She shouldn't be this excited over new plant starts.

After she'd made her list of supplies, Zander had found a catalog and let her leaf through the holograms and pick everything herself. He'd allowed her to buy several types of exorbitantly expensive heirloom seeds, originally grown on Earth, before the planet was destroyed by the overpopulation of the Ocretions. He'd paid for the best soil and beautiful pots, since the "garden" would actually be in his great hall. He'd even ordered two of his servants to assist her. She'd planted the seeds four days ago, and already some had sprouted.

Life as Zander's breeder continued to befuddle her. The confinement and degradation maddened her. The sex, though, while rough and hard, brought her to heights she'd never known existed. She liked it too much.

She checked the timer Zander had given her. He allowed her to leave his chamber on limited excursions without guard for set periods of time. If she didn't return by her curfew, he would punish her. She hadn't dared disobey. She'd pushed hard for the freedom, and fought especially not to have a guard accompany her, not wanting to be alone again with the thief Gunt.

Three minutes until Zander expected her back in his chambers. *Veck*. She'd lost track of time. She ran down the lemon-hued corridor, dusting her hands on her skirt as she went. She arrived at the door and lifted her chin, waiting for Gunt to let her in. She hated the few moments when she had to pass him at his post.

He didn't move, but his horns twitched. "Have you reconsidered my offer?"

Seriously? The dungheap wouldn't give up. "I wouldn't *veck* you if you were the last male in the galaxy," she hissed, reaching past him to open the door herself. Of course, it didn't work. It required the handprint of someone with authorization to open the door, and apparently hers didn't fit that requirement.

His eyes and skin a dark-purple, he shoved her up against the door and curled his fingers punitively, painfully into her clothed sex. "You'll regret that, you *vecking* slave-whore."

She shoved hard against him, but he didn't budge. His fingers groped with bruising intensity.

The door slid open and Gunt sprang away from her. She whirled and practically fell into Zander's arms.

He ignored his guard and dragged an appreciative gaze over her. His hunger showed in the darkening of his horns, the way they tilted toward her. Her body reacted to his nearness, allowing her to put aside Gunt's nasty pawing. Soon, she would tell Zander about it, when she knew him a little better and was sure he would believe her.

"Ah. I thought I might have to punish you."

Her pussy clenched. Zander looked incredible in a body-hugging exercise suit, his huge muscles bulging. It took great resistance not to reach out and touch his hard chest. "No, my lord."

"Come." He pushed her into the room.

She balked. He would put her in the cage. That's what he did when he left her in his room. He didn't trust her alone in there. Probably didn't trust her with his communication devices. "Are you going to exercise, my lord?"

He gripped her upper arm and pulled her toward the cage. "Yes."

She tried to slow their steps with no result. "May I watch you? I'll be good. I'll kneel in the corner and won't make a sound."

He raised an eyebrow, as if suspicious it was a trick.

Well, maybe it was. But the only trick was getting out of the boredom and claustrophobia of the damn cage.

"Please?" She gave him her best pleading slave eyes, which she knew he loved.

His horns stiffened and twitched in her direction. "Promise you'll be good?"

She nodded quickly. "I promise. I won't disturb you a bit."

He tugged her elbow in that commanding way he had. "Let's go."

"Really?" She scurried along beside him. "Thank you."

"Don't make me regret it." He could be gruff, but she'd found he wasn't terrible. Over the past week, he'd only punished her three more times, each time for disrespect. Despite all the new implements Daneth had brought him, he'd only used his hand and each spanking had concluded with a rough breeding session, which she had come to love.

He bred with her once or twice a day. He didn't always hold her afterward the way he had her second day, but when he did, she melted—turning as slavey and submissive as a human who'd been born and bred to serve a man. And she hated herself for it.

Gunt's eyes burned a hole in her back as they walked away, as always. She'd decided he was harmless. If he really thought he could get away with raping her, he would've already accomplished it. Still, she planned to avoid him at all costs.

Zander led her to a room she had not seen before. Like the dining hall, it was lit with natural sunlight magnified by a giant crystal. The room was small with a domed ceiling and raised platform. Seke, the fierce-looking master at arms stood on the platform holding a wooden staff as tall as his body.

Zander pointed silently to a wall and left her, walking up to face the older male and offering a soundless bow.

She knelt with her back to the wall and marveled at Zander's behavior. It was the first time he'd shown subservience to another. In a moment, she saw why. Seke's staff shot out, directly in line with Zander's head. He ducked and swung a foot out to knock the middle-aged male off balance, but Seke jumped, looking as spry as a child.

He swung the staff at Zander once again. Zander dived away into a graceful forward roll.

She bit her lips against the gasp that rose at his magnificence.

The two continued sparring wordlessly, shocking her with their athleticism and the pure art behind the fighting. Clearly, Zander had studied combat arts for most of his life. Watching him fight made her blood heat with desire. Her taut nipples scraped the fabric of the dress she wore, and her pussy soaked her panties with arousal.

She shifted her buttocks over one heel, hoping to press her sex against it to alleviate the growing pressure there. It didn't work.

Zander's gaze flicked to her.

His teacher nearly took Zander's head off with a sword—they'd picked up new weapons several rounds before—but Zander dropped to the ground and rolled out of the way, springing back to his feet and going on the offensive.

Their tussle grew more aggressive, and Zander's fierce determination coupled with the sheer physicality and feline grace of his moves had her clit pulsing, her skin on fire, her breath uneven.

At last, they finished. They both bowed, and Zander spoke to him in their own tongue. The older male's thoughtful gaze flicked to her, but he left the chamber without another word. The moment the door snicked shut, Zander strode over to her and hauled her to her feet. He shoved her against the wall and gripped her jaw, bringing his gorgeous face close to hers. "Bad slave."

She sucked in her breath. What had she done?

"How was I supposed to concentrate when your readouts were flashing your arousal levels the whole time?"

She flushed, her fear at his sudden assault instantly morphing to wanton need.

His thumb slid between her lips and she sucked on it. He attacked her with his mouth, kissing her. It was like no kiss she'd seen or experienced before. His tongue disciplined her, lashing between her lips. His teeth sank into her lower lip before he sucked it into his mouth. He held her head immobile for the onslaught, not allowing her to control any of it.

He pulled back, his eyes a glittering dark-violet. "You're trembling. Are you scared?"

She couldn't make her lips move to speak, but she shook her head no.

"Am I hurting you?"

She licked her lips. "Desire," she managed to rasp out, her voice sounding hoarse.

He seized her again, cupping her ass and lifting her from the floor. "Do you want me to wash first?"

Was he really asking *her*? His slave? If she said yes, would he stop this and clean himself for her?

It didn't matter. She wasn't going to find out, because she needed him desperately, and his masculine sweat only heightened her lust.

"I like you this way," she purred and wrapped her legs around his waist, clutching at his shoulders.

He released his cock from his pants and yanked her panties to the side.

"I'm going to *veck* you right here, little slave. Right here in the exercise room." He speared her, his huge cock filling her and taking her breath away.

With her body pinned to the wall, he slammed in and out of her, asserting his claim over her with each aggressive stroke.

Take me.

She wanted it—needed release more than anything.

"I should take your ass to punish you for distracting me," he said, pounding so hard she thought he might crush her against the wall. Though he continued to threaten anal sex, he had yet to follow through.

"No, no, no," she moaned.

"You were a bad girl."

"No," she protested.

"No? Then you'd better squeeze my cock as hard as you can, little slave...*ungh*," Zander groaned when she obeyed.

He neared climax. She recognized the way his face twitched, his eyes almost black-violet.

"*Now*, little slave. You'd better get ready. Climax, or I take your ass." He orgasmed, thrusting deep inside her and holding her, pinned to the wall by his cock alone.

She screamed, her muscles convulsing around his cock in spasmodic squeezing, milking it for his seed. She'd been ready to come since the moment he began fighting, so the intensity of the orgasm made lights dance before her eyes.

When it passed, she went boneless, a limp rag, hardly able to hold her own head up.

A couple of tears leaked from the outer corners of her eyes.

Zander licked them and closed his eyes as if relishing the taste of her tears. "Did I hurt you?" His voice had gone tender, now. Holy star, how she loved this side of him.

She shook her head, even though he'd surely left bruises all up and down her back. She didn't care. It had been explosively satisfying.

He scooped her into his arms, yanked her dress down, and carried her back to his chamber.

When they passed Gunt at the door, he narrowed his eyes at her, his mouth contorting as if he'd just eaten an insect. She didn't think Zander noticed, but was grateful when the door snicked closed behind them.

Zander arranged her in her cage with a pillow under her hips to keep his seed in. She didn't even mind the cage—her body still glowed from the sex, her pussy pulsing and sore, her blood humming.

He set a timer. "When that goes off, you may move. Take off your clothes and wait for my return. I have a few things to do after I go in the washtube."

Her eyelids grew heavy and she drifted off to sleep, remembering the feel of Zander's large hands on her body.

~.~

"My lord, a word?" Gunt, the guard stationed outside Zander's room stopped him before he went in.

His mind on all the things he was going to do with his naked slave, he stopped with a touch of impatience. "Yes?"

"Your slave, my lord. She's been trying to escape."

He stared, his mind stuttering on Gunt's words. "She can't escape." Every exit in the pod was guarded, and every guard in the pod understood she was not to be allowed out. Even if she found an exit—and he hadn't heard that she had gone anywhere but where she was supposed to go—she would never be permitted through it.

"She offered her body to me in exchange for helping her escape, my lord."

Zander's torso flushed with a flash of cold, followed closely by red-hot rage. He lunged at Gunt, wrapping his fist in the guard's tunic and shoving his back against the wall. "She *what?*"

The guard's eyes widened in shock. "I didn't do it—I wouldn't, my lord," he stammered. "I told her no, of course."

He wanted to skin her alive. Lamira—*his* little slave, *his* breeder—had offered her *vecking* affections to his guards.

He dropped the male and activated the door, striding into his room, ready for battle.

"Cage open." He stormed to it and grasped her ankle, yanking her roughly out.

"Zander," she screamed in alarm.

"Do not speak my name." His voice sounded like cold steel. It sounded more steady than he felt. He dropped her in a cowering heap at his feet.

Veck. Veckity veck veck. Not Lamira. Not *his vecking* slave.

"What's wrong?" She stood up and tilted her deceitful face up to him.

"What's wrong?" he repeated. "I have learned about your attempted escape."

She went still, proving the truth of his words. *Veck.* He'd still somehow hoped it wasn't true.

"I beg your pardon?" Her voice sounded choked.

"Oh yes, you'll be begging my pardon for a long time to come," he raged. The level of his anger was beyond any he'd ever experienced. How could a little human female inspire such depth of emotion in him?

He grasped her wrists and hauled her to the center of the room. With her arms pulled up over her head, he attached her cuffs to a strap hung from the ceiling. He pulled it taut until it lifted her up onto her toes.

"Zander, Zander, please." She twisted and danced from the bindings, her naked body mocking him with its perfection. "Tell me what's going on. What do you mean, my attempted escape?"

He strode to the box of implements and picked up a thick leather strap, sliced at the end to form two tongues. "Why don't you tell me?" Pure ice in his voice. Ice he didn't feel. In fact, he'd never boiled so hot in his life. *Veck,* he'd never felt this much emotion ever—not even when his parents were killed and his planet overtaken.

This was what came of breeding a human. Her overly large emotions had somehow affected his own.

He raised his arm and took aim, applying the strap across the center of her buttocks.

She screamed and twisted away from him, dancing on her toes. A red stripe bloomed across her flesh.

He shook his head. "Hold your position, Lamira, or this strap will fall on your hips and legs and hurt far worse."

Her full lips trembled and green eyes swam with tears.

No. She would not gain his sympathy. Not this time.

He snapped the strap across her quivering cheeks again.

She cried out and danced away, but this time returned to position.

"Tell me about your plan to escape."

"I have none!" she cried out.

If he didn't know humans always lied, he'd think he heard genuine indignation in her voice.

"Liar," he thundered, whipping her even harder.

Her scream hurt his ears, but he gritted his teeth and delivered another stroke and then another. The strap left a crisscrossing of puffy red welts across her buttocks.

"I don't know what you're talking about." She was crying already. He smelled the salt of her tears but had no desire to lick them this time.

"You betrayed me."

Betray was a strong word. She wasn't his mate, she was a slave. And slaves by nature try to escape. It was the reason he kept her in a cage, after all. But he had no rational outlook on what she had done. It burned in his gut, made him want to put his fist through a wall and smash everything in his chamber. Offering herself to Gunt. *Gunt.*

He whipped her again, across the backs of her legs this time.

The terror in her scream did move him, though he wished it did not. He wouldn't whip her there anymore.

Instead, he whipped her ass, three times in rapid succession.

She danced and screamed and wept.

"Gunt told me."

"Told you what?" she screeched. "That he's stealing crystals from you and selling them on the black market?"

"Stop your lies," he yelled, whipping her again. "He told me how you offered him sex if he'd help you escape. You deceitful little whore!"

"He's lying!" she screamed back at him. "He offered that to *me*, not the other way around."

"Zandians don't lie, only humans have such little honor," he shouted and whipped her three, four, five more times.

He stopped, struggling to slow his breath and regain his temper. It was all her fault.

Her ass was a swollen mess—covered in angry red welts. He couldn't go on—not without breaking her delicate skin. He unhooked her wrists and tossed her on his sleeping platform.

She curled up in a little ball, hiccupping.

Unbelievably, his cuff flashed her readout.

Forty percent aroused.

She'd been aroused by the whipping?

Well, he'd breed her then. He didn't care if he hurt her doing it. Hell, he should take her ass for this, but he didn't have the control to be careful enough not to cause her real damage.

His head still swam with the shock of her deceit, her betrayal. He'd wanted to pound Gunt's face in when he told him she'd offered herself up to him.

He grabbed her thighs and yanked her to the edge of the sleepdisk on her stomach.

She turned her tear-streaked face to the side, but stared only at the wall. She was listening, perhaps, for what he would do next.

He nudged her feet apart and she spread her legs, fully compliant, despite her pitiful sobs.

Something in his chest constricted.

No. He wouldn't feel sorry for her. She deserved her punishment.

He shoved his pants down enough to free his cock.

She offered no resistance when he rubbed the head of his cock over her entrance. In fact, he found her pussy slick and welcoming.

He pushed in. His nostrils flared at the glory of her tight, moist heat. Even now, even after what she'd done, he wanted her as much as always.

Damn Daneth and his *vecking* program, picking this *vecking* human for him to breed with.

He slammed inside her, slapping his loins against her flayed ass without care.

She whimpered, still crying softly into his blankets.

No. No pity for her.

He pumped his hips, ignoring her readouts flashing her arousal rate. He didn't care about her orgasm this time. He would leave his seed and she would take it up, like a good slave or she'd never leave her *vecking* cage again.

With punishing strokes, he pounded into her, squeezing his eyes closed to block out the noise in his head and the tightness in his chest. He didn't draw it out on purpose. It certainly wasn't her weeping that delayed his orgasm, but he *vecked* her so long, he grew tired of the position.

He flipped her over.

Her wide, frightened eyes made him grit his teeth. He would not be soft on her.

He clipped her wrists and ankles to the posts on his sleepdisk, spreading her limbs wide.

Her belly fluttered with her sobbing breaths, chest heaved. "I didn't do it, Zander." Her reddened eyelids fluttered.

"Silence," he bellowed and slapped her face. It wasn't a hard slap. He would never mark her beautiful face. He covered her mouth with his hand and mounted her.

~.~

Lamira closed her eyes. She couldn't bear Zander's angry countenance. The only thing keeping her from utter desperation was the tiny voice in her head saying, *this means he cares.* Because surely he would not be so angry over his belief she'd offered herself to Gunt if he didn't feel something for her.

And that knowledge was as satisfying as his angry thrusts deep inside her. She needed this breeding—even as angry as he was. Even as helpless and vulnerable and hurting as she was. Her swollen ass flamed, tender and so raw against his soft sheets.

Zander growled and slammed into her three more times then came.

Her own body responded without any prompting, squeezing his cock, finding her finish in perfect synchronization to his. It was as if, despite all her mental rebellion, her body knew its master. It responded always to his presence, to his touch—whether harsh or gentle.

When he pulled out, he clipped her ankles to a hook on the ceiling, lifting her pelvis in the air with her striped ass on display.

She would have cried again, but she'd used up all her tears. She hung in her ridiculous position as numbness set in, a hollow right in the middle of her chest. She drew in a hiccupping breath and watched Zander turn away from her in disgust and stalk to the washroom once again.

He ignored her when he emerged, freshly washed. Walking to his work platform, he began flicking up holograms.

A light tap sounded at the door and it slid open.

"What?" Zander barked.

"Forgive me, my lord, but Lamira's monitors show signs of stress."

She couldn't see Daneth from her shameful position, but she had no doubt he had full view of her most intimate parts.

"I don't doubt it." Zander's voice was tight.

Daneth walked closer. She turned her face and closed her eyes as if that would keep him from examining her in intimate detail. "What happened?" he asked mildly.

"She offered herself to my guards in exchange for their help in escaping."

"That is not true," she gritted through clenched teeth.

"*Do not speak, slave,*" Zander thundered.

Daneth released her cuffs from their binds.

She rolled into a ball on her side, her legs and arms pricking with pins and needles as the blood returned to them.

"What happened to her back?"

Zander didn't answer for a moment, and then his voice sounded close to the sleepdisk, as if he'd come to inspect her with Daneth. "I bred her up against a wall," he said dully. "She told me I didn't hurt her. Yet another lie." The disgust in his voice made her chest ache.

"I will take her to the lab for monitoring, my lord."

"No." Zander's voice was hard. "She stays here, with me."

Daneth's footsteps moved away then returned. He put the fluid tube to her lips. "Drink."

She did because she was thirsty.

"Has she fed?"

"Not in hours, no."

"I'll send some food in. I recommend you allow her to rest. Stress will adversely impact her ability to breed."

"Yes, well, so will escaping," Zander snapped.

Daneth hesitated. "Of course, my lord." He left and she heard Zander return to his work platform.

Several minutes later a soft tap sounded at the door again. She flicked the blanket across her body to cover her nudity and curled back into a ball.

"Shall I put the food in the cage, my Lord?" a subservient voice asked.

She tensed, waiting for his answer. She really didn't want to go in the cage.

"Leave it over there by the sleeping platform."

A small kindness. She may want to hate him, but he wasn't all bad. She heard the clink of a tray being set on the floating table beside the sleeping platform. She ignored it.

"You may eat."

So imperious. A good slave would sit up and thank him for giving her food despite her punishment.

She wasn't a good slave. She wondered whether he would keep her. Yes his anger indicated he cared, but had he been pushed too far? The imagined loss of her position here, the thought of being sent back to the agrifarm came like a stab in the chest, even with her mother there. She didn't want to go.

Maybe she should beg. She should act more grateful, more slavey.

What would her life be here if she stayed? If she had his child?

She drifted to a semi-dream state, exhausted from the pain and angst, thinking about babies.

She *would* have his baby.

The knowledge came to her, as clear as the light through one of his crystals. *More than one child.*

It brought tears to her eyes. She rarely received information about her own life, and this particular piece of information felt precious, especially considering the ragged state of their relationship. She also hadn't expected the flood of joy she would experience over having a baby. She'd never thought about what it would feel like to bring a child into the world, had only been angry about the non-consensual plan to breed her.

She reached for more information about the child. Was it a boy? Or a girl?

Boy.

Would she raise it? Would she be its mother, or would Zander take the child from her? Would he be done with her once he had a child?

No.

She felt certain she would raise it. It was her baby. Her perfect halfling with green eyes and dark olive skin with a hint of purple. Beautiful in every way—a fat happy gurgling smiling cooing baby doing all the things that a perfect healthy baby should do. Her chest filled with so much love. It banished the grief of Zander's punishment and anger with her. She slipped into deeper sleep, peace settling around her like a blanket.

"My lord?"

She startled awake. Was someone else in the room?

No, Daneth's hologram hovered in mid-air. "Take a look at these data files."

"What's the subject?"

"Lium set up security recordings around the pod this solar cycle. I think you'll find these interesting."

Zander made a grumbling sound in his throat.

"These are the only two files of their kind. There is no other evidence of wrongdoing," Daneth said.

"This is my chamber."

She stilled. That was Gunt's voice.

"I should get back to Prince Zander."

And hers. She rolled over and opened her eyes, cringing to see the hologram of herself and Gunt standing in his chamber doorway. It unsettled her to see herself projected there, the fear and discomfort of the moment returning full force.

"I could help you around here. Protect you from the rest of them. Maybe even help you escape."

"Oh sure. And all I have to do is what? Suck your cock?"

"Not all. But yes. That's a start."

"No thanks."

Even knowing what was going to happen, it shocked her to watch Gunt's huge hand shoot out and grasp her throat. Zander surged to his feet, his huge fist slamming down on his work screen.

"You think you're too good for me, vecking human?"

The hologram flickered off and a second one—the one of her and Gunt that morning—played.

"Repeat." Zander watched the tidbits one more time. When they ended, he stormed to the door, opened it, and slammed his fist into Gunt's ugly face.

She sat up, watching in fascinated horror as the prince followed Gunt to the ground, continuing to beat his face with his fists until two more guards arrived at a run.

"My lord, may we help you? What happened?"

He climbed off Gunt and snapped his head to crack his neck. "Take him to a dungeon cell," he growled.

They rushed in, seizing the unconscious guard's arms and dragging him off down the hall.

When he turned to her, Zander's purple skin looked paler than usual, his worried eyes searching her face. He came in, and the door slid shut behind him. His fingers curled into fists at his sides. He dropped them, though, and walked to the foot of the sleeping platform. "Lamira." His voice sounded strained. He crawled up over her.

She turned her face away. It burned hot with the intensity of the moment. She wanted to hide under the covers, her emotions too raw to meet Zander's eye after all that had passed between them.

"Lamira." He tugged her shoulder when she rolled away, then released her. "Lamira, I'm sorry."

The words sounded larger than the room. They filled the space, filled her.

"I made a...terrible mistake," he rasped. "Terrible." Out of the corner of her eye, she watched him rub his face. "I cannot undo it." This sounded to be as much to himself as to her. He sat beside her, leaning on one arm and gazing down. He stroked a lock of hair from her eyes.

She still refused to turn toward him, feeling too raw, too wronged. *Let him feel sorry.*

"I will grant you a boon to make amends. What can I give you?" He reached out to touch her again, this time resting his palm on her shoulder—lightly—as if afraid she'd shrug it off.

She drew a breath. The most wicked part of her wanted to make him suffer—to drag out his obvious distress and refuse to allow him to make amends. But the image of the baby flashed in her mind again. That image had changed her. Profoundly.

"Hold me."

"I beg your pardon?"

"The way you do sometimes after you breed with me."

He shook his head. "No, you don't understand. I will grant you a boon—make you a gift, or offer some freedom, as recompense for the suffering I caused you." He sounded stiff, formal. Like they were at an official proceeding or hearing.

"All I want is for you to hold me."

Was that moisture in Zander's eyes? He blinked rapidly and pulled back the covers to scoop her up into his arms. With his back against the wall, he settled, cradling her like a baby.

"Like this?" His raspy voice sounded pained.

She leaned her head on the hard, sculpted muscles of his shoulder and drank in his heat, his strength. This was the male who would be the father of her children. "Yes," she murmured.

He stroked up and down her arm in a non-demanding way, as he often did after breeding. "Why didn't you tell me—no, wait—I know you tried to tell me today, but why didn't you tell me when it happened?"

"I didn't want to cause any trouble. I'm trying to find my way here—to make friends. To learn to get along in my new home."

He stilled. "So you have accepted that you belong here? To me?"

Did she accept she was his slave and believe she belonged to him? No. She, like her father, believed humans should be free. But if she had to be someone's slave...she'd pick Zander to be her master over all others. "I am getting used to it," she said carefully.

He shifted her on his lap, and she winced at the pressure of her flayed skin brushing against his pants. He froze and lifted her into the air, scowling.

"Call Daneth," he snapped.

His cuff produced Daneth's head, floating right above her. She flinched.

"My lord."

"Bring something to ease her pain."

Daneth bowed his head. "Of course, my lord." The hologram disappeared.

"You should have told me. You are my slave—my female—and no other male should touch you, especially not from my own guard. I will kill—" He broke off and closed his eyes, as if reining in his temper. "I would have protected you. Did something else happen between you?" His violet gaze was intent.

"No, my lord."

"Is that truth?"

She nodded. "Truth."

He stroked her cheek. "If it had—if he had raped you, would you lie to me about it?"

She tensed. She might lie. She wouldn't want Zander to question the parentage of any child she conceived. "I told you, nothing happened. Remember how I begged you to let me go about the pod without a guard?"

Zander grimaced. "To avoid being with Gunt?"

She nodded. Her stomach rumbled.

Zander reached for the tray of food and picked up a piece of cheese. "You're hungry." He held it to her lips.

She closed her mouth and shook her head. "No, I'm not." She instantly regretted it.

Zander's eyes flashed and his body stiffened. "Even now you lie when I can clearly hear—"

"I meant, I'm too upset to eat."

"I don't understand."

She sighed and rolled her eyes. "My emotions affect my digestive organs. My stomach feels like it's tied in a knot. If I ate, it would make me sick."

Zander's expression grew sober and he drew her closer. "You're angry with me?"

"A little," she admitted.

"And what else? Your pain?" He ran his hand lightly over her swollen buttocks, and she hissed.

It was odd to have Zander always dissecting the things she said, never understanding normal human communication or emotions. It forced her into more self-awareness. And, for once, she wanted to confess the truth.

"You scared me."

Regret made Zander's handsome face droop. "I'm sorry, little human. Did you fear for your life? Your safety?"

She shrugged. "Maybe a little."

"I admit I was...upset." He used her word, as if trying it on for the first time. "But I would never cause you lasting harm. I wouldn't take it too far. I know humans are delicate. I knew when to stop."

She realized she believed him—perhaps she'd known it even at the time. Some little anxiety inside her settled.

A tap sounded at the door, and the screen on the back of it showed Daneth standing outside.

"Come in."

She squirmed, trying to extricate herself from Zander's arms, but he refused to let her go. He must have realized why she was uncomfortable, though, because he tugged a blanket up over her.

"Stress levels are still elevated," the doctor said, leaving out any greeting.

"What can you give her?"

Daneth produced a small gun.

"No." She tried once more to scramble out of Zander's grasp.

He caught her wrists in one of his hands and tugged them up, his other arm snugly around her waist. "Hush. This will make you feel better."

She twisted around, her legs thrashing underneath her. "No, it will make *you* feel better. I don't want to get—"

Zander held her immobile and the shot spiked in and out of her arm—a sharp prick.

"Ow!"

"It works on the central nervous system. It will calm her stress as well as alleviate pain. It should take effect in five minutes."

"I didn't ask you for that, you know—"she growled through clenched teeth, still thrashing against Zander's hold.

Zander ignored her, looking up at Daneth. "How did you know?"

The physician shrugged. "She appeared genuinely indignant—as though she'd been wronged."

Wronged. That was the understatement of the day. Guilt tightened his chest and made his heart heavy. Neither feeling was familiar to him. He made difficult rulings for his people every day, but he hoped he'd never misjudged a situation as badly as he had today.

Lamira stilled in his arms, her body growing heavy.

He watched her eyelids slide shut. "I asked for something to ease her pain, not put her out." He ought to be kinder to Daneth, who had been wise enough to seek the truth and brave enough to show it to him.

Daneth studied her readouts. "She may have been exhausted—stress will do that to a human." The physician glanced at the tray of food beside the sleeping platform. "She never ate?"

He shook his head miserably. "She said she was too upset."

"She will eat in the morning."

Heaviness overtook him. He needed to make amends to his delicate little human. Why hadn't she asked him for anything? He would have made her any gift, though she'd never shown much interest in his wealth or finery. And then he remembered what she did care for. "I want you to purchase her mother. She lived on the same agrifarm where you bought Lamira. Can you arrange it?"

Daneth bowed. "Of course, my lord."

"Has Seke seen the files?"

"Yes, my lord."

"Thank you, Daneth. That is all."

He waited until Daneth left, then said, "Call Seke."

When Seke's hologram popped up, the master at arms inclined his head to show respect, but said nothing. Because Seke was his teacher of battle arts, he did not grovel as much as the others did.

"You watched it?"

"I saw." Seke was a male of few words.

"There are no other data files of the two of them?"

"No, they are the only ones."

"Check on something else for me. Lamira said Gunt has been stealing crystals from the pod. I don't know how she would know such a thing, but I'd like you to investigate before I address Gunt."

"I'll investigate."

"Thank you." He flicked the hologram off and sighed, looking at his lovely slave. He had just flicked off the artificial light when her lids fluttered open and she blinked unfocused eyes.

"You're awake."

"Mmm." She smiled. The light of the giant Ocretion moon shone through the skylight, amplified by his crystal. It gave her a beautiful, bluish glow.

"You must feel better."

She rubbed her cheek on his chest, creating a riot of sensation everywhere she touched him. "I do."

"No more pain?"

Her cute freckled nose wrinkled. "Not much. And I feel happy." Her smile widened.

He'd never seen such a glorious sight. It made him want to work for that smile every minute of every planet rotation.

She reached for his horns.

He choked on a groan, and his cock surged to attention. She ran her dainty fingers around the width of one horn, rubbing it until it grew stiff, then she shifted her attention to the second horn. "Lamira," he choked, doing his best not to throw her on her back and pound her with his cock for a third time that planet rotation. "I don't think you know what you're doing."

Her smile grew naughty. "Oh, I think I do."

Zandian moons. She was smarter than he gave her credit for. He had underestimated her from the start, and now the entire fabric of his existence was unraveling beneath him as their dynamic shifted into something new.

He raised his eyebrows. "You *want* me to breed you again?" This time he was the one trembling from need.

She pushed herself up to her knees and straddled his waist, placing the heat of her pussy directly over his clothed cock. When she took hold of both horns, a shudder ran through him. All Zandian moons, when had she gained such control over his body?

He shoved his pants down and she climbed on, her naked body glowing in the moonlight.

She brought her lips to his and they were sugar-sweet, soft and—he groaned and gripped the back of her head to dominate the kiss, taking over, thrusting his tongue between her lips and nipping her.

She rocked her pelvis, taking his cock deeper into her glorious channel.

"Lamira…" He gripped her hips, careful not to touch her welted bottom, and helped her ride him, lifting and lowering her over his cock.

Soft tendrils of her hair fell against his neck, shocking his skin with the new sensation. Her intoxicating scent filled his nostrils.

He tilted his head to suck one of her beaded nipples then lost his concentration when she moaned, low and lusty.

"*Veck*, Lamira, *veck*."

She gave a keening cry, her inner thighs clamping around his hips, her lush ass undulating, breasts bouncing.

He wanted it to last forever, but the urge to drive to the finish took over. "On your hands and knees," he barked.

Her unfocused eyes blinked slowly, as if she were too dazed to comply, so he helped her, lifting her off him and pushing her down the way he wanted her.

He entered her, gripped her hips and pumped, forgetting to be gentle with her swollen bottom, slamming his loins against it.

Her tight pussy squeezed him like a glove, and she lifted her hips back to meet him. *Oh moons, oh yes.* His thighs tightened; cum surged down his shaft. He yanked her back against him, buried to the hilt, and shot his load into her canal.

She tightened around him, a good little slave, always waiting for his climax before she went off.

"Good girl," he purred, reaching around to stroke her little button and prolong her spectacular finish.

He set off a fresh wave of squeezing and her knees collapsed beneath her, sending both their hips to the sleepdisk, still connected.

"Good little slave," he murmured, biting her neck. "You took my cock three times in one day without complaining."

Not that she'd complained much if at all after the initial deflowering. No, she was a willing breeder—a perfect slave. A loyal slave. She hadn't given herself to Gunt, hadn't wanted anyone but him.

He bit the shell of her ear. "I'm sorry I punished you, Lamira," he murmured in her ear. "I wish I could take it back."

She turned her face to the side and laid her cheek on the sleeping platform, her eyes soft, face relaxed, as if thoroughly satiated. "I'm going to have your baby."

He stilled. "I beg your pardon?"

Her eyes snapped to focus and she shook her head as if shaking off her dreamy state. "I meant someday. Never mind."

He stroked a lock of copper hair behind her ear. As usual, he didn't understand his little human. They spoke the same language, but her words didn't make sense to him. It didn't matter. They had enough for now. He eased them both to their sides, his cock still inside her. He stroked slowly in and out of her, to savor the sensation.

Lamira emitted a contented sound and pulled his arm around her, bringing it to her breast. With a soft sigh, her eyelids slid closed again.

He wrapped his longer body around hers a curious sense of well-being flowing through him. Was it happiness? Did this little human make him happy?

If only they could learn to communicate. If only he could trust her.

~.~

Her dreams were full of Zander. Zander angry, gripping the horrible strap.

Only this time she wasn't scared. *You're mine,* he said. *Mine alone. I will not share you.*

Yes, master. She dropped to her knees and reached for his cock.

Then Zander was buried inside her, murmuring in her ear. Zander fighting with Master Seke, his beautiful muscles rippling, his movement graceful like poetry.

She woke on an empty platform. She sat up. Zander's clothes and gold arm cuff lay on the sleepdisk and the sound of water rushed from the washroom.

She reached for the cuff. On the agrifarm, the foremen had used handheld communication devices. Zander's was state of the art, sleek and beautiful. As a human, she'd never been permitted to use any kind of device, but she'd looked over plenty of shoulders to see how they worked. In fact, she'd longed for one. She had a list a light-year long of the things she'd like to research. But they were mostly farming related. What would she search now, if she could?

Something about her new situation. Something to help her understand Zander better.

"Search Zandian Genocide."

Nothing happened. Right. Because they were programmed only for voice recognition. She remembered, once, seeing someone borrow a device.

"Guest user."

A light flickered on.

"Search Zandian Genocide."

A hologram hovered, showing images of airships bombing the capital of Zandia, Zandians running and screaming from burning buildings. A dispassionate voice over gave the facts of the date, which had been nearly twelve revolutions around the sun ago.

She realized she had something more important to research. With a trace of excitement, she said, "Search Leora Taniaka."

A hologram of her mother appeared, with the name of the agrifarm where they worked beneath it.

Well, at least nothing had changed.

"Search Lily Taniaka."

Her mother had asked every underground rebel for word of her sister for as long as she could remember.

A hologram of a young woman much like her popped up. The words underneath read, "Escaped slave. Whereabouts unknown." Her heart leapt. So her sister had escaped. Good for her. Perhaps she was part of the revolution, like their father.

The water in the washtube turned off.

"Close."

The hologram went on with the projection.

"Off. End." Her voice rose in pitch. How did she turn this thing off? Zander would kill her for using it!

"Stop. Over. Shut down. Close."

She clamped her hand over the light projecting the hologram.

The door to the washroom opened.

She tossed the cuff back where she found it, praying it had turned off.

Zander stepped out, fully naked. He seemed even larger without clothes—not only his cock—every part of him. His muscles bulged and rippled, from his wide shoulders and glorious pecs, to his washboard abs and sculpted thighs and calves. His skin glowed with the beautiful lavender tinge. And yes...his cock. It was huge even in repose, although it twitched to life as his violet eyes came to rest on her.

Her pussy clenched.

"You're awake."

"Yes, my lord."

She scrambled off the sleepdisk and stood to face him, the way he expected. As always, she was naked, except for the soft leather cuffs around her wrists, ankles and neck.

"Come here." He pulled fresh clothing from a shelf and put it on as she crossed the room to where he stood. When he finished dressing, he grasped her nape and pulled her up close to his face. To her shock, he planted a kiss on her forehead and released her. He walked to the sleepdisk and picked up his cuff.

As he fingered it, his head whipped around, eyes narrowed.

Veck. It must be warm, still. Or was a light on?

"Show last."

The hologram of her sister sprang up. He stretched it, looking from Lily's face back to hers. "Who is this? A sister?"

She wrung her fingers and nodded. "Yes," she managed to say. "I've never met her. She was taken from my parents for the sex trade when she was three."

Zander winced. "I'm sorry." His voice held a note of shock that made her believe him.

"Back."

The image of her mother hovered. He spun it around. "Is this your mother?"

"Yes, my lord."

"Back."

The first hologram she'd watched sprang up, right where it had left off, the disembodied voice explaining all the critical data points of what was probably the worst day in Zander's life.

She cringed.

"Back."

The hologram switched to a list of transactions—one of Zander's business accounting records.

"Close."

Her legs trembled when he swiveled his dark-eyed gaze on her. For a long, nerve-wracking moment, he said nothing, simply gazed at her speculatively. "What were you doing?"

It wasn't only her legs trembling. Her whole body shook. She didn't like Zander's dissatisfaction. She opened her jaw to keep her teeth from chattering. "I'm sorry."

He didn't move. Didn't speak.

Right. *I'm sorry* wasn't exactly an answer to his question, was it? For once, she tried for the truth. "I just wanted to understand you better."

He cocked an eyebrow. Once more, he made her suffer with a moment of silence. At last, he said, "Do not touch my things without permission."

She held her breath and waited to hear what the punishment would be. Her poor bottom couldn't take another thrashing, but the cage was almost worse.

He scrolled back to the Zandian invasion and zoomed in. His brow furrowed. "I've never seen this footage." His voice sounded hollow. She sensed the trauma beneath the words.

An image of him as a teenager, being hustled out to an airship flashed in her mind.

"How did you get away?"

He swallowed and rotated the rolling pictures, narrowing in on what must be the palace—his former home. "Master Seke evacuated the palace. He brought most of the servants...and me."

"The servants who are still here?"

"Yes."

She reached out to touch his arm. "I'm sure you wanted to stay and fight."

He turned his amethyst eyes on her, wide with wonder. "Exactly. My parents stayed to fight—both of them. I wanted to stay and fight, too, but they made me go with Seke—" He stopped speaking, his voice choked. "Everyone left on Zandia died that day."

"How many ships got away?"

He shook his head. "Only mine. The rest of the Zandians still alive today were away from the planet for the invasion. Lium and Erick. They were both offplanet."

"You're planning to take it back." She shouldn't have spoken. That was her claircognizance feeding her information she shouldn't know.

But Zander answered. "I *will* win it back." His jaw tightened with determination. "Release cuffs." The locks on her binds snapped open and the cuffs dropped to the floor. He jerked his head toward the washroom. "Go and wash. I have things to do."

She dipped into a curtsy, her heart aching for him. It was a huge responsibility he carried on his shoulders— the liberation of his people, the rightful return of his planet. No wonder he didn't have time for her.

She scooted off to the washroom and stepped into the washtube. The glorious washtube, which she'd come to love. She'd wash three times a day if she thought Zander would allow it. She stood under the warm spray and closed her eyes, allowing it to clean her. The water felt too warm on her still-sore bottom, but she didn't mind. Standing in that tube felt luxurious, indulgent, decadent. She held her breath as the water filled to the top then drained away and the warm air dried her.

She stepped out and combed her hair.

When she emerged from the washroom, Zander snapped her cuffs back in place. "Get in your cage. Today is the pod's recharge day."

She stared at him blankly.

"Once every ten planet rotations, Zandians must bathe in the light and eat a meal to maintain strength. On visitor's day, we open the light bath for outside Zandians. Today is the day those living here recharge. I'm going to the light bath now."

"Can't I come?" It wasn't only desperation at not being left in the cage—well, perhaps it was. But she also wanted to see the light baths and how they worked. She remembered the vision she'd had of the rainbow light and the joy spreading through her.

His dark gaze was unfathomable. Once more he stared at her a long time without speaking. Although she'd never been one to beg, she adopted a hopeful, expectant look.

He sighed and lifted his arm with the gold band. "Call Daneth." When Daneth's head popped up, he asked, "Is it safe for Lamira to enter the light bath?"

Daneth blinked a few times.

She stepped behind Zander to hide her nudity and peeked around his shoulder.

"I honestly cannot say for certain, my lord. I would think yes, so long as she wore protective eyewear. I do not know how well human eyes would withstand the light."

"Thank you." He hit something on the band and Daneth disappeared. "Put some clothes on."

She beamed at him, hurrying to dress. "Thank you, my lord," she said breathlessly.

"Let's go." He pressed his palm to the door.

"My lord." She ran to catch up with him and was startled when he took her hand in his as they walked swiftly down the corridor. She noticed Gunt had been replaced with a different guard. "You do not have to put me in the cage every time you leave your chamber. If you trust me enough to walk about the pod on my own, why not to stay in a room I cannot exit, which is guarded at all times?"

"Cage time is good for you." His deep voice sounded gruff, but rather than frighten her, it reverberated right in her core.

"Why?" she demanded.

"Research says once cage-trained, humans love them. It becomes a safe space. I like it because it reminds you of your place. Makes you happy to see me when I return."

Her pussy moistened and something slithered in her belly. Why? Surely she didn't *like* being trained like a pet by Zander?

He stepped up to a room she hadn't been in before and pressed his hand to the seal. It slid open. "Close your eyes."

She gasped when they stepped inside. A gigantic crystal had been installed in the ceiling, sending rainbow shafts of light all around the dome-shaped room.

"I said, *close your eyes*," Zander snapped.

She covered them with her palm and allowed him to lead her to the center of the room, where she'd seen narrow flat beds arranged in a circular pattern to match the shape of the room.

"Take off your clothes."

She pulled off her clothing and peeked to see him shucking his clothes as well. He guided her into a bed and she heard him settle in one next to her.

"Here," he said, dropping a piece of clothing over her face. His shirt, she thought. It smelled of his clean, masculine scent—a scent she'd come to love.

She breathed in deeply.

"Keep your face covered, just in case. I'd feel terrible if it got burned."

He'd feel terrible. So he must care about her. Or at least he took responsibility for her. Were they the same thing? Not necessarily.

She lay under the great crystal and paid attention to the sensations dancing across her skin. There was a tickling—no, a vibration. A humming of energy that made the hairs on her arms stand up. As the room grew quiet, a whisper became apparent.

King Zander will restore us to our planet. He needs you. Pay attention to all knowing.

She sat bolt upright and opened her eyes.

Zander's lids flew open and he glared at her. He pointed to the door, "*Out.*"

She snatched up the shirt and lay back down, covering her face again. "No, no. I'll be good. I'm sorry."

Her heart pounded against her ribs. No one was in the room but the two of them. Even as her rational brain struggled to answer the riddle, she already knew—the crystal had spoken to her. The *vecking* crystal.

Something about the experience made her weep. There was a lightness, a benevolence projecting from the crystal. Love, in its purest form. She felt grateful to be in its presence, grateful to be spoken to, to be needed by Zander.

Except...no. She couldn't tell Zander. Clearly he hadn't heard anything. Zandians, like humans, weren't supposed to just "know" things. Or "hear" things. Or "see" things. And while it may not be a trait punishable by death for a Zandian, it sure as hell was for a human.

So how would she help Zander with her knowing— the knowing that had never done her a bit of good in her life—when she couldn't reveal how she knew things?

CHAPTER EIGHT

"Gunt has stolen over thirty crystals from the pod in the last three solar cycles." Seke rubbed his forehead, his mouth turned down in disgust. "He sells them to Ocretions for a tidy sum. I'm sorry I didn't catch it."

"Where is he now?"

"He's in a holding cell."

Zander sighed. One of the downfalls of being part of a nearly extinct species was that he couldn't ever cut any being loose. He'd love to banish Gunt, but he didn't want to lose or waste any Zandian life.

"Leave him there. What else did you find? How did my human know?"

Zeke shook his head. "There's no other recording of the two of them, but I told you that before. There's no recording of her seeing him take them—they were all taken and sold before she got here."

Tension ran up Zander's shoulders to his neck. Something tight in his stomach made him feel sick. "But how could she know?" His voice rasped a little. "She was an agri-slave before she came here."

Zandian moons was she not a slave? Was she some kind of plant—perhaps part of the Finns' plot to kill him? But that would mean Daneth was part of it. Or someone had tampered with his program...

Seke's eyes narrowed, and he knew the older man had the same thoughts. He was the one who had taught Zander the art of war and strategy, after all. "I don't know."

Zander stood up. "I'll question her."

Turmoil swirled through his insides as he stalked back to his chamber where he'd left Lamira out of her cage. He wouldn't make that mistake again.

He opened the door and let it close behind him. Lamira scrambled off the bed to stand before him, naked, as he required. Her beauty angered him now.

Was she an elaborate ploy to get close to him? If so, to what end? And how dangerous could she be? He could snap her neck with the flick of a hand.

He stared at her for a moment and watched her fidget. "How did you know about Gunt and the crystals?"

Genuine fear flashed across her face—her pupils narrowed, breath shortened. He smelled it coming from her pores.

It chilled him. So she did have something to hide.

She shook her head quickly and took a step back. "I didn't. It was a guess, that's all. Was I right?"

"Come here."

Something twitched in her cheek. She stepped closer to him.

He picked her up by the armpits and lifted her until they came eye to eye. "Do. Not. Lie to me." He kept his voice even and cold.

A shiver ran through her. It brought him some small satisfaction. Her reactions were so transparent. She couldn't be a spy. At least, not a trained agent. She was a terrible liar and while her emotions confused him, she wore them on the outside. Surely a spy—even a human one—would have more skill.

"Zander, please. I swear—I don't know anything."

"You knew about Gunt. How did you?"

"He didn't seem trustworthy, that's all."

Zander shook his head. "No. You told me he was stealing crystals. That's a specific accusation, and Master Seke has proven it to be true. So how did you know?"

His little slave looked beautiful with tears swimming in her eyes, lips trembling, a wide-eyed pleading look on her face, her naked body vulnerable and available to him. "I didn't know," she insisted, not quite meeting his eyes.

He dropped her back to her feet. "I promised you a whipping the next time you lied."

She blanched, her little hands reaching back to cover her still-marked ass. He should punish her again, but he couldn't bring himself to. Still, anger coursed through his body, much like it had the night before. Once more, this little human had completely thrown off his equilibrium.

"I punished you yesterday when you didn't deserve it, so I won't strap you again. But I am very angry with you. Kneel at my feet and do not speak—I do not wish to hear your voice."

He turned away from her, taking a seat at his work platform, but his mind was on nothing but the docile, delicate creature at his feet. When had she become so submissive? Had he already tamed her in a short week? How?

She sniffed, and he smelled the scent of her salty tears.

"Why are you crying? I haven't caused you pain. Yet."

"I'm not crying."

He grabbed her hair and yanked her head back. "You continue to lie when evidence of the truth is right here on your face?" He flicked his tongue to catch the salty drop.

She jerked her head away. "Stupid master. I'm not"—she huffed out a sigh—"the words weren't intended to deceive."

He let the *stupid master* part slide, only because her face crinkled with distress. "Oh, right, they are what you wish were true. If you do not wish to cry, do not. Is it so hard for you?"

She jerked away. "Yes."

He picked her up and arranged her on his lap, gripping her face to turn it toward him. "Why do you cry?"

The tears continued to swim in her eyes. "I don't like displeasing you."

His eyebrows slammed down. "If you do not like displeasing me, then don't," he thundered, the deep tones of his voice reverberating against the walls.

She flinched, shrinking back from him.

He remembered that he'd truly frightened her the last time. But shouldn't a slave be afraid of her master when she disobeys?

"Tell me the truth."

Again real fear flashed in her eyes. What was she hiding?

"Come here." He pulled her up by her arm and marched her to the spanking bench Daneth had provided. With a shove, he positioned her over it and snapped her cuffs to lock her in place.

"Zander...Zander, please. I didn't know. I don't know anything."

"Stop the lies." He slapped her upturned ass, and she shrieked. After rooting through the box of implements, he found the butt plug and ginger oil to make it burn. He coated the plug in the oil and pressed the tip against her little rosette. "I won't whip you, but you deserve to feel my dissatisfaction, slave."

She squeezed her butt cheeks together to keep him out.

"Open up, or I will change my mind about spanking you."

"Zander..." Her voice shook.

His armband flashed her readout: *Forty percent aroused.*

"Now."

One cheek relaxed then the other. He rubbed the bulbous head of the butt plug over her anus and waited for the sphincter muscles to relax. The moment they did, he pushed the object inside, stretching her slowly.

"No," she cried out. "Ah!"

Seventy percent aroused.

"Bad slave." He eased the plug in farther, and she squealed at the largest part. She took the entire plug into her cavity, her anus closing around the narrow neck, leaving the steel handle protruding.

Ninety-five percent aroused.

He pumped it a few times, the sounds of alarm she made turning his cock rock hard. She tightened around the plug.

Climax achieved.

"Did you come?" he snapped. "Bad slave. You do not orgasm without my cock inside you—without my seed inside you." He spanked her with his hand, the plug jostling as she bucked.

One hundred percent aroused.

He unclipped her from the bench and fastened her wrists behind her back. With a tug, he pulled her to sit on his lap on the sleeping platform, facing away from him. He pinched both her nipples. She threw herself back against him, arching and writhing. He spread her knees so wide they hooked over his, leaving her pussy exposed and vulnerable. With a snap of his wrist, he spanked her wet pussy, his fingers slapping again and again to punish her.

Climax approaching.

"Oh! Oh please. Oh wait—stop—Zander! No... Oh no, I'm going to do it again—"

He shoved his pants down and lifted her onto his cock. She slid on easily, her passageway swollen and wet, more than ready for him. He lifted and lowered her over his cock, the end of the butt plug connecting with his pelvis and shoving it in deeper on each instroke.

Lamira babbled something—nonsense mostly, her gasps and cries one long string of sound.

He moved her just the way he wanted her—grinding over his cock, her back arching and breasts thrusting in the air. He bounced her up and down until he couldn't hold back any longer. Yanking her in, he climaxed, shooting his load. It only took one tap of his finger against her clitoris and his little human came, too, her muscles squeezing his cock, massaging it, milking it for his seed.

Climax achieved.

Since she was still being punished, he didn't cuddle her afterward, but lifted her up and placed her on the sleepdisk, with her ankles strung up in the air, holding her hips aloft.

Ninety-five percent aroused.

Still? Well, so was he.

Somehow, punishment had turned into a glorious game. Yes, he was still annoyed with her, but not enough not to enjoy her luscious body. She looked unbelievably hot strung up like that. He adjusted one of her ankles so her legs were spread wide. The view of her pussy was spectacular. Swollen, glossy, with traces of rainbow colors from his seed. He brought his hand down between her legs and spanked her swollen folds again.

~.~

She couldn't help it. She climaxed again, the moment he slapped her sex.

Of course, there was no hiding it, with his cuff giving off constant data on the state of her vagina.

He slapped her clenching pussy again. "What did I say about orgasming without my cock inside you?"

She couldn't muster any intelligible reply. "Ugn...uh..."

"I will let it slide, since my seed is already planted."

She couldn't decide if he was playing with her or was genuinely still angry. The line had grown blurry during sex. She feared he had come to understand his dominance aroused her. She hadn't yet admitted it to herself, even, but his damn arm cuff didn't lie.

"You will remain in this position for thirty minutes." He set a timer on his cuff and turned away.

She sighed. The position left her still impossibly aroused, despite the multiple orgasms. She prayed no one entered the chamber to see her like that.

Zander worked at his platform while she tried to cool her engines.

The ankle cuffs began to cut into her flesh and her feet went numb. She shifted around, but there was little she could do in the ridiculous position.

Zander turned his violet gaze on her. He didn't seem angry.

"Please, my lord. My feet have lost all feeling."

He stood and sauntered over, grasping one of her feet. She gasped as pins and needles shot through when he touched it. With a quick command, he released the clips on her ankles and scooped her into his arms, carrying her to his sitting platform where he sank back down with her cradled in his lap.

This. Yes. Stars, yes. She loved when he held her afterward. She rubbed her feet together, tensing at the sensation returning to them.

He looked down at her and tweaked one nipple between his thumb and forefinger. "I like when you look at me like that."

She hardly dared breathe. Was Zander actually paying her a compliment? "How do I look?" She spoke softly, not wishing to jar Zander out of his unusual tenderness.

He smirked. "Like I'm your entire universe."

"Well," she said lightly, "you *are* my master."

His eyes narrowed as if trying to determine if she was being sarcastic. For once, she wasn't. She'd meant what she said. He was her master. In the short time she'd been with him, he had become her entire world. Bending to his will meant avoiding punishment, and even earning comfort. So, yes, he had become her entire universe.

"Lamira, you must tell me the truth now."

All the post-climactic languor fled her body in a single moment. She stiffened in his arms, attempting to sit upright. He didn't allow it. "Don't lie again."

She blinked up at him. She wanted to obey. But how could she? It would mean her death.

"Are you really from an agrifarm?"

"Yes, my lord. I swear it." She met his unbelieving eyes.

How could she prove her innocence?

"I can show you the plants I've started in your great hall," she offered. She'd been dying to show him her work but had made herself wait until more had sprouted.

He lifted her to her feet, his lips pursed. "All right. Show me."

She turned big pleading eyes on him. "Take the plug out? Please, my lord?" It still burned, heating her pelvis from the inside out.

"No." His voice had the hard edge to it. He had not forgiven her, no matter what gentleness he'd shown after sex.

"You're still angry."

He nodded. "Yes. I don't see the point of keeping a slave I cannot trust."

She stopped on her way to put on her clothes, a chill running through her. "Zander," she breathed, her vision blurring.

Would he send her back? The thought of returning to the agrifarm, even to her mother, left her empty. That wasn't where she belonged. The crystals had spoken to her. She'd seen the baby.

That's right, she'd seen the baby. He wouldn't send her away. She'd prove her innocence to him. She yanked on her clothing and drew herself up, her head held high.

~.~

Lamira chattered on about her plants, using the Latin Earth names for the little sprouts. The glow on her face nearly matched the sunlight pouring in through the crystals, shining through her coppery hair in shimmering waves.

She walked stiffly, the plug in her ass plainly causing her discomfort, the flush on her face as clear a readout as the one on his cuff.

He liked her aroused. Maybe he'd keep her that way all day until she confessed her secret. It was hard to believe she was a spy. She wasn't good enough at it. But why wouldn't she tell him how she knew about Gunt stealing crystals?

"So you see? Soon we'll have fresh food grown here. The plants love your crystal light—it's amazing how quickly the seedlings have grown. Three times as fast as they would've on the agrifarm. I only wish I had more space. I'd love to have an entire room of raised beds to work with."

He steeled himself against her beauty, against the way his lips fought to reward her excitement with a smile. The more he was around her, the more discombobulated he became. This human was trouble for him.

He gripped her elbow. "It's time for your ass-*vecking*."

Her green eyes flew wide and the color drained from her face. "But, my lord..."

"Unless you're ready to tell me how you knew about Gunt?"

Her expression clouded, worry gathering on her brow.

"Let's go." He tugged her back down the hall, the thought of taking her ass putting a spring into his step.

Perhaps their impasse did not have to be unpleasant. He certainly enjoyed punishing his little slave.

He led her to his chamber and propelled her into the washroom. "Clothes off."

Like an obedient breeder, she stripped, folding her clothes neatly and stacking them in a pile on the counter. She seemed eager to appease him. He could get used to having her around. And that was cause for concern. Because, right now, he should be focused on winning the battle for Zandia.

"Bend over the counter." He spun her around and pushed her torso down on the cool stone surface. Daneth had given him equipment to clean her bowels, and he pulled it out now, attaching one end of the hose to the water line from the sink and filling the water bag.

The handle of the oiled plug nested between her pretty cheeks, giving evidence to her humiliation. She'd be getting an even larger dose now. He eased the plug out of her hole, smiling at her gasp.

"Reach back and hold your cheeks open for me."

"Why?"

He slapped her ass. "Really, little slave? You're going to question me?"

"No, my lord," she mumbled. He met her eyes in the mirror and saw anguished surrender.

Beautiful.

"Open them wide."

"Yes, my lord." She reached back and peeled her lovely cheeks wide, exposing the delicate pink rosebud of her anus.

He rubbed a lubricant—not the ginger kind this time—on the top of the nozzle and inserted it into her anus.

Her gasp of alarm made his cock hard.

He opened the clamp and let the water fill her bowels.

She moaned. "Please, my lord. What are you doing? Please don't…"

He liked her begging.

The bag emptied.

"I'm cleaning you out for me. I need you to hold that water until I say you can let it go."

"I can't," she moaned. "Please, my lord."

"Tell me how you knew about Gunt."

Silence.

"Are you a spy?"

"No, no, no, no," she breathed, her self-control clearly challenged by holding the water inside her. "Not a spy. It was a lucky guess."

"Don't insult me with your lies."

"Please," she whined. "I can't hold it any longer."

"Two more minutes."

"I can't…"

"You will."

He smelled the salty scent of her tears. For a moment, he regretted pushing her, but then he remembered her lies.

She shifted from foot to foot, her anus visibly clenching in spasms around the tube still inserted in her ass. At last, he removed it. "Empty yourself for your ass-*vecking*." He left her alone in the washroom to finish up.

She emerged, subdued and pale.

"On the sleeping platform, on your knees and forearms. Ass in the air."

She crawled up to the platform and assumed the position.

"Spread your knees wider."

She obeyed. The lips of her sex parted wide, swollen and wet.

He ran his finger lightly over her slit, smiling when her entire body shuddered. "What happens to slaves who lie to their masters?"

"I-I don't know," she whispered.

He rubbed his finger over her clitoris, feeling it swell and harden under his fingertip.

"They get their asses *vecked*. Hard. Is that what you want?"

He spread her glossy juices up to her clit.

She made an unintelligible sound.

"Bad slave." He released his cock from his trousers and rubbed lubricant over it. "You have displeased your master."

"Forgive me," she panted, sounding breathless.

He fit a large vibrating dildo in her cunt and flicked it on.

She gave a startled, wanton cry.

"Hold still," he commanded and pushed the head of his cock against her anus, waiting until the tight ring of muscle relaxed and allowed him entry.

Her moans sounded alarmed.

Despite his purpose in punishing her, he experienced a rush of affection. To take his large Zandian cock in her tight ass asked a lot. Her humbled position endeared her to him. From his point of view, her bottom splayed wide, her cunt dripping, her ass taking his cock like a good slave, she was *vecking* gorgeous. He slid in and out, loving the tightness.

"Bad little slave," he murmured, but his tone sounded affectionate. He couldn't help it—he loved taking her like this, loved owning her so completely.

He turned up the speed on the vibrating wand in her twat and pumped harder.

She wailed beneath him, her cries rising to a keening pitch. "Please, master, please. I'm sorry. I'll be a good slave. I swear I'll be a good slave."

His balls tightened. He shot his load, wasting his seed in her ass. It had been worth it. Euphoric victory coursed through his veins.

He eased out of his slave's ass and turned off the vibrator. "You didn't climax," he murmured, gathering Lamira up in his arms.

"No, but it feels like I did." Her lips barely moved. Her body lay limp and spent in his arms. A sheen of sweat gave her skin a glow.

Beautiful.

He wanted to give her the world. He couldn't wait for her mother to arrive.

He wished they were not at an impasse over her lies.

~.~

Zander punished her every planet rotation. During the days, he put her in the cage and left. She had a feeling he was training for war—his plans to take back his planet filtered into her consciousness daily. Since the crystal bath, her knowings had come more often, more clearly. She saw an image of her mother, dressed in luxurious robes, and rejoiced that she was still alive and would know freedom.

At night, he asked her if she was ready to tell him the truth. When she refused, he punished her. The first night he paddled her with a horrible wooden board. She sobbed and begged for his mercy, but, as usual, her traitorous body somehow became aroused at the punishment, ready for him to breed the moment the spanking ended.

The next night, he went easy on her, perhaps taking pity on her still-swollen ass. He spanked her with his hand and forced her to suck his cock until he came down her throat.

The third night, he used a terrible cane on her. That night, she'd wept so bitterly at the pain he had not bred her, instead he'd taken her into his arms on his sleepdisk, stroking her back and hair until she drifted off to sleep.

The fourth night, he used only his hand again.

She couldn't hate him. He took such care with her, even when he punished. It was odd, but while she feared the pain he liked to inflict, she wasn't afraid of him. Not the way she had been afraid of the guards at the agrifarm. Not even the way she was wary of Daneth, though he'd never hurt her.

She woke the following morning with her wrists chained over her head, Zander's hot hands roaming over her breasts.

She arched into them, shivers of excitement rolling through her. Her pussy, which was nearly perpetually wet since Zander had begun breeding her, heated and began to pulse.

"Little Lamira. You're such a bad slave."

No, I'm not. I'm your good slave.

Where did that come from? At what point had she started desiring his approval? Wanting to please him? Right from the beginning, it seemed.

He straddled her and brought his thumb and forefinger to one of her nipples, pinching it. "When are you going to stop lying to me?"

God, would he ever let it go?

Her eyes slid sideways, away from his amethyst gaze.

Slap. His palm swatted the side of her breast. She arched and yanked against her binding.

"Do I need to spank your breasts?" He slapped its twin.

"Oh! No..." She writhed beneath him, uselessly trying to twist away from him, to hide herself.

Despite the pain and what was worse—the fear at this new, untried form of punishment—moisture seeped onto her inner thigh. Her wanton pussy was ready for whatever her large master had to offer.

He slapped her breast one more time but then climbed off, his gaze decidedly cool. "No, I think I'll try something else today."

A fresh ripple of fear went through her and she shivered. "Master?"

"I will deny you my cock. You may have been reluctant to take it at first, but now I think you've grown to enjoy it...perhaps it is too much of a reward."

She ought to be relieved the punishment was so mild, but he was right—denying her his cock left her yearning. Empty. Rejected.

Shifting his tone into the quiet command he used on the electronics, he said, "Release cuffs."

She sat up, whimpering at the pain of the blood rushing fully into her arms.

Zander looked over his shoulder at her on his way to the washroom and she swore she saw a wrinkle of concern on his forehead. He hesitated but then shook his head and entered the washroom.

She flopped back on the sleepdisk and sighed. Living with her master presented a new torture every day. Not the kind she'd expected. No, the emotional kind. Longing and angst. Need, desire...and love? It made her stomach clench to think the word, but, yes, she'd certainly become emotionally attached. Bonded. Maybe it was love, maybe it wasn't. She really didn't know about these things.

Her stomach rumbled. She got up, dressed, and tapped on the washroom door. "Master? May I go to the kitchen to eat?"

"Yes." His answer was short and clipped. "But return in twenty minutes. I'm leaving for the United Galaxies meeting this morning, and you must stay in your cage while I'm gone.

Ugh. A long day alone in the cage. She'd hated the last few days. Servants brought her food and liquid and let her out for a walk and to use the washroom, but she hated staying cooped up. The only way she'd kept from going insane was paying attention to her claircognizance. Something she never used to do.

She walked down to the kitchen. "Good morning, Barr," she chirped. Seeing the friendly chef always cheered her.

He rewarded her with a broad smile. "Lamira. Guess what I made for you this morning?" He set a plate with a beautiful breakfast pie in front of her.

"It's called quiche. Have you ever heard of it? It's a human recipe I researched."

She blinked back tears. "You researched human recipes?"

"Yes, from old Earth. I know you probably wouldn't know them, but I thought perhaps they'd be especially good for your body." He blushed after mentioning her body.

She smiled. "That was so thoughtful of you. What's in it?"

The older Zandian beamed. The crust is made with flour and butter, the inside is egg, cream, cheese and vegetables. He waited with anticipation on his face, for her to take her first bite.

She picked up the utensil and popped a serving into her mouth. "Mmm...it's...absolutely delicious," she said, still chewing. "Thank you so much!"

Barr smiled. "My pleasure."

She ate quickly, partly to show Barr how much she loved it and partly because she didn't want to be late for her curfew. When she'd eaten every last crumb from the plate, she stood. "Thank you again. Really. I am touched by your efforts. You're wonderful, Barr."

His skin turned a darker purple and he ducked his head. "Have a good day, Lamira."

"You too, Barr."

She headed back to Zander's room, running down the hallway in case she was late.

Zander stood outside the door to his chamber, listening to Master Seke tell him something. Their heads were bent together and Zander's forehead wrinkled.

He threw her a distracted look and opened the door. "Go in your cage."

That was it? He was trusting her to go in the cage on her own. Her heart picked up speed as she contemplated disobedience. To be safe, she crawled up into the cage and swung the door mostly shut but stopped before the lock clicked into place. There. If he came in and secured it, that would be that. If not...would she dare leave it during the day? Would his servants know and report her?

Well, she could figure that out after he left.

She listened for the sound of the door opening, but it never came.

As always, she closed her eyes to shut out the closeness of the bars. An image immediately flooded her mind.

It showed Zander's ship docking somewhere—a huge complex—the United Galaxies headquarters, perhaps. The moment it arrived, the dock blew into smithereens.

She gulped for air.

No.

Oh stars, no. Zander.

Kicking open the cage, she scrambled out and ran for the door. For a moment, she feared Zander had locked it so she couldn't leave, but it slid open.

She raced down the hall, her bare feet digging into the luxurious rugs. Where would he be? Had he already gone? Remembering the direction of the dock from Gunt's tour, she charged through space.

There.

At the end of the corridor, surrounding by a group of guards and advisors, about to step out into the docking platform.

"Zander!" she screamed.

He whirled around, a frown creasing his brow.

Ah stars, what would she tell him? She couldn't say what she'd seen.

But she had to stop him—had to.

"What are you doing out of your cage?" he demanded.

"My lord—you can't go!"

She reached him and gripped his forearm, tugging at it. Of course, he was completely immovable. Her heart beat wildly in her chest, the image of the explosion still burning her eyes.

"What in the Zandian moons are you doing? Why aren't you in your cage?"

Under different circumstances, she'd be embarrassed that he mentioned her cage in front of other beings, but she didn't have time to care now. All that mattered was keeping him from getting on that ship.

"Zander—please don't go. You can't!" She probably sounded hysterical. Hell, she felt hysterical. "Please, my lord."

He gripped her shoulders and gave her a shake, like a naughty child. "What's wrong with you?"

She needed to give him some kind of reason. Her brain raced, searching for something, anything she could tell him that would make him stay. "Right now. I'm ovulating. You have to breed me. This is our one chance for the lunar cycle."

Yes, it was a stupid reason, but it was the first thing she could think of.

"I think the crystal bath kicked it into gear."

Zander's brow furrowed even further, but he shook her off his arm. "Go back to your cage, Lamira. *Now*. I have to get to the UG complex and I don't have time to waste with you today."

She grasped him again, holding his arm tight as he tried to tug it away, causing him to yank her forward and into the air. She twisted wildly as her feet grasped for purchase, refusing to let go of his forearm.

"*Lamira*." He shook his arm so hard, her teeth rattled. So much disapproval and irritation rang through in that single word, but she didn't care. If she let Zander go, he'd die. She'd seen it.

"You *cannot* go," she hissed.

His eyes blazed dark purple. A muscle in his jaw tightened.

"This is unacceptable." The room tilted and flipped upside down as she found herself upended over Zander's shoulder. His hand clapped down on her ass, hard. "Start the engines. I will be there in a moment," he barked over his shoulder as he walked swiftly down the corridor.

Think, Lamira, think. There must be a way to convince him to stay. Something she could do or say?

Zander slapped her ass again, his irritation coming through clearly in the stinging blow.

She steeled herself against the continued spanks. If she'd known sooner, she might have disabled the ship. No, that was foolish. She didn't have the slightest clue how to disable a ship, even if she were able to get away with such a thing.

They arrived back in Zander's chambers, where he dropped her on her feet and glowered.

"Don't go," she whispered, her body trembling from her scalp to the tips of her toenails.

Zander put his hands on his hips. "What is this about? Is this because I denied you sex this morning?"

"No—" It was silly to keep the up the lie about her ovulation, but she hadn't come up with a better idea. "It's just now is our best chance—to conceive a baby. It has to be right now."

He glanced at his armband. "I do not have the time right now. I am the ambassador of my species, and I'm supposed to be at a United Galaxies meeting representing our interests *at this very moment.* Are you so foolish you cannot discern what is of the highest importance here?"

Tears of desperation leaked from the corners of her eyes. "Zander...you don't understand..."

He'd lost all patience with her, though, and stalked to the box of punishment tools. He withdrew the cane she hated with every particle of her being.

Well, at least it meant he was staying—if only for a few more minutes.

He grabbed her elbow and spun her around to face the sleeping platform. "Bend over, pants down."

Nothing could be more humiliating than folding her torso over the platform and reaching back to bare her own bottom for his punishment. She gritted her teeth, flinching when the cool air reached her butt cheeks.

The cane sliced through the air.

She cried out, rising onto her toes.

"That is for leaving your cage."

He whipped her again.

"Or did you never get into it?"

"I did, I did!" she cried out, as if that would stop the horrible cane from swinging again.

"Is that another one of your lies?" he demanded, the cane landing again.

"No, master! I was in it, but the door never locked!" *Because I didn't lock it.*

He laid another stripe across her twitching flesh.

Stars, it hurt.

"And that is for refusing to return when I ordered it." Two quick strikes.

She felt certain she was going to die.

"And this is for still arguing with me as if you might pester me into getting your way." Three more terrible strokes.

She sobbed into the sleepdisk covers.

He threw the cane on the sleeping platform. "Now get in that cage and stay there until I return."

No. She couldn't let him leave. She pushed herself weakly to her feet and turned, her pants tangling around her legs. "Don't go," she croaked. "You can't leave—please don't go."

He threw her a look of disgust and stalked out, the door whooshing closed behind him.

She stood there, tears streaking her face, her ass on fire, trying to think of something else she might do to keep him from that meeting. But nothing came. Her brain had frozen in fear, stopped cold with the vision of her master —her lover—exploding.

~.~

Zander drew deep breaths as his long, hurried strides carried him back to the ship dock. He'd thought Lamira was smarter than that. What in the stars had she been thinking? He ought to punish her again when he returned. No. He needed to talk to her, to try to understand why she felt so strongly about breeding with him today. Because surely she understood she risked punishment, and yet she did it anyway.

He glanced at his cuff. *Veck, veck veck.* He should be flying already. They'd assigned his ship a specific garage and dock time to cut down on air traffic problems, and now he'd be lucky if he made it by the end of the window. And he had planned to leave with plenty of time to spare. He hated being late. The UG required each ambassador to dock and remain in their docking area for security clearance. The entire process took at least an hour. If he missed his docking window, he might have to wait even longer to be allowed out of his docking garage and into the Great Hall.

His guards stood at the dock door, looking alert and ready. Master Seke also stood waiting. He would accompany Zander into the meeting and serve as his primary advisor and protector.

They folded in when he passed, following him onto the craft. He sat down in the pilot's chair, not because he didn't have staff who could fly but because he preferred to be the one in control. All the battle flight simulators in the galaxy didn't compare to actual flight. Not that the simple flight path to the UG was anything like a battle.

Seke took the co-pilot's chair. His expression was blank, as always. He wouldn't ask about Lamira, either. He was a being of few words.

"The human is disrupting everything," he complained. He knew he sounded like a petulant, spoiled little prince. She was his breeder. He should be able to handle her without whining to his advisors about it. Zander eased the craft out of the docking station and zipped onto the flight path at top speed. He needed to make up the time he'd spent with Lamira in his chamber.

Seke leaned back in his chair. "Yes, she has affected you."

That wasn't what he meant. What in the Zandian moons was Seke saying?

His aggravation level increased. The spacecraft wove in and out of traffic, maintaining speed.

"She's too big a distraction. I cannot go on—"

"Give it more time," Seke interrupted in his ever-calm voice. "We've never had a female living on the pod before. It's natural for adjustments to occur."

He gave his head a quick shake. Even now he was thinking about her when he should be focused on the assembly meeting.

He slowed the speed of the craft as the traffic grew heavier around the UG pod. Winding his way through the other airships, he circled to the back to his assigned docking station. He glanced at his cuff. One minute late. Hopefully they hadn't opened the inner doors yet.

He cut the engines completely and coasted in toward the dock.

White light exploded in front of them and, a second later, a boom deafened him.

"Cut away," Seke barked, unbuckling his harness.

He flicked the switch for the engines to fire back to life at the same time he wrenched the steering arm to the left. The craft banked, flying into flames.

For a moment, he thought the entire ship would explode—he'd flown too close to the source of the fire. But then the smoke and flames cleared and the craft circled away.

The moment they were free of the flames, Seke ran back to man the weaponry, barking orders at the guards. "Check for incoming."

"We have three on our tail, Master," one of the guards shouted back.

"Fire at will."

Laser fire lit up the windows.

Zander dodged the cluster of airships in his way, dropping down to lure the attacking ships into open territory where his crew could get a clear shot. It must be a Finnian attack.

A flash of light glared behind them as one ship exploded.

"Target one, destroyed," his guard reported.

"Target two acquired," Seke said, his voice still calm, even while the rest of the crew yelled.

Another explosion.

"Target two destroyed."

"Third target has fallen back."

He whipped the craft around. No way he was letting his enemy get away. Chasing the retreating fighter craft, he wove in and out of traffic, keeping his gaze locked on target three."

"A little closer, my lord."

He shoved the throttle open, hurtling forward through space.

"Target three acquired. And..."

Another ship darted into their path, and Zander yanked up to avoid a crash. *Veck.* He swung back around, but the fighter craft had disappeared.

"Where is it?" he shouted.

The area was too congested. Aircraft flew all around. The *vecking* enemy had slipped through their fingers.

Seke returned to the co-pilot's chair and sat down.

"I'm going back to the UG."

"Not advised. That was a trap, laid precisely for you. We must get you back to the pod and tighten security."

"I'm not running to hide like a terrified animal!"

"This is not the war. It was not even a battle. It was a plot to assassinate you before you have a chance to assemble your warriors. Do not give them an additional chance to kill you. Your species need you alive."

He gritted his teeth, but turned the craft and recharted for his pod.

"The bomb must have been set on a timer. If you had been on time, we all would have died."

Ice washed over his skin.

He remembered Lamira's wild eyes as she yanked at his arm. *My lord—you can't go.* She'd seemed desperate to stop him. *"She knew."* He glanced over at Seke, to see if the master warrior had arrived at the same conclusion.

"It seems so."

A heavy silence fell over them. How did she know? Was she part of this assassination plot? Had she been planted as an insider? Perhaps she'd fallen in love and changed her mind.

In love. The thought tore at his heart.

She'd saved his life and he'd whipped her for her troubles.

But who was she? A stone sank to the pit of his stomach. He could never trust this human. Not even if he kept her locked up in a cage for the rest of her life. There were too many unknowns about her unusual knowledge, and too many beings who wanted him dead.

~.~

Lamira jerked awake to the sound of voices in the corridor. She shifted in the cage and gasped at the pain still radiating from her ass. Worse was the incredible tightness in her chest, the heaviness of lead weighing it down.

Zander. Her Zander. Was he already dead? Some part of her wailed inside in mourning.

The door slid open.

Was it already lunchtime?

She twisted and her breath caught.

"Zander!"

Her master looked pale, but unharmed. His haunted gaze raked over her.

"Open cage."

She scrambled out and he caught her and lifted her down, but his brows were drawn together, as if disturbed.

"Zander, are you all right?"

"You knew." His voice cracked.

She reached out to touch his face, still overjoyed to see him alive.

He caught her wrist but allowed the touch, pressing her hand to his cheek. "Were you trying to save me?"

If her emotions were not so wrecked from fear and then joy, she would have played it differently. She would have played ignorant. But his drawn expression made her worry—perhaps his crew had died.

"A-are you all right? Was anyone hurt?"

"Who set the bomb? How are you connected to them?" The lash of his cold voice whipped her.

She jerked her hand away, realizing her colossal mistake. Shaking her head, she backed away. "No...I don't know anything."

"Enough with your lies!" He lunged forward and caught her by the throat, lifting her from the floor and squeezing until her breath died.

She kicked and clawed at his fingers, her eyes bugging out in panic.

As if he suddenly realized he might kill her, he dropped her, pain etched in the deepened lines on his forehead.

She coughed, rubbing her throat.

He stood staring at her, his fingers clenching and unclenching in fists. Were those tears swimming in his eyes?

The sight of him, so reduced from her deceit, made her abandon her pretense and speak more directly. "I'm not working with your enemies—I swear to you, Zander. I have no connections. But I can't tell you how I knew or it could mean my life."

"You are safe here," Zander roared, the muscles bulging in his neck and shoulders as he took a step forward. When she flinched backward, he stopped himself and didn't touch her. Perhaps he was afraid he might kill her. He jabbed his chest. "I will protect you. My enemies won't touch you here."

"It's not your enemies. You wouldn't even believe me, if I told you the truth. I just—I can't tell you."

He stepped closer and grasped the hair at the back of her head, tipping her head back. His face drew very close to hers, his beautiful eyes light-purple. "You must tell me," he whispered hoarsely, his lips centimeters from hers, his gaze so intent, she thought she'd dissolve into a puddle.

She blinked back at him, her knees weak and wobbly, her breath stalled in her chest. "I can't," she finally managed to say.

She expected anger, but instead Zander closed his eyes. He released her hair and cradled her face, bringing his forehead to touch hers. When his lids blinked open, she was certain she saw excess moisture there.

"Lamira—" he began, his throat catching. "You saved my life and for that, I will make sure you live out your life in peace."

Her heart missed a beat as it roared to a gallop, thudding painfully against her sternum. Was he getting rid of her? "Zander—" she cried in protest.

"Shh." He tightened his grip on her face, covering her ears with his large palms. "I...I cannot go on this way." His voice choked. "I can't keep you near me when you cannot be trusted." He thumbed away a tear she didn't realize she'd cried. "I know you care about me. I saw your distress this morning when you thought I would die. I care about you, too. More than I would like to admit." His forehead wrinkled. "Is this what you humans call love?"

Love. Was it? Stars, yes. She loved this being with all her heart, despite her position as his slave and breeder.

She nodded, fresh tears streaming down her face.

He mopped them with his thumbs. Tilting his head down, he crushed his lips to hers, licking and sucking, demanding her kiss roughly.

She gave it to him, hoping—praying it didn't mean what she thought it did. *Good-bye.*

But it did. When he broke away, he raised his voice and called to Herman, the guard who had replaced Gunt outside his door. "Take Lamira and her things to a guest chamber."

"Of course, my lord." Herman flicked a curious glance at her.

She pointed weakly at the shelf where her clothing lay stacked in neat piles. "Those are my only things."

Herman scooped them up and led the way out the door.

"Zander..." Her voice broke. "Please don't do this."

"Go, Lamira. It's not safe for me to be around you."

She choked back a sob and turned to follow Herman, her head bowed in surrender.

This could not be how things ended. She would find a way to prove her trustworthiness to Zander again.

~.~

Zander pulled off his boot and hurled it against the wall. The clunk was not nearly as satisfying as he'd hoped, but he repeated the action with the second boot anyway.

Why?

What did all this mean? His beautiful Lamira...his slave. A spy? How was she tangled up in the political machinations of the Galaxy? What connections did she have that gave her such underground knowledge—information none of his spies had discovered?

He sank down on the sleeping platform and rubbed his face.

He should send her away—far away.

But how would he live without her?

CHAPTER NINE

Zander leaned his head in his hands at his work platform. He couldn't think. Or, rather, couldn't focus on the work at hand. All he thought about was the youthful human female locked in his guest quarters.

He hadn't risked seeing her—he knew where it would lead. Straight to pushing her down and spreading those long, beautiful legs. Straight to pumping his aching cock inside her tight, wet channel until she screamed and begged for release. Straight to breeding. His body craved her nearly every moment of every planet rotation. But more than the loss of the sex, he missed the sound of her voice, her scent, her lovely face. He missed holding her, the sound of her soft sighs as she slept.

They hadn't had enough time together. He had barely begun to understand her. Had only seen her smile and laugh a few precious times. Had barely learned who she was—what she liked and didn't like, what her past held. Why hadn't he tried to discover these things? He'd been impatient and unkind. He'd thought her beneath him, not worthy of his time. Yet she'd still cared for him. Cared enough to anger him, to goad his worst punishment because she feared for his death.

Perhaps if they'd had more time together before the assassination attempt, he'd understand her better. He'd learn to discern her lies from truth, or to understand why she lied or who she protected. Was it her mother?

He'd demanded an update on the search for her mother daily. Daneth said the Ocretions were pretending they couldn't locate her, most likely to get more money out of him. "Then pay it," he'd shouted the last time he asked for an update. He hoped for a clue about Lamira from her mother. But even if she did not provide him with the information he sought, he wanted Lamira to have someone she loved with her. She deserved that. He'd taken her away from her mother and now imprisoned her in his guest room with very little interaction with any other beings. She must be terribly lonely. He'd refused to watch her hologram, but he felt certain she wept there in that room, all alone.

It wasn't a permanent solution. He knew he needed to make a decision about her. The decision should be to send her away. He could find a decent place for her—maybe even some underground location where humans lived free. Once he reunited her with her mother, he would send them both away.

But why did that decision make his heart ache as if it would cease to beat?

~.~

Lamira thought she would die. She'd been cooped up alone in the beautiful room for eight planet rotations, with no word or sight of Zander. Barr himself had come up a few times to serve her food—at least he missed her. He watched her eat with sad, concerned eyes. He didn't know what happened, or if he did, he didn't speak of it, but he kept an upbeat outlook, saying things like, "When the prince lets you out..."

The two servants who had helped her with the garden stopped in, bringing her small plants and showing her holograms of the rest of them.

And since she already felt dead, she considered, at least twenty times every planet rotation, telling Zander she was ready to confess the truth. She'd rather be reported to the Ocretions and executed than have him believe her unworthy of his trust. But her mother...they shared genes. If it was revealed Lamira had aberrant genes, her mother would be executed as well. She had an obligation to keep the secret her mother had worked so hard to help her hide. It wasn't just about her life.

But Zander's promise to protect her kept ringing in her ears, too. How tied to the Ocretions was he? He lived here, but his pod consisted almost entirely of Zandians. She had literally not seen an Ocretion since she arrived. Maybe he could protect her if he knew her secret. He owned her, after all. He'd bought and paid for her, fair and square. But could they take her away from him if they knew? In her experience, they could do anything they wanted. And Zander needed asylum here until he won back his own planet. No, it was best to keep her silence, even if it did mean banishment from Zander.

But she couldn't go on forever, locked in this room. She needed to beg him to let her out, to serve him still as his gardener, at least. He wouldn't have to see her. He could give her a schedule and she would be sure to never cross paths with him... although the thought made her eyes burn with tears.

She couldn't go on this way. She needed to make peace with Zander. Somehow.

CHAPTER TEN

Leora blinked as she returned to consciousness. A doctor with purple-hued skin and horns leaned over her, taking her blood. Her body and hair had been cleaned of the agrifarm dirt and she wore a white tunic or gown of some kind.

She licked her dry lips. "Where's...my daughter?"

She'd seen this same doctor take Lamira away from the agrifarm. It had terrified her. She'd been lucky getting placed in the agrifarm when she was pregnant with Lamira. When Johan, Lamira's father, had died in the rebellion, she'd managed to remain undetected, her position as a factory worker never questioned. The factory had closed shortly after and she'd been transferred to the agrifarm, where she kept her head down to keep them both safe. The farming required limited interaction with the guard and foremen. They didn't have to serve anyone, or scrape and grovel, or—worst of all—serve Ocretions sexually. She'd managed to hide Lamira's beauty and her claircognizance for twenty-two solar cycles there, which had been a miracle in itself.

But then, one day, Lamira had been summoned to the director's office and this doctor took her away.

The doctor didn't answer her. In fact, he pretended she wasn't speaking. Her wrists and ankles were bound to the table, so she couldn't move.

"Where's Lamira? What have you done with her?"

Her daughter was nearby. A mother knew. She'd always had a tinge of the intuition Lamira had to hide. Hunches, nudgings. She was certain, now, Lamira was here.

"Please tell me what's going on."

This, finally got the doctor's attention. He met her gaze. "You have been purchased by Prince Zander. I am sure he will tell what your duties are to be."

A tap sounded on the door, and it slid open. In the doorway stood a massive warrior of the same species. He wore a sword on his belt— a simple weapon for an advanced species. He walked in, his gait more graceful than she expected from a male of his bulk. His eyes swept over her and their gazes locked.

She caught her breath. His irises were blue, rimmed with purple—incredibly beautiful. As she stared into their depths, they darkened to a blue-violet. His horns somehow struck her as masculine and sexy, although she'd never had an affinity for any species besides her own.

The warrior cleared his throat. "Are you finished with her exam?"

"Yes."

"The prince wishes to question her."

"Tell him her health is in order—nothing good nutrition won't fix." The doctor picked up a bag and fit a tube into it. He shoved the other end into her mouth.

She jerked her head away and something sweet smelling dribbled onto her neck.

"Release her," the warrior snapped. "How can she drink when she's bound to a table on her back?"

The doctor's lips twitched, as if amused by the warrior's irritation, but the rings holding her ankle and her wrist cuffs snapped open.

The warrior walked to her side and held out a hand.

She ignored his hand and scrambled up to sit.

The warrior remained still, watching her. When she met his gaze, he inclined his head slightly in the ghost of a bow. "I am Seke." He waited and, for a moment, she wondered if he thought she ought to know him, but then she realized he was waiting for her to introduce herself.

"Leora."

He took the bag from the doctor and held it out to her. "It's not poisoned. You should drink before you meet the prince. You look thirsty."

She rubbed her cracked lips together. They were absolutely parched. She accepted the bag and drank, closing her eyes at the shock of the delicious taste. She meant to take only a sip or two, in case it was tainted, but her body overrode her mind, and she sucked on the tube, drinking deeply until half the bag had disappeared.

The warrior glowered at the doctor. "You kept her malnourished."

Once more, the doctor's lips twitched. "She cannot eat or drink when unconscious."

"Do you require food?" The warrior turned back to her, his eyebrows knit.

"No...not yet. Thank you."

Something about the warrior had disarmed her. He reminded her of Johan —pure masculinity and quiet strength. And her gut told her he could be trusted.

"Come." He beckoned her off the table and grasped her shoulders.

A shock of heat raced through her body at his touch.

He rotated her slowly to face away from him then caught her wrists and pulled them behind her back. His touch was gentle, despite the obvious strength behind it.

The cuffs clicked together and he turned her back around. She stared up at him, studying his handsome features. A piece of her hair had caught on her chapped lips, and she tried to rub it off with her shoulder.

He reached out and brushed it away. She swore his skin had turned darker purple, his horns rougher. He opened his mouth, as if he was going to say something, but then shut it again. Placing a hand at her lower back, he guided her forward. "Come, Leora. Our prince awaits."

He sure as hell wasn't her prince. But she kept her mouth shut. She needed to find Lamira—needed to know she was still alive and well.

The warrior—Seke—led her through beautiful corridors and into a giant domed room. A giant crystal was embedded in a skylight, and the light that came through was natural.

On a throne, of sorts, a young male sat. Also built of hard muscle, he had the beauty of youth. She lifted her chin and dared to look him in the face. She expected to see haughtiness there, but instead found only a haunted quality to his expression.

"Leora, chosen mate and partner of the human warrior Johan Jonas," Seke said as an introduction.

She flinched to hear him speak Johan's name. How did they know? Would they tell the Ocretions? If so, it meant her certain death.

"Daneth said to tell you she's in good health." She thought she heard disapproval in the warrior's voice—as if he disapproved of her inspection. It warmed her.

The prince cocked his head, searching the warrior with a speculative gaze.

Leora lifted her eyes to glare at him and, to her surprise, he flinched.

"I see where your daughter gets her beauty."

"Where is she? What are you doing with her?"

She expected him to ignore her questions the way the doctor had, but the prince spoke. "She is here. You will see her soon."

The prince sat back and knit his fingers. "Leora...your daughter saved my life last week."

Whatever she'd expected, it hadn't been this. She stared up in surprise.

"But she refuses to tell me how she knew of the planned assassination attempt."

Goose bumps stood up on her skin as she comprehended the situation.

"There's nothing special about my daughter," she clipped, her chin lifted. "It was probably a lucky guess."

The prince's eyes narrowed. "A lucky guess," he spat bitterly. "Yes, I've heard that from her before." He folded his arms across his chest. "Tell me, Leora, what connection do you and Lamira have with the Finn?"

The blood drained from her face, and her hands went clammy. She realized, suddenly what species they must be—Zandians. Ousted from Zandia by the Finn. A homeless species, forced to take refuge on Ocretia. "We have no connection, Your...ah Highness." She shot a quick glance at Seke.

"He is addressed as *my lord* or *Prince Zander*."

"My lord." She dropped a curtsy. "Neither Lamira nor I have any connection with other beings. We kept to ourselves on the agrifarm."

"Except for your connection to the underground human resistance movement."

She caught her breath, her heart pounding. Her throat worked as she swallowed. The prince had inside knowledge about things the Ocretion government had not yet discovered. About Johan, and the resistance. Perhaps he was not aligned with them. She took a chance, and offered the truth. "They are not connected with your enemies, my lord."

His eyebrows shot up at her admission. "What sort of information is passed?"

She swayed on her feet, feeling slightly dizzy. "The things you ask could get people killed."

"I don't work for the Ocretions."

Shivers of fear ran through her body. Her gut told her he spoke the truth—that he could be trusted, but she couldn't risk it. Not until she'd seen Lamira and knew what he wanted with them. "I wish to see my daughter."

"How did your daughter know about the assassination plan?"

She stared back at him, struggling to piece the situation together. So, the Finn had attempted to kill the prince and Lamira had saved him? She wondered if he meant anything to her.

"So you, too, refuse to answer?"

"She saved your life, my lord." She spread her palms. "You said so, yourself. Surely you cannot suspect her of treason or doubt her loyalty?"

He shook his head and stood up. "I cannot trust her."

Was that anguish on his face?

A shock of knowledge rippled through her.

He loved her. This alien cared for her daughter.

Frustration crinkled his forehead. "Take her to Lamira."

Surprised to be dismissed so easily, she dropped an uneasy curtsy. "Thank you, my lord."

"Tell your daughter she has one planet rotation to confess or I will separate and sell you both to the worst—" He stopped and pressed his lips together, and she understood. He was bluffing. And it was a lie he couldn't even finish.

Yes, he loved her.

He turned and stalked out of the room, tension radiating from the set of his shoulders and neck.

The warrior stepped forward and once more placed his hand on her lower back. A shiver ran through her. For the first time in solar cycles, her sex dampened as she thought about those hands touching her in other places.

He applied gentle pressure to turn her toward the door, guiding her forward.

"He loves my daughter." She took the risk to speak her thoughts.

The warrior halted and turned toward her. After a long moment, he said, "I believe it is true." He nudged her forward, guiding her to the hall. "But he cannot keep her if she can't be trusted."

"But she saved his life? Does that count for nothing?"

Seke made a grumbling sound. "The Zandians are an honorable species. It counts for everything. But our prince's continued safety is paramount to all else, even love. If you care for your daughter's happiness, you will convince her to speak the truth."

The warrior stopped in front of a door and pressed his palm to the screen there. The door slid open and her heart skipped a beat.

"Lamira!" she cried and ran to her daughter.

~.~

Zander stalked down the corridor and replayed the interview with Leora in his mind. One thing she said struck him as odd.

There is nothing special about my daughter.

Was it a human turn of phrase? Something he did not quite understand? Or did it mean there *was*, in fact, something special about Lamira? If so, what? In what way would she be different?

Different.

His skin crawled as a realization struck him.

Human slaves had been bred by the Ocretions for certain qualities. Docility, obedience, physical strength. Those who were found to be too intelligent, too resistant, too *special* were eliminated.

Is that what Leora had meant? Did her daughter carry special traits? Perhaps that was why Daneth's program chose her as his perfect mate. Perhaps the system had picked her, not because of some human trait, but because she had some *super*human trait. Something special. And she kept it hidden because her life depended on it. Lamira's defiance had surprised him. Did she carry other aberrant traits?

For the first time in ten planet rotations, the heaviness surrounding him lifted. He changed direction and walked briskly toward Daneth's lab.

"My lord, how did you find the new slave?"

"Her name is Leora."

Daneth took the correction in a stride. "Of course, my lord."

"Daneth, it occurred to me perhaps your program selected Lamira for me because there is something special about her genes."

"Certainly," Daneth said, as if he, too, had considered the possibility. "Her father's warrior genes would be considered out of range. If her relation to him had been known, she would have been killed."

"What if there was something else? Some special sensitivity, perhaps? An ability to predict the future? Or know things she hadn't seen?"

Understanding dawned on Daneth's expression. "A psychic ability, you mean?" He stroked his chin. "Some humans once possessed such gifts, it's possible for a recessive trait to resurface." He flicked on a holograph which projected an image of genes into the space before them. "I don't know how to search for such a gene. I would think if it was known, the Ocretions would have already found it and killed her at birth." He tapped his finger to his chin. "Show brain scan."

An image of her brain floated in the space between them.

"Compare with normal human brain activity."

An area of Lamira's brain lit up with a purple hue. "Above average activity noted," the program reported in a clipped, female voice.

"What is this area of the human brain used for?"

"Unknown."

Daneth rotated the brain image in a circle. "Show brain image of a Venusian."

The Venusians were a humanoid species with extra-large eyes and many extrasensory abilities including telepathy and energetic healing.

The Venusian brain hologram popped up. Daneth spun it around and enlarged the area that had more activity than normal in Lamira's scan. The physician's lips stretched into a grin. "Look how much this area is used." He pointed at the normal human brain scan. "Here, it is not used at all, like most of their brain mass. You were right—she has extrasensory receptor activity." His voice rose in pitch with excitement. "It makes perfect sense to breed with a female with these abilities. Think of the increased power of your offspring!"

He didn't care about his offspring at that moment. All he cared about was reclaiming Lamira.

"Thank you, Daneth. This is what I needed to know."

⁓·⁓

Lamira sat on her luxurious sleeping platform, holding both her mother's hands, still weeping with joy.

"But tell me about this prince—you are his prisoner, but he grieves your loss."

She blinked her wet lashes. "He does? How do you know?"

"I sensed it in him. He loves you. Even his warrior agreed."

"Master Seke?"

Was her mother actually blushing at the mention of the master at arms? Well, Seke was an incredible specimen of masculinity, even if he was old enough to be her father.

"But, Mother, he believes he cannot trust me."

"I know—he told me the same thing. Lamira...can you trust him?"

She hesitated. Her mother's familiar and loving face made her chest nearly explode with joy.

"He knew about your father. He knew we are part of the resistance movement, yet we both still live."

Lamira gaped in surprise. He knew? She shook her head. "Did he say why he bought you?"

Her mother shook her head. Mother Earth, which Zandian male would she be given to? Did they believe she was still of breeding age?

"Do you know why he bought me?"

"Tell me."

"For breeding. Daneth—his doctor—ran a program and it chose me as his best possible mate to bear children." She waited for the shock to appear on her mother's face. All those solar cycles her mother had worked to protect her from exactly this fate.

But her mother only touched a finger to her lips thoughtfully. "Why, do you think?"

She could not think. Her emotions were running in too many directions and her brain had overheated into a melted blob of confusion.

"I cannot see him giving the mother of his children up to the Ocretion slaughter block."

"But I haven't given him children," she wailed. "And now I won't."

"What I'm saying is perhaps he can be trusted with the truth of your gifts."

"They aren't gifts," she started to protest, but then remembered the whispering from the crystals.

He needs you. Pay attention to all knowing.

Perhaps they *were* gifts. To him, anyway. Her knowing had already saved his life, after all.

"You should tell him."

"He probably won't believe me, anyway. They don't understand sarcasm, and he's convinced humans lie about everything." She caught her mother's hand. "Wait. You know telling him may risk your life, as well."

Her mother gave her a tight smile. "I know." She squeezed her hand.

. . .

Zander paced the length of his chamber. He'd sent for Lamira and now his body hungered for her, just at the thought of having her near him again.

A tap sounded at the door. The image of Lamira standing outside with a guard, wrists bound behind her back popped up as a hologram above the door.

"Enter."

The guard walked in with her, but he dismissed him with a wave. "Leave her."

Lamira's chin was held high, defiance blazed across her delicate features. He remembered that look from the day she first arrived on his pod. She marched over to him and spat in his face.

Her attack came unexpected, so he registered only surprise, rather than anger.

"My mother will not be your sex slave!"

It was so absurd, he wanted to laugh—and she was adorable angry like this. But he didn't show amusement. Instead, he scooped her up by the waist and carried her to his sleepdisk, where he sat on the edge and draped her across his lap.

He spanked her with his hand, hard and fast. "I have no intention of using your mother as a sex slave," he made clear. "She is my guest—a boon I purchased for you after I gave you that undeserved whipping."

Lamira didn't answer, probably too caught up in wriggling under his punishing slaps.

He'd forgotten how satisfying it felt to spank her. Everything about it lit his senses on fire—the feel of her soft, supple form across his knees, the sight of her perfect little ass bouncing beneath his hand, the gasps she made each time his palm made contact. He could question her about her psychic abilities later, after her spanking. And breeding.

His wrist cuff was still programmed to monitor her arousal rate, and the numbers flashed rapidly.

Twenty percent aroused. Thirty. Thirty-five. Forty.

She liked her spankings as much as he did.

The only displeasing aspect of the situation was her clothing. He lifted her to stand between his knees and yanked down her leggings and panties. "Why are you wearing clothing? What is the rule when you enter my chamber?"

Fifty percent aroused.

Realizing he couldn't remove her shirt with her wrists bound behind her back, he grasped it with two hands at the neckline and rent the fabric down the middle, tearing it from her body.

Lamira gasped and wobbled on trembling legs. Her cheeks flushed pink with emotion, and confusion played across her face.

Sixty percent aroused.

"You are only punished in the bare, Lamira. You shall never be allowed the protection of your clothing."

Seventy percent aroused.

Her nipples stood out in stiff peaks.

He pulled her back over his knee and resumed the spanking, delighting in the contact of flesh on flesh, the crack of his palm against her bare skin, the scent of her arousal. He loved the way she squirmed over his lap, her hip rubbing his throbbing cock.

Eighty-five percent aroused.

Stars, he loved this. He loved that she grew excited when he took her in hand. He loved the heady sense of power punishing her gave him. And, yes, he loved her. He loved her. No matter what her secret, they'd work it out.

Her skin turned pink under his continued onslaught. He wondered if she could orgasm from a spanking alone. Not that it was allowed.

When he heard a sniff, he suddenly realized her back was shaking with sobs. He froze.

Oh veck. Had he spanked her too hard? He didn't think he had used more force than normal. He released her wrist cuffs.

"Lamira," he croaked, spinning her up to cradle in his arms, the way she liked it.

Her face dripped with tears, eyes red. She tucked her head against his neck, where he couldn't see her eyes.

"What happened? What's wrong?"

She shook her head, still pressed against his neck, and wept in ragged, heart-wrenching sobs. Her arousal rate had dropped back down to thirty percent.

He stroked her back and held her tight, rocking slightly. "Does it hurt too much? Should I call Daneth?"

"No," she croaked immediately.

"What do you need?"

"You!"

He stilled once more, drawing in a shocked breath. His heart beat erratically.

This was the wildness she inspired in him. A starstorm of emotions, needs, and desires.

"I've missed you, too, little human." He buried his face in her hair, rubbing his horns through the silky strands, breathing her in. She smelled both sweet and sensual, the fresh lime-citrus of her soap blending with her natural feminine musk.

He loved her.

He stood and walked on his knees up the sleeping platform, settling with his back against the wall, and his little human cradled in his lap. "I can't live without you—I don't want to. I need you here, in my chamber, between my sheets."

"I'll tell you," she sobbed. "I'll tell you everything. I promise. You may not believe me, but I'll tell you what you want to know."

He caressed her nape, pried her head from his shoulder to see her wet face. Using both thumbs, he mopped her tears. "Tell me," he murmured. "I'll believe you."

She hiccupped, trying to regain her breath. Her hand came up to cover her face from his view, but he caught her wrist. "Don't hide from me. No more lies, little slave. I want all of you—your honest truth. You're mine. Even your tears are mine."

She drew in a long, terraced breath and dashed her tears with the back of her hand. "Thank you"—she sniffed and gave a laughing sob at her own tears—"for my mother. Thank you so much."

He pulled her in and kissed her forehead. "You're welcome."

She leaned her forehead against his, looping one hand behind his neck and stroking her delicate fingers lightly over the skin there.

His body prickled with heat.

"Sometimes..." She drew in another shuddering breath. "Sometimes, I know things. About people. Not usually about the future."

"You're psychic."

Her eyes locked on his, startled. "Yes. Claircognizant. I know things I shouldn't. But since I've come here, it's been more—now I see things and hear things, too. I think it's your crystals—they've amplified the trait. You believe me?"

He traced her eyebrow, caressed her temple with the pad of his thumb. "I believe you. Your mother said something earlier today that led me to have Daneth examine your brain activity. He compared it to the Venusian brain and there were similarities."

"Do you think I have Venusian blood?

"Daneth could probably test it to find out."

"So..." She held his favorite expression—the pleading one, with her green eyes wide. "Am I forgiven?"

He adjusted her, pulling one of her legs around so she straddled him. Her hot core pressed against his cock through his trousers, dampening them. Palming her luscious ass, he squeezed it and rocked her into him.

"I'm sorry—" His voice sounded rough—whether it was from lust or regret, he wasn't sure. "For so many things. For the times I hurt you. For—"

"No." She touched his face, stopping him. "You're a prince—the leader of your species. You were right to be cautious. Zander..."

She nibbled her bottom lip, making him want to claim her mouth, to suck that lip between his, to taste her.

"I've seen something...about us." Her gaze was intent, as if measuring whether she could tell him or not.

"Tell me. From now on, you will tell me everything. No more secrets. No, wait. I understand why you were afraid to tell me, but I will never turn you in to the Ocretions. I will not let anyone touch you—ever. You belong to me, and I protect what's mine. Understand?"

~.~

Warmth coiled in her chest, swirled up her neck. She tugged Zander's lips down to hers, attacking him, showing him how much his words affected her. He kissed her back, grasping her head and holding her still as he took over. His tongue licked between her lips, and he claimed what belonged to him.

He pushed her down to her back, crawling over her. "Tell me." His voice sounded gruff, but his eyes shone with affection. He pinned her wrists beside her head. "Now, little slave."

"I saw our baby."

His face went slack, eyes full of wonder.

Her vision blurred.

"When? I mean—"

She laughed. "I don't know. But he was perfect."

"He?" Zander's lips stretched into the widest smile she'd ever seen him wear. His teeth gleamed straight and white against his purple-hued skin.

She nodded. Her chest felt so full, she thought it would explode.

He nudged her knees apart and shoved down his pants, freeing his cock. "Then I guess we'd better keep breeding, so we can meet him soon."

She reached for his cock and guided him to her dripping entrance. He filled her, stretching her wide and making her gasp. After ten planet rotations without sex, she felt virginally small for his large size, despite the ample lubricant.

"Take me," he commanded, his eyes glittering with amusement. He knew, from the cuff on his arm, what his bossy commands did to her.

She arched and offered herself up to him, his for the taking. She craved his touch in every way—not only the tender caresses he'd just offered, but also this—the rough way he handled her, demanding so much yet never going too far.

He pistoned in and out of her, shoving deep on each instroke. "I missed you, naughty slave."

"I'm a good slave," she protested, giving herself over to the force of his instrokes, which rocked her up at least six inches every time.

"You spat in my face."

Oh yeah. She'd forgotten that part.

"I think, when I'm finished filling you with my seed, I will take your ass. You deserve a long, hard ass-*vecking*, don't you?"

Her head wobbled, somewhere between a nod and a shake. While she found anal sex terrifying, it had also been incredibly satisfying—the intensity equaling the pleasure.

Zander pulled out. "On your knees, hands behind your back." He shoved her torso down into the sleepdisk and lifted her hips high. She heard the click of her wrist cuffs fastening behind her legs.

She loved this position. There was something so...objectifying about it. It lifted and presented her sex and anus to him and left her face completely out of his sight.

He gripped her hips and slid into her again, resuming the hard pounding he'd been giving her. His breath grew ragged.

Her pussy gripped his cock in ecstasy.

"Come, slave."

He shoved in deep and stayed, filling her with hot streams of his cum while her pussy spasmed around his length, squeezing and milking his cock for its seed.

Despite his threat to take her ass afterward, he collapsed on top of her, releasing her wrists and laying her out on her belly. His strong arms wrapped around her from behind and he rolled them to their sides. He brushed kisses across the skin at her neck.

"I'm going to have this removed." He rubbed his thumb over the barcode tattooed at the base of her neck. "I want to make my own mark on you, Lamira."

She rolled in his arms to face him. "How?"

He leaned up on one elbow. "Would you wear my crystals?"

The fact he asked her, rather than dictated, meant something—though she wasn't sure what. "Does that mean you would pierce me?"

He nodded, tweaking one of her nipples. "Yes. I'd pierce these. And your navel. Your ears, too, if you like." He brushed her cheek with the backs of his fingers. "You say the crystals make your intuition stronger. Perhaps wearing them will make it even more so. You'll be my own personal oracle."

"Do I have a choice?"

He stilled and his expression grew sober. "Do you not wish to be my female?"

She blinked rapidly, moisture gathering at her lashes, her chest so full it hurt. "Is that what wearing your crystals would mean?"

He nodded. "Zandian males adorn their females to show their attachment."

"I do—" Her voice cracked. "I do want to be your female, Zander."

His lips stretched into a satisfied smile. He stroked a hand up her throat to cup her chin. "I will take good care of you, little human. I promise."

Her heart thudded. She almost didn't ask it—she didn't want to ruin the moment, but she had to know. "Am I still your slave?"

He smirked. "Yes. Always, Lamira. You serve. I rule. You like it that way."

She wanted to deny it, but he had her numbers—literally—in the constant readout of his armband. "Will I ever be allowed off this pod?"

Once more, his lips curved into a wicked grin. "Only if you're a good little slave."

As always, when he reinforced his ownership over her, her pussy clenched. He tilted his head and claimed her mouth, and she lifted her lips to meet his.

Yes, she belonged to him—body and heart and soul. It wasn't perfect, but it was a start.

EPILOGUE

Lamira sat up, the luxurious sheets falling away from her naked form. She slept so much more now that she was pregnant, and Zander didn't mind if she spent half the morning dozing in his sleepdisk.

He sat working on his invasion plans, a hologram of his planet up and slowly rotating.

"My lord—" She could scarcely make her lips and tongue move, she'd been awakened from such a deep slumber by her knowing.

He swiveled and smiled, his eyes dropping to her swollen breasts, now pierced and adorned with his crystals.

"The being you seek is here in the pod."

He lifted a quizzical brow. "I don't understand."

Zander hadn't shared his takeover plans, but she'd gleaned enough through clairvoyance and observation.

"Do you seek someone with an army? Someone you can pay to wage a war?"

He nodded, his gaze growing sharp.

"That being is here, now. In the crystal bath." It was the one planet rotation of the week when the Zandian public were invited to use the crystal baths or visit with the prince. Zander had pushed his visitation time back to afternoon that day because the traffic had been light and he liked to spend more time with her now that she carried his child.

Zander's lip curled doubtfully. "A Zandian? With an army?"

She nodded and scooted out of bed, a sense of urgency driving her forward. "He's been here before but you have not met. I...I don't think he likes the idea of royalty. But he requires the crystal recharge all the same." She yanked on her clothing.

Zander stood and walked briskly to the door. "Will you know him when you see him?"

She swept past him into the corridor. "I'm not sure. Maybe you will." She shoved back the moment of doubt she always had about her claircognizance. There was no mistake. The feeling had been so strong.

Zander strode beside her, one hand at her lower back, the other on the handle of his sword. They reached the crystal baths just as the door slid open and a huge warrior walked out. He did not appear much older than Zander—perhaps five or ten solar cycles, but he bore scars and the lines of a being who had led a tough life.

His eyes flew open when he saw her, then took on a menacing glare. "You," he snarled.

Her heart jumped in her throat. He thought he knew her? How?

Zander shoved her behind him and slid his sword partway out of the scabbard.

The warrior ignored him, even though he was his prince and ruler. "What are you doing here, Lily? I can't imagine you think I'd ever be happy to see you again."

"You're speaking to Lamira," Zander growled.

She craned her neck around to see past her muscled master. "How do you know my sister?"

HIS HUMAN PRISONER

PROLOGUE

Lily flattened herself in the tiny washroom near the old airship's controls. A scrape ran the length of her leg, and her slave's dress had been soiled during her escape from her master's pod. She'd barely made it onto the ship her fellow runaways had selected on the fly to hijack. A bead of sweat ran down her forehead.

Please don't let any being use the washroom before takeoff.

This plan had been eighty planet rotations in the making. It had been a miracle she'd managed to get out at the appointed time to meet the others. They'd chosen a day and a time. Picking the craft to board had been left to the chance of the day, but this one actually seemed to be ideal—a rusty old ship with just six crewmembers to overpower. She'd hidden close to the cockpit to aid in taking the pilot and first mate.

She peered through the slats in the door and watched him—a huge male of a species she'd never before seen—flick on the engines. A small, wizened female entered and settled into the copilot's chair.

Oh *veck*. Was she Venusian? If so, she would intuit Lily and the other slaves' presence on the ship. Venusians possessed extrasensory abilities.

The pilot initiated hover movement, easing out of the dock. If she weren't holding her breath, praying she made it off Ocretia without getting caught, she would admire his muscled shoulders, the bulging biceps and corded muscles of his forearms. He sat taller than an average human by at least a foot and his skin had a purple tinge to it. Two horns on the top of his head gave him a rugged, fierce appearance.

He steered the ship through the incoming traffic, weaving in and out at a speed that made her stomach lurch.

She closed her eyes and said a silent prayer to Mother Earth. If all went well, she'd be free in a matter of hours—a slave no more. Unless he heard about the other missing slaves, her elderly owner wouldn't notice her absence until late that night, and even then, he'd never suspect she'd made it to the dock and onto an airship. Ocretions grossly underestimated human intelligence, and Lily had always played the simple, docile sex slave for him. Not that the old male had been able to use her for that purpose much. No, she'd been lucky with him. She'd only had to look beautiful in her scanty uniform and endure his petting while she served him.

The pilot punched up the speed, zooming into the outer layer of traffic, farther away from the territory of her odious captors. Traffic grew lighter and lighter until, at last, they made it into free space. The pilot set the controls and stood up.

"You should take care of the stowaway in the washroom," the old Venusian said.

"Are you *vecking* kidding me?" He cursed. "Why didn't you say something earlier?" He marched over and threw open the door.

She pointed her laser gun at his throat, but the huge male batted it to the floor as if she'd held a twig. Because it was too far away to reach, and his speed and strength greatly exceeded hers, she held her hands up and put on her best helpless female eyes.

"Please don't hurt me." She feigned weakness, knowing her beauty and slight stature worked in her favor. Seven years as a sexual slave had taught her a great deal about minimizing injury from males.

His brows shot up as he took in her appearance, and she knew what he saw. A slip of a human female, scantily dressed and possessing the qualities considered beautiful by most beings. Though she was used to inspiring hunger in males, the flash of it in his eyes came with particular satisfaction.

He was younger than she'd guessed initially—not much older than she, if she measured by human standards, but his eyes and the scars on his handsome face told a story of a life hard lived.

So they had something in common.

She let the miniscule sex servant's dress she'd stolen to escape slip down her shoulder, revealing skin and the suggestion of one breast.

The pilot's eyes traced down, stopping at the place her nipple lay hidden beneath the cloth.

It puckered under his gaze. Her body's reaction surprised her. She never grew aroused from a male's attention, not even in the throes of sexual activity. It seemed purple skinned and horned was her type. Go figure.

"Oh no, pet." He shook his head, apparently steeling himself against her helpless female act. "You picked the wrong airship to hide on." After picking up her weapon, he grasped her wrist and pulled her out under the lights, giving her another head-to-toe sweeping glance. To the Venusian, he said, "Why didn't you tell me before we took off?"

The old female blinked her protuberant emerald eyes. She smelled of brownbeer, and her short, black hair stuck up at all angles, as if she hadn't brushed it in days. "She means something to you."

His eyes narrowed, and his gaze returned to her. "*Veck*. You know I don't believe in that excrement."

The Venusian shrugged. "Denial will not change your destiny."

He rolled his eyes and gripped Lily's elbow, steering her into the bowels of the ship.

She took note of where in his belt he tucked her laser gun, biding her time.

The pilot kicked a sleeping chamber door open and stepped inside with her. "What's your name?"

"Lily." She made her voice sound breathy, sweet.

"Where do you think you're going?"

"Anywhere. Wherever you're going." Again, she tried to appear fragile, in need of protection.

He scowled.

Holding his gaze with her own, she eased down to her knees.

His eyes changed from a purple-ish brown to a light violet, and the sexy horns stiffened and leaned in her direction.

"I don't have any steins to pay you, but I promise I'll make it worth your while," she purred and worked the bulging form of his cock out of his tight black flight pants.

He swallowed, his large hand dropping to tangle in her hair. She watched him struggle for control. "How did you get on my ship?"

Was he really caressing her ear? An odd sensation moved in her—a small stirring of curiosity or excitement.

"I slipped in through the cargo hatch. Please"—she tongued the sensitive place beneath the mushroom head of his cock—"let me stay. I won't cause you any trouble."

"Well, I guess a female of your talents"—he broke off and groaned as she swirled her tongue around the head of his enormous malehood—"might be of some use on this ship...*ugh*." He grasped the back of her head and shoved her over his length, causing her to gag and her eyes to water.

She'd given hundreds of deep-throat blowjobs or rough *vecks* over the years as a sex slave. She'd learned to simply detach and let her mind float away, to become nothing more than flesh, a body devoid of personality. But the pilot pulled back when she choked, and he brushed his thumb over the moisture leaking from the corner of her eye.

"Forgive me." He rubbed her tears between his finger and thumb as if he found the substance fascinating. "I didn't mean to choke you. Your mouth is smaller than I'm used to."

She blinked up at him in surprise, and he brushed her cheekbone with the backs of his fingers. "Try again. I won't choke you, beautiful."

She took just the head of his cock into her mouth, sucking hard.

His groan of pleasure kicked up her confidence—excitement, even, and she took him deeper, relaxing the back of her throat to swallow him down.

Though his thighs trembled and ball sac had grown rock hard, he didn't thrust again, but let her control the movement, his rough breathing sending thrills of excitement straight to her core. She'd never felt so powerful giving a male oral pleasure before. She'd never enjoyed seeing a male come undone. But this one...his guttural shout made her pussy clench, the way his huge hand cradled the back of her head to hold her in place—so gentle yet capable of snapping her neck with ease if he wanted to. She swallowed his seed as she'd been trained to do and licked him clean.

He gripped her nape and lifted her to her feet as if she weighed nothing. "Blowjobs like that will certainly be accepted as trade." His gaze grew heavy-lidded. "But I do think you deserve punishment for stowing away on my ship." He rotated her to face away from him then picked up her two hands and pressed them against the ship's wall. His exotic masculine spice filled her nostrils. The heat of his torso radiated against her back, and his breath feathered across her bare shoulder.

A surge of lust ran through her body, once more surprising her. What was it about this male that excited her when no male had ever aroused her interest before? Her pulse sped as she waited to see what shape his punishment took.

He tugged up her short slave's gown. She wore the bare minimal under-clothing, as required by her station—a tiny string threaded around her waist and through her buttocks to hold up a slip of spidersilk between her legs.

The pilot made an approving noise in his throat just before his huge palm clapped down on her ass.

She yelped but didn't move from her position.

He rubbed away the sting. "Naughty slave girl, hiding on my ship." He slapped the other side. Unlike punishments she'd received at the hands of her masters, or at the training institute before, his purpose was obviously to arouse her through the pain. She'd heard of such a thing but never understood it.

Now, though, a sliver of interest flickered, her sex actually growing moist from his rough treatment. It didn't make sense. She'd been beaten on countless occasions, for a master's pleasure or as punishment, and it had never had this effect on her.

He continued the slow cycle of slapping and rubbing each side, and she grew more and more agitated. How would that big purple cock feel inside her? Would he be rough or gentle? What positions did he like?

No. She needed to keep her head. Look for the opportunity to grab the laser gun.

He reached around the front of her hips and slipped his fingers under the gusset over her panties.

His middle finger traced up her slit to find her clitoris. She hid her surprise. He cared about her pleasure? Delaying his own?

He brushed a feather-light circle around it, so much less than she craved. A strange itchiness took over her body, sending tingles of heat across her skin and producing a darker, pulsing need in her core. He disappointed her by removing his fingers from her panties.

A sharp slap over her sex made her cry out.

"Have you been naughty, slave?"

A shout sounded from just beyond the door. She whirled and lunged for the laser gun in his holster, the element of surprise giving her the split second she needed to beat him to it.

With the barrel pressed against his chest, she lifted her chin toward the door. Nineteen escaped human slaves would've fanned out over the entire ship by now, taking the meager six-member crew hostage. She'd done her part and captured the toughest one.

"To the cockpit," she ordered. "We're commandeering your ship."

The rage on the purple-skinned being's face should have frightened her—and it did. But it also inspired a sliver of regret. She almost wished they'd had a chance to finish that act she normally detested so much.

Almost.

CHAPTER ONE

Rok glared at Lamira, the human female who looked just like the one who'd stolen his ship and left him stranded on the abandoned planet Pifany eight months ago. It had taken him and his crew three weeks and a lot of sweet-talking to find a lift back to civilization. Then it had taken another six weeks of the most dangerous smuggling work—piloting a borrowed ship loaded with weapons into a war-torn planet of Jesel—to earn enough to buy a new airship.

In fact, he still hadn't recovered financially from the setback.

So to find a human who claimed to be Lily's sister peering from behind the so-called Zandian prince annoyed the *veck* out of him.

"Where is your *vecking* sister?"

Prince Zander drew himself up. "You will speak with respect to my mate."

Mate, huh? That gave him pause. The slip of a human was dressed in finery, but she wore a collar around her neck like a slave. Granted, the collar was embedded with enough Zandian crystal to buy him five new airships.

The crystal was the only reason he'd come to the Zandian prince's pod. His body required energetic recharge through crystal-amplified sunlight, and Zandian crystal was impossible to come by anywhere else.

For one half-moment, he considered picking up that little human—with the collar, of course—and making a break for it to his ship. He had no problem punishing one female for her sister's misdeeds, and this one was certainly as pretty as Lily, although his body didn't have the magnetic attraction he'd experienced the moment he laid eyes on her. That's how the little witch had tricked him.

Too bad Zander had security guards everywhere and, unlike him, they were around the crystals all the time, getting constant recharge. So while he had a lifetime of street fighting behind him, their strength probably outmatched his.

He met the darkened stare of the male who called himself prince. Prince of Nothing. Zandia had been occupied by the Finn for over twenty solar cycles.

The male glaring back did not look as weak or pampered as he'd imagined the royal nothing would be. In fact, he looked every inch the warrior—eyes alert with an assessing, intelligent gaze, hand on the hilt of a sword, not a laser gun.

He had to give grudging points for that. Maybe Zander wasn't just a pretty boy living out his life on his country's remaining wealth.

Rok cleared his throat. "Forgive me, Your Highness." He didn't quite keep the mocking tone from his words.

The prince's eyes narrowed and then, before he had a chance to react, Rok found himself shoved up against the wall, the sheathed blade of the sword pressing down on his windpipe. "My mate asked you a question. How do you know Lily?"

He didn't fight back, knowing it would be useless in the prince's own pod, with his guards everywhere. When Zander let up enough on the sword for him to speak, he croaked, "She stole my ship!"

The prince released him, surprise flitting over his features.

"So she *is* free!" Lily's sister bounced on her heels, looking excited. "Where? When?"

"Eight months ago, leaving Ocretia's capital. She and two dozen escaped slaves overtook my crew and forced us to land and disembark, so if you know where she is now, I'd really love to get my ship back."

Lamira licked her lips. The memory of her sister's lush mouth closing around his cock flashed through Rok's mind.

Yes, that was part of why he was so *vecking* mad. He'd known it was the oldest trick in the book and he'd still let Lily tempt him. His cock had taken the lead, and he had lost everything he'd owned. What had it been about that pretty little human slave that had tempted him?

Mierna had said they had some sort of connection. What in the stars could it be?

"I've never met her, actually."

That surprised him.

"She was taken from our parents when she was just three, before I was born. I've spent my whole life hoping to meet her."

Zander extended his arm, fist raised at a ninety degree angle in the traditional Zandian greeting. "I am Zander."

Something painful tightened in his chest. He hadn't seen the gesture since he'd left Zandia, but he remembered its use. Remembered his father, a palace laborer, using it when he greeted other beings. He crooked his arm into the same shape and touched fists with Zander.

"Rok."

"Welcome to my pod, Rok. Please stay for the weekly meal so we can discuss Lily"—he glanced at Lamira—"and other matters further."

He arched a brow. What in the veck were the *other matters*? He really didn't have time to spare—his crew waited for him in the ship, and they'd made the dangerous trip to Ocretia just for him to recharge.

"His crew," the human murmured.

Smart, for a human.

Zander's gaze flicked to her and back. "Your crew is also welcome."

He nodded once, slowly. "I'll go ask them, then. They may not want to stay." Mainly because he and three of his crewmembers had warrants out for their arrest for smuggling in Ocretia.

"Prince Zander does not work for the Ocretian government," the human said.

A tingle washed over his skin. Did she read minds?

Zander shot her a warning look, but she laced her fingers in front of her, looking serene. "Many of us have reason to hide from them." She met his gaze squarely.

She certainly would, if she possessed mind reading powers. Humans with any aberrant traits were exterminated immediately. The Ocretions bred their slaves for only one thing—servility.

Reason told him to get the *veck* out of there, fast. She knew about the warrants. It was probably a trap. She was Lily's sister, after all, and that human had ruined the past eight months of his life. But his gut said to stay. Besides, curiosity nipped at his heels.

He wanted to know what this quirky human was doing with the prince of his species, and what they wanted from him. Because he sure as stars knew they both wanted something.

~.~

Lily dodged the flying debris from the firebombs, a sob stuttering in her too-dry throat.

Dead. The entire enclave of escaped slaves had just been found and demolished. If she hadn't been out foraging for food, she'd be dead, too.

Tears streaked her cheeks. They'd been like family to her. For the past eight months, she'd been free. Yes, it had been hard. Hiding out on the planet of Jesel, they'd hoped to emulate those humans who had fought for freedom there and won over four hundred years ago.

But Jesel had been in the midst of another war and had fallen to the Republicans once again. And, funny, but the Republicans hadn't cared that she and her fellow escaped slaves weren't from Jesel. They were killing every human they could find.

She needed to get the veck off this planet, and fast. The trouble was, she had no one in the universe. No one to message, nowhere to go that would be safe for an escaped human slave.

Stumbling through the smoke, coughing the polluted air, she scrambled down into a crevasse, where she could at least breathe. Her eyes stung from the smoke and ash, and her knees, elbows, and chin were bloody from when she'd been knocked on her belly by the blast.

A shallow river sliced through the canyon, and she waded right into it, dropping to her knees, cupping the water in her hands and splashing the ash from her face. She screamed when a dark serpent shot out of the reeds and bit her ankle.

Vecking hell. She wished she'd died with the others.

She wouldn't survive out here alone. There were too many wild animals and natural dangers, even if she didn't have to worry about being hunted down and killed by the Republicans. She'd probably be better off using her laser gun on herself to save the terror and suffering of starving to death or being killed.

Veck that.

Her self-preservation instincts kicked in. She was a survivor. She'd somehow kept her soul after all these years in captivity, and now she was sure as veck going to keep it now that she'd found freedom. If she had to learn to live alone in the caves cut into these canyon walls, she would.

She heard a whistle to the left of her—a decidedly human whistle—and then an arrow whizzed by her head and hit the rock beside her. She grabbed the arrow and started running before she'd even figured out from which direction it had come.

In another moment, she was on the ground, pinned down by a large human male. "I got her," he cried triumphantly in the ancient language once used on Earth. "Wait till you see her—she's about as tasty as they come."

A fraction of her fear eased. If they were interested in using her body, she'd convince them to let her live. This was one situation—perhaps the only one—she knew how to handle.

~.~

Rok had never eaten so well in his life. The food served at Zander's table had been exquisite. They dined in his Great Hall, a magnificent room in his palatial pod. The walls were brightly colored, and crystals magnified the sunlight in here, too. Most fascinating, though, was the plethora of potted plants that made the room appear like a lush jungle. Food-bearing plants, from the looks of them.

An exiled prince lived a far different existence than the escaped laborer's son. A large group of Zandians had gathered for the meal along a long row of tables. Almost all were male, save a few elderly females, which explained why the prince had taken an alien mate. Still, his choice of a human surprised Rok. Although Lamira was admittedly special.

Not that he was prejudiced, either. He'd grown up among aliens of all kinds. He didn't have the luxury of presuming his species was better than another. But Zander and his pod were known for keeping to themselves, allowing only Zandians to work there or even enter the pod. The fact that Zander had invited his crew in for the meal meant he must really want something from Rok.

His crew sat at the far end of the table, but they didn't seem to mind being relegated to the lower class section. Janu and Jaso, his two foster brothers, kept raising their glasses toward Rok and Zander in appreciation of the delicious meal. He was grateful they'd shown some modicum of manners, as the small but ferocious Stornigians could be as rowdy as animals, especially when there was wine involved.

Mierna, his Venusian copilot, had also obviously indulged in the wine, but then she functioned half-drunk on a regular basis, so that was nothing new. His giant, one-legged friend Gaurdo, an Elau, ate heartily but watched the entire affair in wary silence. Rok had rescued him from a pack of wild beasts outside a trading station once. That was how he'd lost the leg.

Depri had also taken in everything, particularly the opulence of the palatial pod. He'd probably already devised a hundred schemes for how Rok and his crew could benefit from trading with Zander.

When the meal ended, Prince Zander, his human mate, and her mother remained, along with four older males. Lamira was as beautiful as he remembered Lily, but without the fire behind her eyes. Lily had been magnificent— her treachery as impressive as the way she'd handled a weapon, burning determination in her gold-flecked green eyes. And her scent...he still remembered that feminine musk. He'd stroked himself off to fantasies with her in the months since she stole his ship. Particularly to the thought of punishing her soundly for her misdeeds.

Lamira and her mother had grilled him on everything he knew about Lily, which was little. Their excitement at hearing about her was not diminished by what he considered the considerable unlikelihood she was still alive. Escaped slaves didn't last long in this universe, or any other, for that matter.

Still, he had a feeling there was something else Zander wanted from him, so he wasn't surprised when, at last, the prince asked if he and his advisors might have a word in private.

Lamira and her mother, Leora, stood. "Your destiny is woven with ours," she murmured, as if only half intending him to hear. "And it is great. You were born to lead armies."

Zander seemed to take this prediction in stride, as if his mate normally spoke in riddles like a Venusian. Rok frowned, but didn't have time to respond, as Lamira had already glided from the room, one hand on a slightly swollen belly, signaling what he'd missed before—she was pregnant.

His crew waited for his command. He gave a single nod, which they would understand to mean, *retire to the ship but remain alert.*

When they all had left, Zander touched his fingertips together and leaned back in his chair.

"Your primary occupation is as a pilot?"

Rok narrowed his eyes. If this was coming back to the smuggling warrant, he needed to leave.

"Any battle experience?"

"Why? You planning on taking Zandia back?" He snorted.

The prince didn't answer.

He sat forward in his chair, interest spiking. "You *are,* aren't you?"

Zandians didn't lie. Well, *he* might lie, to get himself out of a pinch with officials, but true Zandians didn't. He watched Zander closely, waiting to see what he said.

The prince chose not to answer, which, to Rok, was as good as confirmation.

He tried to remember the vow his father used to give and lifted his fist, elbow bent at ninety degrees. "On Zandian honor, I will not speak of anything I hear here."

Zander and the four warriors all held their fists aloft to acknowledge his vow.

"You have a battleship?"

"I may have access to a number of battleships."

Rok's eyebrows shot up. "Is that so? And you need pilots to fly them?"

"We are all experienced and battle-ready pilots," he said, indicating the males present. "But I need hundreds more. There aren't enough Zandians alive to build such an army."

"Do you have the coin to hire such an army?" It was a rhetorical question, really. The Zandian prince was known for his enormous wealth, gained not only from what he'd escaped with, but from years of savvy investments.

Zander nodded.

He considered. Stornigians trained in combat flight were easy to come by, but they'd be unlikely to engage and fight with another species. If he led them, however, they *might* be willing. Still, could he find hundreds? He could only think of a dozen he might ask.

"I may be able to round up an army. I'd be their commander, though."

Zander inclined his head. "How soon will you know?"

"How many do you need, exactly?"

"One hundred and fifty."

He pursed his lips. If he were a wise male, he'd tell Zander no, thank you, and leave as quickly as he could. The possibility of taking back Zandia seemed slim, even with battleships and financial resources. But Zandia was his home. It still danced in his dreams—the vivid colors, the honor of the species.

"It may take a few months," he hedged. "I have another job to do first." They didn't need to know it was another illegal weapons smuggling job.

Impatience flitted over Zander's face, but he nodded. "I'll be awaiting your reply." He stood and bowed.

Rok barely resisted rolling his eyes at the pomp, but the prince had earned a grudging respect from him. Far from sitting on his cushioned throne, it appeared the male had been amassing his fortune for a reason—he sought to regain his kingdom.

Rok had to appreciate that goal, whether he believed it attainable or not.

CHAPTER TWO

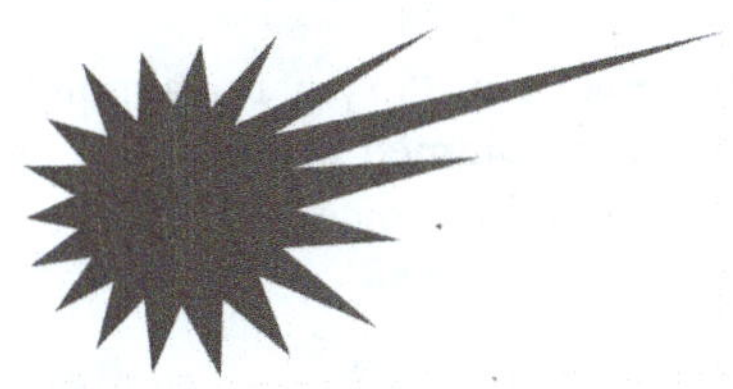

Lily dozed on hard ground, where she'd spent the past forty-eight hours being taken multiple times by each and every one of the eighteen human rebels. She hadn't resisted—she knew better than that. Instead, her mind had drifted off to her "safe place"—the one with rainbow-hued light beaming through crystals onto her skin, rejuvenating her, healing her. This was how she'd survived since the day she'd been placed into sexual servitude.

The humans who had taken turns on her had smaller cocks than Ocretions, so she hadn't torn or suffered physically. Not that she'd know if she had —numbness inhabited every limb.

The sound of an airship forced her onto her hands and knees, and she staggered to her feet. One of the rebels grabbed her elbow and propelled her forward, toward the landing craft.

Every man in the camp ran forward, lifting weapons that didn't match the primitive lifestyle they led in the wild.

The door to the craft lifted, and she blinked several times. *Could it be?*

No, she was delirious.

But the huge purple-skinned warrior who emerged *had* to be the same pilot whose ship they'd stolen when she escaped. How many horned purple-hued smugglers could there be?

His eyes swept over the group, and though his expression showed nothing, his gaze bounced over her twice—three times. Of course, it could be the fact that her clothing had been torn off so she stood naked in a crowd of clothed beings.

The smuggler addressed the men's leader, bringing out several cases of weapons. She couldn't hear any conversation, but it was obvious the rebels had expected the male and wanted the goods he brought.

He closed up the cases and stacked them on the ground outside the ship then stood directly in front of them and folded his arms. This would be the negotiation stage.

The rebel leader said something.

The smuggler shook his head and answered.

More head shaking and speaking. The smuggler lifted his chin in her direction, and all the men turned.

The rebel holding her dragged her forward.

"No deal," the rebel leader said. "We've only had her for two planet rotations and there are no other human females alive on the planet. We need her to breed."

The smuggler appeared bored. "So pay the appointed price."

The rebel leader's brows slammed down. He bent his head together with one of his friends to consult in low voices.

"Fifty thousand."

"And the female."

He was negotiating to buy her? Her idiotic heart gave a leap of excitement, right before she remembered that the smuggler surely didn't intend to pick up where they'd left off. No, she'd stolen his ship and left him stranded on an uninhabited planet. He intended to exact revenge.

"We keep the female."

"Then the price is one hundred thousand." He had the bargaining face down pat, boredom sprawled over his features.

More downturned mouths and angry gestures. "Forty thousand and the female."

The smuggler considered. His purple gaze swiveled to her.

Unaccountably, her nipples stiffened, as if excited by his disinterested up-and-down sweep. She folded her arms across her chest, but not before the smuggler noticed, a momentary twitch at the corners of his lips making her humiliation complete.

"Forty-five. Bring me the female." He made an imperious gesture in her direction, no longer looking her way.

Her captor shoved her forward, and she fell to her knees. As she crawled up to stand, her mind raced. Was she walking to her death? She figured there was at least a 50 percent chance of it.

Why, then, did hope keep fluttering in her chest?

She stumbled through the rebels and walked right up to the pilot. Though she ought to know better, she held her head high and met his gaze squarely with her best look of defiance.

She expected a face slap at best.

Instead, she found herself upended over his shoulder. His huge hand clapped down on her bare ass. The sting enlivened her, bringing awareness back to her abandoned body, sending prickles all across her flesh. Dearest Mother Earth, did she really hope he wanted her for sex?

The pilot collected his money and carried her, still slung ignominiously over his broad, muscled shoulder, up the ramp.

"What in the *veck* just happened out there?" a short, hairy humanoid—Stornigian if she knew her species right—demanded. "If you really just accepted a female in exchange for..." The male trailed off when the pilot dropped her to her feet. "*Her?* No vecking way. What are you going to do with her?"

The pilot's grin held menace. "Anything I want."

A shiver ran down her spine, but her pussy clenched. Why did this male always succeed in arousing her?

His huge hand dropped onto her nape, and he steered her forward, into the ship. A door slid open revealing a tiny washroom with a toilet and shower. "Clean yourself," he growled. "I don't want to smell those *vecking* males on you."

Excuse the *veck* out of her. Like she could help it. She'd just been used as a *veck*-doll for forty-eight hours straight.

"Jaso"—he turned to face the Stornigian trailing them—"stand guard at this door while I take off. The sooner we clear Jeselian airspace the better."

She was grateful when he shut the door on her, leaving her alone in the cramped quarters.

Washing off the residue of the sex and the men was a luxury she hadn't expected, and she didn't plan to waste it. She flicked on a spray of water and stood beneath it, letting it soak her hair and sluice over her skin. The water felt hotter than she was used to, but she loved it, her muscles unknotting and releasing.

She closed her eyes, imagining the water cleansing not just her body, but her *vecking* soul. Like the rainbowed light of her imaginary safe place, it cleared away the muck, the foul experiences and beings she had contact with, leaving only her pure essence.

She paid special attention to the serpent-bite on her ankle. It had reddened over the past two planet rotations and now throbbed under the heat. *Veck.* She hoped her body could work out the poison on its own because she doubted this ship carried antidotes or antibiotics and seeking care elsewhere would be akin to turning herself in.

The door banged open and she braced herself, expecting to see the small hairy Stornigian. Instead, the enormous pilot squeezed into the room.

Her nipples beaded at the sight of him, her mysterious attraction to this being heightened by the intimate proximity.

His irises appeared more violet than before, and his horns stood as stiff as his cock, which bulged beneath his flight pants.

He stripped his clothes off without a word.

She hid her mild surprise. Fine. She knew how these scenes worked. "Couldn't wait, huh?"

His lips twisted into a sour expression. "Apparently not."

Her pulse quickened. His words implied he was there against his will—as if he couldn't stay away—and that idea thrilled some part of her. Especially because her body continued to respond to his nearness, heat flooding her core at the sight of his magnificent, muscled, and scarred body.

He grabbed her around the waist, turning her at the same time so she faced away from him, her ass pressed back against his muscular legs, his thick cock jabbing her lower back. "I believe you owe me this," he rumbled just before he shoved her up against the shower wall.

"Yes," she gasped.

"You agree?" He pulled her hips backward and pressed the head of his cock against her pussy.

"Yes."

"Good. Then we don't have to quarrel."

Unlike the eighteen males who'd just pummeled her sex, this one took care with her, rubbing his cock head over her entrance several times to test her readiness before easing in.

She gasped—his cock was far bigger than anything she'd taken before.

He froze, halfway in. "Take it," he growled, yet he didn't press further and his hand slid around the front of her hips, fingers questing for the button at the apex of her entrance.

He was the only male who had ever touched her there. She shrieked at the sensation, immediately pushing her hips back to take in the rest of him then shuddering at the shock of it.

He stayed buried deep inside her, not moving. His fingers slapped her clitoris several times until she began to move her hips up and down, trying to gain more friction.

"Ready for me?"

Her internal walls contracted. *That voice.* Deep, masculine, powerful. Just like the cock he began to pump in and out of her.

"No," she gasped, though it wasn't from pain. It was all too much—the sensations of being filled by his huge length sent frissons of pleasure through her core and down her inner thighs.

He vecked her harder, faster.

"I'm sorry," she gasped. "For what it's worth. I'm sorry I stole your ship."

"You will be, Lily." The words were threatening, but the guttural tone promised sex.

She was surprised he remembered her name. But, of course, he'd probably been hunting for her.

"I plan to punish you in at least five hundred ways, and when I'm through, I know someone who will pay a great deal for you. Maybe enough to even cover the cost of my ship."

If he hadn't been moving inside her, stroking her inner walls with his long cock in a way that made her eyes roll back in her head, she might have grown chilled by his promise to sell her. As it was, lights exploded behind her eyes as his enormous length rammed her inner walls and stretched her wide.

She noticed that while he had her mashed up against the wall, his own arms took the brunt of his force, protecting her from bruising her pelvis each time he shoved deeper. Like the other small considerations he'd shown, it added to her growing opinion that he might be a decent being.

Not nearly as cruel as he'd have her believe.

"Veck, Lily, you're so...*vecking*...tiny...so tight."

His pleasure and obvious loss of control gave her confidence, made her feel powerful—which was a first for her during sex.

He thrust upward with each word, lifting her off her feet, speared by his cock.

One of his huge palms closed over her left breast, and he squeezed her nipple between his thumb and forefinger.

It was too much. Her body convulsed under his hold, pussy clenching and releasing around his enormous cock, shudders of shock and pleasure running down her legs, up through her torso.

Holy Earth. Holy Mother.

He withdrew and shoved deeper, deeper still, vecking her with a force she thought certain would crush her, and then he, too, found his finish. Hot streams of his seed filled her, leaking down her legs in a splash of pearlescent rainbow.

She stared at the substance, fascinated by the beautiful colors swirling down the drain.

He panted behind her, thankfully still holding her up, or she'd collapse on the metal floor.

"Did those humans hurt you?" His breath came hot against her ear, voice a deep rumble that went straight into her chest and reverberated.

The question surprised her. "No. I know better than to resist."

"Good. Did I?" He shut off the spray of water and warm air blew at them from all directions.

Did he what? *Oh.* For some unfathomable reason, her face grew warm. A sex slave felt no shame. Yet there she stood, blushing from a simple question.

Simple, yet complex.

"No." Her voice cracked. "It was no more than I can take."

He spun her around and shoved the wet hair from her eyes. "Good," he grunted. "Because I plan on putting my cock in every hole of yours daily until you beg for mercy."

He must be very foolish if he thought threatening her with sex would frighten her.

"Between beatings, that is."

Her breath halted.

His hand had dropped to cup her mons, though, middle finger gliding over her slit, spiking her temperature again, confirming her suspicion that this was all a game to him. He didn't harbor deep resentment; he was enjoying himself.

Stars, how did this male elicit such reactions from her?

She licked her dry lips.

He stared down at her mouth, as if disconcerted to see her tongue. "I'm looking forward to punishing you, Lily."

There. She'd known it.

"Let's get your first whipping taken care of. That way you can sleep it off and we can start again in the morning."

Truthfully, it didn't frighten her. As a slave, she'd been punished in far worse ways than whipping, and she'd already begun to trust him enough to believe he wouldn't go too far. In fact, she almost looked forward to submitting to his punishment without a fuss. Would he find her unable to resist again?

Her gaze tangled in his amethyst one, and her breath hitched as all thoughts rushed out of her brain. She became nothing but naked, trembling flesh, a blank canvas for him to paint upon. "I—I don't know what to call you."

"Rok."

She dropped her eyes and dipped a curtsy. "Master Rok," she murmured submissively.

His posture went rigid. He cupped her chin and lifted it. "Just Rok." His eyes had returned to dark brown. "I'm not your master, I'm a male exacting punishment in the way he likes best."

A shiver ran down her spine at the note of sadism. He made everything sound sexual. She remembered the spanking he'd given her the first time they'd met. Measured pain made to arouse. Yes, this male enjoyed blurring the lines between pain and pleasure. Strangely, that ignited far more excitement than fear.

"What species are you?"

Already dry, Rok pulled on his clothes. "Zandian."

She'd never heard of it.

He bent both her wrists behind her back and pinned them there with one hand. With a push of a button, the door slid open, and he maneuvered her, completely naked, out through his ship.

A good slave would drop her eyes and walk humbly past the crew. But she didn't think it necessary to pretend. Something about the Zandian made her think he didn't care about those things. The game he played was his own, and she'd have to learn the rules.

She lifted her chin and stared haughtily back at the crew as they passed. Two Stornigians, the old Venusian she'd seen last time, an Elau, and the thin one—a species she didn't know. They all gaped as she padded past in bare feet. He shoved open the door to a tiny sleeping compartment.

What in the stars was he doing? Rok hadn't meant to barge into the washroom and *veck* the little human against the aluminum wall.

He'd seen the dead in her eyes back there on Jesel. He'd wanted to kill those *vecking* human men. She'd been ill-used. Enough that half her soul had fallen away, by the looks of it. But then he'd returned to relieve Jaso of standing guard, and the thought of her, just beyond the door, naked save for droplets of water gliding over her skin, made him mad with desire.

The same thing had happened on their first meeting. He'd known she was playing him, offering to suck his cock to keep him from sounding the alarm that she'd escaped. He'd been ready to wrap a fist in her thick copper hair and tell her to smarten up. That he couldn't be so easily manipulated. That he might not return her to her owner, but she'd sure as *veck* have to barter something to keep him from turning her in.

Except he'd caught her scent. Watched those full lips part. Drowned in the depths of moss green eyes. And then he just had to let her barter the skill she had obviously perfected.

And it had cost him his ship.

Yes, he certainly planned to thoroughly punish the little human for the trouble she'd caused, and he'd let her think he planned to turn her into the Ocretions because she deserved a little stress. But she had family yearning to see her. A younger sister who spoke like a Venusian and a wistful mother, still beautiful despite what had obviously been a hard life.

Her sister's beauty had not affected him like this. What was it about Lily that made her impossible to resist?

He guided her to his sleeping platform and pressed a hand between her shoulder blades, forcing her to fold at the waist and present her delectable little ass to him. It was skinnier than he'd like to see it. Perhaps on their twenty-six planet rotation journey to Ocretia she would add a little roundness to her elegant curves.

He wound a leather band around her wrists, tying a knot so could not escape. He slapped a second leather band against his palm, measuring its sting.

Not horrible. He slapped it against his leg. Yes, it would do.

"I'm going to whip you, Lily." He thought it only fair he explain what her punishment would entail. "It will be a hard punishment. You stole my ship and left me and my crew stranded for weeks on an abandoned planet."

In her vulnerable position, folded naked over his bed, hands bound, she appeared pale and penitent. But he wasn't fooled.

"This won't be your last punishment for your crimes. I intend to exact revenge in a variety of ways during our trip to Ocretia." He ran his large palm over her lovely ass, drawing a measured breath to still the surge of lust touching her incited.

The muscles in her back bunched up at that. Yes, he'd let her believe he planned to turn her in. She should be worried for her life. He stroked up her back, soothing her before he caused her pain. He liked her nervous, not terrified.

He brought the leather strap down across her buttocks, holding her wrists to contain her lurch of pain.

She cried out then ducked her face into the bedcovers.

"This punishment"—he brought the strap down again, making a second puffy red line below the first one—"will probably be the most severe, unless you anger me again on the trip."

Her muffled cry sounded from the covers.

He held her hip and applied the strap, whipping her over and over again. He liked hurting females, especially if they enjoyed it, but this time he didn't intend to play. He'd whip her thoroughly and get the rancor out of his system. A true punishment for a real crime. After that, he'd let himself enjoy having her at his mercy. That had been his initial plan, anyway. Of course, he'd already diverged from that course and *vecked* her, not waiting more than two minutes after he'd cleared Jeselian airspace and set the controls on autopilot.

Well, this should set things straight between them.

He snapped the thick leather strap across her lower buttocks.

She screamed.

He leathered her shapely ass from the top of the crack down to her thighs and back up again.

She didn't beg or plead, but she did make plenty of noise, yelping each time the strap slapped her flesh.

He whipped her, watching her pale skin turn a deep shade of red, then continuing for another ten strokes.

By the time he finished, her back shook with sobs. He steeled himself against the pang the sound produced in his chest.

He worked the knot on her bonds and freed her hands. Her little fists curled under her body, face still pressed in the bedcovers. He sat beside her and ran his hand over her slender back, admiring the delicate lines of muscle, her narrow waist, and, of course, her beautiful welted ass.

"That's over with. Now, we can move forward."

Her back continued to heave with ragged breath.

He slid his fingertips into her thick hair and massaged the back of her head, her neck, one shoulder.

She turned her face to look at him, and he was surprised to find her eyes dry and a questioning expression on her face.

He stroked her flushed cheek with his thumb. "It's over now, pet."

Her breath slowly quieted. She still lay folded over the edge of the bed, rosy red ass on display.

His cock stirred. He wanted her again. But he wouldn't take her. She needed a good meal and some rest. Tomorrow, he could whip her again, if he liked. Take it slow and show her how pain could bring pleasure when applied just right.

He stood up. "I'll get you some food. Crawl up in the bed. Don't move from it, or I'll punish you again when I return, and I'll make that last beating seem like a caress. Understand?"

She immediately obeyed, crawling up to flop on her belly on the bed.

He gripped one ass cheek, thumb nested down against her anus, and gave it a possessive shake. "Answer me, pet."

"Yes, master—I mean, Rok."

"Good girl." Satisfaction at her easy obedience made his chest hum. She didn't seem resentful over her punishment, which came as a relief.

He slipped out and locked the door from the outside, setting the controls so only his handprint opened the door from either side. Almost immediately, his body rebelled at being apart from her. He wanted to keep her close, as if her body provided some energy he required just to live.

Jaso and Janu were in the kitchen, preparing a basic meal of grain, dried fruit, and erk bird meat. Both his foster brothers narrowed their eyes and watched him with an accusing stare as he walked in and dished a helping into a bowl.

He didn't require food as often as most species—only once every dozen planet rotations, as long as he stopped at Zander's pod for a crystal recharge at least once a month. Growing up on Stornig without the crystals, he'd had to eat more frequently, and even then had been weak and unhealthy. He hated that he needed to recharge with something he didn't control, although Zander never charged his species for their use, and made his palace open once a week to those who needed it.

"I seriously hope you have a plan for recouping the steins you just lost us in taking that ship-stealing piece of human filth," Janu said.

"You're going to turn her in for the warrant money or sell her to the Zandian prince so he has a twin set, right?" Jaso challenged.

His lip curled, annoyance flashing through him. He may very well have been planning to bring her to Zander, requesting, of course, compensation for the loss he took in "rescuing" her. But his brother's insinuation that Lily would become Zander's second sex slave bothered the piss out of him. So did the reference to her as human filth.

He didn't know much about humans, but they seemed to be of great use to the Ocretions, and this particular one was not unpleasant to look at. To say the least.

"Yes," Janu jumped in. "Please tell us this isn't about getting your big purple cock sucked by a pretty little mouth, because we could've bought you a human slave a year ago and saved all of us a world of trouble."

He scowled, tempted to stalk away without giving either one of them an answer.

But that wasn't fair. They had suffered as much as he had as a result of Lily's deception. Of course, it wasn't all her—there had been close to two dozen other stowaways who'd helped her take the ship.

"I plan to punish her, which you know I shall enjoy, and then, yes, collect a ransom on her, either from Prince Zander or the Ocretion slave enforcement."

A smirk formed on Jaso's lips, appeased now that Rok had admitted to his fetish.

"I'm not thinking entirely with my *giant* purple cock."

Janu tossed a cleaning cloth at his face. He ducked and let it fly over his back.

"You sharing her?"

That same current of irritation ran through him. "*No,*" he growled. Then, realizing he'd spoken too sharply, he tried to make it light. "I thought you considered her filth, anyway."

Now Janu smirked, too. "Beautiful filth. That Zander knew what he was doing when he bought her sister."

His teeth clenched. "Right."

Discussing Lily and her sister had become no less annoying to him, so he picked up the food and left the twins to their own meal.

In his chamber, Lily appeared to have obeyed, still lying in the position he'd left her. The sight made something high in his chest squeeze. A fierce, protective urge rose in him. This fragile human, this delicate, lovely female's safety lay in his hands now. He would make sure to keep her safe.

She lifted her head, eyes on the food, and a pang for not feeding her first ran through him. She hadn't eaten for several planet rotations, judging from the attention she paid the bowl. She eased up to kneel, wincing when her ass hit her heels then choosing instead to stand on her knees.

The sight nearly undid him.

She looked every inch the sex slave—pert breasts offered up, her sex—permanently made bare through laser hair removal, as was the custom with Ocretion sex slaves—gloriously inviting between her legs, copper hair tumbling across one shoulder. If some being told him that she was actually a mystical, magical creature, capable of seducing males of every species and bringing them to their knees, he would've believed him. Her sister had possessed some extra-human ability to read minds. Why couldn't this one possess some quality that made her irresistible to him?

He stepped closer, and she reached for the bowl, but he pulled it back, out of range. "Uh uh. I'll feed you, or you'll eat too fast. How long has it been since you've fed?" He scooped up a spoonful of grain and fruit and held it out to her.

Her lips closed around the utensil immediately, and she answered with a full mouth, "Since they captured me, two planet rotations ago."

"You were only with them two planet rotations? That's good." Though he shouldn't care, the idea of her being mistreated by those men made him uncomfortable.

She watched the spoon expectantly, but he paused, not wanting her to make herself sick by eating too quickly.

"It was time enough for each one of them to take me several times."

The bitterness in her tone ripped his chest open. He'd half convinced himself that as a sex slave, she'd known no better—apart from her brief freedom when she'd stolen his ship. He hadn't wanted to pity her for her station in life. Because if he did, it would make everything he'd done to her wrong, as well.

Veck.

"I'm sorry."

Her eyes shifted from the bowl to his face, surprise flickering there.

He swallowed and picked out a piece of meat. "Chew it slowly," he warned. "How often do humans normally feed?"

She chewed frantically and swallowed. He rolled his eyes.

"Three times a day, if we can. Sex slaves are generally well-kept. They want us looking healthy, of course. But we'd been foraging on Jesel for half a solar cycle, so we didn't eat as often as we liked."

"You and who? The rebels?"

She shook her head and made an impatient jerk of her chin toward the bowl. He smiled. She was adorable. He loved when she showed him this real side of her, what lay beneath the slavish meekness. Lily, the warrior. The one who'd stolen his ship. He fed her another bite.

"The escaped slaves. The ones who took your ship."

"Hold on," he barked. "Is my old ship back there on Jesel?" He would turn around and recover the thing, if it was.

"It didn't survive landing."

He growled his displeasure.

She shrugged. "They'd only learned to fly by scanning databases. No one had any practical experience, so we figured we were lucky to walk away from the landing."

He swore several times and walked a tight circle around his small chamber.

She climbed down from the bed and followed him, attempting to take the bowl from him with adorable supplicant eyes.

Once more, he jerked it back, but offered her a bite. Her little tongue darted out to catch a spilled piece of grain on her lip, and he watched it, fascinated.

He really shouldn't be so turned on by this silly human.

"So what happened to the rest of them? The escaped slaves?" He wasn't sure why he wanted to know, but he did. He wanted to hear all of her stories, too—how they'd planned the escape, what her life had been like. But that was just bizarre.

Her pretty face clouded, and her muscles hardened. "They were killed," she said stiffly.

"By whom? The rebels?"

"No. By a bomb. I was away from camp." Her gaze turned distant, like she was reliving the moment.

He didn't want her to.

"Again, I'm sorry."

The long dark lashes lifted, and she studied his face as if checking for sincerity. "I don't understand you," she muttered.

He fed her another bite of food and handed over a bladder of juice with a tube attached. She bit the end off and drank the entire thing down.

He lifted his chin. "Get on the sleeping platform. I think you've had enough food for now."

She opened her mouth as if to protest, but he shook his head. "I promise I won't let you go hungry."

~.~

Lily whimpered as the rebel slapped her face and pushed her backward, forcing her to the ground. Her wrists were tied together and he held the end of the rope, which he jerked above her head, until she lay flat. "Spread your legs, slave. You don't get to walk around our camp."

His force came down on her too hard, and he stank of the worst body odor she'd ever smelled. Her former masters had at least been clean and kept her in comfortable surroundings. They'd been upper class, so they possessed the wealth to own their own pods and have steady access to food.

He came down on her, ready to shove his cock in her mouth.

"No," she moaned and turned her head to the side.

"Hush, Lily. It's a dream."

Confusion twisted through her consciousness as she tried to match the voice to the filthy human holding her down.

Her body jerked, and she blinked up at a horned alien warrior. *Rok.*

Her wrists were still bound together with the other end of the rope attached to Rok's wrist, the way he had secured her before they fell asleep.

Holy one true sun, he was beautiful. His hairless jaw was square and strong, hair sandy brown around the stiffening horns. His eyes glowed with violet-rimmed irises. He leaned against the wall behind his bed with his magnificent chest bare.

His eyes traveled from her face down to her bare breasts and grew more violet, hunger evident in his gaze. She was accustomed to being ogled in every way, had learned to use a male's interest to guide or distract him into some form of sex act that might be the least invasive at the moment.

Never before had a lustful gaze made her body heat in response.

Her nipples beaded, breasts grew taut.

"You're finally awake. I've been waiting to torture you for hours."

She wasn't sure how to take that statement. It produced a shiver, and the memory of the past night's whipping returned to her in full force. Yet a tinge of excitement coated everything as well.

He unwound the leather strip that bound his wrist first, then the one around the two of hers. His examination of the red marks and the way he rubbed his thumb over them as if trying to erase them made something flutter in her belly.

Did she hope he cared? She considered showing him the serpent bite on her ankle. It had continued to fester, the throbbing a dull background pain to everything. But she didn't want him to take her somewhere for medical care, because it would mean her immediate arrest. No, better to wait it out. Hopefully, she would recover on her own.

Looking to Rok to save her was stupid. She was his captive, and he was bent on exacting punishment in a way he clearly enjoyed. When he was through with her, he planned to collect the warrant on her, which meant her certain death.

So, basically, she needed to find a way to escape or she'd be dead when they reached Ocretia.

Rok tugged her torso over his thighs so she lay facedown, ass up. His large hand traced over her buttocks. "Is this normal for a human?" His voice choked with shock.

She twisted around to look. Her ass still wore the splotches from his whipping—patches of red standing out brightly on her normally pale skin.

Did he regret it?

If so, she wasn't going to tell him that it no longer hurt and probably wouldn't unless he picked up his strap and used it again. She opted for a sulk, instead. "You whipped me—*hard*." That was not a lie.

"How long does it take you to heal?" He still sounded choked.

"I don't know, seven to ten planet rotations, probably."

Rok abruptly lifted her from the spanking position and plopped her beside him. Some of the color had drained from his face. "Well," he said stiffly, "Humans are more fragile than I knew. Not good for punishing at all."

She hid her amusement. "Most find us extremely good for punishing. The pain of a lesson lasts for a long time."

His lip curled. "I suppose if you're training a slave, that's useful." He sounded disdainful.

Perhaps she'd taken it too far. He enjoyed delivering punishment and now believed she was unfit for it. She didn't want him to lock her away until he collected the warrant. She'd have a far better chance of escape if she remained in his chamber as his slave. And she didn't care to examine that other, small part that *might* enjoy being near him. Even craved his attention and his touch.

She rose up on her knees and reached for one of his horns. She'd seen how they stiffened and leaned just like his cock during arousal. They must be a sensual part of his anatomy.

He shuddered when she fisted it, allowing her to tilt his head down.

She pressed her breasts in his face and swirled her tongue around the horn.

Rok's breath turned ragged. He palmed one breast, squeezing harder when she took the entire horn into her mouth. Though as short as her thumb, it was the same girth as a human cock, and it stiffened and grew as she sucked it. His lips closed on her other nipple, tongue flicking it.

Rok looped an arm around her waist, pulling her closer as the fingers of his other hand slid between her thighs.

Surprise flitted through her when she realized how wet he'd found her pussy—it practically dripped, her folds swollen and slick. He screwed one then two digits inside her, making her gasp with pleasure.

"Suck harder," he grunted and plunged his fingers in and out of her, filling and stretching her.

She obeyed, hollowing her cheeks and sucking as hard she knew how, bobbing her head up and down over his horn.

Rok found the bundle of nerves on her inner wall and her inner thighs trembled. She moaned over the horn. He shifted the arm around her waist to bring a finger to her anus.

She stiffened.

"Keep sucking." His voice sounded low and gravelly.

She whimpered, but obeyed, both wanting and not wanting him to continue working her with his fingers. It seemed she had no choice—he finger*veck*ed her pussy as he worked one digit into her back hole and *vecked* her there, too. Her insides fluttered. Heat flooded her pelvis.

He shouted a curse, and she realized he was coming. He withdrew his fingers from her and shoved his sleeping pants down to fist his cock.

"No, don't stop," he gasped when she adjusted her mouth. In two pumps, he arrived, ribbons of rainbow-hued seed spurting like a fountain from the slit of his cock.

She continued sucking his horn until he finished and his eyes went heavy-lidded.

He grasped her waist, tossing her to her back and climbing over the top. "Good slave," he purred. "Very good girl. How did you know about the horns?"

She attempted a shrug, which was impeded by his weight pressing her down onto the sleeping platform. "I guessed."

"Clever female. You've been trained very well, haven't you?" His cock, though he'd just orgasmed, prodded her entrance.

She rocked her hips up to meet it, desperate for her own release after the incredible fingering.

"If I weren't still angry with you for stealing my ship, I would let you have my cock right now. I can see how much you need it."

She frowned at his arrogance and turned her head sharply to the side.

He chuckled. "Don't think you can hide it, little female. You're going to be on edge until I allow you to orgasm. Since I can't punish that pretty little ass of yours, I'll have to torture you this way." To her shock, he bent down and took her nipple between his lips, sucking and nipping at it until both her breasts ached and her pussy wound tight with need. "There will be no touching on your part. If you touch yourself, I will whip you again, sore ass or no. The only way you're going to get satisfaction is when I decide you deserve it, understand?"

She blinked at him. This was not a game she'd ever played. On the surface, it sounded deceptively easy. All she had to do was not touch herself or orgasm? Fine. She never did either of those things.

Yet he had inspired a restlessness in her, an itchy desire that, for the first time, she needed to scratch with something bordering desperation.

He pushed the tip of his cock inside her, and she relaxed. He'd just been teasing. It was some form of joke. But then he withdrew it again, watching her face closely.

Damn him! She certainly showed her frustration when he pulled out.

He repeated the torture once, twice. On the third time, she turned her head to the side, determined to float away, as she'd learned to do during sex, but he caught her jaw.

"Look at me," he growled. "You want my cock?"

She thrust her jaw forward, not wanting to answer.

He shoved in all the way this time, his cock stretching her wide, stroking her inner wall. "Answer me, Lily." He pulled all the way out.

She gave a sob of frustration. "Yes! Okay? I want your cock. Are you happy, you arrogant—"

He covered her mouth with his large hand.

It was a sign of her growing comfort with this being that she dared call him names. Even so, she wouldn't have been surprised if he'd slapped her at the least.

He cut off her breath with that hand over her mouth, plunged in again, rocked his hips to scythe in and out three, four times, then released her, pulling out and climbing off the sleeping platform, his back to her.

She gasped, her pussy clenching around emptiness, her lungs filling and releasing without satisfaction. She'd been so. Close.

Rok's sleeping pants hung low in back, showing the top of his muscular ass. His broad shoulders stretched a mile, built of solid muscle, and scars, large and small, covered his skin. Something about those scars made him all the more appealing to her. They proved him to be the rugged warrior he looked like. Or maybe it was because he'd known as much hardship as she had.

"I suppose you're hungry again?"

"Yes, master."

He turned around with a frown. He didn't like that title for some reason, but she didn't understand why. There were so many things she didn't understand about him. Like how he could enjoy hurting females and act so caring at once? There was something so darkly treacherous, so seductive about him.

She feared, more than any threat facing her welfare, she would grow attached to him. To his attention, his consideration. The way he'd fed her, watching to make sure she didn't overeat, his reluctance to continue punishing her when she still showed marks, the way his eyes turned dark purple when he wanted her.

He rummaged in a cabinet. "There aren't any flight suits that will fit you, but you can wear my undershirt." He tossed her a thin synthetic shirt in white.

She pulled it over her head.

Rok's eyes traveled to her breasts, and his lids drooped.

She glanced down. Though the shirt was huge on her, falling to mid-thigh, the thin material made it hug her breasts, her steepled nipples poking through.

Rok pinched one nipple through the shirt and the silky fabric slid over it, sending a shiver straight to her core.

She glared up at him and crossed her hands over her chest, not wanting to show how hot and bothered he had her.

He picked up her hand. "I don't need to tie you up, do I, Lily?"

She loved when he called her by her name. Some masters had, but most called her "slave." Even those who had used Lily always made it sound disapproving, like her name was a bad word. In Rok's deep rumble, though, it somehow sounded sensual or even like an endearment.

But that was crazy. She was definitely reading too much into this male. He was a species she hadn't encountered before and she wasn't used to his ways, that was all. Soon she'd learn how to get by and come up with a plan to free herself.

"Do I?" He arched a stern brow.

"No, Master Rok."

His lip curled at her use of the title master again, but he didn't say anything. Her hand fit in his palm like a child's in the larger one of a parent. There was both comfort and safety in the gesture.

A memory of her tiny hand encased in a man's flitted in her mind. Her father, perhaps? Before she went to the institute to be trained as a slave? It must be, because she had no memories of anyone ever holding hands at the institute. All they knew there were complete subservience and swift and painful correction when they protested.

She couldn't remember a mother, specifically, but she knew she'd had one. She didn't remember a face or an incident, but she seemed to recall a feeling of love and safety. The energy of a mother. Some larger force that cared for her in a sweet and tender way.

Did Rok embody some essence of that? Was that what disturbed her so much about him?

She shook off the thoughts. They would not help her survive this. She needed to concentrate on a plan. She had to get free.

~.~

Torturing Lily by withholding her orgasm also tortured him. At least he'd taken the edge off when she'd sucked his horn. Holy Zandian star, he'd never had a female do such a thing—hadn't even known what it would do to him. Yes, he liked to rub his own horns, and he particularly liked to run them over the flesh of a willing female, but when she'd sucked it into her hot little mouth, he'd been in pure ecstasy. Yes, he planned to make her perform that task at least twice a day until they reached Ocretia.

He looked down at the beautiful little waif padding barefoot beside him.

"You're more agreeable than I'd expected," he observed.

She tilted her face up to his, her sensual lips curving into a wry grin. With her free hand, she touched the barcode at the back of her neck. "I'm a slave, aren't I?"

"Yes, but you're not particularly subservient, either." He stopped and pushed her up against the wall, trapping her there to show his far greater strength.

She tilted her lovely face up to his, her green eyes flashing with spirit. He loved that he didn't find fear or resentment there. Excitement, yes. And curiosity. She liked being his prisoner, he was sure of it.

"I like the rebellion in you," he rumbled. He was so *vecking* hard for her again, her scent filling his nostrils, her soft coppery hair brushing his face. "I'm surprised it was never beaten out of you." The idea of some previous master punishing Lily both enraged and turned him on. He hated to think of any master abusing Lily, yet the idea of taking her to task himself kicked his lust into overdrive.

"I usually hide it better."

He *vecking* loved that answer. He heard flirtation in her voice, as if she fully understood his game and wanted to play. "Do you think I should act more slave-like to my new master?"

She knew he didn't like her calling him that—he could tell by the wicked glint in her eye. Well, he preferred that feistiness to the docile show. He eased away from her and tugged her down the corridor.

He didn't want her to call him master. That was what Taraw had called him —Depri's sister, the female he had once loved. Besides, he didn't believe in keeping slaves. Zandians never had kept another species in slavery—he remembered his father being proud of that, even though it meant his father had to put in hard labor. "Other species would use slaves for physical labor, Rok," he would say. "But, on Zandia, we aren't afraid to use our bodies to build things." His father had been proud of his station, low that it had been. "I built the palace the royal family lives in," he would say proudly. "I keep things running there. I'm part of a system that works without degrading other beings."

That was why it had bothered him so much to see the prince with a collar around his human mate.

They entered the kitchen, and he pulled out a meal pack, unwrapped it, and added water to reconstitute it.

Mierna drifted in, a tube of cheap grain alcohol in her hand. "Good," she said, jerking her head at Lily. "She belongs with you."

He rolled his eyes. Mierna always had predictions about his future—some great destiny he had to fulfill. Excrement, all of it. He didn't believe in destiny, and he sure as stars didn't see any higher purpose in his life. He'd been cobbling together an existence as a smuggler for the past ten solar cycles, and the one thing he'd learned was never to make plans for a future, because excrement happened. He'd learned to play things by the seat of his pants, taking every moment he remained alive as a win.

"You sure she belongs with me? Last time she put a laser gun to my chest and stole my ship."

The old Venusian nodded sagely. "There will be more trouble before it's done. Much more."

Despite his steadfast determination that fate did not exist in a universe of free will, her words made him tighten his lips. Would he have more trouble from Lily?

Probably so.

Her docile demeanor belied a quick-witted and devious character. One not unwilling to sacrifice others for her own gain.

He scowled at her, surprised when she shrank back from him. She was more sensitive to his thoughts than he'd expected. Another reason not to underestimate her.

Which didn't mean he wouldn't be sure to wring every bit of pleasure he could out of punishing her.

"Yes, have your fun," Mierna said, waving her hand as if to dismiss it all. "No harm in it. Both will enjoy."

He looked back at Lily and wondered if Mierna actually knew what he wanted to do to the human. He rather hoped not.

He handed Lily the paper tray with the reconstituted meal and watched her eat, wondering how else he might torture his little prisoner.

A wicked idea formed in his head. He searched the cabinets until he found the things he wanted—bree oil—a flavoring used by Depri for his food. It had a spicy, warming quality that would work perfectly. He also used a root vegetable as an aromatic spice. It, too, produced heat. Of course, the human was delicate. He'd have to watch her closely. But if it worked, it would be perfect for keeping her on edge.

She finished eating and deposited her waste in the incinerator, which immediately turned it to dust.

"Lift up your shirt."

"Isn't this your shirt?" she shot back, but her fingers reached for the hem.

"Did you get mouthy like that with your old masters, Lily?"

"No, Master," she conceded.

"Good. Higher." He nudged the shirt above her peach-tipped nipples.

He uncorked the bottle of oil and dabbed a circle on each breast.

"Why good?"

"I'm glad you're willing to give me a little sass. It gives me reason to punish you." He watched her face flush an enchanting shade of pink.

"Why do you like to punish?"

He dropped his hand to her pussy and rubbed the oil that remained on his fingers onto her clitoris.

She clung to his arms, her legs wobbling as he stroked slowly over her slit.

"Because"—he bent his head and murmured close to her ear—"it's so *vecking* hot to control all the responses of a female."

Her breath had quickened, fingers tightening until her nails dug into his skin.

"But why punishment?" She let out a sexy whimper and her eyes rolled back in her head.

He shoved her back against the wall and plunged his fingers deep inside her. "Because some little females deserve to be punished. Don't they?" He pumped them in and out.

"Oh!" Her face had flushed a deep pink and her fingers flew to her breasts. The oil had started working.

"Do you deserve my punishment, Lily?"

The involuntary twitch near her mouth made him yank his fingers out of her. She'd been about to orgasm.

She sobbed, her big eyes both pleading and accusing as she doubled over and reached one hand between her legs.

"Ah ah," he said sharply.

Her hand stopped just before it reached her sex.

"What did I tell you, pet?"

"No touching," she whispered. She took on a feverish appearance, eyes glassy, body shivering. She cupped her breasts. "May I—"

He shook his head, and she froze.

Her brows came down in frustration, and she shoved at him, throwing her entire weight into his chest.

It was delicious. He loved the fight in her, He caught her up into his arms and held her off the ground while she kicked and scratched.

"Careful, pet. I don't want to have to spank you again, not until that pretty bottom heals."

"Oh the entertainment is in here," drawled Jaso from the doorway. Janu stood beside him, and they both wore smirks.

Lily instantly stopped fighting, dropping her chin and turning sullen, her face still flaming.

He tucked her against his side, protectively. He didn't mind a little humiliation, but any more would work against him and his plans to enjoy his lovely pet. Because truthfully, he needed her to enjoy his game, too, or else it wouldn't be fun for him. She might fight him, curse him, say she hated him, but as long as her sensuous body continued to show signs of arousal and excitement, he considered her to be playing along. He knew, though, if he took things too far —if he gave her more pain than she could handle or humiliated her too much, that part of her would shut down. He'd already seen glimpses of how she checked out of her body. And he definitely didn't want an empty *veck*-doll.

Not in the least.

"Come, pet. Let's not give them a show. You may either have some alone-time, locked in my chamber, or you may come to the exercise room with me."

"Exercise room," she said immediately.

Her answer pleased him, though he wasn't stupid enough to believe it was because she wanted to be near him. He needed her close, though. Liked to look on her pleasing form, to feel her closeness, smell her scent.

Yes, the little human pleased him a great deal. Far more than he'd expected, although he might have guessed based on his initial reaction to her the day she stole his ship.

~.~

Lily had never been held against a male's side while he walked. Even more intimate than the way he'd held her hand, it once more stirred her oldest memories. She'd been held. Picked up. She almost remembered the snippet of a song a female had sung to her.

To push back her panic at the swelling emotions within her, she searched for stable footing. "So how did you become a smuggler?"

He shrugged. "Scrappy trade for a scrappy male."

"And your crew? You seem close." She noticed he had the same crew as when she'd stolen the ship, despite the fact that they must have been grounded while he scrapped for a new craft.

"Jaso and Janu are my foster brothers. Their parents took me in after I escaped genocide on my planet."

She nearly stumbled, so surprised by this revelation. So his scars didn't lie—he had lived a rough life, like her.

"How old were you?"

"About eight solar cycles in Ocretian time."

"How did you escape?"

They entered an exercise room. It had equipment along the walls, but the center had been left as open space and contained only a floor mat.

"I got lucky. I lived in the palace because my father was a worker there. A guard scooped me up with two other children—daughters of an important advisor—and got us to an underground tunnel the moment the invasion started. He tried to go back out and fight, but the tunnel was sealed from the palace end by an explosion. We walked in the other direction for many kilometers and exited through a long-abandoned docking station. The guard loaded us on a ship and flew us out of there. I don't know how—it seems a miracle to me now." Rok rubbed his face. "Then we got shot down over Stornig and I was adopted by those dogs."

"What happened to the girls—I mean, the female young?"

His face clouded. "I never knew. I don't even know if they survived the crash. I was thrown from the ship and knocked unconscious. My foster family found only me when they came upon the wreckage."

Jaso and Janu filed in, along with the other three crew members. It seemed this was an appointed exercise time.

The wizened Venusian peered into her face. "Do you like to fight?"

"Wha—? Oh, no." She shook her head. She'd had docility trained into her at a young age with shocking forks. Any slave-child who showed aggression found herself immediately immobilized, pain shutting down her central nervous system.

"Me neither. Come—we'll exercise on the equipment."

She didn't know how to use the equipment, either, as exercise also had been forbidden, unless a slave required certain training by her master, but she followed the Venusian after shooting Rok an inquiring glance.

"What are you called?"

She bit her tongue to keep from muttering, "slave." Something about this crew made her far more at ease than she would normally be. "Lily."

"I am Mierna."

"Why haven't you introduced your prisoner properly, Rok?" one of his foster brothers taunted.

She enjoyed their playful banter and the way Rok ignored it. She hadn't been around such lighthearted ribbing before. Ocretions were always formal and stiff, with the class system fully regimented. No one teased in the pods where she'd lived.

Rok sighed and rubbed the back of his neck. "Come here, Lily." He beckoned her back to his side.

She dutifully returned, keeping her eyes lowered out of habit.

"Lily, you've already seen Jaso and Janu, my brothers. This is Gaurdo." He lifted his chin at a giant, rock-like being, almost as wide as he was tall. One of his legs had been amputated, and he had a metal post in its place. "And Depri." He indicated the tall, thin being with brown skin and green eyes. "He is also a brother, of sorts."

"Also from Stornig?" She wasn't sure what made her think it was appropriate to quiz them, but no one seemed troubled by it.

"No, we met them on one of our early expeditions." She wondered who "them" was, but something had clouded in Rok's expression so she no longer felt comfortable asking.

"How about you?" she asked Mierna as the old female steered her back toward the equipment. "How did you become a part of this crew?"

"They freed me from imprisonment in Bangi. I had nowhere else to go, so I joined them."

Her words sent such a streak of longing through Lily's chest, she almost couldn't breathe. Her present situation was not unlike what Mierna described. This crew had helped her escape slavery—although not willingly—and she had nowhere in the galaxy to go. She did not have a single friend or family member. Nothing. To be invited in as a crewmate on this aircraft would be a fate beyond her dreams.

She thought back to the day she'd escaped. What would've happened if she hadn't stolen their ship? Rok had seemed content to accept payment for her fare in sexual trade. Would he have offered her a position when she told him she had nowhere to go?

She shook her head to clear the thoughts. She couldn't think this way. Her situation wasn't the same. She was wanted by the Ocretions—Rok couldn't keep her aboard a ship that traveled through the galaxy on dangerous trade missions. She'd threaten the safety of all of them. He'd be accused of transporting runaway slaves and put to death along with her.

The males had begun sparring in hand-combat in the center, one on one. Her eyes followed Rok's graceful movements. Though he was large, he moved with fluidity and ease, as if born fighting. The twins fought fast and dirty, lunging in, clamping sharp teeth on their opponent, but apparently not biting down.

Mierna handed her one end of an elastic band attached to the wall. She followed Mierna's action, pulling an elastic band out and in with her arm in different positions, mimicking it. Her muscles grew tired after only a few repetitions, but she kept at it. If she planned to escape and survive, she needed to become strong. These beings could show her how. Perhaps even teach her to fight.

The old Venusian nodded as if she knew Lily's thoughts. "Your destiny is much bigger than you see now. Do you know that?"

A tingle ran across her skin. She'd always had the sense that something came *after*. That sexual slavery wasn't her only episode in life. That belief had kept her from desperation or depression. Kept her from contemplating suicide, like some of the other girls.

But the Venusian might say such things to everyone. She hadn't said anything specific, and it probably didn't mean anything.

"I-I don't know," she murmured.

The old being nodded again. "You do know. You have always known. A great destiny. You will help many other beings find freedom and peace. Rok does not believe in destiny, yet he, too, has one he must face."

Her doubt increased, even as the hairs on her arms stood up. For a few months, she'd believed such a thing. She'd been a part of an escape plan and had learned to survive in the wilderness. She'd thought they might build a new human community of free beings.

But it had been too good to be true. Just when she'd started to care about something, it all had been destroyed. Every being she'd grown to care for, every hope and dream crushed.

And now she was on a ship, rushing to her death.

"You will not die yet," the old Venusian said softly, turning away to repeat the exercises with her other arm.

Lily's breath caught.

The female did read thoughts.

CHAPTER THREE

Rok couldn't wait to get Lily back into his bedroom for her final torture. Keeping her on edge all day had been his own delicious deprivation, as well. He'd been hard for her all planet rotation. Stars, just having her in the exercise room while he sparred made his aggressive hormones flow to a height he'd never before experienced. He'd nearly harmed his brothers twice, throwing them to the ground. In the end, they'd gone four-on-one instead of the usual two-on-one, because no one, not even Gaurdo, could hold him back.

They'd accused him of showing off for his slave.

Perhaps he had been. Her green eyes followed every move he made, though he sensed neither approval nor disapproval at his performance. All he knew was her mere presence in the room gave him the knife-like certainty of winning. He supposed it was a primitive response to enable a male to protect his mate.

Not that he considered Lily his mate.

He kept her close to him all day, pinching her nipples and rubbing between her legs every moment they were alone to keep her wet for him. Her scent filled his nostrils, inciting lust sharper than the crack of a whip.

Which, sadly, he wouldn't be using on her.

He didn't mind—what he had in store was far better.

He fingered the aromatic root he'd cut into perfect form and wrapped for her punishment. "Come, Lily." He picked up her hand.

She glanced up at him through her thick lashes, lips parted, the copper sheet of her hair falling over one shoulder. By the Zandian moons, she was lovely. So *vecking* lovely. Maybe he wouldn't return her to Zander. The prince didn't deserve two females this beautiful. He could make it part of his price for leading an army of airships on the Finn. One hundred thousand steins and your mate's sister as my...what? Slave? No, he'd been thinking *mate*.

Vecking excrement.

He ushered his slave into his chamber and locked the door. "Since your bottom is too tender for more punishment, I had to devise another means to exact retribution on you today."

She didn't flinch, but her pupils narrowed, and she tensed. She was a little warrior of sorts, too. The kind who remained alert to all dangers, bending but never breaking.

He shifted the sitting platform to the middle of the room and sank into it. "Take off the shirt."

She pulled it over her head in one fluid motion and tossed it on the floor in a small show of defiance.

His lips twitched. "Pick that up and fold it neatly, pet. You know I won't tolerate insolence."

Something deadened behind her eyes, and he regretted whatever he'd said that had triggered her emotional shutdown. He definitely didn't want her disengaged.

"Or, rather," he tried to fix it, "I'll punish you for insolence. That doesn't mean I don't expect it now and then."

It worked. She returned, curiosity flickering behind her eyes. "What made you like this? How did you learn you liked..." she swallowed, seeming unable to finish.

"To punish?" He smiled. "I had a lover—Depri's sister, actually. She loved pain. Loved to have control forced away from her, to be held down and hurt in a way that didn't cause lasting harm."

"What happened to her?"

He'd known she'd ask the question, and braced himself for the sharp jab that always lanced through him when he thought of it. This time, though, it seemed less painful than usual. "She was killed during a transaction." To the day he died, he would regret not going instead of her. It should have been him who had fallen that day.

Lily paled. "I'm sorry," she murmured.

He shrugged. "It's been a long time. Almost four solar cycles now." He needed to redirect this conversation before his mood went south. "But I learned many things with her. How to torture a female in the ways that fulfill the most." He flashed a wicked, promising smile. "Now, lie over my lap."

Her eyebrows lifted. "I thought you weren't going to spank me."

He grinned. "That doesn't mean I don't still own your ass. So when I say bend over, you'd better obey quickly, pet, or I'll make the punishment more challenging than I already planned it to be."

A shiver visibly ran through her, but she did as he commanded, gingerly folding herself over his thighs and presenting her perfect little ass.

"Reach back and pull open your cheeks."

"What?" He sensed more confusion than disobedience in her tone.

"You heard me."

She shot him a questioning look, but reached her hands back and prized her cheeks apart.

He unwrapped the root and worked the freshly peeled end, which he'd carved in the shape of a finger, against her anus.

She clenched her back pucker, tightening her ass.

He slapped the back of her thigh. "Do you need a spanking, too?"

"No." He loved the sullenness in her tone.

He popped each cheek once, anyway. "Open up." Wiggling the end of the root against her back entrance, he applied steady pressure.

She gasped when it breached her tight muscles and entered. He pushed it in until he reached the end he'd notched to keep it from entering all the way.

"Now stand up." He gave her ass a pat.

She stood up, the little root sticking out from between her ass cheeks. Soon it would begin to produce heat, even burning.

"Straddle my knees," he ordered.

She adjusted and started to climb onto his lap, but he held her back with a hand at her hips. "Not sitting. Standing." He lowered his knees, hoping she'd manage it.

"Oh." She lifted her weight onto her feet, which forced her legs to be spread wide.

"Good, pet." Her bare breasts bobbed right in front of his face, her pussy was spread between his legs, and he checked with his fingers to make sure the spicy root he'd inserted still protruded from her ass. The sight was so erotic, so lovely, he wanted to capture it forever.

He reached behind her and pumped the root in and out of her ass, watching her face flush and nostrils flare.

"What is that?"

"Anal punishment."

She tossed him a suspicious look—probably guessing there was more to it than that.

"You'll find out soon enough."

Wariness scrawled over her visage.

"Your bottom is too sore, but there are other parts of you I can spank. Can you guess what they are?"

Her belly fluttered with a rasped breath. "No." Her voice was little more than a whisper.

He slapped her left breast with a quick, arcing open palm.

She jumped and moved to step back, but he caught her waist. "Ah ah. Where are you going? You stay right here for your punishment." He slapped her right breast.

Her breath quickened, making her breasts rise and fall at an alluring rate.

He yanked her forward and applied his mouth to her left nipple, twirling his tongue around her nipple, scraping his teeth across the delicate flesh then sucking it into his mouth. The moment he released it, he slapped his fingers across it again, watching it bounce under his treatment.

"Which is better? Breasts or..." He clapped his palm up between her legs, connecting with her wet, plump folds. "Pussy?"

She cried out, wobbling, but he held her up with the hand on her hip.

"You've been naughty, pet. Your pretty little pussy deserves to be punished." He slapped it again. "So does this ass." He pumped the root in her anus.

"Oh." Her startled look told him that the root had begun to heat inside her.

He slapped her pussy again, which dripped with arousal. "I told you I would punish you every day until we reach Ocretia. I wouldn't lie. If your ass is still too sore tomorrow, I'll tie your legs open and whip those inner thighs until you scream for mercy."

The wariness had gone from her face, replaced by desire. Her eyes glowed glassy, breath came in pants. "Please," she breathed.

He screwed two fingers inside her hot channel and watched her face. Judging from the way her muscles contracted around his fingers, she was ready to blow.

He shoved down his flight pants, allowing his cock to spring free. "Climb on it."

The relief in her expression was almost comical. Or it would have been if his own desperation didn't match hers. He gripped her ass and impaled her on his cock, unable to wait for her trembling movement.

She gasped at the sudden intrusion. He let her adjust to his size by pumping that wicked root in and out of her ass, twisting and turning it to renew the burn.

"Oh stars, oh *veck*," she moaned, rocking her hips up to meet his.

He nearly died from the rightness of it.

"That's it, beautiful. Take me deeper," he growled, moving her hips forward and back over his erection, using the length of his cock to rub her clit each time she moved out.

"Oh *veck!*" Her gaze flew around, a frantic wild quality to her movements now.

He took her right nipple into his mouth and sucked hard, still yanking her in and out over his cock so fast her teeth probably rattled.

The sound of her gasping breath, the desperation of her gyrating hips sent him over the edge. His thighs tensed, balls contracted. Stars danced before his eyes.

"Come, Lily," he roared, unable to wait for her.

He yanked her body against his and held her tight, his cock buried deep inside her as he came and came.

She, too, found her release, shudders bucking through her lithe body until she lay limp as a rag doll.

He bit the place where her shoulder met her neck and laid a kiss behind her ear. To his surprise, she pushed off his lap, limbs jerky with anger.

Oh *veck*. Had he hurt her? A sheet of cold doused his body.

~.~

Lily stalked away to face the corner, arms crossed over her chest, shoulders hunched.

Get it together, Lily. Get it together.

Tears burned in her eyes, and her heart jumped erratically in her chest.

What had just happened? She'd never lost control like that. *Veck,* had she ever even been present during sex before?

"Lily?" She heard Rok surge to his feet behind her, and his two beefy forearms appeared on either side of her, caging her against the wall.

"*Veck*, Lily. Did I hurt you?"

The shocked concern in his voice only made the restless emotions ricocheting through her body worse. She had to get a grip on them before she unraveled completely.

When she didn't answer or turn, he shifted to catch her shoulders. "I went too far. I'm sorry."

His apology only ratcheted up her confusion. Why did he care about her feelings? Wasn't this supposed to be retribution for her crimes against him? The icy truth that her suspicion it was something altogether different sent her tumbling headlong down the mountain of uncertainty.

What was this male playing at? And why—by the Earth's one true moon— *why* did he have such an effect on her?

He turned her slowly, and the soft regret on his face undid her.

"Get off me," she shouted, shoving his hands away. "I don't know what you're playing at, but I want no part of it."

"Tell me what I did. Why are you angry with me?"

Because it wasn't what he'd done but this very concern that had her chest in shreds, she slapped his face.

He let her. Yes, she actually saw him start to withdraw the target then let the slap fall. But he'd had enough. He caught both her wrists and yanked her against his chest.

"Did you like it too much?" his face was grim, and the knowing in his tone nearly dropped her to the floor.

Tears spilled down her cheeks like a valve had opened.

Rok caught her around the waist, holding her up. He plucked out the vegetable that burned and heated her ass, leaving her entire pelvic region warm, her pussy dripping. Even after that vigorous ride, after taking his huge Zandian cock, she wanted more.

And it terrified her.

She shouldn't desire her captor. Find pleasure with her master. Receive comfort from the male who planned to give her over to her death in just a few weeks.

This maelstrom of conflicting emotions made it impossible for her to think, to reason her way out of this bizarre entrapment with a tender captor who liked to cause her pain.

Except she hadn't noticed the pain because the driving force of the need, the *vecking* edge he'd had her on all planet rotation had her begging him for it. And the humiliation of it all—the burning root he'd pumped relentlessly in and out of her ass, the pussy spanking, the breast spanking—it all replayed in her mind so loudly, in such vivid detail and color and sensation, she couldn't *breathe*.

This wasn't her.

Rok scooped her into his arms and slid her onto the sleeping platform. He popped a tube in a liquid pack and pressed it to her lips. "Drink."

She hadn't known she was thirsty, but the sweet liquid cooled her mouth and throat. She pulled hard, swallowing in quick bursts until she'd finished the entire pack.

"Look at me." Rok stood beside the platform, a crease between his brows. His shirt was off, and his bare chest rippled with muscle.

She obeyed.

"Are you hurt?" He asked the question slowly and clearly, as if her answer was of the utmost importance.

She shook her head.

"Did I take things too far?"

She couldn't bring herself to say yes. It hovered on her lips, both a truth and a lie.

She dropped to her side, offering her back, and stared at the wall.

"Oh no, you don't." Rok caught her upper arm and rolled her over to face him. "Don't you *dare* turn wax doll on me, Lily. Not after that *vecking spectac-ular* display of sensuality. Sexuality—whatever. We're going to talk about this. You liked it. I know you liked it," he said fiercely, as if the universe depended on him convincing both of them. He brought his palms to her face, bracketing it with a soft touch. "It was intense for me, too."

Her breath stalled. Stuttered. Stalled again. Their gazes locked, his amethyst eyes boring down into hers, nothing but dead sincerity on his hand-some face.

After a long moment, he flicked off the light. "I'm going to crawl up there beside you, and if there's anything you want to tell me in the dark, while you don't have to look at me, I'll be listening."

Her heart hammered against her ribs. What did he think she would say? What was he inviting her to say?

She had no experience to help her navigate this male, nor the feelings still swimming around her gut.

He lay down beside her, catching and tying her wrists so easily in the dark she wondered if she was the only one who couldn't see. The blackness did provide some measure of safety, though it also seemed to give her emotions room to expand, which she didn't like.

"I got scared," she admitted.

Rok slid his hand across her breast in a light caress. "You haven't let go before."

She considered his words, plopped like stepping stones in front of her, to help her find the way out of the hole she'd descended into. "No, I haven't."

"I did humiliating things to you, and you're not sure how you feel about that."

Even as her insides squeezed in the agony of embarrassment, her pussy clenched. "Yes," she whispered. This might be the crux of the problem. Her sexual response was not in line with her mental one. "Why do you enjoy that?" she snarled. "Hurting and humiliating females?"

"Lily…If you hadn't responded, if you'd cried or begged me to stop, if you'd turned to stone, as I've seen you do, I would've stopped. But you liked it. Your pussy dripped for me. You begged me to take you."

Her face grew warm in the darkness. Yes, she had begged him.

"Is that what you like? The begging?"

"I love all of it, pet. I love being in charge. I love frightening you. Hurting you. I love making you cry and then I love making it better."

She curled into a tight ball on her side. "That's just wrong."

The light came back on, and she yelped from the intensity, blinking as the sheet of white blared across her vision. "Very well." His clipped voice made her sit up and pay attention.

He stood from the bed and made an impatient gesture. "Get up."

"Why?" Her heart thudded; somehow it knew this consequence would be her worst yet, and it wasn't going to involve pain. At least not the physical kind.

"I'll lock you in a different room. You can stay there until we arrive in Ocretian territory." His expression was closed and stony. She saw the warrior in him now—huge, fierce. Terrifying. Not a being she'd want to cross.

Cold waves of panic ran through her. "No." Her rational mind said she needed to stick with Rok if she wanted any chance of escape. Her heart screamed the same. Her insides had dropped to the floor, leaving her an empty shell, cold and paper-thin, ready to blow away at Rok's next breath.

He arched a brow. "No?"

She shook from head to foot. Since her rational mind had left, she reverted to her training, dropping to her knees at his feet, bowing her head low. "Forgive me, master."

He hauled her back up so quickly she yelped. He lifted her by her upper arms until they saw eye-to-eye, her feet dangling in the air.

"Ouch." She squirmed. Somehow she knew this wasn't one of the ways he meant to hurt her.

She was right. He dropped her like she'd scalded him and stepped back. His eyes burned dark purple with anger.

She wanted to rub her arms, knowing there'd be finger bruises there soon, but her bound wrists made it impossible. She tried it less formally this time. "I'm sorry, Rok. Please don't send me from your chamber. I won't complain of your treatment of me again."

But that still wasn't what he wanted to hear. He put his hand to the screen and his door slid open. "Let's go." The coldness in his expression cut her like a blade.

Her throat closed and her nose burned. She thrust her jaw forward. "No, I won't go. I belong here. For your punishment."

He remained wooden. No, stone. "Don't feed me what you think I want to hear."

She winced and held her breath to keep from crying. "I'm speaking the truth. You were right. I like what you do to me. Maybe too much."

There. That was the most raw veracity she knew.

The harsh lines of Rok's face gentled, though he didn't move.

"My ass isn't really sore," she admitted. "It just looks bad. You could spank me tonight..." The heat of a flush crept up her neck.

Rok stared at her for a long moment. Then the corners of his lips twitched and he cupped her nape, dragging her against his huge, hard body and pressing his lips to her hair. "It's not sore, hmm?"

"Not so much. A few twinges now and then."

"I'll punish you for that deception, too, then. Tomorrow."

The door swished shut as he released his hold on the hand-panel. He spun her around to face the sleeping platform and forced her torso down. She held her breath, waiting. He'd said tomorrow for the spanking, so what was this? More sex?

But his huge palm clapped down on her ass, landing a flurry of spanks that sent her to her toes. Six, seven, eight. He stopped and rubbed her screaming flesh.

"Tomorrow, I'm going to fuck this pretty little ass. Teach you to mean it when you call me master."

Rok scooped his little human onto the sleeping platform and crawled in beside her, wrapping an arm over her waist and molding her soft body against his. Despite the difference in their sizes, in their species, she nested perfectly with him.

He hit the button on the wall behind his head to extinguish the artificial light in the room. He hated that weak light—his cells longing for the crystal-amplified sunlight Zandia had featured.

"Is that why you don't like when I call you master?"

His chest closed, the ache every time she said that word automatic. Taraw had called him that, with complete surrender and total submission. She'd look up at him with adoration, waiting for his command.

"*She* called you that."

He sucked in a breath, startled. Did the human read minds like Mierna?

"Who?"

"Depri's sister. You never said her name."

"Taraw. Yes."

Silence stretched between them as his throat closed with grief and guilt. "I'm sorry for your loss."

He couldn't speak. Taraw had been as different from Lily as a female could be. Willowy and tall, like Depri, she'd been a warrior, as forceful as any. Only on the sleeping platform did she surrender. Lily had been a slave, trained in subservience, but she resisted her real surrender. That was the part that had frightened her earlier.

"I've never loved anyone." Her voice sounded hollow. The emptiness of it scraped at his chest.

"No?" The image of her sister and mother's faces, pinched with concern over her flashed in his mind. "No family? Friends?"

"None. The closest I came to friends were those slaves I escaped with. But..."

"But what?"

"Things turned divisive with them almost as soon as we settled. There wasn't enough food to go around. Things were hard. We took care of each other, but there was a lot of infighting and resentment."

"They all died in the explosion?"

"Yes. I was out foraging for food. We weren't supposed to be out alone, but I'd needed some time away. I was still enjoying my freedom." The bitterness in her voice made him wince.

But she wasn't a slave anymore, not really. If she didn't realize that yet, she would soon. Even more when she was reunited with her mother and sister. He smiled, knowing she couldn't see him in the darkness. Giving her that gift—one she'd never had, or could no longer remember—would be sweet.

CHAPTER FOUR

Lily woke in Rok's chamber just as mixed up as she'd been the night before. The lights were on half-strength and she was alone, but he'd moved a hover seat close to the bed and a plate of food sat upon it.

Her heart squeezed uncomfortably. She wasn't even sure why. Just because Rok had been thoughtful enough to leave food? Or was it something more?

She'd been broken, but not in any way a master had broken her before. Last night, Rok had made her *choose* to stay with him. Choose to submit to his punishment, to serve as his sex slave. And she had chosen.

As much as she'd like to believe she'd chosen with her cool, rational mind because staying with Rok offered greater chance of escape, deep down, she knew it wasn't true.

It went far deeper.

She needed to see where this thing with Rok was going. To understand the emotions he stirred in her, as disturbing as they may be. She spent the morning trying to identify them and came up with one word: need.

He created desire in her—not just for his touch, for sexual release, but also for his attention, his approval, his nearness. She wanted to be with him at all times, to watch the grace of his hulking body in motion, to admire the easy command he had of his ship and crew. Because they didn't act subservient to him, yet they all still deferred.

They've chosen him, too.

A tingle ran through her when she realized it. This was the sort of master he was. The kind others chose to follow, not because they were forced by station or threat of punishment, but because he was the one who led best.

It brought home the problem that plagued the escaped slaves—lack of a clear, trusted leader. They'd all been so eager to be free, to follow their own will, they couldn't get organized around any authority. Decision-making had been impossible because the group wouldn't even agree to a democratic rule of majority vote for each decision.

The night before, when she'd realized his dead lover called him master, jealousy had gutted her. She'd swallowed back the hurt because his pain was palpable but sent up such a longing for what he'd had, for what they'd had together, she could scarcely breathe.

Love.

The only inkling she had of its meaning was when she tried to conjure up a picture of her parents. Though no specific memories came up, she was certain she'd been loved. She had known love, once.

The beings who hadn't—girls brought to the training institute as infants— never could be trusted. They never made friends with the other girls or helped each other out. She had had friends there.

She'd forgotten in that moment of self-pity the night before when she said she'd never known love.

Though the trainers separated any slaves they suspected of forming bonds with each other, the children had formed bonds, nonetheless. They comforted each other after punishments, protected one another's emotions and souls, even when they couldn't protect each other's physical bodies.

Remembering them renewed in her the vision that had died on Jesel—a free human race. She still believed it could be done, wanted to participate in the liberation of her people.

It strengthened her resolve. She still did have a purpose beyond her own basic survival. She must escape and find a way to help others to escape. There had to be a way. If only she could stop Rok's craft from entering Ocretion airspace.

She knew nothing about spacecraft, but maybe there was a way to disable this one—enough that he'd have to land somewhere sooner rather than later. Create a slow leak in the fuel supply, perhaps.

She climbed off the sleeping platform and pulled Rok's shirt on. She liked that he'd worn it, that it belonged to him.

Like she did.

No—he wasn't keeping her. Was that what made her heart squelch so? She'd finally been claimed by a master whose touch she *wanted*—craved, actu- ally—but he didn't have any interest in keeping her around? Worse, he planned to send her to her death so he could claim the bounty on her head.

Jagged pain slashed her chest. She had to escape. Either that, or she had to make him change his mind. Somehow, escaping seemed the less daunting task.

She ate the food. It had the deadened taste of food that had been reconsti- tuted, but wasn't horrible. She wondered what and when Rok ate.

The door slid open, and the alien in question leaned against the frame, looking sexy as hell in a skintight black undershirt and matching black flight pants. His gaze fell on her, cool and assessing.

"How are you feeling?"

A riot of emotions rippled through her. She realized she didn't know her role. He didn't like when she "played" at slave, nor could she bring out the steely revolutionary who'd stolen his ship. She didn't owe him anger after the kindness he'd shown her the night before.

Thankfully, he let her off without answering. "Care for a shower this morning? I imagine you need the washroom, at least."

She exhaled. "Yes, please. That would be wonderful." A new shyness made it too difficult to look at his face, so she settled into her usual slave-gaze in the direction of his feet.

He caught her chin when she approached and lifted it. His expression held curiosity, and he seemed to see right into her soul. She shifted on her feet and swallowed.

He lowered his head and brushed his lips across hers.

She went still. A kiss. The tenderness of it rocked her right down to her bare feet.

Rok groaned against her mouth and shifted the hand at her chin to the back of her head, holding her still as he deepened the kiss. His other hand gripped her ass, squeezing hard.

She lifted her thigh to wrap it around his legs, and he immediately palmed her entire ass and lifted it higher, until her core met the hardened bulge of his cock through the flight pants.

"*Veck*, little girl. I'm hard for you already." He inhaled deeply with his face at her neck. "Your scent drives me mad. You'd best get to the washroom fast before I decide you need a hard *veck* up against this wall first."

She wasn't sure she *didn't* need a hard *veck* up against the wall first, but her bladder protested so she ducked past Rok and padded toward the washroom.

.

Rok waited for his little slave to emerge from the washroom, her freshly washed skin just as intoxicating in scent as it had been before her cleaning. She still wore his shirt, which he adored on her.

"Have you ever played walnees?" he asked.

Her blank look told him she had not.

"It's a strategy game. Come, I'll teach you. It's fun." But as he led her to the exercise/game room, the lights flashed a warning amber and the mechanical voice of the flight computer announced, "Approaching space debris. Repeat, approaching space debris. Adjust flight course immediately."

He grabbed Lily's hand, and they sprinted to the flight controls. Mierna was already snapping her safety harness in place in the copilot's seat.

Janu and Jaso sped around the corner, followed by Gaurdo and Depri.

"Everyone buckle in," he barked and shoved Lily into a seat, yanking the harness down around her.

"I've got it." She snatched the buckle from his hands and fastened it for herself.

"Activate protective shields," he barked at Mierna.

"Already on it," she sang out.

He slid into his seat, buckling with one hand as his other reached to flick on manual control. Taking the directional knobs, he dodged the debris flying at the ship from all sides, jumping to the right, then left, swooping around, flipping to fly sideways between two large pieces. Smaller pieces hit off the outside of the ship, sounding far worse than they probably actually were. In his experience, the space junk had to be big and heavy enough to throw them off course when it hit to cause any external damage. So far, he'd avoided those largest pieces.

But the debris field became thicker.

"Fastest way out is 120 degrees," Mierna reported. "But the debris is thickest in that direction."

He angled north, but almost immediately dropped back down to avoid smashing the ship. "Negative. Too hostile. What are my other options?" He slowed their speed to navigate the heavy influx of space trash.

"Incoming," Mierna shouted. "Spacecraft, appears unfriendly."

"Gaurdo and Depri, prepare to fire on my command." He kept his clipped tones calm, although it appeared they were under attack. Space pirates sometimes used the cover of debris to lie in wait.

"Three more—shots fired."

He dodged the laser fire from the first ship, swung around and lined his ship up to fire back. "Fire at will," he commanded.

His world narrowed to the razor sharp reflexes necessary to maneuver the ship in and out of debris and enemy fire. "Take the *veckers* down," he growled when he provided a straight shot for his crew to fire.

Their laser fire hit the enemy ship, and it exploded in a burst of flames. Immediately, the three other ships charged his, obviously intent on revenge.

He dropped straight down, swerving around a piece of debris. Unfortunately, a huge piece caught the top of the craft, sending them into a spin. With a curse, he wrestled the controls to ease the ship out of the spin.

Laser fire struck their shields on the starboard side.

He flipped the ship one hundred and eighty degrees, making them hover upside down directly in front of one of the enemy ships.

Jano and Jaso fired on the ship and it exploded into flames, blinding him.

He eased off the speed and righted the craft. The other two enemy ships retreated. An alarm bell sounded, signaling damage to the craft.

Gaurdo unbuckled from his seat. "I'll look at it," he rumbled.

Rok dipped the craft to the right, finally escaping the field of debris.

"Clear," Mierna reported.

He shoved the thrust to full throttle, and the ship sped forward out of the treacherous territory. "Status, Gaurdo?" He sent his voice through to Gaurdo's flight collar.

"Not yet," came his gruff reply.

"Are we talking life-threatening damage?"

"No."

The rest of the crew unbuckled and left the cockpit, presumably to help Gaurdo.

He glanced over his shoulder. An unfamiliar urge to protect the female behind him made him itchy over the damage to the ship. Lily's lovely face had gone pale, but it was the look in her eyes that made his heart stall.

She appeared to be in awe...*of him.*

"Where'd you learn to fly like that?" She moistened her lips with that pretty little tongue of hers.

He shrugged. "Always flown. It's all I know how to do."

"You know how to fight."

Her insistence on being impressed by him made something lodge in his throat. Though he'd never sought meaning or purpose in his life, some odd desire to become or do something more rose up in him.

"All I know how to do is lie down and take it."

The bitterness in her voice shredded him. A great, dark anger surged within him at all the idiot masters she'd had who hadn't seen her as a being. Hadn't treasured her. He'd be *vecked* if he wasn't going to try to show her something different.

"Come here." He beckoned to her.

Surprise flitted over her face, and her fingers fumbled at her harness. When it popped free, she came to him. It pleased him how easily she obeyed —and not out of fear. She was beginning to trust him.

He pulled her down onto his lap and buried his face in her neck, breathing in the scent of her silky hair. "You want to learn how to fly?"

She pulled back, eyebrows raised. "Really?"

He shrugged. "We both know you're capable of far more than lying down and taking it. You're intelligent. You're quick. And you know how to follow the path of least resistance."

Her blush made him want to take her long and hard just to prove he'd meant it, but he restrained his desire. This moment was for Lily to be something other than a receptacle, for once. "Let's start with flying a ship. That way, the next time you steal some idiot's ship, you won't have to crash land it."

She choked on a laugh. He swore light beamed from her face, her smile was so bright. He arranged her on his lap and placed her hands on the controls, explaining what each one did.

"It's not on autopilot now, so any movements you make will be real. Go ahead and try it."

"But is the ship okay? We're not going to lose a wing or anything are we?"

"If we do, I promise I'll take over." He grinned.

She shifted the directional thrust and the ship wobbled, one wing dipping. "Help!" she gasped.

He covered her hand and nudged the plane back into balance. "It's touchy, but you get the feel of it after a while."

Gaurdo's voice came through on his collar. "There's been damage to the outer shell. We won't make it to Ocretian airspace. We'll have to stop sooner."

He cursed. "How much sooner?"

"Two to four planet rotations."

"Mierna, research possible landing locations."

"Already working on it," she sang out, implying she'd already known this outcome.

Lily shifted and settled on his lap, sending his cock into false expectations about what they were doing.

Soon, he'd *veck* her. She was his to take any time he liked. But, right now, he loved her pleasure and delight.

~.~

After showing her how to fly and feeding her a midday meal, Rok led her to his chamber and pulled her only covering—his thin undershirt—off her. His gaze dropped to her nipples, which tightened the moment his horns stiffened and his lids drooped.

Rok didn't miss the change. "They're begging for my mouth, aren't they?"

Heat flooded her core.

He tweaked one between his thumb and finger, pinching just hard enough to make her lips part. "You'll have to beg me for that later, little human. Right now, I want you to make yourself comfortable with your fingers between your legs. You get that pussy nice and slick for me because, when I come back, it needs to be wet and ready. Understand?"

She didn't understand, not really. The instructions, yes, but not his game. But she nodded anyway. "Yes, master."

His gaze sharpened, and he studied her face, perhaps searching for her sincerity. She thought she'd meant it, but whatever he saw didn't convince him. His eyes narrowed. "Don't call me that," he growled. "I'll punish you when I return."

She didn't experience dread at that promise. More of a morbid curiosity bordering on excitement. She wondered what more the sadistic alien had in mind for her.

He left her in his chamber.

She climbed on the sleeping platform and gingerly reached down to touch between her legs. The truth was she had no experience with pleasuring herself. It had been forbidden at the training institute, and afterward, she'd never had an interest. She'd spent most of her time disassociated from those parts of her body—from all of her body, really.

Until Rok, she'd never known pleasure of any kind.

What made her wet and ready? She explored her folds with a sort of scientific curiosity. Unpleasant memories of being used while completely dry and ill-prepared rushed in, and a wave of nausea made her stop.

She couldn't do this.

Rok could do whatever he wanted with her, but she wouldn't willingly pleasure herself. She just didn't need that sort of thing.

With her arms stiffly by her sides, she closed her eyes, removing herself from her body and the situation she didn't know how to handle.

She didn't know how long it took Rok to return—her sense of time had floated away with her mind.

He frowned when he saw her position on the bed.

She sat up quickly.

"Spread your legs and show me your pussy."

She bent her knees and opened her feet wide.

"Is she wet for me?" Rok crossed the small space and dragged his thumb across her slit. It caught in her folds. He raised an eyebrow. "What happened?"

Sullenness stole over her—an unfamiliar emotion. Certainly one she'd never allowed herself to reveal to a master. "I didn't know how," she said stiffly.

"No?" Only polite surprise tinged his voice. "I'll show you, then." He climbed onto the platform and sat with his back against the wall. After widening his legs, he grasped her around the waist and pulled her back flush against his front, her buttocks nested against the bulge in his flight pants.

He tapped her clitoris lightly with the pad of his index finger. "You know about this spot, I presume." *Tap, tap, tap.*

Her sluggish arousal sputtered back to life, blood rushing to the area.

"Did you touch yourself here?"

"No."

He slapped her pussy, and she yelped, squeezing her thighs around his hand.

"Naughty slave." He picked her knees up and draped them over the outside of his legs, so they were pinned wide open. "Keep them here, or there will be consequences. I expect your full cooperation with your punishments."

He slapped her pussy again.

She sucked her breath in across her teeth and threw her head back on his shoulder.

"When I tell you to prepare yourself"—he spanked her poor sex with even, firm slaps— "I expect you to obey me." He delivered five more and swiped the pad of his finger across her sex.

This time, it slid easily, her natural lubricant flowing.

"That's better," he murmured, spreading the moisture up to her clit and tracing a slow, torturous circle around it. "Maybe all you need is my punishment to get you hot."

She flushed. That couldn't be true, could it? Yet she couldn't remember ever growing moist, except with him.

He flipped her around so she lay across his lap then threaded her hand underneath her hips and between her legs. "Stroke yourself, beautiful. Keep it wet while I spank you."

She touched her sex, surprised at how plump and swollen her folds had grown.

Rok brought his palm down on her right cheek, hard.

She yelped and curled her fingers back into her hand, bracing for the pain.

Though the hand was underneath her, somehow he knew. He slapped the back of her leg, which hurt even worse, and reached around to replace her fingers. With his digits tangled over hers, he gave her a quick tutorial on how to touch herself, making a tight circle over her clit then thrusting a finger inside her.

"Keep it going or I'll spank down here." He popped her thigh again.

"No," she shrieked.

He chuckled. "Be a good pet, then. Do as you're told. I need you to learn how to pleasure yourself."

Her head swam, as if the concept itself made her dizzy. A master ordering her to pleasure herself was a most bizarre and backward experience. Fingers fluttering between her legs, she tensed her shoulders, every cell in her body listening intently to the sensations created from simultaneous spanking and masturbation.

He spanked with a heavy hand, slow, measured strokes, without any rubbing or petting in between. The steady and predictable cadence helped her settle into the pain, accepting it, even though it set her bottom on fire.

After what seemed like an endless duration, Rok picked up speed.

She cried out in protest, but he once more set up a rhythm, just twice as fast as the last one. Her own fingers picked up the pace as well, matching his thorough spanking with a frantic, jerky pulse. Need coiled inside her, dark and hot. The sensations mingled, pain and desperate desire.

"Rok," she gasped, hips bobbing on his lap—whether they were reaching to meet his hand or move away from it, she wasn't sure.

"That's it, beautiful." His voice sounded deeper than usual. "Say my name when you come, say it."

"Rok...Rok!" she shrieked. All the muscles in her pelvic floor tightened. Her thighs tightened, squeezing her hand tightly between them. Her butt cheeks clenched. Under her fingers, her pelvic floor contracted six, seven times. All the while, Rok kept spanking her, even harder, now, and so fast the sensations exploded into one giant tumultuously satisfying event.

She lost track of time, of herself, of everything. Not in the way she normally "went out" during sex. Not like that at all. She felt only pleasure—glorious, satisfying. Bone-deep.

When awareness came filtering back in, she was lying collapsed over Rok's lap, with his large hand running slow circles over her flaming ass.

"Rok," she croaked.

Once more, she wanted to cry. Not out of sadness. Not out of humiliation or frustration or anger. Not for any reason other than that she felt wrung out. Maybe that had been what happened last night, too.

A blanket fell around her shoulders, and when Rok rolled her up against his torso, she was cradled like a baby.

"Good, pet. Sweet, beautiful female."

She squeezed her eyes closed and tucked her face into his chest, unable to bear looking at him.

"I'm going to let you hide for about ten more seconds, and then you're going to let me look in your eyes so I can see what's going on."

Another mini-orgasm ran through her at that. This new brand of mastery, of dominance that demanded she bare her soul, not just surrender her body, gave him a terrible power over her.

A terrible, wonderful power.

Her body began to shake, and Rok wrapped her up tighter. Her eyes fluttered open.

"You're fine, beautiful. They're just aftershocks. It will pass soon. I've got you." He offered her a tube of sweet fluid, which she sipped.

"I have something that might help, actually. A human food—medicinal—originally from Earth." He rocked her close. "After the shakes go away, I'll get you some."

Tears burned behind her eyes. *Veck.* She didn't want to cry—not again. She struggled to keep it in, holding her breath, but Rok gripped her chin and tipped her face up to his. "Are you crying again?"

She shook her head but the torrent released in a ridiculous snort-sob, tears leaking from both eyes.

He wrapped his hand around the side of her head and kissed her hair. "Let's get you that treat."

She pressed her body against him, not wanting him to put her down, but he seemed to understand. He climbed off the bed with her cradled in his arms then swung her around to carry her on one hip, like a child carried by a parent.

She felt ridiculous and tall and pleased all at once. A giggle escaped her lips.

Rok smiled up at her, his violet eyes warm.

Her chest swelled so large, she thought it would burst.

He carried her to a cabinet, which he unlocked with his palm print on the panel. Inside were stacks and stacks of black bricks. "I received them in trade. I'd planned to sell them to the wealthy in Ocretia, but once I tasted it, I decided to keep it for myself." He unwrapped one brick, sliced the end off it, and popped it into her mouth.

She puckered at the bitterness and made a face. "I think it's gone bad."

He shook his head. "No, it hasn't. It's just better sweetened. I'll make you a nice drink with it, later, but let this melt on your tongue. You'll be restored in no time."

She let the bitter dark slice dissolve in her mouth. "What's it called?"

He grinned. "Chocolate. It was considered a food of the gods and an elixir of life in ancient human civilizations. You ought to know these things—" He'd been teasing, but he broke off, probably realizing she'd have no chance to know anything about her species as a slave. "I'm sorry," he muttered. "Of course you wouldn't know."

Her body began to hum, energy from the chocolate enlivening her.

"You're feeling it."

She'd never had a master—or any other being for that matter—pay so much attention to her. It was addictive—more heady than the chocolate buzzing through her veins.

To reward her thoughtful master, she gripped one of his horns and sank her mouth down on the other one.

"Holy *veck*," he growled, lurching and sending her unbalanced weight careening in a circle. "Little girl, you have exactly twenty planet rotations to stop that."

She gave a husky laugh, her mouth still stretched wide over his horn. Her tongue laved the side, lips suctioned over it.

"Veeeeck, little pet." The arm under her ass boosted her higher. The position was perfect, as she sat high above his head and it was easy to angle her mouth down around the frisky horns.

"Other side, other side, other side," he rasped. He'd leaned his hip against the sleeping platform and had his free hand in his flight pants, stroking his length.

She switched horns, staring at his enormous malehood when he pulled it from his pants. It grew, a drop of rainbow pre-cum glistening on the tip. She wanted to have that huge organ in her mouth instead.

"Do you want me to suck him instead?"

Rok groaned. "Yes—*no. Veck*, I don't know. I wish there were two of you." His slipping control encouraged her and took the bite away from the insinuation that she wasn't enough on her own. "Lily..." He made a quick reverse, so his opposite hip faced the sleeping platform—the one with her on it. She climbed onto her knees, the blanket that had hung around her shoulders falling down.

She worked faster, using both hands now—one on each horn, her tongue switching between the stiffened protuberances.

He barked a curse then thrust her away.

Her momentary offense drained away when she saw the dark lust in his eyes. He shoved her to her ass then pushed her on her back and dragged one horn down the center of her naked body, groaning the entire time.

When he reached her core, he rubbed her clit clumsily with the horn then adjusted his head and penetrated her with the other one.

She gasped and gripped his free horn, pulling his head up, disappointed when the horn did not sink deep enough inside her to satisfy.

"Roll over." His deep, gravelly voice reverberated through her entire body. "I told you I'd take this luscious little ass today. The time has come." The swish of his palm over her still heated skin made her arch her bottom up to him and purr.

He moved from the sleeping platform, and she watched him walk to one of the cabinets, his huge member bobbing in front of him. A pang of anxiety twisted.

He would never fit.

Not in her anus.

He returned with a jar of some kind of oil or salve, which he slathered over his enormous cock.

"Rok...I don't think...it's too big."

"I don't think it's too big, either." He smirked, deliberately misunderstanding her. "It's punishment, remember, pet? You'll have to stretch to let me in. You'll find full surrender when I master you this way, little slave."

Her anxiety only ratcheted higher, but she didn't dare argue with him.

He stuffed two pillows under her hips to raise her backside. "Hold your cheeks open, pet. I'm going to *veck* you until you scream."

His words did not reassure.

Her fingers twisted into the worn fabric of the platform covering.

Please don't hurt me.

"Lily." His voice cracked with sharp command.

She jumped then replayed his previous command in her mind, listening this time. Reluctantly, she opened, realizing the full humiliation of holding her own ass wide for his plunder.

He rubbed some of the lubricant on her anus.

She closed her eyes and did what she did best—disappeared. Dropped out of her body and hung in limbo, somewhere else. No—nowhere.

Rok nudged her rear hole with the head of his cock and she observed it as if from far away—noticing, but with complete detachment.

"Lily." The sharpened tone brought her back again.

What command had she failed to obey now?

Abruptly, her world spun, and she found herself on her back, looking into Rok's angry face.

"Where did you go?"

She blinked at him. *Vecking* excrement. This male was far too perceptive.

"Don't you dare go dead on me like that. You think I want to *veck* a wax doll?"

Figuring the question was rhetorical, she didn't answer. Or maybe it was because she hadn't fully returned.

Rok picked up her ankles and held them in the air with one hand, leaving his other hand free to punish her. He slapped her ass, the backs of her legs, and her exposed pussy with hard, attention-demanding spanks. The poisoned bite on her ankle throbbed, but Rok hadn't noticed it.

All her numbness dissipated as the shock of each stinging slap set her nerves on fire.

"Rok, please," she gasped, twisting her hips to dodge the blows to no avail.

The moment he stopped spanking her, his thumb penetrated her ass, sinking to the knuckle.

The invasion wasn't nearly as unpleasant as she'd expected. In fact, her pussy pulsed, clenching and releasing on air with excitement.

"You don't want my cock in this ass?" he growled, pumping his thumb inside her. "This ass that I own for the next twenty planet rotations?"

"I..." Her tongue worked in her dry mouth. She couldn't quite bring herself to admit she wanted it, but flames licked her core, need growing larger.

"Look at me." His voice snapped like a whip.

She gazed around her legs at him.

He removed his thumb from her ass, and she registered its loss with disappointment.

"Don't look away." The command came softly this time. He pulled her cheeks open and pushed his cock against her anus. Her feet found his shoulders, and he wrapped his huge hands around the front of her thighs to brace her for his thrust.

She whimpered her protest, not daring to move as he stretched her wide. "Rok...please."

He held her gaze, easing forward. "Whose ass is this?"

She thrust her breasts into the air and moaned.

Her reaction to his words shocked her. Why did she *like* the dominant way he claimed ownership of her? She'd never gloried in being owned by any male. Yet, his possessiveness tweaked her. For the first time, she felt desirable, not as just an owned body, but as Lily, the female locked in Rok's violet gaze.

He pushed the head of his cock past her entrance, providing slight relief. She curled her fingers into the fabric of the platform and let her eyes roll back in her head.

"Look at me, Lily." The growl made her lids jerk back open.

"I can't," she moaned, but forced her eyes to remain wide while he slid in and out of her ass. "Too much," she whimpered.

"No, it's not. You're taking it. Taking it like a good slave." The raspy, broken quality of Rok's voice signaled his impending loss of control.

A foreign surge of female pride at being the cause of that loss of control rolled through her.

"Touch yourself," he growled.

She obeyed, threading her fingers between her legs and rubbing her clit as he'd shown her. Her cries grew more desperate, keening louder and higher with each of his thrusts.

"Whose ass is this?" he roared.

"Yours," she screamed back. "*Veck* me, Rok!"

He slammed in deep and remained there, stretching her wide and filling her ass with his hot, rainbow cum.

Her muscles were unable to clench around Rok's enormous girth; it felt as if a climax went through her, nonetheless.

Mercifully, he eased out. "Don't move," he murmured and left the sleeping platform, and then the chamber.

She couldn't have, if she'd tried. The chamber spun as she lay on her back and let the aftershocks of his plunder roll through her.

Rok returned with a damp cloth, which, unbelievably, he used to clean her. She bit her lip to keep it from quivering, hating these tears that seemed to leak each time after he forced her surrender.

Because she liked it too much. Liked the tenderness of his touch and the softness of his gaze now. The solid strength he provided when he pulled her onto his lap and held her against his chest.

She couldn't get used to it. Rok wasn't a real master—he planned to turn her in for the warrant. She wanted to ask him what it would take to convince him to keep her, but she was too afraid of his answer. She didn't think she could bear to hear him say his plans out loud.

Especially not now—after what they'd just done.

She feared she wouldn't survive it.

CHAPTER FIVE

Rok maneuvered the ship onto a small landing platform on a trading outpost. He'd have given anything just to stay in space, enjoying his little human who surrendered more to him with each passing planet rotation.

But their ship couldn't withstand the flight without repairs. He flicked off the engines, unbuckled his harness, and swiveled to survey his little prisoner. He hated to lock her up, but he also didn't have proper clothing for her.

"I'm coming with you," she said instantly, as if guessing his thoughts.

He smiled. He liked when she showed her real self—not the slave persona she'd perfected. "Mierna, do you have any pants Lily might squeeze into?" The Venusian was short but rounder around the middle from her excessive drinking. Pants of hers just might fit his long-legged human in the waist, though they'd be too short.

Mierna muttered something and beckoned Lily to go with her. Lily flashed a grateful smile his way, which made him feel all kinds of warm. He hadn't considered taking a mate. He hadn't even come close with Taraw. But now the thought of ever being apart from Lily rankled him. He wasn't even sure he'd be able to give her over to her mother and sister.

He waited for Lily to emerge. The pants came down to her knees and were a close fit, molding to the shape of her ass and thighs in the most delicious way. He couldn't wait to tear them off her later. He held his hand out and took her palm, tugging her off the ship and onto the arid, desolate station. Beings of all species wove through the station, chattering in hundreds of different languages. His crew flanked him, hands at their weapons, ready for trouble.

There was no reason to expect trouble, but this was wild, ungoverned territory, which meant anything could happen.

He made inquiries about getting replacement scrap to mend the outer hull of his ship, and they were led to a toothless being of an unknown species.

"Five hundred stein," the turtle-like creature demanded.

He shook his head. "Fifteen."

The turtle shrugged his shoulders and turned away.

Rok, too, went silent, waiting. In his experience, persistence often won the wrangle.

Turtle turned back. "Give me the female."

Lily shrank against his side, and he immediately cursed himself for bringing her. She was far too beautiful to be safe in a wild place like this.

He took a risk and pulled a dagger, lunging forward, stopping with the tip just a millimeter from Turtle's throat. "Don't look at her," he growled. Beings around them stopped their conversations to stare. Many reached for weapons far more deadly than a blade.

The Turtle showed no sign of fear. He stared at Rok for several moments with watery eyes then shoved his wrist and the weapon away. "Fifty."

Rok sheathed the blade. "Done."

Half a planet rotation later, they had a stack of the material outside their craft. Gaurdo and Janu argued over the best way to patch the hole while he ignored them and went to work. He'd love to have the job finished before nightfall. He had no desire to spend more time at the trading station than necessary.

When the ship docked near them took off, he threw an arm over his eyes to keep out the flying grit. His protective instincts kicking into gear, he looked around for Lily.

Where had she gone?

"Lily?" He turned in a circle. She'd been hanging around behind him a short while ago. He jogged onto the ship. "Lily?" Maybe she'd gone to the washroom?

But no, he didn't find her there, nor anywhere on the ship. His heart picked up speed. Back outside the ship, he called her name. "Lily?"

Gaurdo, Jano, Jaso, and Depri stopped what they were doing to look around.

"Where in the *veck* is Mierna?" Lily must be with her.

But Mierna came walking calmly toward them, a pouch of brew clutched in her little hand. "She's gone." Mierna waved a hand in the direction of the ship that had just taken off. For once she didn't appear serene when imparting information others didn't know.

"What in the *veck* do you mean?"

Mierna pointed again. "She's been taken—she's in great danger. We must follow, before it's too late."

Vecking excrement!

He threw the material haphazardly over the hole, welding it with a ray gun. He didn't care if they had to repair it at the next stop; he just needed to get them in the air. Before he lost the first bright spot he'd had in his life in ages. Maybe ever.

~.~

Lily lay on the floor, hands bound behind her back, ankles trussed together and attached to her wrists. The serpent bite on her ankle throbbed in time with her heartbeat. It had taken a turn for the worse that planet rotation, and now she began to feel the poison flowing through her veins. Her head ached and lips felt cracked and dry. A fever made her alternately hot and cold.

This was it. Her life was over.

She'd made the mistake of wandering over to the ship beside them to inquire in which direction they were headed. She'd thought she might stow away on their ship if they were going in the opposite direction from Rok.

The moment the lizard-like beings saw her, though, they'd gone crazy, chattering in a language she didn't understand. Within seconds, they'd surrounded her, and one of them shot her with a stun gun. She'd woken in this storeroom closet, tied on the filthy floor.

Veck. She should have stayed with Rok. He wouldn't really have turned her in. He didn't have it in him to send her to her death. Not with the way he cared for her. She should have had the courage to ask him what his intentions were, or if they'd changed.

Instead, she'd walked into this. Whatever it was.

She was probably speeding on her way to the Ocretion authorities right now. Or perhaps to be sold as a slave to yet another master. Of course, she might die before they even arrived because she needed medical care for her ankle wound.

She thought of Rok and wondered what he would think. Would he know where she'd gone? He'd probably believe she ran away. He probably wouldn't try to look for her.

Even so, she clung to the tiniest sliver of hope—something she shouldn't allow herself. Rok might come for her. Somehow, he might deduce which ship she'd left on and he might follow.

Please, sweet Mother Earth, please.

Things felt incomplete. She wasn't supposed to die this way—to leave Rok in the way she had. She needed to see him again. All her life, she'd been searching for meaning. She'd thought it was about escaping, about setting up a free human colony. Now, she thought it might be much simpler than that. Maybe the meaning in life was just love. Connecting with another being. Sharing oneself. Trusting.

She coughed against the dust filling her nostrils and lungs.

Love. She'd almost had it.

***

Rok managed to catch the ship with Lily on it. He attempted communication with it, but either it didn't have the same channels or they deliberately chose to ignore his messages. Though he wanted nothing more than to shoot their *vecking* ship out of space, but that wouldn't help him get Lily back. He chose to follow at a distance, locking all tracking on their ship.

The moment it landed, he'd *vecking* storm the craft and incinerate every last one of them until he found Lily.

Mierna stared out into the space in front of them, her lips pinched. "You failed her," she declared.

His fingers curled into fists, horns stiffened with anger, even though he'd been thinking the same thing. "What in the *veck* do you mean?"

"You let her believe she might come to harm. She was looking for other options when they took her."

Ice flooded his veins. He clenched his teeth, his vision spinning. "No."

"No? Did she not think you would turn her over to her masters?"

"Yes," he snarled. "But I—"

"She is ill, also. Poisoned. She may not last another planet rotation."

"She will last," he gritted. She had to. He wasn't going to lose another female he loved. Especially not this one. Lily was his mate.

He knew that now. His body had known it the moment he'd first seen her, it just had taken his mind a while to catch up. He'd never felt this way for any being before—so in need of her that taking his next breath without knowing she'd make it seemed an impossibility.

Yet he did breathe. One inhale, one exhale. Again and again as they zoomed through space.

***

They landed at an air station in the far outskirts of Ocretion territory. Rok docked beside them and went tearing out of the ship, weapon in hand, only to find an enormous troop of Ocretion soldiers crowded around Lily's ship.

"Lily," he shouted when he caught sight of the soldiers leading her out, wrists bound behind her back, head hanging forward. Her hair looked limp and dirty.

She looked up at his cry, and what he saw terrified him. Her face was pale and sweaty, dark hollows lay her under eyes, and her lips were cracked and bleeding.

Janu and Jaso yanked him backward, into their ship, when the soldiers turned and pointed toward him.

"Shut the *veck* up," Janu hissed. "Do you want them to come and arrest you, too? How will you help her then?"

He fought them, not because he believed they were wrong, but because it felt good to fight. He needed to rip someone to shreds. Gaurdo and Depri joined the tussle, and he continued to fight until the four of them had him pinned to the ground, panting and cursing them like a crazed animal.

"Think. Think," Depri shouted at him. "Think your way out of this. How can you help her? Who can help?"

Who.

His body went slack. "Get off me."

They must have seen the return of reason, because his friends helped him to his feet. "We need to see Prince Zander. He has battleships, and he wants Lily, too."

CHAPTER SIX

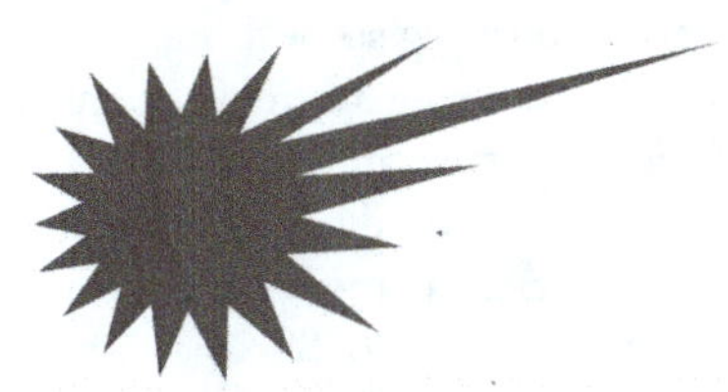

Lily sat on the hard plastic bench, shoulder to shoulder with other prisoners in the death pod. Her head still pounded, but one of the soldiers had taken pity on her and run a medical scanner over her bite wound then delivered the antivenom.

No one knew how long they had to live. The Ocretians kept the death pods largely a secret and, obviously, those who went in, never came out. It seemed they were still filling it, though. Prisoners had been filing in for three planet rotations.

Crazy though it was, she felt certain Rok was working to get her out. He'd been there when they took her. She'd heard his anguished shout, seen his friends wrestle him back into their ship. He did care about her—she knew it!

That thought alone kept her from sinking into the darkest despair. Rok had to get her out, because they belonged together somehow. She didn't know how, nor did she care. Even if he wanted nothing more than to keep her as his sex slave for his entertainment on his flights, she'd be on board. But he'd already been willing to teach her to fly. Perhaps she'd find some use other than sex. She could be one of the crew—have a family of sorts for the first time, ever.

A human mother and child were led into the pod. The guards split the two, putting the child in Lily's cell and taking the mother away.

"No!" the woman screamed. The walls echoed with the ripping pain in her voice. "Carmeela! Give me my baby back!"

Something scraped at the back of Lily's memory—her own mother's cries. Someone had screamed for her like that. Someone had screamed herself hoarse while Lily was carried away, kicking and crying, from some kind of factory housing.

There'd been another, too. A man had tried to block them, had reached for her as she screamed his name, but he'd been stunned.

Tears burned behind her eyes. She had been loved, once.

The little girl, who couldn't be more than six sun cycles, appeared in shock. She didn't cry—perhaps she'd already had that response beaten from her.

"Hey," Lily said softly. "It's going to be all right."

The girl stared at her, brown eyes wide. Her dark hair fell across her face in matted clumps; her skin was too pale. "You can sit over here, with me," she offered, though there was no room left on any of the benches.

The girl ignored her offer, though, and sat down on the floor, cross-legged. She began to rock, silently mouthing something.

"That just isn't right," the being beside her muttered. "Separating them like that. Why not let them die together?"

Lily lifted her chin. "We're not dying," she said firmly. She didn't know what made her say it, except it seemed important to keep that child from floating off, the way Lily had learned to. She didn't want her to stop living until her body died. And she sure as hell didn't want that body to die any time soon.

The old human male on her left snorted.

"It's true. We're all going to get out of here, and we're going to live on a planet free of slavery. Things will grow there—beautiful plants and flowers. And the light will come down in rainbows."

The little girl lifted her head and stared at her.

She nodded, emphatically. "Everyone will be free there. No slaves. Different species will live in harmony, with a fair government that never puts beings to death. The worst punishment will be exile, and no one will ever want to earn that punishment because it's so wonderful there."

"People will sing," a cracked voice spoke from the corner.

Lily peered around to see an old Stornigian. The reminder of Janu and Jaso squeezed her chest, but she smiled encouragingly.

The female cleared her throat. "Music will be everywhere. Songs and instruments. And dancing."

"There will be enough food for everyone. Delicious food they grow right there," another being chimed in.

The little girl listened, eyes round, expression rapt.

"Are you hungry, girl-child?" Another being produced a bit of a nutrition bar and offered it.

The girl looked at it warily then glanced at Lily, as if for permission. Lily nodded and Carmeela took it, unwrapping it with grubby fingers.

"There will be water. Enough water to sink your body into. And colors. Every kind of color you've ever seen, everywhere," a middle-aged human female offered. "And art. Artists from all over the galaxy will go there to create beautiful works."

The child spoke for the first time. "What is art?"

The woman smiled. "Art is when you make something you love, just because it's beautiful. Just because you want to."

"Why?"

"For others to enjoy. Or for your own enjoyment. It could be something you look at, or listen to, or watch."

"I made a house, once, out of mud," the child said. "They said it was forbidden."

"You see?" The woman sounded triumphant. "On the planet we're going to, it will never be forbidden. You can make whatever you like."

"Will my mother be there?"

"Yes," Lily said immediately. "Your mother will certainly be there."

She held her breath to keep the tears from choking her throat. It had to be true—every promise they'd made. It just had to be true. She would give anything to make it true.

~.~

Rok and his crew disembarked onto the landing dock of Zander's palatial pod. He had requested permission to land on the basis of having urgent news about Lily, the sister of the prince's mate.

The Zandian guards met them and bowed as if they were honored guests. He hid his surprise and returned the bow, following the males briskly through the halls to the Great Room, where Zander sat on a raised dais. He wore a white tunic and pants, made of a finely woven material that probably cost more than twice what Rok's ship had. A ceremonial sword hung at his waist. The prince's copper-haired mate and her mother stood nearby, and the four male advisors from his previous visit flanked him, also dressed in white.

He bowed to the prince and went straight to the *vecking* point. "I had her and I lost her. She's on an Ocretion death pod. I need your help to get her free."

Zander surged to his feet and stepped down from the dais, responding to the urgency in Rok's tone. "What death pod? Where?"

"Outer limits of the territory."

One of the advisors, the huge, battle-scarred warrior named Seke, moved closer to Lily's mother, Leora, in what appeared to be a protective stance. The woman, whose beauty shone as bright as her daughters', had gone pale, and she clutched the back of Zander's unoccupied throne with white knuckles.

Zander addressed one of his advisors. "Daneth, contact the authorities and attempt to purchase her. Tell them I will pay any amount."

Daneth bowed. "I will do my best, my lord." He swiftly exited.

Zander paced a few feet then stopped and rubbed his face. "Tell me."

"She was on Jesel, captive of other humans there. I bought her." *And tortured her.* Pain seared his chest. He had mistreated her. After everything she'd been through, he'd used her as a sex slave, had caused her to suffer in the belief she was on her way to her death.

Lamira's green gaze locked on him, and he felt certain she read his thoughts, knew his sins. "She knows you're coming for her," she murmured.

A shudder ran through his body.

If ever he believed in a *vecking* destiny, he knew this was his. He *would* rescue Lily. It was an impossible task, but he would do anything and everything he could to get her out of there. She was his destiny.

"I wish to use some of your battleships." He'd never been one to pussyfoot around.

Zander folded his arms across his chest, mistrust evident in his gaze. "What is your plan?"

He didn't have a *vecking* clue. "All six of us can fly." He indicated himself and his crew. "We'll attack and force the death pod out of territory. There's a unincorporated planet not far from there. If we can get them to land, then I'll storm the pod and rescue Lily."

"That will never work."

He glanced at Lamira, hoping she'd entreat her mate, but she remained silent, breath held, watching them both.

Zander, too, looked at Lamira. She didn't move, didn't blink, but her wide green eyes pleaded.

With a frustrated gesture, Zander turned to one of the guards. "Show them to guest quarters." To Rok, he said, "We'll see what Daneth finds out from the Ocretion government. Then we'll talk."

Rok wanted to smash the colorful walls of the well-appointed palace. He didn't have time to wait. Lily was speeding to her death as they stood there. But what else could he do? Gnashing his teeth, he stalked out behind the guard, knowing courtesy demanded he bow first but not giving a *veck*.

"Rok." Zander called him back.

He stiffened.

"The crystal bath will be made available to you if you need it."

This time, he forced a stiff bow, though he couldn't bring himself to thank the male. His body did crave the crystal light, though. Just being in the palatial pod, where the crystals were embedded in every skylight, made his body hum with energy and vitality.

He made his way straight to the crystal bath, stripped his clothes off, and lay down on one of the beds, absorbing the rainbow light. He closed his eyes, allowing the color to permeate his skin, to recharge his life force. He wanted Lily to see this room. Though before, he'd hated that he had to come here, seen his need for the light recharge as a weakness, now he imagined it through her eyes. She would find it beautiful. He would feed her chocolate while she lay in a bed beside him and... What?

What was this ridiculous future he was imagining? Did he think he'd be living here at the palatial pod with Lily and her family? As if Zander would have him—a smuggler with three warrants out for his arrest and a ragtag scrappy crew.

And yet, he knew for certain that if—no, *when*—he got Lily back, he would never want to let her leave his side again.

Veck.

~.~

Lamira watched Zander pace the length of the Great Hall, his muscular shoulders tensed into hard knots. The rest of the gathering had exited, leaving them alone in the lavish hall. Her plants grew in pots all around the room—banana plants, tomatoes, peppers, fig trees. So many incredible rare varieties of Earth-based food-bearing plants grown from heirloom seeds. She would plant these on Zandia, when they recovered the planet.

Zander stopped and scrubbed a hand across his jaw. She knew his affection for her was clashing with his singular purpose in life—to take back Zandia. Giving up six airships to a probable death mission would not only hurt his chances, but if his involvement was linked to it, it would endanger his position as a recognized ambassador and his chances of mounting an army against the Finn—the species who had taken over Zandia when he was a boy.

"Lamira, you know I want to help..." he began.

She stiffened, sensing the *but* that was sure to follow.

He stopped speaking, regret washing over his face, probably at her expression. He had not always been so in tune with her emotions. When he'd first purchased her for breeding, his inability to decipher her human complexities had angered him and resulted in many misunderstandings. But he was learning. He blew out his breath.

"Tell me, have you foreseen this? Any of it?"

She sucked on her lower lip, debating what to say. She had once hidden her claircognizance from him, but now believed she was destined to use it to aid in his purpose—regaining Zandia.

She, too, saw danger, even death facing the warrior Rok and his mission. But if he had Zander's full crew as part of the mission...well, she didn't see the outcome, but the energy felt enormous. Powerful. As if great things might happen.

But it would be hard enough to convince Zander to give Rok six ships. For him to throw in his own life, and the lives of his best warriors as well, would be an impossibility. Especially when this was not his battle.

She dropped a hand to her abdomen, sensing their baby's peaceful energy. Could she gamble that little life in order to save her sister's?

The baby seemed to agree.

"Rok will be successful," she said. It was not a lie. A misdirection, perhaps, but not a lie. He would be successful if everything fell into place. But in order for that to happen, she would have to force Zander into action.

CHAPTER SEVEN

Rok slipped into the pilot's seat of Zander's gleaming state-of-the art battleship, and his cock nearly grew hard at the power he felt.

How he had convinced Zander to let them take the craft, he still wasn't sure. He had a feeling the prince's little human mate had a lot to do with it. After his luxurious crystal light bath, and Mierna's disastrous one—she had asked to try it out and had become violently ill, throwing up for the rest of the planet rotation—Zander had informed them that Daneth's request had been denied and he would grant them four ships. Rok had argued again for six, but Zander held firm. Clearly, he thought they wouldn't return.

Veck him.

Rok had a date with his *vecking* destiny, and her name was Lily. He fired up the engine, closing his eyes to savor the ferocious purr. He flicked all the switches on, adjusted the controls, and eased out of Zander's hanger. Touching the control on his collar, he established communications with Gaurdo, Depri, and Mierna, his other pilots. Janu and Jaso had split to ride with Depri and Gaurdo, respectively.

He eased out into the dense traffic surrounding the capitol, keeping it slow so his friends could follow. Gradually, they fought their way up, into clearer air space, and eventually, he punched the speed and they exited the planet's atmosphere in the direction of the death pod. He'd started to switch over to autopilot when a beep sounded over the ship's controls.

"Rok, this is Zander." The prince's clipped tones came through.

He rolled his eyes, wondering what warning the prince had for him. "Yes, my lord?"

Silence ensued then Zander snapped, *"Where is my vecking mate?"*

A door swishing open behind him made him groan. *Vecking* stars, did stowing away run in the family?

He leaned forward. "I *vecking* swear I didn't know she was on the ship. I did not take your mate."

"Confirm, now. You do or do not have my mate on board that ship?" The panic he heard in the prince's voice made him wince.

"I do have her," he groaned. "But I didn't invite her."

"What about her mother."

He hadn't made eye contact with Lamira yet, but he did now, brows raised. The pretty human stood framed in the doorway, her mother behind her.

"Yes, her, too."

"Turn the ship around and return, immediately."

He ground his teeth. Zander might be able to disable the ship from afar. He also was likely to kill him for kidnapping his mate. And Lily's life was hanging on the line.

"Negative, my lord. My mission is still intact. I will return after I have reunited your mate with her sister."

Zander's curses and the sound of something smashing came across the speakers. "You *vecking* get back here now or I will cut your *vecking* cock off and shove it down your throat. My mate is with child, do you understand me?"

Veeeeck.

He started flipping controls to cut off the prince, but the male's curses and threats still came through. Finally, he found the right switch, and the board went silent.

He slumped back in his seat, ignoring his uninvited guests.

"He will follow. Give him time to catch up. You'll need all the ships you can get to attack the death pod."

Shock shot up his expression, raising his brows right to horn level. "You planned this? To get him involved?"

She slid into the seat beside him, her palms pressed over her abdomen protectively. "It was the only way."

"What *are* you?"

Leora drifted in and settled into the seat behind them.

"I have gifts similar to those of a Venusian. The Zandian crystals enhanced them, which may be why Mierna grew sick from them."

"It probably sent her into a detox," he muttered. "You do realize Zander is going to kill me now?"

"He won't kill you. Zandians are on the brink of extinction—all Zandian lives are important to him."

He didn't want to ask the next question, but curiosity got the better of him. "So what does he do with criminals?"

"He has a dungeon in the pod. He keeps them there." She spoke lightly, as if his fate to spend the rest of his life in a pod dungeon wasn't worrisome.

He touched the communications device at his collar. Zander probably had access to this frequency, but he didn't mind. "We're going to modify speed until the prince and his fleet join us."

"Copy that," they each replied.

He flipped the switch joining him to Zander's communications back on. "Waiting for your arrival, my lord. Do you need our coordinates?"

"I don't need your *vecking* coordinates," Zander growled over the lines. It sounded as if his teeth were clenched. "Estimated arrival, 1600."

"Copy that."

~.~

Singing.

The entire death pod was filled with singing. Beautiful, mournful songs.

The guards had attempted to stop it at first, shocking the woman in Lily's cell who began it, but once others picked up where she left off, their leader had shrugged and said, "There's no harm in it. Let them sing. It's better than wailing."

Now, voices joined together in song after song. They came in different languages, repeated until everyone learned the words. Chants, songs, spirituals. Suppressed religious songs. She'd never heard any of them before, but the effect on her was enormous. The voices carried her away. Not in the absent-from-body way she'd refined, but in a sort of euphoria. Joy. Solidarity. Communion. Peace.

Rok would come for her. She knew it in her bones. Just like she'd always known her life had more meaning than being a colorless sex slave. He was her *after.* The life she hadn't yet begun. The promised land she'd described to the sweet child now sleeping in her lap.

Rok would come, and they all would be free.

~.~

Their ten cloaked battleships surrounded the death pod. Rok sent out a communications jammer to interrupt any signals they might be sending or receiving. He didn't need them calling for help or identifying the battleships.

"Fire without incurring damage. We don't want to cause any explosions or even disable the ship, only to force it out of territory," Rok barked over the communications. "On my count, one...two...three, and *fire.*"

Laser fire blasted, and the huge death pod rocked. It lacked the ability to fly quickly or nimbly, so it simply made a slow bank to the left.

Good. Exactly the direction they wanted it to turn.

"Keep the pressure on the right. Keep it turning!"

Beside him, Lamira was strapped in, hands gripping the control panel. She'd gone pale. "I think I'm going to be sick."

"*Vecking* excrement—do it that way." He pointed to her other side.

Leora rubbed her back and offered a container of fluid.

"Now, stay right on it! Oh *veck*."

Smoke issued from one of the pod's turning vents and it wobbled and spun in a circle.

"Push it back. Push it back toward the land mass." He prayed the pilot of the death pod was good enough to get control of the thing and land safely.

But the giant death pod began to plunge, spinning out of control through the atmosphere of the land mass below.

"Send out magnerays to stabilize it!" He sent his battleship into a dive after the pod.

Veck, he had no idea if their ships had enough power to stabilize the thing, even with them all working simultaneously.

He aimed and shot the magneray, which struck the pod and interrupted the spinning. It still wobbled horribly, but— There. Depri's magneray caught the pod from the opposite side, providing more stability. One by one, the other battleships sent out magnerays that attached until, together, they held the pod stable and aloft.

"Lower her slowly," he barked, easing his own craft toward land.

The ships worked together, bringing the pod down by degrees, tipping and tilting it as they went. Sweat dripped down Rok's brow. It took every bit of his concentration to maintain contact with the pod and keep the thing from crashing to the land mass below.

"That's it...keep going. Easy now... Whoa!" The far side of the pod dropped when three ships lost contact with it, but Prince Zander swooped down below and sent a beam upward to catch them and steady the fall. "Good work, my lord."

They continued to descend, meter by meter. An alarm went off, warning his engine was too hot from the exertion of the magneray. "Almost there," he muttered, trying to turn the *vecking* sound off.

"Move out of the way, Your Highness, or you'll be crushed," he barked as they got close to the ground. He shifted his ship around to another side to help stabilize the side Zander would drop. "On three. One...two...three!"

Zander moved out, and the pod dipped sharply. The alarm screeched, lights flashed, but they got the thing to the ground. Smoke issued from every side of it.

He brought his ship to land beside it.

"Outside atmosphere is unsafe for breathing," spoke a robotic female voice of his ship. He wasn't surprised, otherwise the land mass would be inhabited, but it made things difficult, especially with the smoke issuing from the death pod. The passengers would need fresh air to breathe, and soon.

"My crew—board with arms drawn. Prepare to fight. Depri, destroy all tracking devices on the pod."

Zander issued a similar order to his men.

He unbuckled his harness and pressed ray guns into each of the women's hands. "You two stay here. Do not open the door for anyone but myself or Zander. Understand?"

Lamira nodded, but he wasn't sure he trusted her. "I mean it. If anything happens to you, it's on my head."

She rested her hand on her belly. "Nothing will happen to me."

With a curse, he fastened a helmet with controlled air delivery over his head, left the ship, and sealed the door, sprinting to the entrance of the death pod, which Depri already had burned halfway open with a laser ray.

~.~

The moment the death pod had been impacted, she'd known Rok had come for her. Now that they'd landed, smoke filled the corridors in thick plumes, making it impossible to see even a hand in front of her face.

She scooped Carmeela into her arms and cradled her against her hip, holding her tight, as if that might somehow protect her from suffocation. Far away, she heard the muffled sound of Rok shouting her name.

"Rok!" she screamed but choked on smoke, coughing and wheezing. "Rok...Rok! I'm here!"

"Rok!" one of the males in her cell shouted.

"Rok!" Another one cried. Someone thumped the heel of his shoe against the wall repetitively.. "Rok! Rok! Rok!" More voices joined, creating a chant of his name.

Tears moistened her eyes. They were doing this for her. Well, her rescue might free all of them, but they were working together. It never happened. Ocretions kept lower caste beings from organizing, developing relationships. They forced separation, but, in this moment, they all cried out as one. "Rok! Rok! Rok!"

A door burst open at the end of the corridor. Every cell door slid open.

"*Lily!*" Rok's deep voice rang with urgency.

Hands jostled her and Carmeela forward, thrusting her in the direction of Rok. "She's here!" someone yelled. "Right here."

Through the black haze, Rok's hulking figure appeared. His face set with ferocious intent, he appeared like a demon. No, like a god.

"Rok!" she shrieked and threw herself at him, Carmeela still in her arms.

Momentary surprise registered on his face at the sight of the child, but he promptly wrapped them both up in an embrace, his arms like steel bands around her, lifting them off the ground and swiftly carrying her back out the door.

"You came for me."

"Of course I came for you," he said gruffly. "You belong to me."

The sensation those words produced was all warmth. It wasn't the twisted knife in the chest that came with being considered an object for trade and use, but the soaring joy of *belonging*. What she'd longed for from the moment she met Rok—to be a part of his circle, his crew, his life. Being owned by Rok carried an entirely different meaning than slavery to her, and she knew it did to him, too.

"Every being follow me. Remain calm and orderly. Help those who are having difficulty," Rok's loud voice echoed off the corridor walls as he swept forward. They entered a large antechamber with less smoke.

"Every being get down on the floor, where the air is most clear," Rok ordered. He immediately unclipped his helmet and reached to put it on her, but she deflected it and put it over Carmeela's little head instead.

"We have to find her mother," she said urgently.

Two males of the same species as Rok strode in, swords in their hands, appearing as fierce and deadly as Rok.

She gaped.

The younger one gave her an assessing sweep. "You have found Lily."

She started at his use of her name. Was this Rok's brother? No, he'd been orphaned and taken in by Janu and Jaso. Who, then were these males?

"Where is my mate?" the handsome Zandian demanded.

"On my ship. Is the pod secure?"

Lily blinked, utterly confused.

"Yes," the older Zandian answered.

"Let's go together, then." Rok hooked an arm around her waist just as Carmeela's mother screamed her name from across the room.

Lily started toward her, and Rok instantly followed, providing protection as she moved through the crowded chamber.

"Carmeela!" the mother screamed again.

"It's all right," Lily shouted. "She's safe."

Rok shouldered through the crowd, delivering them to the weeping mother.

"Oh thank you, thank the stars." The mother claimed her little girl, hugging her tightly against her chest.

Before she could answer, Rok tugged her back through the crowd, his broad shoulders and extra height making it easy for him to cut through. In this setting, it hit her full force what a magnificent specimen of male warrior he was—solid muscle, radiating strength and confident capability.

He'd come for her. She hadn't been wrong about his feelings for her. Something beautiful took flight in her chest, and the tears burning her eyes weren't only from the smoke.

The other two Zandian warriors waited near the door, and Rok steered her in their direction. "Come on, beautiful. There's several beings you will want to meet."

~.~

Rok's hand trembled on the hilt of his sword. The death pod had been packed with beings—perhaps six hundred in all, with the cells set up as waste receptacles—designed to open at the floor to dump all the prisoners into outer space. No wonder they'd flown to the outer region of the galaxy. Stars, if he'd been even a minute late, he would have lost Lily forever.

My Lily.

Lily had not been a helpless victim; she'd led the group. Somehow she'd won the support of everyone in her cell, and taken on the welfare of a small child. By the one true Zandian star, he loved this female.

He kept her close as they traversed the corridors, which were gradually clearing of smoke as the pod's oxygen systems circulated and cleaned the air. He grabbed a couple helmets from dead guards and put one over Lily's head and one on his own to protect them on the short trip to the battleship. Zander followed close, asking Seke to stay behind to keep the peace, if necessary.

His heart thudded in his chest as they traversed the rocky terrain. Guilt over keeping Lamira and Leora's existence from Lily twisted like a knot in his solar plexus.

He wished he had a moment alone with her to prepare her, but things were never easy.

He activated the hatch, and they entered. Lamira launched herself at Zander. Although the prince clutched her tightly, his face remained as if made of stone.

Leora's attention was only for Lily, though. She stepped forward, tears glinting in her eyes. "Lily?" she rasped.

Rok cleared his throat. His poor female appeared lost, brow furrowed, shoulders tense. "I should have told you," he said immediately, before she could say it herself. Of course, she still didn't know what in the *veck* was happening.

"Forgive me, Lily. I knew you had family searching for you. I was selfish. I wanted to surprise you."

"Surprise me?" she repeated blankly, looking from Leora to Lamira. She surely must recognize her own features in their faces.

"Your mother, Leora. And a younger sister, Lamira, mate to Zander, exiled prince of Zandia."

Lily's knees buckled, and he snapped her up against his side to keep her from falling.

"I understand it's a shock. And I know if I would've told you, you might not have tried to escape me. I will forever bear the guilt of losing you."

"Mother?" Lily whispered, confusion still etched on her face.

"And sister."

Lamira stepped forward beside her mother, after casting a worried glance at Zander.

Leora's eyes shone with tears. "I feared we'd never find you," she choked and opened her arms.

A bewildered Lily stepped into them but didn't return the embrace. When Leora released her, Lamira stepped forward, but Lily accepted only a cursory embrace before turning back and staring up at him.

"You knew?" she rasped.

He tried to swallow, but the knot in his throat made it impossible. "Forgive me, Lily. I met them before I bought you on Jesel."

"So...so you never intended to turn me over to the Ocretions?"

Regret stabbed him. "I shouldn't have let you think that."

To his shock, a slow smile spread across her face and then a manic laugh bubbled out of her. "You were going to surprise me?" She threw her arms around his neck, jumping to reach. He caught her under her seat and boosted her legs around his waist.

"You're not mad?"

"You *did* intend to keep me." Triumph and joy bubbled up with more laughter.

"You're mine," he said gruffly into her neck.

A few tears dripped down Lily's face, but she was still laughing. Lamira and Leora wore faint, curious smiles.

Zander cleared his throat. "You are welcome on my pod with your mother and sister, Lily."

It was everything he could do to keep from growling *"Mine!"* at the prince.

Lily twisted, and he reluctantly placed her on the ground, turning her around so her back pressed against his front with his arms wrapped around her. "What will happen to the other prisoners? They can't go back to Ocretia. Where will they go?"

When Zander's expression showed nothing, she turned pleading eyes on Rok.

She wanted his help. Trusted him to solve her problem. She believed in him. His heart swelled too big for his chest. He suddenly owned his destiny—

the complete one Mierna had always predicted. The one Lamira, too, had promised.

Your destiny is woven with ours. You were born to lead armies.

Rok cleared his throat. "I will train them as soldiers and pilots. They can help us take back Zandia."

A tiny jerk of Zander's head showed his surprise.

Lamira's face broke into a broad smile. "I knew you would be the one."

But Lily frowned. "And what then? They will be slaves of Zandia?"

Zander stiffened. "Zandians do not keep slaves."

Both Rok and Lily's eyes traveled to Lamira's collar, but they kept their mouths shut. She was obviously far more than a slave to Zander, whatever their situation may be.

"Any human who fights for Zandia will be considered a full and free citizen," Zander declared, though it appeared to cost him.

The three lovely humans rewarded Zander with brilliant smiles. "Thank you, my lord," Lamira murmured.

"We can remain in the death pod, so long as you provide us with supplies. Training can begin immediately." He cleared his throat, hating—despising—what he had to offer next. "Lily, if you want to go with your family—"

"I'll stay and train with you," she cut in immediately, and something akin to fireworks exploded in his body, warming him, sending sparks of happiness showering everywhere. He squeezed her so tight she had to slap his arms so she could breathe.

This was it—his destiny. He knew because Lily was at his side.

Purpose and direction had never been clearer. Achieving a goal never easier.

"My lord, I have one personal request."

Zander arched a brow. "Yes?"

His throat tightened. "I wish to mark my mate with a Zandian crystal, as is our ancient tradition."

Zander's expression softened and he glanced at his own mate with the same fierce need Rok felt every time he was near Lily. "Of course, Rok. I will send it with the first supplies."

Lily twisted in his arms to gaze up at him. "Am I your mate?"

He brushed her coppery hair from her face. 'Yes, pet. You're mine. Only mine. Always mine. Forever mine." He cupped her chin. "Any arguments?"

She shook her head and whispered, "No."

CHAPTER EIGHT

Rok escorted Lily into one of the guards' sleeping chambers he'd selected as their own. They'd spent the most of the planet rotation convincing the humans that Zandia was the promised land, and all they needed to do to earn their freedom was to help win it for Zander. Though doubt lingered in the air, it wasn't as if they had any other options or choices. Lily just hoped, after they received fair treatment, they would come to believe.

"You have to the count of five to get those clothes off," Rok growled, his eyes glowing deep-violet with desire.

Her gaze flicked to his stiffened horns then dropped lower to the considerable bulge in his flight pants. He'd been sending her hungry looks all planet rotation, along with keeping her pinned to his side at all times as if he feared she might be taken from him again.

Prince Zander had left with her mother and sister, who had promised to send her clothing and supplies.

She shimmied out of her filthy slave dress and Mierna's flight pants. Her nipples pebbled in the cool air, pussy clenched under Rok's lustful stare. "I really should get cleaned up," she murmured.

Rok groaned, and his huge hands palmed her ass, lifting her to straddle his waist. "Can't wait...." He nipped her neck, licked up the column of her neck to suck on her earlobe.

Her bare core rested against his hardened cock, and she rocked her hips, trying to rub her clit against the fabric of his flight pants.

"You want this cock, Lily?"

"Yes," she moaned.

"You're going to get it. You're going to get it so hard and so long your eyeballs will flip backward in your head. And then you'll get it some more. I'm going to pound that little pussy until you understand this is the last cock you'll ever take. Understand me?"

A wave of heat washed over her at the possessiveness he showed. Each time he asserted his ownership of her, it healed some small part of her that feared she'd always be alone, separate.

She reached for one of his horns, but he stopped her. "You do that, pet, and your first *vecking* will be remarkably short. And I just promised you a rough ride."

She laughed, the huskiness in her voice echoing in the small chamber.

He whirled and pushed her up against the wall, shoving his pants down to free his cock. "You take this cock deep now, beautiful." He rubbed the head over her slit, testing her readiness. There was no need. Her sex dripped for him, slick and open.

Despite his harsh words, he eased into her inch by inch, giving her time to adjust to his enormous size. "You're so *vecking* tight, Lily." He withdrew a little then thrust in and up, shoving her higher on the wall. "I will never grow tired of this beautiful little pussy."

Hooking her legs over his arms, he shoved her knees high and pinned her in place while pistoning in and out of her.

Her head lolled on the wall, eyes already rolling back as he'd promised. "Rok," she croaked in alarm, already on the edge of an orgasm.

"Go ahead, pet," he husked, still slamming in and out of her. "I'm going to keep you orgasming all night long."

Her internal muscles clamped down, squeezing and pumping his cock.

He drilled deep and held, allowing her to climax.

She reached for one of his horns, and the shocked pleasure that contorted his face pushed her over the brink. She squeezed and rubbed the horn until his mouth opened on a roar and he shoved in and up five times, fast, then filled her with hot streams of his luminescent cum.

She cried out, eyes closed, her senses overloaded. Sparks of light danced before her eyes.

"It'll be part of your punishment," Rok murmured, rocking slowly into her again.

Her eyes fluttered open. "What will? What punishment?" she panted, her brain unable to make sense of his words so soon after their mind-blowing sex.

His smirk was wicked. "Forced orgasms. I'm going to make you come until you cry, my little prisoner."

She came again, her internal muscles pulsing around his cock.

"What for?" Her voice cracked, though not from fear—only from spent desire and the building tension of renewed lust.

"For leaving me, pet." Rok eased away from the wall, taking her with him, still impaled on his cock. He carried her to the sleeping platform where he settled with his back against the wall. He lifted her easily by the waist and flipped her over so she lay sprawled across his thighs. His huge hand clapped down on her upturned ass, and she cried out in indignation. "It's a lesson I'm going to make sure you learn very well, Lily."

"Wait—"

But Rok continued to spank her, his paddle-like hand clapping down on first her right cheek then left. In her post-orgasmic state, she registered the pain acutely, her nerves sizzling under the hard, continuous spanks. After more strokes than she could count, he paused and rubbed her blazing flesh, tipping her hip up to slide one hand beneath her. His middle finger slid seductively along her plump, wet folds.

"Are you sorry, Lily?" Both taunting and seduction rang in his tone.

"Yes," she warbled. "So sorry."

His finger found her clit, and he rubbed the swollen nubbin, causing her to squirm with excitement. She thought she could manage the building tension until his thumb pushed against her anus.

"No," she cried, squeezing her buttocks.

He slapped the back of each thigh, making her shriek. "Naughty pet." He couldn't have sounded more loving. Affection glowed in his words. He spit on her crack and parted her cheeks with two fingers then pushed again at her back pucker while he made a tight circle around her throbbing clitoris.

"Rok!"

His thumb penetrated her ass.

She gasped at the sensation.

Rok worked his thick digit in and out of her ass while flicking and rubbing her clit. For a second time, explosions of sensation blinded her. The wave of pleasure sent her crashing into another orgasm. She bucked, squeezing her cheeks around his hand, pussy contracting around nothing.

"Rok." She sobbed his name again.

"That's it, beautiful. I love to watch you climax." He eased his fingers out of her.

She felt as if she were soaring, her body suspended in the air, floating on the power of Rok's attention.

"Now, we'll get you cleaned up." He rolled her up into his arms and stood. "And don't think I won't *veck* you hard from behind in the shower again. Stars, I'll never forget that first *veck* for as long as I live."

"Why not?" She held her breath, dying for his answer.

He paused by the door and gazed down at her with such a fierce expression of love, it made her heart stall. "Because I knew right then I'd never be able to live without you. Your little body fit with mine like we were made for each other. Do you feel the same way, Lily?"

"Yes." She touched his scarred face. "Rok, despite the fact that I've been a sex slave for the past seven years, you're the first and only male who ever aroused me."

A satisfied smile crept over his face. "Say it again."

She giggled. "You're the only male."

"Say you belong to me—with me. You know I meant that, don't you?"

"I know," she whispered. "I belong to you. And with you. I'm yours."

"And I'm only for you," he said gruffly. "Freeing Zandia?" He shook his head. "It's for you. Not for Zander or this pod full of humans. It's what you want for them, so it's what I will do. I'm yours to command, as much as you're mine."

Tears welled in her eyes, but she blinked them back, laying her cheek against his heart. "I love you, Rok."

"Do you, beautiful? I'm not sure how that's possible, but I sure as *veck* will take it. I need you like breath. If that's love, it's what I feel."

EPILOGUE

Leora answered Zander's summons, finding him in the Great Hall staring at one of Lamira's plants without appearing to see it. He'd been silent on the flight back to his pod, and her daughter's anxiety had grown when he refused to speak with her.

Her daughter had expected punishment for putting herself into danger. Zander was quick to deliver physical correction, but, judging from Lamira's blushes, they weren't entirely unenjoyable.

Lamira had been in tears that morning, saying he'd acted like a stranger, hardly acknowledging her when they returned to his chamber.

"Perhaps he needs time to think about how best to punish you," Leora had suggested over breakfast.

"The last time he doubted me, he set me aside," Lamira fretted.

"You are carrying his young. He will not set you aside," she'd promised. But, looking at him now, she wasn't so sure. He still wore the withdrawn, stony expression he'd had since the previous planet rotation.

"You asked for me, my lord?"

He fingered a leaf absently. "Yes."

When he said nothing, she approached him, stopping a few feet away.

"You are my guest here, Leora."

"Yes, my lord."

"When I bought you, it was as a gift to Lamira. I have not made any demands of your service other than as her companion."

She dropped her head, sensing the rebuke that was coming. "Yes, my lord."

"As her mother, I would expect you to hold her health and well-being as the utmost priority. Even more so because she is with child."

"Yes, my lord, that is why—"

"No," he cut her off. "Do not give me any explanation—I have no patience for your excuses. Allowing Lamira to risk her life as she did was unacceptable."

She kept her eyes trained on the floor. "Yes, my lord."

"You have displeased me, and I require that you be punished."

A knot tightened in her middle. Would Zander punish her himself? Lamira had suspected, when he'd first bought Leora, that he intended to use her, too, as a sex slave. How would her daughter react to hearing Zander had punished her.

A movement drew her attention to the doorway. Master Seke, the warrior, stood in perfect stillness. How long had he been there?

"I have asked Master Seke to punish you."

Her belly fluttered as Seke's deep-amethyst gaze held hers.

"As it seems you require a direct master, and it is inappropriate for me to take that role, you will now answer to him. He will take responsibility for you and your behavior."

She couldn't seem to breathe.

"Your obedience training begins today."

TRAINING HIS HUMAN

CHAPTER ONE

Veck, no.

Seke wasn't taking on a human slave.

It had been one thing for Zander, the prince of their species, to purchase and breed the human slave, Lamira. Her genes best matched his for producing offspring. But Seke had no desire for offspring, not after the pain of losing three.

Nor did he have need for a sex slave. Or a mate.

He'd sworn celibacy when he lost Becka, his mate and the mother of his children, during the Finnian invasion of his home planet, Zandia.

But Prince Zander stood, moody and dark, at the palatial pod window, ordering him to take control of Leora, Lamira's mother. The proud and beautiful female human. The one who had captivated him from the moment she arrived. At fifty solar cycles, he was still in his prime for a Zandian, and his libido had not slowed, despite his vow.

She fascinated Seke with her delicate, soft features and exotic looks. Her proud demeanor befit a queen more than a slave. It showed strength of character. Power and self-control. Things he didn't expect in a female. But that didn't mean he wanted to own her or train her. To keep her in his room as his sex slave.

"I'm not a slave-keeper." He sounded stiff. It was not often—perhaps never—he and Zander crossed hairs. Though his role as master at arms was that of loyal protector, as well as director of all war strategy and security, the prince was like a son to him. He'd practically raised him since he rescued him from Zandia during the takeover. He'd saved Zander, rather than his own family—a choice he had to live with every day.

Zander usually demonstrated a deep respect for Seke, who functioned not only as a friend and mentor, but also as his Master at Arms, who'd trained him in battle arts. Now, though, he made an impatient gesture. "Nor was I, but circumstances necessitate adaptation. I believe you've told me that at least once."

Seke closed his eyes, debating whether his sense of honor would allow him to outright refuse this order. "You wish me to punish her and train her to obey me as her master?"

"Exactly so."

"Do you imagine I will breed her?" The Zandian species was nearly extinct, with no females of breeding age remaining, which was why Zander had taken a human for breeding.

Zander at last turned from the window and leaned back against it, folding his arms over his chest. "No. I promised Lamira that when her mother arrived she would never be used that way. You will honor my word in that respect."

He ought to be relieved by the pronouncement—breaking the vow of celibacy he'd made in Becka's memory would be cause for quarrel. Besides, as a Master Warrior, he believed sex had the effect of scattering one's energy. Before Zander had bought Lamira, Seke had advised him not to dally with females until it was time to breed. But the fact Leora was off limits niggled Seke, too.

"So why don't you do it? You already keep and discipline one slave. How different—"

"Punishment arouses them."

Seke's jaw went slack, visions of a humbled and aroused Leora making his cock thicken. "Pardon me?"

Zander nodded. "You understood me. Daneth inserted sensors in Lamira to aid in breeding. I discovered—"

Seke's chest had constricted, and he waved a hand, not wishing to hear more. The thought of any male monitoring Leora that way—or observing her arousal during a punishment—made him clench his fists. It was an odd reaction for him—a highly trained and disciplined warrior who usually kept all emotion in check.

"So I cannot punish her, as I am mated to her daughter. It would be wrong. You seemed like the next best alternative."

"Why?" he demanded, though he already knew the answer. He'd shown a proprietary interest in Leora since the day she arrived. That didn't mean he wanted her, though.

He had no desire for a female—not for mating or for sex.

"Shall I ask Daneth?"

Vecking Zander! Too *vecking* observant for his own good. He knew Seke wouldn't stand for any other male touching Leora.

"No," he clipped. If the *vecking* physician so much as thought about putting monitoring devices in Leora or punishing her, he'd tear his limbs off.

Seke changed tactics. This order to train Leora wasn't about the human being unruly or undisciplined. It was about Zander's unresolved anger with his own slave-mate. The pregnant Lamira had essentially run away—leaving with her mother and the warrior Rok in pursuit of her sister, causing Zander to give chase and enter a war between humans and Ocretions they could not afford to engage in.

"Have you punished your mate yet for leaving?" He knew Zander had not, because the prince had hardly spoken to her that morning, acting like a stranger. Both Leora and Lamira had been quiet and subdued, Lamira's sad eyes following her mate with longing.

Zander's eyes flashed dangerously purple. "That is not your concern."

Like veck, it wasn't. If the leader of the Zandian species allowed his personal relations to affect the way he led and the decisions he made, it was exactly Seke's concern. But he didn't say that. Respect, honor, obedience. He had pledged himself to Zander's father and to the crown of Zandia. He did not give of himself conditionally.

He rubbed his ear. "You wish Leora punished. And trained."

"Daneth will send the equipment to your chamber and can instruct you in its use. You will keep her there, with you, until she demonstrates complete obedience and bonding with you as her master."

Bonding. Was that why punishment aroused them? Was that how the Ocretion slave masters had enforced obedience? Punishment and breeding? Was their arousal at punishment the trait that made humans good slaves? He'd always thought it was their weaker physical and over-emotional constitution. The thought made him want to kick down a wall. Who else had punished Leora? Had they used her for sex? For breeding?

But no. Both her daughters had been sired by Johan, the human revolutionary, killed during the last slave revolt. Seke relaxed by a degree. Still, the need to know each and every master who'd ever touched her, to seek those masters out and destroy them, rose like a hot flame, giving him a restless, angry energy. He flexed his fingers to keep them from clenching.

So Zander expected him to punish her to arousal, not have sex with her, and still establish a bond. He supposed it was possible. He'd trained many males in battle arts, establishing a master-student bond. But with Leora, the female who already tempted him from his vow of celibacy on a daily basis...veck.

"Very well. I will do as you command. But with all due respect, I suggest you resolve matters with your own mate. Humans have delicate constitutions. Lamira appears stressed by your disregard, and it could affect the young she carries."

Zander's eyes flashed, and he surged forward on his feet, his chest nearly bumping Seke's. "You worry about your slave, I'll worry about mine."

Veck.

His slave. One he had to punish in the most intimate manner, who would become aroused when he did so. How in the stars would he manage?

. . .

Leora entered the Great Hall of the palatial pod, summoned there by Prince Zander. "You asked for me, my lord?"

He had called her to his opulent throne room, no doubt to inform her she had displeased him by allowing her daughter—the prince's pregnant mate—to risk her life in pursuit of her sister. She'd expected his rebuke, even punishment. So had her daughter Lamira, yet she'd chosen to act, anyway. They had succeeded in rescuing her elder daughter, Lily, thanks to Zander's forced influence, and no one had been harmed. But they'd returned to the pod the night before, and the time for the reckoning had come.

He fingered the leaf of one of Lamira's potted plants absently. "Yes."

She approached him, stopping a few feet away.

"You are my guest here, Leora."

"Yes, my lord."

"When I bought you, it was as a gift to Lamira. I have not made any demands of your service other than as her companion."

She dropped her head, sensing the rebuke coming. She had accompanied her daughter on an unauthorized, dangerous mission to rescue Lily, her other daughter. "Yes, my lord."

"As her mother, I would expect you to hold her health and well-being as the utmost priority. Even more so because she carries my young."

"Yes, my lord, that is why—"

"No," he cut her off. "Do not give me any explanation—I have no patience for your excuses. Allowing Lamira to risk her life as she did was unacceptable."

She kept her eyes trained on the floor. "Yes, my lord."

"You have displeased me, and I require that you be punished."

A knot tightened in her middle. Would Zander punish her himself? Lamira had suspected, when he'd first bought Leora, that he intended to use her, too, as a sex slave. How would her daughter react to hearing Zander had punished her?

A movement drew her attention to the doorway. Master Seke, the warrior, had been standing in perfect stillness. How long had he been there?

"I have asked Master Seke to punish you."

Her belly fluttered as Seke's blue-violet gaze held hers.

"As it seems you require a direct master, and it is inappropriate for me to take that role, you will now answer to him. He will take responsibility for you and your behavior."

She couldn't seem to breathe.

"Your obedience training begins today."

The prince's words rebounded in her head, ricocheting around like a rubber ball.

Your obedience training begins today.

Master Seke stepped forward from the shadows to claim her, his expression inscrutable. Like all Zandians, he stood taller than a human male, with purple-hued skin and two small horns on the top of his head. The master at arms' face was worn and scarred, and always composed. He moved with a feline grace belying his size. His broad shoulders stretched the fabric of his tunic, and a sword hung at his belt. Purple rimmed the blue irises of his eyes, which was unusual. The rest of the species she'd seen had brown-purple irises.

Against all reason, her pussy clenched at the mere idea of the scarred warrior punishing her. She'd always thought of him as *her* warrior, though they'd exchanged few words.

He placed a supple animal hide collar around her neck, caramel in color. It fit perfectly, snug but not bothersome. With a swift, easy movement, he gathered her hands behind her back and cuffed her wrists together with bands of what felt like the same supple leather. His touch was impossibly gentle, considering the strength behind it.

Cuffing her was entirely unnecessary. She'd never win in a struggle against his species, and there were guards everywhere. Nor could she ever leave the Zandian's guardianship. They had knowledge about her past that would have her executed by the local species, the Ocretions, immediately. She could only assume cuffing her was for effect. To show his dominance, his mastery over her.

This male Zandian will soon punish me. Her sex tightened again.

He propelled her forward, his touch still light, but the direction plain.

How would he do it? Intimately? Or publicly? It would be physical punishment; she had no doubt. Lamira had intimated Zander spanked her.

In the factories where she'd met her human mate, Johan, and on the agri-farm where she'd raised their daughter Lamira and hidden her beauty from the greedy Ocretion masters, they'd used a shock-stick to keep the human workers in line. The pain from the shock was unbearable. Overuse caused permanent damage in the nerves and eventually in the brain.

But in the short time she'd been, as he put it, a *guest* on Zander's pod—since he'd bought her as a gift for her daughter, whom he loved—she'd seen no shock-sticks. There'd been no abuse. She and Lamira had always been treated with courtesy, even though it was understood they were slaves. They ate delectable food, slept in luxurious surroundings, and were not required to labor in any manner. Though her daughter wore a collar and cuffs, they were decorated with priceless Zandian crystals—part of the Zandian mating ritual, and she'd been well cared for here. Leora knew Zander punished Lamira, but in private. They hadn't spoken of it, but Lamira had never seemed to resent it. In fact, from her blushes, Leora suspected there was an enjoyable aspect to his mastery.

Was that why Seke was in charge of her? Had he *asked* to be the one to punish her? Since the very first planet rotation she arrived, he'd been solicitous with her, almost protective.

Am I to become Seke's sex slave?

The moment that thought tumbled through her head, she stumbled. Master Seke steadied her, slowing and showing a patience that, again, implied concern. Something in her core pulsed with excitement, even as her mind rebelled. She stiffened her spine, preparing her resistance. Though she had little choice but to ultimately submit, that didn't mean she had to make it easy on Seke.

He led on, down a brightly colored corridor, the polished marble floors covered in expensive, hand-woven Ostrion rugs. Everywhere she turned, the opulence served as a reminder of the comfortable life she'd led there. This pod, no more than a giant spacecraft parked over Ocretia, was the sole seat of the Zandian kingdom until their species reclaimed their planet from the Finn.

He stopped before a door, which swished open when he placed his palm against the panel beside it. He pushed her into what had to be his chamber.

It was beautifully appointed, as was every room in the palatial pod. An oval sleepdisk hovered on one side, suspended as if by magic. The thick mattress was draped in the finest fabrics of amber, green, and midnight-blue. Crystal-amplified light shone through a skylight, making the room, with its high ceiling, light and airy. A workstation hugged one wall.

But what made her breath stop and her solar plexus twist was the cage suspended in the corner. The punishment apparatus on the bed. The tall basket filled with various manual implements, all designed to inflict pain.

A trembling started in her knees and traveled up her legs to her core. It turned her hands clammy and cold. To hide her terror, she lifted her chin and met the eyes of her new master. "So, am I to be your sex slave? I'm past the ideal age for breeding. Surely you know that." At forty-one solar cycles, her body could still reproduce, but the risks were higher.

Something in Seke's face tightened, a slight strain showing beneath the marble mask. "No," he clipped. "You have displeased your host. Prince Zander ordered your punishment and training, but he gave his word to Lamira you would not be used as a sex slave."

She wondered if he inserted the part about the prince ordering it as a subtle means of letting her know this wasn't his own idea. Did he find it distasteful? She couldn't tell.

"Release cuffs." The cuffs, which had to be voice-commanded like the doors and locks in the pod, separated. "You will refer to me as *master* at all times. You will keep your eyes lowered and your hands behind your back unless otherwise instructed. I expect your obedience and complete submission. Defiance will be immediately punished. Remove your clothing."

Even though she should have expected this treatment, his words struck her as if she'd been punched in the gut. From another male, it would not have wounded so badly, but from Seke, the male who had always shown her such courtesy, it came as a betrayal. Before she could consider the wisdom of it, her hand shot out to slap him.

He moved even faster and caught her wrist, twisting it behind her back so she had to either spin around or have it wrenched in the socket. She whirled, and he flattened her against the closed door, with one wrist pinned to her back, the other to the cool metal. Her cheek pressed against the door, and his body covered hers, pinning her with the whole of his chest, his torso, the bulge of his cock against her lower back.

So. He did find this arousing. His hard muscles met most of her body, unyielding and warm.

The trembling in her legs grew stronger. "Seke," she whispered.

She didn't know what made her speak his name so intimately, as if they were lovers, not almost-strangers ordered by another to complete this strange scene.

And his breath was at her neck, hotter even than his flesh. "Defiance will be punished every time, Leora." He, too, sounded more like a lover than a keeper. She didn't hear anger or even danger in his threat. Only promise—sweet promise, as if he looked forward to conditioning her to his command.

She struggled then, terrified, not of the punishment, but of him and her body's reaction to him.

He took her hand from the door and folded it behind her back with the other one, fastening the cuffs together once more. "Come." Again, there was no bark to his words, only quiet determination. He turned and guided her to the sleep-disk, where he sat and pulled her across his knees, her torso resting on the mattress.

She understood immediately what he meant to do, but held back from struggling. Perhaps, if she was honest with herself, she'd admit her curiosity, her fascination with the scenario—of being held so intimately on a male's lap to have a private part of her anatomy touched, punished by him.

When he pulled up her white robes, though, she came back to life, fighting against his obvious intent. Of course, her struggles were no match for him. He had only to scissor one leg over her kicking limbs to pin her in place. Her robes slithered up her back, the fine material sliding over her skin like a caress. The modest panties went in the opposite direction, down her thighs. He lifted his leg to wiggle them past it, and the cool air of the room hit her bare bottom.

She twisted, contorting her torso in an effort to bring her mouth to his arm to bite, but she couldn't reach.

The first slap of his enormous palm came almost as a relief—the actual punishment was better than the anticipation that had been twisting and coiling in her belly. Then pain bloomed, and she started to fight anew. He spanked her fast and hard, a steady pace that covered every inch of the lower half of her buttocks.

Though she tried to keep her lips closed, not wanting him to know how quickly he'd conquered her, grunts and gasps slipped out and, at the loudest, he stopped and rested his paddle-like hand on her blazing skin.

Her back heaved with panting, and she arched, lifting her head to protest the ignominious position.

"Tell me something, beautiful female. Did you fight your Ocretion masters this way?"

Beautiful female. She wished his words didn't affect her, but she liked hearing the endearment far too well.

"No," she admitted after a moment.

Abruptly, his hand crashed down on her bottom again, slapping hard and fast.

She let out a mewl of protest.

"No, *master*," he corrected. "Try it again."

She stilled her struggles and closed her eyes. Something stubborn in her didn't want to give in, even though she knew she'd never win this battle.

"You may keep resisting, little human, but I will break you in the end. And your punishment for displeasing the prince has not even begun."

Tears began to smart her eyes, not from the pain—the spanking wasn't light, but it wasn't unbearable—but from the humiliation.

"No, master!" she croaked angrily.

He stopped spanking, smoothing his rough, calloused palm over her twitching buttocks.

"Is this rebellion for me alone?" His words came softly, as much a caress as the hand circling her burning bottom.

Her heart thundered. Heat swirled in her core. She didn't understand his question, or the angle behind it, but the truth tumbled out before she could stop it. "Yes...master." Again, the tears burned.

And just like that, Master Seke righted her, letting her robes fall back down over her bared ass as he plopped her on his lap, one arm looped around her waist. Her panties were still lowered, tangled around her thighs, which kept her humiliation in place.

He rubbed his knuckles over her cheek, and she resisted the irrational urge to lean into the touch. "This training was not my design, Leora." Regret echoed in the heaviness of his voice. "But it must be. You will humble yourself to me. I will punish you. And I will care for you, for that is the role of a master."

Her pussy clenched at the same time something twisted in her solar plexus. Desire in conflict with pride. Fear smeared around and between both. She almost wanted to give herself over to him, to let him punish and care for her.

Almost.

"Will I be allowed to see Lamira?"

"After your initial training, yes. Keeping you from her will be used as a punishment only—for both of you."

If this training was her fate, she wondered what punishment her daughter had met at her mate's hands. He'd be careful with her because she carried his young. Even without the pregnancy, he'd be fair, though. She'd seen his love for Lamira.

Seke pushed her to her feet. "Release cuffs." The wrist cuffs sprang apart. "Remove your clothing. Being naked before me is part of your training."

Her eyes narrowed. "Why? I thought I was not to be used for breeding or sex."

He landed a swat on the back of her thigh. "I will tolerate your questions today because you are adjusting to the change in our relationship. In the future, I expect obedience without question. The reason I require you naked is to humble you."

Again, something twisted in her solar plexus and anger flashed. Her hands free, she lunged for his face, fingers curled into claws, aiming for his eyes.

He caught her wrists, and one of his feet pushed the backs of her knees so she plunged forward. Her strangled cry morphed into a groan as her knees hit the finely woven rug at his feet.

Seke's expression hadn't changed—his eyes glowed purple, but his face remained an inscrutable mask. He lifted her twisting hands to his face and stroked his cheek with them. She could have clawed his skin, could have inflicted that small wound, but her fascination with his action made her go quiet.

What was he doing?

"These hands," he murmured, still rubbing her fingers over his cheek, across his open mouth.

Was it her imagination, or had his horns stiffened and changed their angle —leaning toward her?

"These hands will learn to serve."

Enraged, she tried to pull them away, but while his grip wasn't harsh, his strength made it impossible. The next time he dragged her fingers across his mouth, he bit down—not hard—more sensually. Her eyes flew wide, heart stilled as she froze, staring up at him.

Shock danced over his features, as if he hadn't meant to nip her. His blue-violet eyes locked on hers, and time stopped. The room spun. Desire throbbed between her legs as insistently as her bottom burned.

And then Seke released her. Suddenly. Violently. He tossed her hands down so hard they bounced in her lap, and he stood, lifting one leg over her head. He moved away from her, toward the door, where he stopped and folded his arms over his massive chest, turning back.

"Stand. Disrobe. I am losing patience." His tone was much colder now—so unlike his usual courtesy, it wounded. And yet it made it easier to obey. This was a nameless, faceless master. Not her Seke. Just one of the hundreds of masters she'd had in her lifetime as a slave.

She clenched her teeth as she stood and pulled off her white robes, slid out of her tangled underpants, then stood facing him, hands neatly folded behind her back. She didn't lower her eyes, though. They both knew her submission wasn't genuine.

Something flickered behind his eyes. Pain or regret. He looked sickened, yet nothing in his expression had changed. Somehow, she read it, though. Perhaps it was the hint of instinct she had—that fraction of the psychic ability her youngest daughter possessed in spades.

His throat worked to swallow. He scrubbed a hand over his face then cleared his throat. "You will obey me."

She lifted her chest. "Yes, master."

CHAPTER TWO

Yes, master.

He hadn't expected to enjoy hearing those words on her lips quite so much. The throb in his thickened cock from seeing her naked did not come as a surprise, however. He'd known she would be a terrible temptation.

She was even more beautiful than he'd imagined. Though her body was still too thin from her enslavement at the agrifarm, her breasts bounced, ripe and lush, the peach-tipped nipples standing alert. Her arms and legs were lean, muscled, and her hips flared below the slender waist. Her skin—like many humans'—was peachy pink in tone. Delicate and fresh. Her scent clung to his clothing. He wanted to snatch her up and breathe it in again, to touch the softness of her flesh.

He had enjoyed spanking her—*stars*, he had enjoyed it. He wouldn't like giving the serious punishment he owed her for the prince's displeasure, but punishing her over his lap with the flat of his hand had been a delight. The way her muscular buttocks flattened and sprang back under his hand, the way her tender skin blushed pink, the sounds she'd made. Yes, he enjoyed chastising her that way.

But he couldn't take her. No matter how tempting this lovely human was, he would master his urges. A master at arms had self-discipline, if nothing else.

And so her training had to begin. He stepped to his workstation and settled in a hoverseat. "Kneel at my feet, Leora."

She hesitated just long enough to register her protest but came before he issued any threat. Her knees cracked as she sank to the floor by his feet. He resisted the urge to bury his fingers in her coppery waves, to stroke the slender column of her neck. The reality of her belonging to him had begun to settle in, and with it, crept a heady sense of power, excitement at the possibilities.

No. He had to steel himself against the temptation she presented. He served the prince and his memory of Becka, not his cock aching for her lush lips to close around it....

Wrenching his attention back to business, he flicked open the first hologram blinking on his wrist cuff.

Lundric, his chief of security, sprang out of the cuff, his head hovering in the room.

"Master Seke." He inclined his head to show respect.

"Report, Lundric."

"I've arrived. Supplies and crafts have been delivered."

Zander had sent Lundric to the uninhabitable planet Shooku where the Ocretion death pod carrying Leora's daughter Lily had crash-landed. After rescuing Lily and two hundred other humans from their death sentence, Lily and her Zandian mate, Rok, had somehow convinced Zander to take responsibility for all the humans, training them to be the army he needed badly to take back Zandia.

The past planet rotation had been a nightmare of coordination—setting up full cloaking of the death pod and sending out false reports of its destruction via a meteor to throw off the Ocretions.

"Is everything in order there?" He half expected to hear Rok and Lily had disappeared again. After all, Rok may have been a Zandian, but he wasn't aligned with them. He'd been raised on Stornig and had been a smuggler and rogue pilot for most of his life after escaping Zandia's invasion.

"Yes, master. Many of the humans still appear in shock, but Rok and his mate have things under control."

"Ask Rok to contact me. I told him I want a daily report."

Lundric inclined his head.

"You will stay to serve Rok but also to report directly to me. Understand?"

Again, Lundric bowed.

"Thank you. Disconnecting." He closed the hologram, and Lundric's head disappeared.

Leora shifted her weight over one heel then the other.

"Are you uncomfortable, little slave?"

She lifted her green eyes with a baleful glare but modulated her voice into respectful tones. "My knees are too old to kneel this way...master."

Studying battle arts for most of his life had given Seke an excellent appreciation for body mechanics. He pushed off the hoverseat and crouched beside his slave. "Kneel up." He lifted her until she lifted her naked bottom away from her heels. He stabilized her with an arm around her waist and gripped one of her heels, testing how freely it swung right and left. He repeated the action with her second heel. They didn't swivel freely.

It took all his concentration to ignore Leora's quickened breaths, the scent of her arousal, the softness of her belly against his arm. She required his care now, not his lust. He nudged her fibula toward the outside of her calves, following the slender bone from her ankle up toward the back of her knee, then back down again until it moved freely. He did the same with the other leg then retested the swivel of her heels and found them easier to move.

With the arm at her waist, he guided her back down to sit. "Better?"

Surprise flitted over her face. "Yes, actually." A blush colored her cheeks. "Thank you. Master."

He nodded once. "Masters take care of their slave's needs," he reminded her. "When you're in discomfort, I want to know." He cupped her chin. "If I give you pain, it should be purposeful."

Her eyes narrowed, and for a moment, he thought she would fight him again, but she clamped her lips shut, chin lifted.

"You may sit on your heels, on your hands and knees, or forearms and knees. I grant you permission to change positions as necessary. You may also lie prostrate over my lap."

"Only humiliating positions." Her voice sounded tight, and it pained him because she was right.

"It's part of the training, little human. You learn your place in relation to me. Once that is established, you will be granted more freedom."

He'd learned humility as a young student of the battle arts. Had knelt at his master's feet. Had endured physical discomfort and endless tests designed to strip him of pride. Warriors were disciplined, honorable. He had trained Lundric and even Prince Zander this way—though with more respect as befit his station. He knew how to train pupils and didn't believe what he required of Leora to be too cruel.

But the hurt on her face slayed him. Literally slashed across his chest like the wound from a sword blade.

He supposed the worst of it for her was the shift in their relationship. He'd shown her only respect in the past. Now he debased her. But she would learn, like Prince Zander had, the context of their different roles. In the battle arts studio, Seke was master to Zander. Outside of it, Zander ruled him, as he ruled all the Zandians and would rule their planet, when he retook it. Yet training Zander had been important. Their young ruler had to be an able and capable warrior if he was to lead their species to recover their rightful place in the galaxy.

Once Leora had learned submission, once Zander was satisfied with her training, she would be free to roam the palatial pod at will, and he would treat her with the deference her gender and beauty called forth.

His cuff lit up with another incoming hologram, and he launched it. Rok's head sprang into the air.

"Master Seke." Rok inclined his head slightly. Not raised with other Zandians, he lacked the reverence and understanding of the workings of their culture, but he'd proven himself extremely battle-ready and capable of great leadership. Lamira's psychic vision had predicted he would lead the army necessary to take back Zandia. "The supplies and ships have arrived. We have sorted the beings into groups related to skill and interest. There are at least a dozen who require medical care. Can you lend a doctor?"

Lily appeared behind Rok, as breathtakingly beautiful as her mother and sister. "There are fifteen in all. We require antibiotics and bandages at the very least," she said.

Leora, hearing her daughter's voice, lurched up from her knees to see, but he pressed her back down, modulating his strength so he didn't injure her, but using enough force that she couldn't resist.

"I wish to see my—" she spluttered, clawing at the hand on her shoulder, her nails sinking into his flesh. She twisted and bit him, her teeth tearing through his skin and drawing blood.

He didn't release his iron grip on her shoulder. "I will have them sent immediately." He flicked the hologram off before more of Leora's struggles could be seen and heard on the other end. Without even looking at his wound or wiping the blood off, he swiveled in his chair and lifted her across his knees.

"Stop it, you overbearing oaf!" She kicked and struggled, her anger unchecked.

He didn't mind her rebellion. After a life of servitude, she knew better than to resist a master. The fact she did, showed she trusted him enough to reveal her emotions. He clicked her wrist cuffs together behind her back. He didn't spank her. The moment seemed to beg for something different. First, he needed her to understand. In the future, she would learn to trust his judgment, not requiring explanations.

"Did you wish your daughter and her mate to see you this way? Naked and collared? In my chamber at my feet?"

Leora stilled, panting.

He slapped her ass and made his voice sharp. "Did you?"

"No, master." The sullenness was adorable. He loved all her resistance only because it told him she felt safe enough to rebel. He'd seen her interact in the palatial pod. She had self-control. Intelligence. Reserve. So her anger with him felt personal. Precious.

Or maybe it was just his own ego wanting to believe they'd shared some spark.

"So when I keep you from appearing in a hologram and revealing yourself, it is for your protection. I am your master. I make the decisions about what's best for you. Do I not?"

She sagged over his legs, more defeated than if he'd lit her bottom on fire again. "Yes, master." Her voice came as little more than a whisper now. "I'm sorry," she croaked. "I did not understand the technology—that I would be seen."

Of course she didn't. The agrifarm where Daneth had found her had been highly primitive. The slaves had dwelled in tents and worked with their bare fingers tending plants. When they'd seen holograms of them, she and Lamira had been covered in mud; possibly they did it themselves to hide their beauty from the guards.

He stroked her slender back. She'd just found Lily, who had been taken from Leora when she was three to be conditioned and trained for sex slavery, only to have her daughter take little interest in the family reunion—choosing instead to stay with Rok to train the humans. She still had to be hungry for any contact with the girl.

He lifted her to her feet. For the first time, she appeared subdued, her head bowed, the lovely copper waves falling in her face. With her wrists cuffed behind her, her breasts were pulled apart, showcasing their pert shape even more. His mouth watered because he longed to suck those pretty little nipples until they grew stiff and hard.

"Do not move."

He stood from the hover chair and strode to the box of implements Daneth had brought for her punishments. He selected a butt plug with a bushy animal tail attached and coated it with lubricant from a pump bottle. Daneth had provided the implements and explanations of why they worked well for human females. He chose the animal tail because it would serve the purpose of humbling Leora without causing her pain.

Leora eyed it as he returned, but he doubted she understood what it was.

"You have displeased me, Leora. Lie back over my lap."

To his delight, she went easily, accepting his discipline. He pried her butt cheeks open and worked the rounded tip of the plug against her anus.

She immediately seized up, squeezing her cheeks together, her back bowing, legs lifting in the air, her body stiffened over his knees.

He had to suppress a chuckle as he slapped the backs of her thighs three times each.

"Ow, you brute," she spluttered.

"Leora." He made his voice hard and firm, disapproval and disappointment lacing the words. "Open your bottom for your punishment. Now."

"Wh-what is it?"

"A tail. If you are going to bite like an animal, you will be treated like a beast. The tail will remain in place until you've shown me you deserve to be treated as a human again."

She whimpered but gradually, by degrees, relaxed her legs and bottom until she sagged over his lap.

He rubbed the tip over her anus once more. "Take a deep breath."

She obeyed.

"Exhale."

As she blew out her breath, he pushed the plug forward. She gasped and tried to clench again, but it was too late, and she must have realized clenching only hurt her rectal muscles because she immediately let go.

He eased the plug forward, going slowly as he stretched her wide to pass the largest part of the bulbous plug through.

She mewled, rubbing the toes of one foot against the other in agitation but otherwise remaining perfectly still for him. The plug sank into her, the largest part inside now, only the neck stretching her little ring of muscle. The bushy tail trailed down the back of her legs. It would not cause any damage, only discomfort, and probably quite a bit of arousal.

His cock jumped and lurched with excitement—it looked so beautiful, as if her ass had been begging for this adornment, which showed off her exquisite round curves.

"You will take your spanking with the tail in place, which should remind you who you belong to. Will you bite me again, little one?"

"No, master," she said immediately.

He drew a breath, already dizzy with lust for her. But he, of all males, had self-control. He would complete her punishment without defiling the beautiful human. He lifted his palm and let it smack down on one cheek of her ass. The tail bounced fetchingly.

He bit back a groan and slapped the other cheek. Another bounce. His cock hardened and pressed insistently against her hip. She surely felt his desire for her. What would she think? Did it frighten her?

His heart pounding, he drew several steadying breaths. He'd have to get this spanking over with quickly. He already cursed his decision to keep her naked. How would he survive this training?

He paddled her, striking right side and left, fast and hard. Her hips bobbed on his lap, and the tail shook and quivered, bounced in her ass.

"Open your thighs." His voice sounded raspy and hoarse.

She obeyed, inching her legs apart over his lap.

He slapped the undersides of her cheeks, the tender insides of her thighs, punishing her intimately and thoroughly while her fingertips danced on the floor.

One of his fingers contacted moisture, and something skidded and lurched in his chest. Yes—her pussy leaked arousal onto her inner thighs, the glossy substance coating his finger.

His inner thighs shook with need. He wanted to drop her onto her knees and *veck* her from behind, pound into her until they both lost their minds and she screamed herself hoarse.

Because he couldn't—wouldn't—anger spiked. He lifted her from his lap and dropped her back to the floor by his feet.

"You may fetch a cushion from the bed to help you kneel." He sounded curt, and the bewilderment on her flushed face gave him a pang of regret. It wasn't her fault he wanted her so badly.

She dropped a curtsy, eyes lowered, and fetched the cushion. It took her a while to situate herself on her knees, but he didn't help. She ended up folding the cushion in half and placing it between her heels to lift her bottom slightly higher. The scent of her arousal still filled the air, and the way she rocked on the pillow told him she suffered as much as he did at that moment.

He flicked through his communications but didn't see or understand anything he reviewed. All he could think about was Leora, the image of that tail bouncing in her perfect ass as he spanked her permanently burned on his retinas.

~.~

Leora's brain swam in confusion. She truly had been reduced to an animal, as no thought could formulate or take hold. Her entire body trembled, though less from pain than...something else.

Need.

The plug stretched her anus in the most erotic manner, and it had moved inside her as he'd spanked as if she'd been ass-*veck*ed at the same time. Every firm slap of his hand had registered not as pain, but as foreplay. The throb in her ass matched the one in her clit. Now her entire body buzzed and tingled; her ears rang, and her eyes were unfocused. She needed to orgasm. Sweet Mother Earth, how she needed release! The urge to cry—not out of pain, but out of frustration—pressed behind her face.

She closed her eyes, trying to rein in her errant emotions. She had gone eighteen years without sex. Just because a handsome alien warrior had stripped and spanked her didn't mean she needed to turn into a wanton sex slave.

Johan would be horrified...except even that thought didn't stick because something about this incredible warrior reminded her so much of her long-dead human partner. While Johan had never spanked her or required her submission, he had been strong and determined, dominant as a decision-maker for all those around him.

Was it crazy that she wanted more spanking? Wanted to be back over Seke's lap, those powerful hands slapping open her inner thighs, the undersides of her butt cheeks, the area just below her anus, right over her sex, making the tail jostle and pump in her ass? This had to be why Lamira blushed and smiled when she spoke of Zander's punishments. It was as much pleasure as it was pain.

She rubbed her clit over the pillow between her legs. Would Seke notice if she—

"Don't." His voice sounded harsh. Almost alarmed.

She froze, her chest rising and falling with shortened breaths. Her breasts felt heavy and tight, swollen and aching as much as her sex.

"Your punishment aroused you," he rasped, "but you are not a sex slave. I will not be enjoying the juicy little pussy that's swollen and wet for me."

Blessed Mother Earth. She neared orgasm just from his words, from his acknowledgement of her state.

"And so you will not be allowed release, either. Consider it part of your punishment."

She nearly wept. "Evil," she muttered under her breath. "Mean. Twisted. Wrong." Louder, she said, "You should not have aroused me, then." She half-wished to goad him into spanking her again.

"You should have behaved." He stood abruptly. "You shall be confined to my chamber while I'm gone. I will have food sent to you."

Her stomach clenched as she watched him stride to the door. "Release cuffs," he muttered before he left without a backward glance and her wrists fell apart.

Had she pushed him too far? Or had his own sexual frustration driven him away?

Briefly, she considered offering herself to him. Since Johan's execution after the human revolt he led, she'd never desired another male. She hadn't missed sex, as she'd been too busy trying to keep her younger daughter from getting picked up for sex slavery like Lily had been.

She'd kept her head down and survived.

But now that the Zandians had bought her, now that they owned her entire family, life had improved significantly. They were treated well—at least she had been until this punishment. The surroundings were beyond comfortable, the food plentiful and delicious. With her improved conditions, the desires of her youth reawakened. She wanted love, like Lamira and Lily had found. Sex. Freedom. Purpose. Things she'd never even dared to dream of when she'd been owned by the Ocretions.

She rocked over the pillow once more. Would Seke even know if she pleasured herself here, alone, with him gone?

She didn't want to, though. Somehow, the idea of them both suffering the same need hurt in the most delicious of ways. She wanted to feel the effects of his punishment, and know he, too, had wanted something more.

She eased out of the position, taking time for her knees to unbend and shaking life back into them. Walking to the washroom, she stood in front of the looking glass, gazing at her naked form, imagining how it looked through Seke's eyes.

Though she'd lived a hard life, she'd always been healthy. Her breasts still had a spring to them, her skin still had a youthful glow, and her hair fell thick and wavy over her shoulders. She had fine lines around her eyes and stretch marks under her belly button but, otherwise, was unmarked.

She had a distinctly erotic look now, though, naked save for Seke's collar and cuffs. Her nipples pebbled in excitement, and a flush painted her cheeks. Her pubic hair had been removed by laser by the Ocretion slave masters when she'd hit puberty.

She turned to gaze at her backside. Her bottom had been painted pink by Seke's large palm. It tingled now, the memory of that spanking eliciting shivers of excitement. The long, fluffy animal tail hung down between her legs, and gave her ass a perky, cheerful look.

She cupped her breasts, squeezing her nipples gently between her thumbs and forefingers. She imagined Seke doing the same, perhaps bringing his mouth to one of her nipples and sucking...or biting.

She hadn't meant to bite him so hard. She'd tasted his blood, which had run thick and violet from the wound. She rubbed her ass. An Ocretion master would've shocked her and put her in isolation. Or worse.

Seke had put a tail in her ass and given her a spanking. She touched her sex and found it dripping and swollen, terribly sensitive to the brush of her fingertips.

She groaned. How long would he leave her like this? Would he ever allow her release?

She wondered, again, about Lamira's fate. Was she locked in Zander's chamber now? Or was it worse—had he banished her to the guest room as he'd done before when she'd lied to him about her psychic abilities?

Their plants would need tending. Lamira had planted nearly a hundred food-bearing plants in Zander's pod, utilizing the incredible quality of light his crystals provided to produce healthy plants. Zandian crystal was the reason the Finn had taken over Zandia. It had applications in technology and energy generation. Traditionally, Zandians used them to amplify sunlight, providing the energy their bodies required for fuel.

Lamira's rare and exotic trees and plants, many grown from heirloom seeds and some even from Earth, flourished here. Her work served as preparation for when Zander took back his home planet, because it would require re-cultivation after the horrific crystal mining by the Finn.

Every afternoon, she and Lamira checked on the plants, providing water or moving their location to provide optimal conditions. If she and Lamira were both locked up, who would look after the plants?

She paced around Seke's chamber, but the movement of the tail in her ass and the rubbing of her clit between her legs only made her agitation grow.

After a stretch, an elderly servant entered, averting his eyes as he delivered a tray of food for her. Not hungry, she let it sit.

Hours passed. She changed her mind a dozen times about how to greet Seke when he returned. Sometimes she planned to lash out at him in anger for leaving her alone so long with nothing to do. Other times, she thought it would be best to appear as subservient as possible to prove her training complete so he might allow her to see Lamira again and roam about the palatial pod.

There was still the matter of her punishment on behalf of the prince. Seke had alluded to it, saying it had not yet begun. Was it more than this training? It seemed so. She eyed the spanking bench and the implements laid beside it. One was a flat paddle, thin and smooth and shaped like an oval with a long sturdy handle. The other was a terrible-looking crop or club, made of woven animal hide, as thick as one of Seke's thumbs and half the length of his arm. She weighed it in her hand and shuddered. It would surely leave mean welts.

The door swished open. She dropped the implement and turned like a naughty child, hands flying behind her back, just as he'd ordered. So it seemed her body had made the choice of how to greet him. *Submissively.*

His eyes raked over her body, turning more purple. This time, she saw the horns move, actually thicken and grow taller, leaning in her direction. Did they reflect arousal? Interest? She licked her lips.

Sexy Zandian.

"Little human." His voice sounded raspy, almost pained. The door swished closed behind him, and he sauntered forward. "Have you been good?"

There was the promise of punishment in his voice, a delicious promise, as if he knew they'd both enjoy such a thing.

She licked her lips. She considered issuing her complaints, but the words fluttered away under his dark stare. Instead, she forced herself to make a plea. "Master...the plants need tending every planet rotation. Has Lamira looked in on them?"

Surprise registered, as if he'd never considered the plants. He tapped one finger against his sensual lips. "I'm not sure. Put on your robes, and we'll go check together."

Though it shouldn't have, his decision excited her. Any excursion with him sounded better than one alone and much better than being cooped up in his chamber.

She picked up her panties and started to thread one leg through before she realized they might not fit over the tail. She glanced over and found him frowning. He shook his head. "No panties. The tail stays in to remind you of my displeasure with your behavior. Just robes."

She swallowed and dropped the panties, tossing the robes over her head. They brushed against the tail, which made it jiggle inside her. Her sex flooded with fresh heat. She feared the tail would show beneath the robes, but there was nothing to be done for that.

Seke opened the door and ushered her out. His hand at her back only served to press the robes more insistently against the tail. When his palm drifted lower and he twiddled the fluffy end of the plug, giving it a shake, she jerked away from him, whirling with flashing eyes. It was bad enough to make her walk about the castle with a tail in her ass, but to tease her with it— to further humiliate her—was not fair.

Of course, *fair* didn't exist for a slave. She knew that, and yet Seke somehow made her believe it might. His adherence to some old Zandian code of honor, perhaps, encouraged that thought.

Seke stopped, facing her. "Eyes down, hands behind your back. Give me your submission or I'll lift the robes and let every being here see the punishment you're enduring."

Her face burned, her ears and neck flushed and tingled with anger and embarrassment, but the consequence he described was too horrible. She obeyed, lowering her head and clasping her hands behind her back, holding them above the tail.

"Better." His deep voice resonated in every cell of her body. "Don't test me, little human. I wish to protect your dignity in public, but if you offer resistance, I will not hesitate to strip you of it. Are we clear?"

Her cheeks burned even hotter. "Yes...master."

"Thank you." He placed his hand behind her back, fingers twining over hers in no particular pattern. It was an oddly comforting gesture, and it took the bite away from his sharp remonstrance, though her belly still twisted.

They arrived in the Great Hall, which was empty. She checked the soil on the large banana plant just inside the arched open door and found it moist. Either Lamira had already watered or one of the servants had. She said nothing to Seke, though, not wanting to return to the confinement of his chamber yet. Instead, she walked around, pinching off dead leaves, examining fruit and harvesting the few that were ready, placing them in the enormous copper bowl the palace chef Barr kept on the long table for the purpose. He would use them either for the meal the Zandians ate once every ten planet rotations, or, more likely, to feed her and Lamira, as they required food multiple times every planet rotation.

"Oh, you're looking beautiful today, aren't you?" she murmured to a particularly vibrant tomato plant, whose stalks hung with heavy fruit. Her fingers caressed the leaves as she tested the plump, red fruit to see which were ready to drop. On the agrifarm, they'd raised many crops originally from Earth, but all had been genetically modified to survive on Ocretia. These plants had been grown from heirloom seeds Zander had somehow managed to procure at great expense. The result was the most succulent, delicious fruit she'd ever tasted. All the food served in Zander's pod was like that—flavors that exploded in her mouth. She almost felt as if she were eating sunshine each time she savored a fresh fruit or vegetable. Her skin had taken on a new glow, hair and nails growing faster since she'd arrived.

"Hmm, thank you for these. They are perfect," she cooed to the plant.

She caught Seke's look—half bemused, half fascinated. "You talk to them?"

She shrugged, ducking her head. "I know it's silly. On the agrifarm, the plants were all we had for company for most of each planet rotation. We worked alone, each with our own plot. I suppose, to me, they became like friends."

She looked up, prepared to see his amusement, or worse—scorn.

But he fingered a leaf, thoughtfully. "They are living beings, I suppose. I wouldn't be surprised if things grew so well here because of the love you and Lamira impart to them every day."

A caress of warmth swooped through her chest at his understanding, even appreciation for the small service Lamira had found she could provide to Zander and his pod.

"So how do you know when they're ready—color?" he asked, turning a half-green tomato on the vine.

"Yes, and touch." She picked up his hand and guided it to a tomato ready to drop. "Test this one. Give it a small tug. When it's finished growing, it practically falls from the stalk." She half-feared he'd pull too hard, his strength being so much greater than hers, but her warrior had a light touch, no doubt honed with all his study of battle arts. He plucked it gently from the vine and held it up with an uncharacteristic smile.

It sent shocks of pleasure right down to her toes. Had he ever smiled before? A big smile like that, with white teeth gleaming? She hadn't seen it.

He brought the tomato to his mouth. She followed the motion with her gaze, enthralled by the softness of his beautiful lips, the straight white teeth opening to take a bite. Juice and seeds spurted out, hitting her in the face, dribbling down his chin.

He shouted in pleasure and surprise, laughing as he reached to thumb the mess from her face, his tongue sweeping down his chin to lick the rest. "Delicious. It's better when you pick it yourself, isn't it?"

She beamed, irrationally pleased he understood. "Yes, it is."

He held the half-eaten fruit to her mouth. "Here, you must be hungry. Daneth tells me you eat two to three times per planet rotation."

She tried to take the tomato from him, but he didn't relinquish it, insisting on feeding her. Face growing warm, she nibbled and bit at it, trying to look dainty as juice spilled down her front and splattered on the floor.

Seke chuckled again, the rich sound of his voice echoing throughout the hall. He popped the rest into her mouth, and she closed her lips, trying to manage the huge mouthful without looking ridiculous. Still chuckling, Seke moved away, initiating his own examination of the plants growing in huge, beautifully painted pots all around the room.

She picked plump lemonberries, cultivated from seeds from the Earth-like, human-populated planet of Jesel. They grew on small, heaping bushes covered in tiny, hair-like thorns. Normally, she was adept at plucking berries without catching a pricker, but she looked over her shoulder to see what Seke found interesting and brushed up against a patch of thorns.

"Ouch!" She yanked her thumb back and held it close to her face, angling it into the light to see how many of the culprits had embedded in her skin.

"Let me see it." Before she could refuse his help, Seke took her hand and brought her thumb to his mouth, closing his lips over the area. His tongue brushed along the offended flesh then he sucked, hard. Her body heated by several degrees, as if his mouth had been on her nipple. Or two feet lower, on her sex.

Her pussy clenched.

His tongue swirled again, teeth scraped along the finger. His violet eyes met hers, and a shock ran through her. Her knees went weak, body shivery and feverish, as her anus closed around the plug and his skilled tongue lapped at her thumb. He released her finger and swiped his lips with the back of his hand to rid his mouth of the stickers. "Did I get them all out?" His voice sounded deeper than usual, raspy.

"I-I'm not sure." She'd lost her breath.

"Leora." He spoke her name like a lament, like being with her made him sorry for something. "I'm not sure I'll survive training you."

"Nor am I," she whispered.

~.~

Seke wanted to shove Leora against the wall and pound his cock into her until she screamed for mercy. The way her breath caught, the flutter of her pulse at her throat as he stood so close to her, and her wounded flesh in his mouth, had him shaking with lust.

Fortunately, the palace chef, Barr, entered, and Leora pulled back from Seke. "Any harvest, Leora?" Barr sounded cheerful, as always. Like most of the Zandians who'd lived in the pod since Zandia's demise, he seemed to find the new presence of females invigorating.

"Ah...yes." Her voice sounded shaky. She gestured toward the bowl. "Some fruit."

"Lamira picked some earlier, so I'll add these to the bounty."

Seke caught Leora's eye, the pink flush of her cheeks deepening. "Did you realize your daughter had already been here?" He already knew the answer by the way she turned from him, taking an intense interest in the leaf of the plant in front of her.

Humans lied. They didn't have the same sense of honor as Zandians, a fact that had bothered Zander immensely when he'd taken Lamira as his breeder. But if you watched them closely, it wasn't too hard to see beyond their words.

"Leora." He kept his voice soft, so Barr wouldn't turn back as he bustled away with the fruit.

"Yes, master," she whispered, still not looking at him.

Veck, she was sweet. He *vecking* loved when she called him *master*. Which was wrong on so many levels. For one, Zandians shouldn't take slaves. It wasn't part of their culture, and had been Zander's original objection to buying Lamira. For another, his pleasure at her subservience surely showed an ego-driven desire for power. Masters of the battle arts had no use for ego or power. They served as honorable beings.

He tunneled his fingers into the back of her hair and gripped her by the nape. When she still didn't look at him, he put a finger under her chin. "Were you going to tell me?"

Her lips looked full and lush—close enough for him to ravish with a bruising kiss, if he let himself. But he wouldn't. She hesitated.

"I punish for lies, lovely." He kept his words soft and light, banking on the tenuous bond he'd established to win her honesty.

"No, master."

He kissed her forehead. "Thank you for your honesty, little one. It saved you from further punishment this time. But you've dawdled enough." He turned her and propelled her out of the Great Hall. "We have Zander's punishment to deal with before I put you to bed in your cage."

She stiffened. Whether it was from the mention of punishment or the cage, he wasn't sure, but the woven magic between them dissipated.

He didn't want to administer Zander's punishment—the serious whipping she'd earned for allowing or encouraging her daughter to leave the pod and put herself and their unborn young in danger. Slapping her with the flat of his hand while holding her snug against his lap was one thing. Binding her to the apparatus Daneth had provided and using various implements was another.

But it had to be done. He served Zander and had taken Leora on as his slave, his responsibility. And no, he wouldn't want or allow any other being to do it in his stead.

He brought her to his chamber and leaned his back against the door. His nervous system had been abuzz since the moment he'd taken charge of her that planet rotation—fight or flight hormones dumping into his system, making his pulse race, his skin flush. And, yes, keeping his horns stiff and his cock thick and heavy for her. *Stars*, he didn't want to desire her so.

He drew what he wished was a calming breath and began her lesson. "What do you do when you enter my chamber?"

She lifted those green eyes, her expression puzzled. He didn't help her. Dawning bloomed, and some of the openness on her face hardened, chin lifted as she peeled off her robes, letting them drop to the floor.

Far from appearing humiliated by her forced nudity, she faced him and squared her shoulders and if the challenge hadn't been so dead on the mark, he might have laughed in wonder at her brilliance. But she'd pinned him—she hadn't missed his agony every time he was near that perfect, petite human body and had to resist flipping her onto her back and burying his malehood into her tight, moist heat until she screamed for mercy, for more. He wanted her calling his name as he spanked her ass red and then *vecked* her hard and rough from behind.

"That's right." He summoned the whip-like control again, pacing slowly toward her—no, *prowling*. "When you're in my chamber, you're naked. Why is that, little slave?"

Her nostrils flared as she drew a breath through them, as if to calm her ire. "To humble me."

"Very good, Leora." He stepped close to her and allowed himself a slow, lingering gaze up and down her body. His palm reached of its own accord to cup her breast, thumb strumming her hardened nipple. "It didn't work, though, did it?" He pinched the nipple, and the scent of her arousal filled his chamber, drugging him like an intoxicating gas. The kind that made him only attuned to Leora. Her body. Her pleasure. And, for the moment, her pain.

"No," she whispered.

He continued to worry her nipple, rubbing it between his thumb and forefinger, longing to lower his head and give it the full treatment with his mouth, with his tongue. His teeth. "No, you know you're a torture to me, too, don't you?"

Her eyes drifted closed, and her head lolled back, as if his touch brought her too much pleasure to stay present. "I'm glad," she murmured.

"I'm sure you are. Don't push me too far, little one. If I fail at training you, tempting human, Zander will give you to another."

Her eyes flew back open, and he was satisfied to see the alarm he felt about such an arrangement mirrored there.

With a gentle touch, he turned her and gave a little shove toward the spanking bench positioned on his sleepdisk. "Climb on, beautiful female. The time for your punishment has come."

He didn't like the fear flashing in her smoky eyes, but it couldn't be helped. A serious punishment was a serious punishment, and that was what he'd been charged to deliver.

She obeyed him, climbing onto the contraption and holding still as he locked her legs and wrists to it. With her knees spread, ass lifted and presented for punishment, she made an incredibly erotic sight. The spankings he'd given earlier in the planet rotation had faded in color, leaving him a fresh, pale canvas on which to paint once more. He eased the tail out of her ass.

More of the hormones that had kept him on edge all day surged. He knew his skin and eyes had to be dark purple, horns harder than stone.

To cover his desire, he adopted a clipped, terse tone. "This will be a harsh punishment, one that will cause you significant pain, perhaps for several days. You will endure it as your penance for betraying the trust of your host, Prince Zander. Do you understand?"

"Yes."

With a whack of the smooth, thin paddle he'd picked out, he made her gasp.

"Yes, master!" she cried out, self-correcting.

"Good girl."

He applied the paddle with sharp, quick slaps, keeping the force light and letting the wood do the work. The thicker paddles in the box would leave pain farther below the surface, but he preferred this one, which was more like a cooking utensil—a large, flat spatula. As Daneth had explained to him, the beauty of punishing humans on the buttocks was their ample padding. All punishments inflicted on the surface caused great pain but left no lasting damage.

Leora's breath came in quick gasps and pants as he peppered her lovely posterior. He took his time. A long, carefully measured punishment would be more effective than a short, severe one. It would achieve the emotional submission, which was all that mattered. Punish too cruelly and the student would harden rather than soften. Too many masters failed to understand that. He'd give her a long warm-up to ensure her bottom was properly prepared for the whipping that had to come at the end.

If he hadn't seen the dew glistening between her nether lips, he might have survived it. But her body's reaction to his dominance *vecking slayed* him. It was all he could do to keep his head, to not pounce on her like a feral animal in rutting season and turn her inside out with his malehood.

He spanked harder, sweat gathering around his horns as he drew long, slow breaths in an effort to regain his brain.

She gave a little whimper, which helped to ground him, remind him he served the prince and also had a duty to Leora to keep his head and do this right.

When her whimpers became more frequent and pitiful and her ass glowed red, he stopped. "Good girl, Leora. You took that well." He ran a palm over her heated backside, lightly stroking, soothing. "We're almost finished, but this will be the worst part." He laid the wooden paddle down and picked up the braided leather whip. Normally used on large riding beasts with tough hides, it would mark her, leaving deep welts that would last for several days.

"Ten with the riding whip. You will count them. After each one, you will repeat, *I will not betray Prince Zander's trust.*"

"Yes, master." Her words didn't seem forced this time.

"Good girl." He stepped to her side and took aim then drew back the whip and brought it down across both her buttocks.

Her scream set off alarms in every cell of his body, adrenaline flushing his system, demanding he rescue her from the pain.

But he could not.

Veck Prince Zander and this *vecking* assignment. He would *vecking wreck* the boy next planet rotation in the studio.

It took Leora several beats to regain her breath, and when she did, the injury in her voice was evident. "One. I will not betray Prince Zander's trust."

All he could do for her was offer encouragement. "Good girl. Nine more. You can do this." He whipped her again.

Another scream set his teeth on edge. "Two." Her voice shook. "I will not betray Prince Zander's trust."

"That's it, beautiful. You're doing so well." He struck her again.

A broken moan this time instead of the scream. It was worse—so much worse. His chest tightened with agony.

"Three." Her voice caught on a sob. "I will not betray Prince Zander's trust."

He ran a hand up and down her back, which now glistened with a light sheen of perspiration.

"Faster," she croaked. "Get it over with. Please, master."

He gritted his teeth and lifted the whip, striking again.

She screamed the words this time, as if to get them out fast, so he applied the next line before she'd even finished, then another and another. Her words toppled over one another in a panicked screech, echoing off the walls of his chamber, surely carrying down the hall. She couldn't finish the required speech after he reached seven, and he stopped, waiting for her to catch her breath, absorb the pain.

Her back shook with sobs, but no tears dampened her face.

"Please, no more," she moaned, drawing shaky, terraced breaths.

He leaned over her, weaving his fingers into her thick copper waves and resting his forehead against hers. "I'm sorry," he whispered. "The mercy is not mine to give, or you'd have it."

"Seke..."

Veck—hearing his name on her lips made his heart lurch. He wanted to protect her from all this. To rescue her, to keep her safe.

"Ready, lovely girl?" he murmured in her ear.

"No," she moaned, but she braced herself, lifting her head and drawing her shoulders down.

"We're on eight." He moved to her other side to be sure he kept the pain evenly distributed, and applied the whip again.

"Eight! I will not betray Prince Zander's trust."

The next one he laid just beneath her buttocks on the backs of her thighs, and her screech and shouted count rang with anger. "One more, little slave, and you need never see this whip again, so long as you keep your masters happy." He laid the last welt, hardly hearing her refrain as he spoke over her to release the voice-activated bonds.

He tossed a soft blanket around her and scooped her into his arms, carrying her to a sitting area of two hoverchairs nested together. Her little body trembled, and she hid her face in his neck, but he did not smell any tears. His chest tightened—she was so fragile, so *vecking* sweet.

~.~

She'd drifted to sleep—not for long, at least she didn't think so. She still lay cradled in Seke's arms, his huge hand stroking circles over her back. Her ass throbbed and burned, but desire also thrummed in her, hot and insistent, as if the pain had been simply foreplay.

What about Seke's punishments made her body turn so wanton? It woke sleeping desires in her, made her hungrier than she'd ever been in her life. She shifted, squeezing her legs together in an effort to alleviate the ache there.

"You're awake." Seke's lips were close to her ear, his breath warm and comforting.

She shifted on his lap and winced.

He picked her up as if she weighed nothing and adjusted her so her spread legs hooked over the tops of his knees and her bottom hung freely between his thighs, touching nothing. His huge, hard cock flexed against her sacrum.

"I smell your arousal, little human," he murmured in her ear.

She tensed, shocked to hear her personal secretions were so evident. Zandians had to have a finer sense of smell than humans.

"Why are humans aroused by punishment?" Seke bent over, picking something up from beside the hover chair.

She spluttered. "We're not! At least, I've never heard that before..." Where to take her protest? She couldn't deny her own reaction to his punishment, but she didn't think it was a given with humans and discipline.

Seke remained silent.

"Why do you think so?" she asked.

He brought one large digit between her legs and brushed the seam of her sex, slick with need. "You deny it?"

She groaned at the featherlight contact, dying for more. "No," she gasped, lifting her hips in hope he might return that blessed finger to her core. "I feel it with you, but..."

Something in Seke snapped to attention. He tightened the arm around her waist. "Only with me?" he rasped.

"Yes," she breathed, still bucking her hips, her pussy clenching on air.

A buzz sounded, and Seke brought a vibrating capsule between her legs and pressed it against her clit. She'd never seen such a thing before, and she flinched, fearing pain, but it brought only instantaneous pleasure. She jerked, thrusting toward it and throwing her head back against his shoulder.

He brought it slowly up and down her slit.

"Oh...*oh!*" she shrieked. "What are you doing?" Panic rang out in her voice.

Seke immediately took it away, and she sagged between his knees. "Does it hurt?"

"No—stars, no. Please, do it again."

He didn't require more encouragement, returning the little device to the apex of her sex, where he circled her clitoris with a slow-quick motion that drove her wild.

She gave a cry of excitement.

Seke moved the capsule to penetrate her pussy. When she pushed up at him, seeking more, he stood abruptly, still holding her around the waist, her feet dangling above the floor. With a quick movement, he carried her to the bed, forcing her down on her belly beneath him.

A thrill of heat surged from her core upward—the knowledge Seke was going to *veck* her. And she had no doubt about her interest in that action. She wanted him—desperately.

But instead of his cock nudging at her entrance, the vibrating capsule returned, his heavy erection still contained by his leggings pressing her welted ass down and forcing her pussy against the hard plastic he held in place.

She gave a choked cry as the device penetrated her, Seke's pumping hips thrusting her pussy over it and back, the vibration setting every nerve ending on fire.

"Seke," she cried out. "What are you—?" But she couldn't finish the words. Her orgasm came hurtling over her, core clenching, bottom bucking against Seke's contained cock.

She collapsed, taking the capsule deeper into her still-squeezing channel, her thighs shaking, body limp. "Seke," she repeated again, knowing she was babbling and not able to stop herself.

She hadn't orgasmed in years. Hadn't masturbated or even considered sex after Johan died. Not until she'd met Seke. Now, the part of her she thought long dead, or at least broken, surged up, in perfect repair.

The capsule stopped vibrating, and Seke eased his weight off her and pulled it out. "As your master, I control everything. When you're obedient, I'll give you release."

Maybe if he hadn't just scrambled her mind with the most potent climax of her life, she would have contained her fury at those words. Maybe if she hadn't assumed a closeness over what they'd just shared. But his words brought her reality crashing back down on her, and she suddenly hated herself for letting him please her.

With all the force she could muster, she twisted and aimed her heel at the bridge of his nose.

~.~

Seke dodged the kick without thinking, but he should have let it fall. To wound Leora like that was unconscionable. She'd just given herself to him. Beautifully. Had just surrendered, allowed him to pleasure her, opened to receive everything he gave. It had been a *vecking* privilege to watch her go off. And because he'd felt so much more than he expected, because he should not have taken her that way—because even though it hadn't been sex, it had been *vecking* close—he'd sought to justify it as something a master does. Not a lover. And he'd hurt his little human.

Veck.

If he could take it back, he would. But it wasn't possible—he couldn't apologize without undoing the training he'd worked all planet rotation to establish. And if he apologized, he would show his hand—his real feelings for her. And where would that get them? They were feelings he couldn't act on. Not without breaking his vow of celibacy and debasing the memory of Becka. Not without breaking Zander's word to Lamira. And Zandians didn't break their vows.

No, it was better this way, even though seeing how he'd hurt Leora flayed him, gutted him like a sword to the chest.

He took control of her swiftly, capturing her wriggling body, cuffing her wrists together, then doing the same with her ankles to limit her wild fighting. He didn't have it in him to punish her again. She'd been through enough already, and he couldn't bear driving them further apart.

"In your cage, now, little one." He forced a tender tone, even though anger and hate poured off her in waves.

"No," she screamed, bucking and kicking as much as she could with the cuffs binding her.

He carried her to the cage. "Open cage." The voice-activated door swung open. When he tried to slide her through the entryway, she thrashed even harder, striking her head against the pale rock-wood bars, which were as hard as marble. She grunted in pain, and he drew back, not wanting her to hurt herself more.

She stopped her fighting, panting and warily watching him with narrowed eyes.

Veck.

If she were a student of his, there to seek his training, he would impart the lesson until she learned it, never bending, never deviating from his plan. But she wasn't. She wasn't truly a slave. She was Leora. Honored mother of the prince's mate. Lovely, proud human, who held herself with the dignity of a queen. His Leora.

He sighed, knowing he'd lost the battle. Probably had lost it before they'd even begun this training.

He walked away from the cage and over to the sleepdisk and lowered his beautiful, naked slave onto the mattress. She curled up on her side in a defensive position. If he were a wise male, he would leave her now. Leave the chamber, let her settle on her own.

But it seemed his wisdom had been blown out of the chamber when he'd witnessed Leora's climax because he lay beside her and curled his larger frame around hers, noting how perfectly she fit, notched against him, her trembling body soft, the citrusy scent of her hair soothing his frayed nerves like a drug. He wrapped a beefy arm around her waist and tugged her closer.

"Sleep, Leora. Tomorrow, we'll discuss your resistance."

He wasn't sure whether to log it as a success or failure that she did not even tense at the threat. Her breath slowed and became easy, and within a few moments, the female who had just overtaken his life dropped into sleep.

His cock throbbed, pressed against her bare ass, the heat from her punishment searing even through his leggings. This was his penance. Suffering her constant presence, her nudity, witnessing her explosive orgasms, taking care of her vulnerable human body, would punish him for the liberties he took with her. He would pay in blue balls and a petrified cock. Which he could only reason he deserved beyond measure.

CHAPTER THREE

Lamira rubbed her belly, swollen below her newly pierced belly button. She was naked and on her knees, as Zander required when he entered his chamber, but her huge purple-skinned mate didn't even look at her when he entered. He'd been ignoring her since their return to his pod the previous planet rotation.

It was better than being banished from his chamber, as he'd done when she'd refused to tell him the truth about her psychic abilities. Sort of. Still, suffering his continued silence made her chest ache.

"Zander—"

He held up his hand. "Do not speak unless spoken to."

She nibbled her lip. So they were back to this. After he'd taken her as his mate, pierced and adorned her with Zandian crystals, after he'd admitted his love for her, now he was back to treating her like nothing more than a breeding slave.

She tried to build a wall against the pain lancing her heart. Should she fight him? Insist he communicate with her?

But no. Zander retreated when something bothered him. If she pushed, she only risked him sending her farther away. Only, there was one question she couldn't hold back. "Have you taken my mother from me?" she croaked.

"No." He didn't turn to face her, giving her his back as he stripped out of his clothes.

"Where is she?"

"I've given her to Seke for punishment and obedience training."

Lamira sucked in her breath, shocked. Every cell in her body went on alert, protectiveness for her mother overriding her concern for her own well-being. "My lord—"

"Do not speak." His voice lashed like a whip.

Tears gathered in the corners of her eyes, but she blinked them back, her mind turning over what he'd said. *Punishment and obedience training.* Her mother could handle that, if anyone could. She had managed to make their lives as slaves as easy as possible on the agrifarm, teaching Lamira how to blend in, keep her head down and her rebel heart well hidden. Seke would be a kind and humane master compared to the foremen and directors of the agrifarm. Besides, Seke cared for her mother. Everyone had noticed. He took special care with her—with little chivalrous acts like escorting her through the halls, opening doors. He always had an eye on her, standing silent in the shadows, his large presence more comforting than any guard's.

"Go to sleep, Lamira." Zander sounded weary. He still hadn't looked at her, or even faced her, moving about the chamber with heavy purpose as he readied for bed.

She rose to her feet and padded to the sleepdisk, curling up on her side.

Zander voice-commanded the lights off and lay down without touching her, just as he'd done the night before. This time, she couldn't hold back the tears. Daneth said the pregnancy made her more emotional, and it seemed to be true, although she'd always cried easily when it came to Zander. He'd turned her inside out from the day he sent Daneth to purchase her.

"Why won't you just punish me, Zander?"

He flipped over and lunged for her, covering her mouth with his hand, her body with his long, muscled one. Despite the violence of the move, the anger behind it, her body responded to his nearness, to his touch.

She arched into him, the pointed tips of her breasts brushing against his beautiful, sculpted chest.

He didn't cover her nose—she could still breathe, and though he easily dominated her body, nothing about what he'd done had hurt or scared her.

A light on his cuff flashed, probably telling him how much he'd aroused her.

His eyes flashed violet, but not with arousal—with anger. "I told you not to speak," he hissed.

Fresh tears flooded her eyes.

"Don't." He always said humans were too emotional, and he particularly didn't like when she cried, although he'd grown to understand it in their time together.

She turned her face away, as if she might hide her emotions, and he released her with a muttered curse.

He remained still, braced on his arms, his body poised over hers for a long beat, then he lowered himself to her side. When one of his long arms came around her waist and tucked her back against his front, all the tension in her muscles eased.

Yes.

This.

She needed him, needed the closeness, his touch. Even if he wasn't ready to talk or to punish her, at least he didn't deny her this. She closed her eyes and let the remaining tears run down her nose onto the pillow.

The following planet rotation, she'd try again.

He couldn't block her out forever.

~.~

Leora woke to the sound of Seke holo-conferencing with one of his heads of security, Lundric, a handsome young Zandian who had to be around Zander's age. She remained lying down, remembering she might be seen on the hologram if she got in the view.

There hadn't been such fancy technology on the agrifarm, nor in the factory where she'd been enslaved. She supposed the directors had access, but the humans never saw it. It certainly wasn't wasted on them.

The human resistance movement used the most ancient form of communication—word of mouth among those trusted. She'd been a link in a long chain of communications. She wondered if they'd filled the gap since she left. She wanted to be on that death pod with Rok and Lily, helping ready the humans who'd escaped death, thanks to Rok and Zander.

But they were readying them for a war no one in the human resistance had foreseen—the war to regain Zandia.

The dull ache that had been with her ever since Lily's rescue flared to life. Her daughter hadn't recognized her, hadn't remembered her. Of course she hadn't—she'd been only three solar cycles when one of the factory guards grabbed her to sell into sexual slavery. Still, Leora had wanted to reestablish a relationship—immediately. But she understood. Lily had fallen in love with Rok, the Zandian pilot who rescued her. Their relationship was new and fragile, exciting. And it had been their idea to utilize the humans to make up Zandian troops, her daughter as committed to human freedom as her father had been. It hadn't been the time to go quietly back to Zander's pod with her mother and sister and get to know two strangers who looked just like her.

Leora understood. But it still hurt. She wanted to know her daughter, to learn what she'd missed. To be as integral a part of her life as she was of Lamira's.

Seke disconnected the communication, and Leora sat up, pulling a blanket up to her armpits to cover her nudity. She winced at the contact of her sore bottom with the mattress. The surface still burned and, below it, a dull ache made her infinitely aware of every stroke Seke had administered.

Her new master swiveled in his hover chair and gave her one of his inscrutable gazes. "Drop the blanket," he said after a pregnant pause. His blue eyes darkened to smoky purple.

She looked down at her hands, fisting the fabric; the small mounds of her breasts shifted beneath it. It felt incredibly wrong to be naked, after all those years dressing in the most loose-fitting, ugly sacks she could find, to disguise her shape and form. When she'd first met Johan, he'd made her feel beautiful, and she'd loved her feminine body then, but in the years since his death, she'd become disassociated from her body. Being female meant danger at every turn.

She closed her eyes and reluctantly lowered the fabric, little by little, until it rested at her waist, her fingers still gripping it as if her life depended on hanging on.

"Thank you for your obedience. Remember, when you are in my chamber, you will be bared to me."

She couldn't muster anger toward him at that statement, just the beginning pulse of interest between her legs. Damn him.

"You may use the washroom, then come to me."

Her tummy fluttered. What did he have in mind for her this planet rotation? She climbed off the sleepdisk and headed to the washroom. Once there, she eyed the washtube. He hadn't said what she could and couldn't do in the washroom. A nice hot shower might feel good and would delay whatever torture he had in mind.

She used the facilities then slipped into the washtube, which closed and automatically filled with water. Lamira had shown her how to use it when she'd arrived, after regaling her with the comedic story of her first panicked use of one, in which she thought she would drown.

Water swirled around her, but far from soothing, the heat of the water stung her sore bottom, making her gasp and dance around. She gritted her teeth as it rose up over her head then drained a moment later, leaving her bottom more tender and prickly than before. Even the warm air blowing across her skin irritated her marked ass as it dried her. A sheen of oil blew over her skin while hot air concentrated on her hair until it, too, had dried. The door slid open, and she stumbled out, feeling more fragile than when she'd gone in. And now she had to face Seke.

She desperately wanted clothing. What she'd tolerated due to shock the previous planet rotation now seemed an even higher penance to pay, but there was nothing for it. With her chin lifted, she stepped out of the washroom and walked to where Seke sat, busy at his calculations.

He ignored her for a moment, but when he turned, she saw the effect of her closeness, or more likely, her nudity on him. His sexy horns thickened and tilted in her direction, eyes glowed, changing color. Even his skin seemed to darken. She longed to touch that purple skin. Did it feel like a human's? It was hairless, as far she could tell. Except for the dark closely-shorn hair on his head.

He reached out and rested his huge hands on her hips, drawing her forward between his knees. "How did you sleep?"

She flushed, not expecting him to be solicitous. "Well, thank you." She lowered her eyes, fidgeting with her cuffs.

"I need to examine your posterior." Before she could protest, he'd hauled her forward over one of his long thighs. Her legs parted for his knee, bottom raised, toes leaving the floor.

She stifled a gasp, shocked at the pressure of his hard thigh on her clit. She rocked her pelvis, grinding the sensitive nub against his leg, sparks of pleasure shooting off behind her eyes. Apparently her traitorous body had not lessened its wanton attraction to Seke during the night.

He ran his large palm over her sore bottom, and the tactile reminder of what that palm had delivered the previous planet rotation—his firm-handed spankings, the butt plug, the whipping—had her grinding again, harder this time.

He stroked her with both hands, one on each cheek, up and down, kneading and massaging. "You like your inspection, don't you, little human?"

"No." She sounded like a petulant child and a liar.

He popped her on the ass with a quick spank. "I will not tolerate lies, beautiful female, and I know you don't want a spanking on this already sore bottom, do you?"

He waited when she didn't answer.

"No, master," she finally forced herself to say.

"Good girl. First we must deal with your defiance last night." He parted her butt cheeks.

She flinched at the vulnerability of it.

He gave her ass another pop—not hard, more like a warning. Something liquid dribbled down her crack, and Seke rubbed an oil or lubricant over her anus. "You're going to wear this plug and spend an hour in the cage as punishment. If you accept it without protest, I will consider your slate wiped clean."

Something smooth and round probed her most private hole. The tail again? No, she didn't feel the hairs brushing her legs.

"Deep breath in." Stars. Seke's deep rumbling voice seemed to go inside her and speak to every cell.

Her body obeyed without her command.

"Exhale."

She tensed, failing to exhale.

He waited.

Realizing she hadn't followed instructions, she slowly blew out her breath. Seke pushed the plug in, stretching her wide. She whimpered but inhibited her urge to resist, remembering tightening against the intrusion would only cause discomfort. Instead, she focused on relaxing, exhaling again, allowing Seke to insert the—*veck! Vecking thick* plug inside her.

Once he'd pushed the widest portion of the plug through, it seated easily, a cool metal handle applying pressure against her back hole, held open by the neck of the plug.

"Seke." She literally had never whined before in her life. It wouldn't have been tolerated by any Ocretion, but the tone carried from her lips now, shaping his name into pleading.

"Good, little human." He patted her bottom, which jiggled her ass, and hence the plug inside her.

She bit back the moan on her lips.

"On your feet, sweet girl. Into your cage."

Her face burned with humiliation when he righted her and wiggled the plug in her ass where she stood fully bared to him.

"I didn't think I'd like to see you this way." His voice sounded clogged, even deeper than usual. He brought his hand to the swelling bulge of his erection in his trousers and gave it a quick stroke. "I didn't think I'd want to see you debased." Another stroke, and his eyes rolled back a little in his head.

He hadn't received release the previous planet rotation. She wanted to give it to him now.

"But it turns out I *vecking* love it, Leora." He pulled her forward, using the plug as a handle once more. Her bare breasts danced right in front of his mouth, and his eyes locked on them like a wild beast on prey.

"Only for me, though. No one else will ever see you this way." He spoke the words fiercely, as if fending off the other potential viewers as his competitors.

His jealousy told her he may have been bluffing the previous planet rotation when he'd said he would show her bare spanked bottom and tail plug to the entire pod. She wasn't confident enough to test him on it, though.

He brought one fingertip between her legs, curling it along the seam of her pussy as he drew her even closer with the plug, plunging the hardened bud of her nipple into his mouth. He sucked—hard.

The sensation shot straight to her pussy, which gave a tug as if an invisible string connected the two. Her knees went weak, and she fell into him, her hands flying to his massive shoulders, catching herself just in time, as he finger-tapped the swelling bud of her clit.

"You're all wet for me again, Leora." His voice sounded dark and satisfied. "I won't use you for my own satisfaction, but it's within my right, as your master, to decide if and when you shall be offered release."

She had a feeling he was making up the rules as he went. Apparently, her body *vecking* loved his rules because her inner thighs trembled. Heat gathered in her core, swirling and pulsing as the simultaneous sensations of the plug stretching her bottom hole, his tongue laving her nipple, and finger twiddling her clit had her dangerously close to begging for release.

And she'd sworn to herself before sleep the last planet rotation never to allow him to pleasure her again.

So much for that vow.

Desire coiled tighter with each powerful suck of his mouth on her nipple, each stroke of her clit. Just as she was about to go off, he stopped.

"Get in your cage, little one." His deep, raspy voice sent a fresh wave of desire through her, but he removed his mouth and his fingers from her.

"Wh-what?" She couldn't see straight, dizzy with lust, confused.

"You heard me. One hour in the cage with the plug in your ass. Get in."

Her mouth fell open in shocked outrage.

"Now, Leora, or you'll never get that release."

Her sex clenched at just the mention of a climax. It was a powerful motivator. She wanted his hands back on her almost as much as she wanted to kick him in the shin for his arrogant manipulation. She didn't want to want him.

But humans didn't often get what they want in this galaxy, did they?

With as much dignity as she could muster, she walked to the cage and climbed in. The idea of being imprisoned that way horrified her, but it was only an hour. Thank the great Mother Earth he hadn't forced her in there the previous evening. She wouldn't have survived it.

Seke placed a plate of food in the cage and shut the door. "Lock cage." It clicked shut. He glanced at the readout on his cuff. "I will be back to release you in an hour. Be good, little human."

She ignored him, turning pointedly to the plate of food and picking up a slice of handmade bread slathered in a delicious sweet paste. She took a bite, keeping her concentration solely on the food, but the moment Seke left, she pushed the plate away.

Did he really believe she could go from the verge of an orgasm to eating breakfast?

She supposed the answer was he didn't know. He only had to eat once a week, which was ten planet rotations on Ocretia. He wouldn't know about hunger. She wondered what he knew about a human female's release. Maybe it was completely different from a Zandian female.

No.

He knew. He'd known just where and how to touch her. How to make her scream, how to arouse her in the most wonderful and humiliating ways.

She didn't want to give him credit for the incredible way he played her body, but she had to. He knew female pleasure.

She rolled onto her belly. There wasn't enough room in the cage to lie straight, but she fit with her knees bent. With her face pressed against the soft woven rug at the bottom of the cage, she slid one hand between her legs.

As he walked swiftly to the battle arts studio, Seke brought up the feed of Leora in her cage so it displayed on his arm cuff.

And then he nearly tripped and fell flat on his face.

Leora—his glorious, naked slave—lay in her cage, not eating, but with one perfect, delicate hand between her legs.

Oh, one true star of Zandia.

Holy *veck*.

He wanted to return immediately to his chamber to watch—no, to tell her she was never, ever allowed to orgasm without him. The urge to be with her for every second of her pleasure made his body flush with heat, sweat to break out around his horns.

But Prince Zander arrived behind him. "Everything all right, Master Seke?"

He gulped a breath and struggled to regain his sanity. He would chastise Leora for giving herself a release when he returned, and he'd make it an enjoyable punishment for both of them. Cheered by that thought, he gave Zander a curt nod and motioned to the battle arts studio.

Zander preceded him into the studio and took his position, bowing to Seke, his master in this chamber.

Seke bowed and then swept a foot out to drop Zander to his back on the floor before the prince registered he'd begun. He'd trained the boy well, though, and Zander sprang to his feet, at once on the offensive, coming for Seke.

He parried the kicks and blows, waiting for the right moment to again take Zander by surprise, this time flipping him to his back.

His pupil did a back handspring to rise. This time, his eyes narrowed, watching his master with the awareness Seke played a different game today. This wasn't practice. It was punishment.

Zander proved his understanding with his next move. As he picked up a wooden staff and twirled it, swinging it in Seke's direction, he asked casually, "How goes it with Leora?"

Seke grabbed his own staff and lunged, forcing Zander back into a corner with swing after swing of the staff, which met Zander's with increasing force each time.

"That bad, eh?" Zander dodged the strike Seke aimed for his temple and dive-rolled away, out of the corner, his wooden staff clacking on the floor as he took it with him.

It probably would've ended normally—he would have exercised Zander harder than usual, but they would have bowed to each other and parted with reverence, except he saw the read-out of Leora flash on his cuff. How the feed activated again, he wasn't sure. As a Master Warrior, he didn't allow such things to distract him.

But—*true Zandian star*—Leora had one hand between her legs, one stretched behind her to grip the plug. She writhed between them, pleasuring both holes, her flushed face *vecking* gorgeous.

His cock sprang against his leggings, and he must have moved instinctively because, the next thing he knew, the crack of wood on bone rang out, and the young prince crumpled and went down flat on his belly, unconscious.

Oh *vecking* excrement. His heart surged into his throat.

What had he done? Had he really just struck Zander on the temple?

"Daneth to the studio," he barked into his wrist cuff, kneeling beside his royal pupil.

Zander's eyes blinked open, irises purple from the pain. "You're more angry than I thought," he mumbled, pushing himself up to sit with Seke's assistance.

He wished he could laugh at Zander's attempt to defuse the situation, but he found no levity. He'd lost control of his emotions, of the situation. He'd allowed a female—a human female—to distract him into striking the sole living Zandian of the royal bloodline. It was unforgivable. He could have killed him with that blow!

"Forgive me, my lord," he choked.

Zander touched his fingertips to the bruise already swelling near his eye.

Daneth burst in the room, pale and determined. "What happened?"

Zander defied their concern by jumping lightly to his feet, causing both Daneth and Seke to stand close, ready to catch him if he fell. He pushed their hovering hands away. "Seke let me know what he thought of my latest order," the prince said mildly, his lips twisting into a rueful grin.

"Staff blow to the temple," Seke clipped to Daneth, impatient to see Zander treated.

"A mild painkiller, no more," Zander ordered for himself as Daneth ran his scanner over his body.

"Single contusion. Due to the location, it may cause temporary dizziness, headache, loss of vision, nausea. Requires analgesic, anti-inflammatory, and bed rest until patient has recovered," Daneth's scanner read in a crisp, female voice.

"I don't need bed rest," Zander said. "Just the painkiller."

"I insist on rest for at least an hour," Daneth said, looking past Zander to Seke for support.

But Seke wasn't going to quarrel with Zander—not after what he'd just done.

"The painkiller," Zander snapped. "And put me on your monitor." He indicated Daneth's cuff, which provided him with constant feedback about Lamira's medical state so he could monitor the growing baby. "That way, you'll know if I need anything."

Daneth's lips closed in a thin line, but he removed the medication gun from his medical case and shot Zander's neck with it. "Rest. One hour."

"Go back to your lab." Zander waved him away, walking out of the room without waiting for either of them to bow to him. Daneth's obsession with keeping the Zandian species from extinction had led him to sequester himself for long hours in his lab, studying genes, reproduction, and investigating the possibility of producing test tube young.

Daneth turned a cool, assessing gaze on Seke. "The human female is affecting you."

"*Leora*," he growled, ready to knock another friend to the floor with a blow to the head. "Her *vecking* name is Leora. You know that."

Daneth gave a faint smile, and he realized the physician had purposely goaded him. "Human females do seem to have this effect on Zandian males, do they not? I'd be interested in testing further pairings."

Now Seke did grab Daneth, wrapping his fist in the male's lab coat and yanking him close, so they stood just a hand's distance apart. "It's not a pairing, and you're not testing any more—" He spluttered, not even sure what he was saying. "There will be no further purchases of human slaves here," he thundered.

Unruffled, Daneth continued his bemused, curious study of Seke. "Is it the slavery that bothers you, or your attraction to the human?"

He released Daneth, suddenly disgusted with himself. He was a Master Warrior, a self-disciplined teacher of the battle arts. A male who never lost his temper or acted with emotion. What had happened to him?

It was true, Zander had also suffered as he'd become attached to his human mate. He'd become irritable, irrational. Did this mean Seke had grown to...*love* Leora?

But he couldn't get attached. He wasn't free to mate—he'd made a vow of celibacy in his dead mate's memory. Breaking it would be dishonoring himself and her.

"It's both," he muttered to answer Daneth's question, and walked away before the male could probe him further.

"If you like, I could run the gene-matching program on the two of you."

"No," he barked, unnecessarily loud. "She's not for breeding."

"Of course not," Daneth murmured to his back as he strode swiftly away.

Veck. Veck Daneth and his *vecking* gene-matching program that had brought the humans upon them in the first place.

He just needed to get through Leora's training, and then he'd leave. He'd go to the death pod and help Rok train their new troops. Far away from Leora and those beautiful, moss-green eyes.

But even that thought sickened him. How would he leave her after training her in such an intimate way? He was conditioning her to bond with him, to attach herself to him as her master. He could hardly abandon her after putting her through this humiliating training.

And it seemed even his thoughts of resistance were futile because his feet had carried him not to find Zander to ensure he suffered no ill-effects from the blow, but straight to his chamber, to punish his wanton little slave.

~.~

She'd been touching herself since the moment Seke had left. Even though she'd brought herself to orgasm, once through touch alone and once by touching and replaying the eroticism of the position he'd had her in earlier for her inspection, she still had found no relief.

With a low moan, she rolled to one side and lifted her top knee open to give herself better access to her sex. It had never been so wet, so swollen, so *vecking needy* before.

You're all wet for me again, Leora.

Stars, the male *infuriated* and aroused her at every turn!

The door panel swished open and Seke strode in, dark and purposeful. He stopped in the middle of the floor and stared at her, horns tilting in her direction as the door swished closed behind him.

"*Vecking* stars, Leora," he choked.

He wanted her. She enjoyed the surge of power that came with that realization. In a flash, he was at the cage, spinning it so the door faced him and barking for it to open. He grabbed her ankle and tugged her backward out the door, until both legs were out and she'd folded at the waist, her torso still in the cage. "Lower cage." His deep command caused the cage to float gently downward, until her toes reached the floor.

Within seconds, he had two fingers curling inside her, the swell of his cock bumping the plug in her ass. "Leora, did I say you could give yourself release?" His lips were right at her ear, the growl feral.

Her internal muscles started to quiver around his fingers. He withdrew them, leaving her panting, desperate. A sharp slap on the ass made her cry out.

"Did I?"

"No, master," she gasped, desperate to say the right thing, to please him so he would return to touching her. She'd been so close.

He slid his fingers over her slit again, pinched her clit.

"Ugh!" she groaned. "Please. Please, master."

"*Vecking* stars, I like it when you beg, beautiful human." He spun her around to face him.

She wobbled on her feet, knees weak with desire, eyes glassy and unfocused. She licked her lips suddenly hungry for him to take her mouth the way he'd claimed the rest of her.

But he didn't. He picked up her wrists and clasped them together, then pulled them high, yanking down a cord she hadn't noticed hanging from the ceiling, and clipping her to it. He tugged until it lifted her arms straight in the air above her head.

"I'm going to have to punish you, little one." His heavy breathing and dark eyes betrayed excitement, not anger.

Her nipples pebbled up, pointing toward him as much as his horns leaned toward her. He rummaged through the box of implements and produced a soft leather strap.

Her eyes went wide, and she danced away from him as he approached. Her poor bottom could not take a spanking with that—she was sure of it.

He slapped it against his palm as if testing its weight. "I know your bottom is too sore, beautiful. I'm going to find other places to spank."

"Seke," she whimpered. "No."

He stroked his free hand down her side, resting it at her hip. "Open your legs wide, Leora, so I can punish that naughty pussy of yours."

She made a little sound of protest, but when he nudged her bare feet apart, she obeyed the command. She realized her excitement outweighed her fear. Seke had been careful with her, even when delivering the horrible whipping last night. This would not be nearly so bad, whatever it was he had in mind.

He rolled most of the strap around his fist until he'd shortened it to no more than a hand's length.

He struck lightly, slapping the leather against one of her breasts, kissing her skin with the leather.

She shrieked and danced away, spinning around the rope connected to her wrists. It hadn't hurt so much as it frightened her. In reality, only a light sting and warmth remained where he'd struck her.

"No, no." The correction was soft, patient. His hands steadied her, planted on her hips to hold her still. "Open your legs."

She didn't move, her breath rising and falling in short pants, body trembling.

He brushed her hair back from her face and caressed her cheek with his thumb. "Be a good girl, Leora. Open your legs and stay in position, and I will give you the release you still crave."

She flushed, embarrassed he read her so easily. Did he know how many times she'd tried to satisfy that itch while he was away? Drowning in the liquid violet pools of his eyes, she drew a shaky breath and obeyed, widening her stance.

He offered a slight smile. "That's it, little one. Good girl." And then he struck her squarely between the legs with the leather strap.

She screamed, but his hand shot out to her waist, held her steady.

"Don't move," he murmured, catching her gaze once more.

The sting had already faded to a hectic buzz, desire swirling and pulsing beneath it all.

"I'm responsible for your orgasms, Leora." He snapped the strap up again. She screamed in her throat but held still. "You will never, ever orgasm without me present." Another spank to her pussy.

She moaned and leaned against the ropes. The pain had morphed into molten need.

He whipped up one inner thigh with short, measured slaps. Whipped down the other. When a drip of her arousal landed on the back of his hand, he looked up, appeared almost as wild as she felt. Would he *veck* her now? She needed him to.

"Please," she whispered. "Please, master. Please, Seke."

"Look at me," he ordered, standing in front of her again. He held her gaze as he whipped her pussy, once, two times, three. Five *vecking* times, and she didn't move, held captive only by his beautiful amethyst stare. "Good girl," he breathed as if in awe. "Now your breasts." He slapped her right breast from the outside then backhanded it to whip the inside. One more swing and he spanked the underside.

Her eyes smarted from the pain, and her pussy throbbed and ached.

Seke gave her left breast the same treatment then dropped the strap and shoved his leggings down so he could grip his cock.

She wanted that cock, needed it inside her so desperately. It was huge—bigger, even, than she'd imagined. Her mouth watered, looking at it. She wanted to take it in her mouth, to offer him pleasure.

"How many times did you climax while I was gone?" he demanded. He looked fierce now, like the warrior he was, even while fisting his cock in his hand.

"Two," she whimpered. "But they..."

He stroked his hand up the length of his cock and down, eyes growing darker purple, nostrils flaring. "But?"

"They weren't good...didn't satisfy." She licked her lips, watching his slow, deliberate movements.

"No," he growled. "That's because you were being naughty. Naughty humans don't get satisfaction." He stroked up and down a little faster, and she began to fear he wasn't planning on giving her that cock, that this was all a big tease.

"You said if I—"

He flashed a dark grin. "Your master will satisfy you. *After* he satisfies himself."

She closed her eyes, willing her breathing to calm down, reining in her desperate need.

He pumped faster now, a glimmer of precum glistening and slicking the way. "Don't you ever, *ever* touch yourself without my permission." He spoke through gritted teeth, his cock straining and thick beneath the beating of his fist. "You don't orgasm unless I allow it. And you never orgasm without me there. Understand?"

"Yes, master, yes," she agreed, as frenzied and excited to see his release as she was to earn her own.

He came, showering her belly and thighs with his luminescent rainbow-swirled cum as he threw his head back and roared.

"Yes...yes, master," she encouraged, dancing closer to him, arms still suspended from the ceiling. She reached out her legs to wrap around his waist and bring that beautiful cock against her hot core. But he deflected her attempt, pushing her back and shoving his cock down inside his leggings.

"Seke..."

He gripped her hips, sliding his hands down the outsides of her thighs as he sank to his knees.

One lick of her pussy and her internal muscles started to quake.

"Does my little human need to come?"

"Yes," she panted. "Yes, master. Please."

He dragged his tongue up and down her slit and sucked on her swollen clit. At the same time, he gripped both her buns with his hands and squeezed. She tightened on the plug still stretching her anus as he ground in the pain of the previous whipping, all the while sucking and licking her straight to ecstasy.

"Seke, oh no! Oh please! Oh, dear, sweet Mother Earth."

Somehow her legs had hooked over his shoulders, and her thighs now clamped around his ears. He found the plug in her ass and pumped it in and out while his tongue performed a kind of magic she hadn't known possible.

She screamed, thrusting herself against his mouth. He locked on her clit, sucking so hard she thought he might pull it off, all the while still pumping the plug in her ass. She screamed and screamed, kicking his back with her heels, her trembling thighs opening and closing spasmodically as wave after glorious wave of climax bucked through her. Lights danced behind her eyes, blinding her. She lost all sense of herself—where her body ended and his began. Where she was, what they were doing. She rode the glorious release until the last tremor had shaken through her and she was left hanging from the rope, body sagging between her suspended wrists and her knees, where they were slung over his shoulders.

He released her clit from his suctioned hold and lapped her a few times with his wide tongue, soothing away the tenderness.

She whimpered, an achy sob of release coming out of her throat.

Seke stood, lifting her with him, shifting one of her thighs over his head to hold her cradled in his arms. "Release clip, release cuffs." The cuffs detached from the rope and sprang apart. He carried her to the sleepdisk and laid her on her back, lifting her ankles in the air.

"Relax for me, sweet girl." He tugged on the butt plug.

She tightened instinctively instead.

"Exhale. Open. Give it to your master." His encouraging commands made it easy to let go, and she focused on keeping her bottom relaxed so he could remove the large plug.

It stretched her too wide as it came out, and she whined, but then it was gone. Her body felt empty, battered, well-used.

Content.

. . .

Seke stared down at his ravished slave. Her knees had fallen open when he'd released her ankles, and her arms were flung over her head, hair a wild halo around her. Her flushed cheeks made the green of her shining eyes even brighter.

Vecking beautiful.

The trust she'd exhibited had been beyond his expectations and had produced the most powerful sense of dedication to her. He'd protect her above anything—or anyone—else at this moment. Even his prince.

He brought his thumb to stroke slowly along her slit—not to arouse, just to caress.

Her inner thighs tensed and quivered, green eyes flashed to his, questioning. But trusting.

He *vecking* loved seeing that trust there.

"Beautiful female." He trailed a finger around one nipple, tracing the red lines left by the strap. "You please me."

He'd known it would be hard to train Leora. Hard because his attraction to her was powerful and the punishment required would be arousing to her.

But he hadn't known how much he would *vecking* adore seeing her come undone and knowing he'd been the one to bring her over the edge. He hadn't known how much he would enjoy hearing her call him *master*, or seeing the moment when she chose to trust and obey. That moment he'd swung the strap between her legs and she'd held them wide for him had meant *vecking* everything to him. Her submission and trust made him feel whole and virile and strong.

He leaned over and rubbed his cum into her skin. He stroked both hands up her sides to cradle her breasts. "Such a good girl." Stroked a hand along her back to cup her ass. Down her thighs. He stroked her all over, savoring the feel of her soft, smooth skin, the way her flesh still trembled beneath it, her purring noises as he did it.

How much longer would it take him to train her? For instant obedience at his every command, for her to show deference and respect, to look to him for orders and answers?

Not long enough, he feared.

Because now that he had her, he didn't want to give her up.

But that was foolish. He couldn't possibly maintain a relationship like this. She'd tempt him into breaking his vow too quickly. *Veck*, he'd already half-broken it today by coming all over her.

"So tell me, little one, why the fit over the cage last night?"

He kicked himself for it because she stiffened and pushed herself to sit, wariness returning to her face. Scooping her up by the armpits, he lifted her to wrap her legs around his waist and carried her over to a hoverchair, where he sat with her naked body agonizingly close to his.

"What part bothers you—being locked up or the confined space?"

A little shiver ran through her, but she sat up, her beautiful back sleek and straight as she met his gaze. "A little of both, I suppose. Despite my slave status, I haven't endured much of either. On the agrifarm, we lived in a tent and worked outdoors. I don't even like being confined in this pod, particularly, beautiful though it is."

Of course. He should have guessed. He stroked his palm up her back. "Thank you for sharing that with me. So let's see if we can get you over your fear of it."

She lurched as if to climb off his lap, but he held her fast.

"Why shouldn't you conquer your fear of the cage? If you've mastered every punishment I can give you, you have nothing to fear from me."

It was a mistake—he'd fallen back on training her like a pupil, a student of the battle arts, not a slave. He wanted to give her tools to overcome her fears, to master her heart in adversity. Keeping another being, especially one he cared about, in weakness, in fear, went against a lifetime of training.

Her pale-green eyes narrowed.

He shrugged. "You've already mastered the spankings. They arouse you, so long as they're not too harsh."

"But they still hurt."

"Feeling pain is a choice. You can reprogram your mind to perceive it differently. When I see you aroused from your punishment, it does something powerful to me."

She flushed and looked away.

"So you see, you've already mastered me." He cupped her chin, bringing her eyes back to his. "But that is how it should be," he said softly. "The master should be as bonded as his pupil." He didn't choose the word *slave* because it didn't fit—he didn't see her that way now. Perhaps he never would again. "He should be willing to take any of the punishments for her in a heartbeat if he thought it would help the learning."

Skepticism scrawled across her features. "And you would do that for me?"

He nodded. "I would."

"Strip naked and put a tail in your ass? Allow yourself to be cuffed and slapped in your intimate places?"

None of those things would affect him. He did not suffer humiliation or pain, had learned many solar rotations ago how to maintain his spirit with the least resistance and maximum strength. Perhaps she saw the fierceness in his eyes, understood he'd take any amount of pain, would risk his life for her to keep her safe, because her eyes widened and her lips parted, as if in awe.

She nodded.

"Yes, you're ready to try the cage again?"

She hesitated a moment. "If my master wishes it."

The riot of emotion produced by those words nearly choked him. His chest twisted up, turned inside out, and then burst his heart right out of his body. It made him want to swear every solemn vow he could think of to her.

But that reminded him of the one he'd sworn to another.

Veck.

He was in too deep now, and he couldn't see the way out.

He commanded the cage door to open and lifted his chin toward it, directing Leora to enter.

She shot him an uneasy glance but dutifully climbed in, her chin firming into a resolute line.

He walked to the cage, lifted and spun it so they were face to face. She lay curled on her side. "I could test you now. Leave you for growing lengths of time, but it's not necessary, is it?"

She leaned up on her forearm, considering him. "No, master."

"You've already conquered your resistance and taken the pain from the punishment."

"Is this a punishment?"

"No. Nor was it ever intended to be. There are many who find small, enclosed spaces comforting. A safe place."

She considered him for a long moment then gave a single nod.

His cuff beeped with an incoming hologram from Rok. He pushed the cage higher so it floated closer to the vaulted ceiling, removing her from the viewing space.

"I received the training plan you sent," Rok said without greeting.

He waited.

"With all due respect, I don't fly that way."

Still, he said nothing.

"I appreciate you putting it together, but I'm more of a seat-of-my-pants kind of pilot. You don't learn by studying, you learn by doing. I'm planning on giving them the basics and then just getting them in the crafts for practical experience."

He sighed and rubbed his forehead. On one hand, he agreed with Rok—there was no better or faster way to teach a student than to throw them in and see what happened. But... "You risk human life and Prince Zander's air fleet."

Rok interlaced his fingers and sat back. "Life is risk, master. This entire plan is heavy on the risk. And, meanwhile, we're in danger staying on this sorry excuse for a planet. If the Ocretions come looking for their missing death pod..."

"We circulated reports of the death pod crashing into a smuggler's with no survivors. Inside sources say that information was accepted by the Ocretion empress."

"Any smuggler in particular?"

"One who matched your description."

The corners of Rok's lips lifted, and he visibly relaxed. The Ocretions had warrants out for his arrest for smuggling. "Thank you."

He blew out his breath. "Teach them as you see fit. The prince's mate foresaw you leading an army for Zandia. I will trust you to lead."

Shock washed over Rok's face, then he flushed and inclined his head. "Thank you, Master Seke."

"Anything else?"

"Yes. I received the crystals and the gun to pierce Lily. Please thank Prince Zander for that."

He waited because it seemed Rok had more to say.

"Lily is torn, thinking of her mother and sister and how she did not get the chance to be reunited with them in the midst of the new training plan. I thought we could arrange a time for them to conference?"

He heard Leora's head bang against the cage bars as she must have tried to sit up.

"Yes, I'm certain they would like that, but neither is available at the moment. I will let you know when it can be scheduled."

Rok wasn't a fool. He sat up straight and leaned forward, his brows slamming together. "What has he done with them?"

When Seke hesitated, Rok noticed. "That's it, isn't it? Zander's got them locked up somewhere as punishment? What has he done? Put them in that dungeon of his?"

Seke modulated his face to keep from showing surprise Rok knew of the dungeon. It was a punishment they had devised on the pod. Even though they lived as refugees in Ocretion airspace, the Zandians preferred to keep their own government, which meant Zander issued his own punishments to their species. He also had a "no Zandian blood spilled" policy, since their species was in danger of extinction.

"They are both in excellent health," he said carefully.

"But?"

"They are on temporary social restriction."

Rok's jaw tightened. "Tell me the truth, Seke—is Lamira a mate or a slave?"

He noticed it hadn't taken Rok long to drop the "master" part of Seke's title, although he'd suspected his use of it wasn't genuine to begin with. Rok hadn't been raised as a Zandian, and he lacked the honor and manners of their species.

His question was one Seke had known would come, and he had to answer it with care. When Rok had first shown up on Zander's pod, he'd shown scorn for the prince and the palace, only coming to use the crystal bath out of necessity. But he'd fallen in love with Lily and had returned to request Zander's help in rescuing her, knowing she was his mate's sister. They'd intercepted the death pod carrying Lily and two hundred other humans condemned to die. Lily's attachment to saving the humans and providing them with a place to live had forced Rok to offer to train the humans as Zander's army to free Zandia. So while Zander and Seke needed Rok, their bond with him was precarious, at best.

"Lamira and her mother were Ocretion slaves. Zander purchased them and mated Lamira." None of that was a lie.

Rok narrowed his eyes. "When can Lily see them?"

"Soon. I will arrange it." He ended the communication before Rok pushed for more. Before he even turned to look, he sensed Leora's outrage from the cage.

He stood and went to the cage. Her lips were tight; furious tears brimmed in her eyes.

"Oh *veck*. I've lost you now, haven't I?"

She turned away from him, but he spun the cage to see her angry-hurt expression, the tears spilling down her cheeks as she held her mouth and jaw firm.

"Look at me." He adjusted the cage again to keep her face in view. "Do you trust me? I give you my word—and a Zandian never lies—I will arrange calls and meetings with your daughter. As many and as often as you desire."

Her nostrils flared, anger still simmering there. More tears spilled. Their salty scent overpowered his senses and gave him an itchy sense of urgency.

"Do you believe me?"

She sniffed, looking stonily past him.

"Leora." He made his voice a little darker, more forbidding. "You do understand why I did not allow it in this planet rotation?"

Her throat worked to swallow and failed.

"Look at me and tell me why." He added a sharpness to his tone now, praying he had enough of her trust, that they were bonded enough she'd respond to his displeasure.

She did. Her eyes dragged slowly to his face, lips twisted in a bitter line. "Because I'm still being punished?"

He gave a single nod.

More tears spilled. "I hate you."

He reached through the bars and swiped a tear with his thumb. "I do know how much it means to you. You still suffer the loss of her, even though she's been found. You wish to know her."

At this, Leora burst into honest, heartbroken tears. And it *vecking* ruined him to see her that way. He spun the cage until the door faced him and commanded it open, plucking her out, holding her cradled to his chest.

"I do understand, little one. I will take care of you."

To his relief, she wrapped her arms around his neck and buried her wet face against it, her back shaking with her tears.

"I lost her. And I still haven't found her."

He stroked her beautiful waves. "I know you haven't, sweet female. I know you haven't." He settled on the sleepdisk and rocked her gently. "But you will."

"You promise," she whispered, confirming.

"Yes, I promise."

"What if the prince forbids it?"

Some old hardened rock inside him shuddered a bit at the question. That place in him he'd had to petrify in order to go on living with himself after he'd left Zandia with the young prince instead of his own family. Would he choose honor over love again?

But that was foolish—he wasn't in love with Leora. Except his heart said something different.

"I would persuade him," he said softly into her hair. "If Lamira didn't first."

She lifted her head, her red eyes scanning his face, measuring him. She appeared to have another question, but she closed her lips and settled her cheek against his chest, as if choosing not to ask it.

CHAPTER FOUR

When Leora emerged clean and fresh from the washtube the following morning, she found Seke had returned to his chamber.

"Are you ready to apologize to Zander? Show you have accepted your punishment and training?"

Her jaw dropped. A heaviness pressed against her chest.

Was he serious? Every time she thought she might understand Seke, might forgive his high-handedness, even be able to surrender to him as her master, he did or said something that made her want to kick him in the teeth again.

She'd been furious—*vecking* furious he'd kept her from speaking with Lily earlier, and having Rok demand to know whether they were slaves or not had been humiliating. Clearly, he didn't think they should be.

She agreed. If Zander loved her daughter enough to mate her, he had to treat her as an equal and free both Lamira and Leora from slavery, at least in Zandian eyes. Obviously, they'd never be free under Ocretion law.

"Do you want to see your daughters?"

She scowled at him.

"Then let's complete this *vecking* training and move on."

He said it with a little too much force, causing her chest to hurt in a different way. Did he want to be through with her? What would happen after Seke and Zander deemed her "trained"? Would things return to the way they'd been before? Or would she still belong to Seke? Sleep in his chamber, obey his every order? Take off her clothes for him and bend over and take his spankings, his butt plugs? His—*vecking stars*—his climaxes?

The way he'd spoken made it sound like he couldn't wait to move on, and that disturbed her on a level she didn't care to examine.

"You may wear your robes, but no underclothing."

Scowling, she pulled the white robes on.

He approached her, carrying...was it a leash?

She jerked away when he attempted to attach it to her collar. "What the *veck*? You want to bring me to Zander on a leash? Is this more humiliation training?"

Seke appeared unruffled. His indigo eyes remained cool, face smooth. "Master it and you master us both."

She stared at him a moment, her breath quickened, her mind tumbling in somersaults. And then she understood what Seke had been trying to teach her. A punishment only bothered her if she let it. She had a choice. The leash could humiliate her, or she could simply accept it and choose not to let it wound her pride. Either way, Seke would still be her master and would still be leading her around like a pet.

Fine.

She lifted her chin, offering access to the collar at her throat.

Seke's lips twisted. Was it admiration she saw there? Or pride? She'd pleased him, if she read him right. And judging by the spike of excitement surging through her, she liked pleasing him. Far too much.

She held her head high, following Seke, who kept a steady, gentle pressure on the leash, never tugging it too hard or at an angle that hurt her neck.

The first guard they passed flicked his eyes over the leash and quickly averted them, as if embarrassed. Her own face flamed in response, but she stiffened her spine, not faltering.

Seke led her to the Great Hall, where Zander sat. It was his receiving day, the one planet rotation of the week in which Zandians who didn't live on the pod could visit to request his assistance, or seek justice and permission to use the crystal bath, which was necessary to maintain their energy. As she understood it, Zander settled disputes, acting as both lawmaker and the arm of justice for his species, who preferred to keep to themselves, rather than engage with the Ocretion justice system. As an ambassador to the United Galaxies, he represented their nearly extinct species and used his influence to assist any Zandians entangled in problems with other ruling bodies.

An elderly Zandian female bowed to the prince and exited, presumably for the crystal bathing room their species used for recharging. No one else waited to see the prince.

Thank the stars. It would be embarrassing enough without an audience.

Seke led her up to the throne, where Zander sat, his large hand curled in a fist at his mouth, his eyes vacant.

He wore the same troubled, pained expression she'd seen on him when she first arrived, when he'd been ready to send Lamira away for deceiving him. He hadn't known the secret she kept—that she had special psychic abilities—was not a danger to him, but a complement.

She dipped into a low curtsy. "My lord."

His eyes traveled from the leash to its holder and back again. "Leora."

"I have come to beg your pardon, my lord. I owe you my service and loyalty. I should have warned you of Lamira's plan to leave with Rok." She found it easy to speak the words because they were true—at least from the Zandian's perspective. It didn't mean she would do anything differently if she had it to do over again.

Zander's jaw tightened at the mention of Lamira leaving. He stared unseeing over Leora's shoulder for a moment. Obviously, he hadn't forgiven Lamira yet.

He ignored her, flicking his gaze to Seke. "How is the obedience training going?"

"Well, my lord. Nearly complete."

"And her punishment?" His cool gaze returned to her, assessing.

Her belly tightened, even though the punishment was over. Or was she excited by the humiliation of having it discussed? She worked hard to keep her breath even, her gaze lowered, while her cheeks burned.

"Complete."

There was a moment of silence, as if Zander expected Seke to expand on his statement, but her new master did not. She had a momentary fantasy of Seke lifting her robes to display her marked buttocks, and while she'd never forgive him for such treatment if it really happened, the idea tweaked her. Moisture gathered between her legs.

Zander rubbed his forehead. "Leora, I expect your loyalty. You will inform me if Lamira puts herself or the young at risk again. Agreed?"

She curtsied. "Yes, my lord."

"Dismissed," he muttered, closing his eyes as if his head pained him.

"Thank you, my lord."

Seke led her by the leash down the main hallway and turned into the private corridor leading to his room. He stopped a few paces down it and turned to her. He released the clip of the leash from her collar and cradled her face with both hands, tipping her head forward to meet his lips—a chaste, fatherly kiss on the forehead.

Veck, she wanted those lips on her mouth, demanding her attention. She remembered the way they'd felt on her sex—oh sweet Mother Earth! She'd never forget the pleasure he'd brought her.

"Well done, Leora." He did not release her head but stared directly into her eyes. "Beautiful female. You have such strength. Awareness. Just a fragile human, yet you are more powerful than most warriors."

A shiver tingled down her spine, as if he'd just issued a benediction.

His eyes dropped to her lips, and the irises turned to a dark amethyst.

Kiss me.

One moment she was sure he would pull away. She watched indecision dance there, and his gaze shutter. And then he slammed her up against the wall, his mouth on hers, stealing her breath, teeth nipping her lips, tongue demanding entry.

She lifted one leg and wrapped it around his waist, and he palmed her ass, still kissing her like they could die tomorrow. Steadying herself with her hands on his shoulders, she picked up the other leg and straddled him, bringing the hard bulge of his cock to her dripping core.

He kissed and sucked down her neck as he rocked his hips and pushed his heavy erection right where she wanted it.

"Seke," she gasped. "I want..." She didn't want to say it. It seemed crass or vulgar. But she also sensed Seke required coaxing.

"I want your cock inside me."

A shudder kicked through Seke, but he pulled away as if in pain. Her feet dropped to the floor to hold her weight.

"Leora, I can't."

"Because the prince said I'm not to be used that way? Surely with my consent—"

"No. I'm sworn to another."

Her breath stopped, choked by the tightness in her throat. Or was it her lungs? She couldn't breathe with the heavy boulder that had landed on her chest, crushing her with its weight.

~.~

Leora looked as if he'd struck her. Her face drained of color, and her mouth opened in shock.

Stars, he wished to absorb the pain he'd caused.

I want your cock inside me.

Had she really said that? *Veck!* Pulling away when she'd uttered those words had nearly killed him. His balls ached, heavy with repressed *vecking* need. But his own discomfort was inconsequential compared to the damage he'd just inflicted on Leora.

He caught her chin. "She's dead," he said quickly, before her shock morphed to anger, and she unleashed a star storm of fury on him. Because he had no doubt it would come. "But she has my vow nonetheless."

Shock eased into something softer—was it sympathy? "You lost a mate in the Finnian takeover. And a child?"

A steel band cinched his throat, barely allowing oxygen to pass. "Three children. An infant boy and two girls, seven and eight solar cycles."

"I'm so sorry," Leora whispered.

He didn't want to tell her—he'd never spoken of it, although Zander had tried, on occasion, to acknowledge the sacrifice he'd made. Yet Seke felt compelled. Leora had to know why he could not take her. A strong and beautiful female like her never should feel rejected or betrayed.

"As Master at Arms, I was sworn to protect the king, the royal bloodline. When the Finn attacked, it was a coordinated hit from all sides of the planet. I was able to extract Zander, but there was no time to find my family. I asked one of my guards to get them out." He couldn't finish it—not the rest. The guilt and sorrow rising up nearly swallowed him.

As if she was willing to take on the pain he'd held at bay for so long, her beautiful green eyes swam with tears. It ripped open the wound he'd thought long closed. Pressure built behind his eyes and nose.

She touched his forearm. "I'm sorry you had to make that choice." Her lips trembled so sweetly.

He was glad she hadn't said he'd made the right choice, or the wrong choice. Hadn't told him he'd done the honorable thing. Or that the survival of his species and, hopefully, one day, recovery of their planet were more important than saving his family. All the things he'd been telling himself for the past twenty solar cycles.

He pushed her back up against the wall and leaned down to rest his forehead against hers. His fingertips brushed down her cheek. "If things were different, Leora..."

She turned away from him and, this time, nothing he could say or do sheltered her from the rejection. She heard it, understood him. And protected her heart.

Veck!

He didn't want her closed off from him. Didn't want to agonize now over how he'd betrayed her, in addition to his family. *Vecking* Zander shouldn't have put him in this position.

But no. He should have played it differently. Should have remained impersonal with his mastery of her. Won her respect with pain and consistency alone. Except he knew that was an impossibility.

He eased back and let her go. When she glanced over her shoulder, waiting for him to lead, he wanted to drop to his knees and weep. How could he have won her allegiance, bonded with her, and yet not keep her?

"Would you like to see Lamira?" His words came out sounding forced, throat still clogged with unchecked grief.

The startled joy on her face worsened the ache in his chest. "Yes, please." Her soft voice held no stiffness or rancor.

He dropped an arm around her waist and guided her in the direction of Zander's chamber. The prince normally worked from his chamber, but he'd been away from it almost constantly since they returned to the pod. Staying away from Lamira, no doubt.

Zander may not approve of this visit, but Leora deserved it, and Lamira probably needed a friend to talk to, as well.

He tapped on the door first, knowing their holograms would be projected into the room to let Lamira know they were there. He doubted she could open the door herself, though, so he pressed his palm to the panel by the door for the scan. As Master at Arms, his handprint worked everywhere in the palatial pod, even on Zander's door.

Lamira flew at her mother the moment the door opened. "Mother," she breathed, wrapping her arms around Leora's neck. When she drew away, she fingered the collar, her eyebrows drawing together.

Something in his solar plexus tightened. He didn't want to see the accusation on Lamira's face when she realized he'd been the one to punish and train Leora.

She turned to him, her face tight. Her beauty struck him even more, now that he'd memorized every line of Leora's perfect bone structure. Lamira's was the same, only she was younger and pregnant, so she radiated vitality, too. Even so, she didn't hold a candle to Leora. *His* Leora.

"What does the obedience training entail?" Her voice came as little more than a whisper, and she worked to swallow as she watched him.

He found he didn't want to answer. Every answer he could think of would degrade Leora. Because he *had* degraded Leora. Still, what happened between them had been behind closed doors. No one else, save Zander, need know. Instinctively, he moved to place a protective hand on her shoulder, as if he might shield her pride.

Lamira's expression softened, though, and he wondered if she'd "read" something with her psychic ability. "Of course you'd take care with my mother," she murmured. "Thank you."

Her acceptance, her thanks, made something uncomfortable slither in his belly. He didn't deserve her gratitude, and yet, the fact she'd offered it felt like forgiveness, of a sort. His throat constricted. Unable to speak, he bowed deeply and stepped backward, out the open door. "I'll come back for you, Leora," he managed to say.

She curtsied. "Thank you, master."

Thankfully, the door swished closed before she saw his surprise. She'd called him *master* easily, without hesitation. And in front of her daughter. Had he truly won her allegiance? Her bond? Her...

No.

Love had nothing to do with this. Or anything else.

˜.˜

Leora looked into her daughter's wide-set green eyes, wondering what she knew.

"He's protective of you," Lamira observed.

A trickle of warmth swirled in her chest. "Yes." He always had been, though. On that first planet rotation when Daneth had brought her to the pod, Seke had defended her against Daneth's probing, soothing her with a form of chivalry she'd believed long dead in their culture.

Of course, the Zandians weren't part of their culture. Their species may live on Ocretia, but they lived by a code far different.

Lamira grabbed her hand and tugged her toward a sitting area with a small hover table for two. "It's not been too horrible, then?"

Her face grew warm. She perched on a hover chair across from Lamira, who pushed a pouch of juice toward her. "Some parts, horrible. Some parts..."

Wonderful.

Did she really think so? Yes. Seke had offered her something she'd never experienced before—such pleasure, such...wonder. With him, she'd discovered the paradox of finding strength within surrender. She'd learned to trust a being other than Lamira, and had her trust rewarded. But more than that—Seke truly *saw* her. He looked into her very being and understood her, perhaps better, even, than she understood herself. And despite all the humiliating and painful things he'd done to her, there had always been an underlying respect and care.

She didn't want her training to be over. Being with Seke had become an addiction. She craved his touch, his attention, his nearness at all times. He occupied her every thought. She wanted more of him.

"He won't have sex with me," she blurted.

Lamira's eyebrows shot up, and she choked on the juice she'd been sucking from a long tube. "Why not?"

"He's been mated. Remember? You told me once you thought he lost a wife and child."

Lamira nodded. "I remember. I had a flash of it when I first met him. An infant."

"It was actually three young. He carries enormous guilt because he saved Zander instead of them."

Her daughter's eyes rounded with the same sympathy she experienced for Seke.

"I believe his sense of honor made him choose his duty to the throne over love."

"Sweet Mother Earth. That's a terrible thing to live with."

"I know."

"No wonder he never smiles. But what does that have to do with having sex with you?"

She frowned. "He told me he was bound to another. He meant his dead mate. It's another honor thing— I don't know. Maybe a Zandian custom. Don't they mate for life?"

Lamira tapped her lips. "Yes, but wouldn't *for life* mean until one of them dies? If she's dead, can't he mate another?"

She shrugged, her chest a hollow locker, empty for Seke. "Apparently not. He seemed sorry about it but told me he couldn't be with me. And I know he wants me." She hadn't expected it to be so easy to talk to her daughter about sex.

A tap sounded on the door and Barr, Zander's amiable chef, entered carrying a tray of fragrant food. "Master Seke told me you two might like to share a meal," the elderly Zandian said with a bow.

They both beamed at him. "Thank you so much, Barr," Lamira said. "That was thoughtful of both of you."

He lifted the lid from the dish to reveal a beautiful savory pie of some sort. "It's egg and vegetables. An ancient recipe from Earth. It's called *quiche*. Should be very nourishing for the young."

Everyone in the palatial pod doted on Lamira as the carrier of Zander's young. Both Daneth and Barr constantly researched human nutrition and sought traditional foods to strengthen her constitution.

Lamira touched his arm. "Thank you. Truly, Barr. It looks and smells delicious. I can't wait to try it."

Skin blushing lavender, Barr bowed several times and backed out the door.

Leora served Lamira a piece of the quiche and took a slice for herself. Even though she'd grown Earth-based produce on the agrifarm, they hadn't had access to the fresh food, relying on tasteless, packaged nutrition packs provided by their masters. Here, everything she ate burst with flavor. The love with which Barr prepared their food, combined with Zander's access to high quality meat and produce, meant they sampled the finest foods available in the galaxy. Eating had become a nearly euphoric experience. She took a bite of the egg dish, trying to dissect the various flavors. A light, flaky crust, rich, creamy middle with some kind of herb to enhance the flavor of the vegetables. A layer of thinly sliced nutmeat covered the top. "Mmm," she said, her eyes rolling back in her head. "So good."

"It's better with company," Lamira said, a note of despondency at her confinement in her voice.

She reached out and squeezed her daughter's hand. "Tell me about Zander. He hasn't forgiven you, has he?"

Lamira set her fork down, and Leora regretting saying anything that stopped her daughter from eating when her body needed the nutrition for the baby. "He won't talk to me. He forbids me to speak when he's in here, and he's never in here anymore. I don't know what to do. I think he truly feels like I would leave him—or would choose my family first over him, but that wasn't it." Lamira's voice had taken on a pleading quality, as if Leora was the one she needed to convince. She wrung her hands, and her eyes grew watery. She dashed at them with one finger. "I'm so emotional anyway with the pregnancy," she explained.

"Of course you are. Maybe you could write him a message. We could have Seke send it, perhaps? Explain you would never leave him, and you'd known it was the only way to get him to engage in the battle to save Lily."

Lamira sighed. "It doesn't sound much better that way. I put my life and his unborn young's life in danger and manipulated him into doing something he didn't want to do. It's no wonder he's hurt and angry."

"Your sister's alive because of what you did," Leora reminded her, the burn of her daughters being strangers to each other still smarting. "She wants to visit us," she blurted.

Lamira brightened a bit. "Does she? When?"

Leora took a bite of quiche to give her a chance to order her emotions around Lily. As she chewed, she sank into Seke's reassurances. "Soon. Seke will arrange it." *When we're no longer being punished.* Lamira didn't need to know that.

～．～

Zander sifted through holograms, looking for any he had not yet viewed or dealt with, but there was nothing new. He had moved his business operations to the meeting room where he normally sat with his council. The chamber was round, like many chambers in the pod, but it extended beyond the main body of the pod, jutting out into space. The half of the room that extended consisted of floor-to-ceiling windows, but the crystal embedded in the skylight provided the bright light.

The Ocretion atmosphere wasn't ideal for his species, which required sunlight, rather than food for energy. The sun was filtered and weak, at best, but his crystals amplified the light, which was why Lamira had been so excited to grow things on his pod.

He looked around at all the flowers, food-bearing plants, and small trees clustered by the windows. She'd brought new life to the pod. His servants and subjects had accepted her—some of them even before he had. They doted on her, especially now that she carried his young.

He stood from the round table—so large for one being. It seemed to mock his intense loneliness. Being near Lamira pained him too much. He paced to the bank of windows and stared down at the polluted planet below, watching airships navigate through the space.

He'd nearly gone mad when Lamira had jumped onto Rok's ship in pursuit of her sister. But he should have remembered how much she loved her mother, and that she'd apply that same love to the sister she'd never met. Would she ever love him that much? Or was she making the best of a situation? He'd bought her as a slave for breeding. After they'd mated, she'd asked for her freedom and he'd refused it, saying she loved to be his slave.

And it was true. The monitoring device Daneth had inserted inside her had scientifically proven she grew excited by his dominance—she loved his mastery. But perhaps he had misunderstood. Perhaps her sexual arousal at being kept subordinate to him wasn't enough.

Clearly, she'd felt she had to flee from him, rather than seek his permission or request his assistance to save her sister.

The door slid open, and Seke entered, his cool gaze assessing. He strolled over and leaned one shoulder against the windows, looking down with a casualness Zander knew better than to trust.

"What is the root of your trouble with Lamira?"

He had to flex his fingers, which curled automatically into fists any time another male spoke of his mate. "I don't want to have this conversation with you."

"What fear is behind it?"

He ground his teeth. *Vecking* Seke and his *vecking* lessons.

Losing Lamira.

Losing Lamira forever was his *vecking* fear.

"How do you master fear?"

Lean into it. Own it so it can't own you. He knew well his lessons with Seke.

"*Veck* off, Seke." He purposely didn't call him Master Seke. Though he was a mentor, a teacher, and a father figure, he was also Zander's servant. "What were you so afraid of when you nearly knocked my head off in the studio?"

There. He'd flip it back on Seke and see how he likes a taste of his own teaching.

"My desire." Seke's voice sounded thick, and Zander jerked his head up in surprise, not expecting the older male to answer. They stared at one another, the accusation behind Seke's gaze tarnishing the shine Zander had been polishing on his question.

He had to admit, he'd known Leora's punishment would torture his mentor. Seke considered himself bound to his dead mate by an antiquated code of honor, which Zander thought unnecessary, especially considering the near extinction of their species.

He'd also noted Seke's interest in Leora, and knew the male would never allow another to punish her. But if he was completely honest, He supposed part of him wanted someone else's suffering to match his own. Wanted someone to understand how difficult it was to love a human female.

Both their arm cuffs blinked with incoming messages from the death pod. Grateful for the distraction, Zander launched the hologram.

Lundric, his head of security, appeared, his torso hovering over the round table, face grim and splattered with blood that appeared too red to be Zandian.

Another incoming message light blinked on their cuffs.

"What is it?" Seke asked sharply.

"I killed one of the humans." Lundric's face was flushed, with emotion dancing behind the expression, which was unusual for him. Guilt and anger simmered there, projected from the shimmering image.

"What happened?" *Veck.* He didn't really need more human drama at the moment.

Lundric swiped a large hand across his cheek as if just now sensing the blood there. "He forced himself on C—one of the females. I ended it."

Seke raised his eyebrows. "By killing him?"

Lundric's nostrils flared. "Their necks break easily."

Zander almost wanted to laugh. Everywhere he looked, human females had turned Zandian warriors into beasts, himself no exception.

"And the female?"

"Cambry. I want her."

"Excuse me?"

Lundric cleared his throat, looking as if it took great effort to rein in the wild beast he'd become. "May I take a female slave, as you both have done?"

They both stared at him.

As if he'd just realized his lack of manners, he added, "Please, my lord?"

Seke lifted his chin to catch Zander's eye, and Zander knew, after years of learning to rule as he went along, this meant Seke had something to advise him about the matter.

"You are not in a position to beg any favors of me, Lundric." He made his voice flinty. "We need the strongest allegiance possible from these humans or they'll never serve as an army for us. Right now, you'd better be thinking about how to control the damage you've done to Zandian-human relations on that pod."

Shame crept over Lundric's face. He bowed. "Yes, my lord."

Zander moved to end the hologram transmission, but Lundric stubbornly persisted. "What about the female? What about Cambry?"

"I've granted you nothing. If you want the human female, cultivate a bond."

Lundric paled, but the crazed emotion drained from his face, and his features hardened into determination. He nodded, once. "Thank you, my lord."

The moment the hologram disappeared, Seke held out a staying hand. "Do not answer that next communication. It is from Rok."

Zander waited.

Seke paced around the table. "You cannot promote Zandia as the promised land to the humans—and I know it was Lily and Rok who built that story, but what's done is done."

When they'd rescued Lamira's sister, Lily, from an Ocretion death pod, she'd come as a package deal with two hundred other humans sentenced to death. She and Rok rallied them to join the fight to recover Zandia, promising them all freedom there.

Seke went on, "You cannot promise them freedom and at the same time keep slaves in this pod. Rok is already questioning the nature of your union with Lamira. If word got out on the death pod that your mate is your slave..."

Zander pursed his lips. He'd already considered the possibility of the humans on the death pod refusing to fight for Zandia. But they had no choice.

Zander had rescued them from an Ocretion death sentence. They had no resources, nowhere to go. They were, in essence, at his mercy. If he wished to call them slaves, he could. But it was better to have them fight for Zandia willingly.

"Lily wants to visit her mother and sister. She may be shocked by what she finds here."

An itchy feeling crept over him.

"Zandians have never kept slaves," Seke said flatly.

"That was exactly what I argued when you—yes *you*—promoted Daneth's plan to purchase Lamira for breeding."

"Just because you acquired her as a slave does not mean she must remain one."

A deadly anger settled over him. He wanted to throat-punch Seke for talking about his mate, for mentioning the very issue that had been gnawing at him ever since Lamira left. He couldn't keep her prisoner, and yet he didn't want to let her go. He picked up one of Lamira's potted plants—a raspberry bush, he believed she called it—and hurled it across the room.

The moment it shattered, he felt ill. He'd just destroyed a living, beautiful thing. Much like he'd destroyed his relationship with Lamira.

CHAPTER FIVE

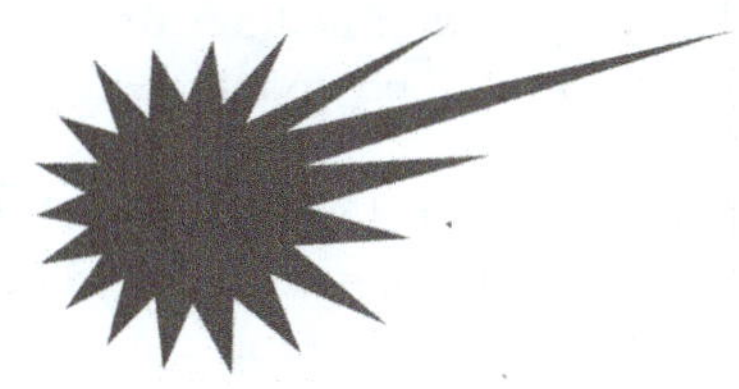

Seke walked back to Zander's chamber to retrieve his human, starved to see her beautiful face, smell the light citrus scent of her hair, touch her soft skin. He wouldn't make her strip for him—not anymore. For one, he couldn't take it. His rock hard balls were probably going to explode if he had to suffer any more unfulfilled lust.

For another, she didn't require it. She'd proven her submission, had paid penance for her crime. He wanted to return her dignity to her.

But even as he had the thought, pictures flitted through his depraved mind. The image of her naked on her knees at his feet. The way she'd looked strung up by her wrists with her legs spread for her pussy whipping, the sight of her upended over his lap, her golden skin turning pink under the slap of his hand.

He'd known he would find training and punishing her arousing. *Veck,* just being in the same room as the female had his cock thickening. But the incredible satisfaction he'd taken in mastering her, in winning her submission and seeing her subjugated had surprised him. If it hadn't been arousing for her, too, he would think himself disturbed. But she couldn't hide her physical reactions to him. Those had been honest and as charged as his own.

He tapped on the door then pressed his palm to the screen to open it.

Leora stood from the little table where the two sat—more radiant than any of the spectacular flowers they grew in their pots. She curtsied prettily, a slight tinge of pink rising on her cheeks.

Veck, seeing that blush on her produced the same sense of masculine power dominating her had. As if his greatest achievement as a warrior had been conquering Leora. No, not conquering. Winning.

But he couldn't keep her. *Veck*—it would kill him to release her from his care. In just two short planet rotations, she'd become his entire universe. He'd become obsessed with thoughts of burying his cock balls deep inside her tight channel. She'd squeeze those internal muscles, milking his malehood until he erupted, pounding her harder than he should, reminding her of his mastery.

Leora.

"Seke, thank you," Lamira said, gliding over to him and standing on her tiptoes to plant a kiss on his cheek. "Take good care of my mother," she murmured, squeezing his arm.

"I will," he promised, although half his heart crumbled and fell away at the words. The half that had already returned her to her chamber, dismissed her from his training. The other half stood up tall and gripped his sword, ready to kill or die for her.

He wrapped an arm around Leora's waist and guided her back to his chamber, without daring to look down at her face. Afraid he might stop and throw her up against the corridor wall again, and push his cock into that notch between her thighs.

Veck him, the moment they entered his chamber, she pulled off her robes.

"No," he barked, bringing her head snapping up, eyes locked on his.

Veck, she was waiting for instruction, proof their bond was solid. He worked to swallow but couldn't. "Keep them on. Please. I don't have the willpower to look at that sweet little body and not lose all control."

She held his eyes and resumed stripping, slowly this time, the robes falling at her feet in a meringue of soft white material.

"I said, *no.*" He tried to make his voice sharp, but instead it came out thick, choked. Because he'd already received an eyeful of naked Leora.

Small, leggy, beautiful. Her breasts jiggled, dancing as she walked to him, the sway of her hips pure, purposeful temptation.

"I told you, I *can't,*" he rasped, sounding as pained as he felt. He clenched his fists to keep from touching her, nails digging into his palms.

"Seke," she murmured, grazing his chest with her fingertips. "My master." Her eyelids drooped to half-mast, making his cock surge powerfully, horns stiff and tilted toward her.

"*No.*"

"Seke, I understand you are honor bound. I admire and respect your dedication." Her fingertips touched his arm, not sexually this time, but it had the same result, sending a zing of electricity through his body. "I just wonder…if you could honor *yourself* as much as you honor others?"

His brows slammed together, the breath knocked out of him. Where was his infamous self-control? The discipline he taught his pupils? All of it fled when faced with a naked Leora, entreaty in her posture, love in her expression.

Love?

A shock of something ran through him, raising his skin into gooseflesh. What made him think Leora loved him?

But, yes, it was there, shining from her face, radiating from her heart. He literally felt it flowing from her to him.

And the last time he'd felt that from a female had been...

With massive effort, he turned from Leora, forcing himself to move his feet toward the door before he did something he'd regret.

"Seke, please." She followed on his heels. "You're worthy of so much more than you allow yourself. You deserve satisfaction."

Pain lit behind his eyes. He didn't deserve anything. He'd left his mate and children to die—had not managed to protect his own family when disaster struck. How could he ever believe he deserved anything but the agony that had become a living beast in his heart?

"Please don't go." She wrapped her arms around his waist from behind—as if to catch him, but without the strength to hold him.

He started to shake her off, but then somehow he turned, picking her up by the armpits and pushing her against the wall behind him.

He crushed his mouth over hers, sweeping his tongue between her lips, giving her all of him—teeth and lips and tongue. *Vecking* her mouth in the same rhythm he shoved the bulge of his cock against the heat between her legs.

She wrapped her legs around his waist, inviting him ever closer to her sweet, bare sex.

His vision tunneled, muscles and movements quick and fluid, as if in the middle of a fight. He lost all capacity for speech, plunged too deep into the inevitability of *vecking* Leora. He shoved his leggings down and fisted his cock, guiding it to her slick entrance.

She wouldn't get gentle. Even if he'd wanted to be careful with her, he couldn't have held back. Not after waiting so long, after so many uninterrupted hours of purple balls. One quick thrust, and he was inside her.

She screamed, but the sound reached him as if from a distance, like he was underwater.

His head dropped back and eyes closed at the launch of lust rocketing through his body from being sheathed in her tight heat. His hips snapped, cock plunged deeper, higher, shoving her body farther up the wall with each thrusting slam.

She'd gone soft and pliant, her pussy squeezing and welcoming, the heels hooked behind his back drawing him in, even though he had to be leaving bruises on her spine and the back of her pelvis from the wall.

He *vecked* her, and her breasts bounced, sweet breath panted. Her lips parted in surprised pleasure. He wouldn't last long. It was like he was fourteen solar cycles again, fisting his cock for the first time and learning how it worked. His thighs flexed; blood rushed in his ears. Stars exploded behind his eyes, and he roared between clenched teeth as he came, filling his female with ribbons of hot cum while she tightened and squeezed around him, riding his cock to her own finish.

He palmed her ass and pulled her in tight, helping her lift and lower on his length until her internal muscles squeezed in spasms of release.

And it wasn't nearly enough.

Not after nearly twenty solar cycles without sex. Not with Leora, the human who'd forced him, unwillingly, into this act.

He dropped her to her feet and ripped off his tunic.

⁓·⁓

Leora stared at Seke, hard muscles rippling as he tore off his clothing. A twisted study of anger and lust, his glassy eyes held both hunger and satisfaction, promise and punishment.

She barely managed to stand, her legs rubbery and weak, body buzzing from his claiming. The heat of his large hands still lingered on her tingling flesh. Her thighs and back ached, her more intimate parts throbbed. Yet she triumphed, gloried, in seeing her controlled master finally undone.

She'd done that to him. Seeing her effect on him—the way he'd lost control despite his vow and honor—thrilled her.

He lifted her by the armpits once more and stalked to the sleepdisk, where he tossed her onto the middle of the bed. He hadn't spoken a word since she'd stopped him from leaving and still didn't speak. Far from dissipating, it appeared his passion had only grown. His cock still jutted out, thick and stiff —so much larger than a human cock. Just the sight of it made her pussy throb at the memory of being parted and pounded.

A dark need brewed like a storm, just below the surface. He climbed over her, pinning her wrists above her head with one hand and guiding his cock between her legs with the other.

Despite how soon it came after the last coupling, her body welcomed him, shuddering with pleasure at the way he filled her so completely, the head of his cock bumping her interior walls even deeper. He arced in and out, no less rough in this position.

"Is this what you wanted from me?" he growled, anger flashing in his deep-amethyst eyes. "You wanted to see what's underneath the control? What I've been holding back from you?"

"Yes," she gasped, her body lifting with each hard shove.

He *vecked* her hard, punishing her with each stroke, making it painful and too rough.

She'd pushed him too far. He hated himself and her for his broken vow. Though it was the hardest thing she'd ever done, she absorbed his anger. With her body loose and accepting, she opened to receive everything he had to give her—his pent-up frustration, his fury, his need.

When he plowed in deep and came a second time, she burst into tears.

Seke froze, and his eyes flew open. Horror scrawled across his face, and he pulled out of her, rearing back on his knees. "Oh *veck. Veck...* Did I hurt you?" He scooped her into his arms and crossed the chamber in two strides, heading for the door. "What have I done?"

He opened the door as if he intended to carry her out, both of them stark naked. She threw her arm out to catch the doorframe. "No. Stop. Where are you going?"

"To Daneth."

"Stop. I'm not hurt. Close the door." She wriggled in his arms, and he seemed to come back to his senses, realizing their state of undress.

He shut the door. Misery blared from his eyes. "What is it then?"

She dashed at her tears. "Nothing. It's nothing."

He gripped her shoulders and shook her, a male clearly at the edge of his sanity. "Don't tell me nothing. What have I done to you? Speak the truth, Leora."

"You're frightening me," she whispered.

He set her down, slowly composing his face. "You're not hurt?"

She shook her head. "A little bruised. A little sore. But, no, not hurt."

In a flash of relief, he yanked her into his arms, cradling her head against his massive chest with one huge palm, his other arm snaked around her back to her hip. His face dropped into her hair. "I didn't mean to hurt you. Or scare you." The rise and fall of his chest was uneven, his breath erratic. He shifted to cup her face with both hands. "But I am angry with you."

She drew a sharp breath. His anger was what had made her cry—even though she wouldn't change a thing if she had it to do over. She wasn't sorry. Seke deserved to seek pleasure, and she wanted to give it to him.

With a hard swallow, she lifted her wet lashes and met his azure stare. "So punish me."

It was his turn for an intake of breath. His irises changed to violet, horns thickened. It was hard to imagine after two orgasms he might be aroused again, but the evidence was irrefutable.

With a swift, sure movement, he looped an arm around her waist and carried her to the sleepdisk where he arranged her facedown over his lap. Without preamble, he started to spank her, fast and hard. He'd recovered his normal control, because there was precision to the assault. He struck one cheek, then the other, then right in the middle, over her sex, over and over again.

She worked hard to submit, despite her body's intense desire to fly off his lap and find someplace to hide. Her breath jackknifed in her throat, caught there, straining, as if it might somehow buffer the explosion of pain Seke inflicted. She now knew he'd held back before—the other times he'd spanked her with his hand.

His free hand tangled in her hair, not pulling but holding her head still while her bottom bounced and jerked on his lap. To keep her hands from flying back and covering, she clawed at the coverlet, wrapping the silk fabric in her fists.

"You're not breathing, Leora." Ever the teacher, her Seke. "Is this more than you can take? You asked for this, didn't you?"

Fresh tears smarted her eyes. "Yes, master."

He stopped abruptly, and the sound he made almost reminded her of a sob.

"Leora," he rasped, the word like an entreaty. "*Veck*, Leora."

But the spanking began anew, this time with additional swats on the backs of her thighs.

"You knew I did not want to break my vow." He kept slapping her bottom, so very hard.

She squirmed and panted, tears wetting her lashes.

"You knew I had been struggling to withhold my desire for you. This is not what I wanted." He continued to spank her with steady hard slaps.

"I'm not sorry!" she cried out, wincing at the way her hair pulled when she tried to move her head.

Seke's breath drew in with a quick stutter and, mercifully, he paused, resting his hot palm on her even hotter flesh. He rubbed it up and down, stroking down the backs of her legs and up to her bottom, first on one side then the other.

"You're not sorry," he muttered, sounding bitter. "But I am. Does that count for anything, Leora?"

"Yes," she whispered. And then the words "I'm sorry," rose to her lips, even though she'd just sworn them untrue. She tried, "Forgive me," instead. A better sentiment.

Seke's lips pressed against her shoulder blade, but he didn't speak. Didn't say whether he forgave her or not. "Facedown. On the middle of the sleep-disk." The command sounded both soft and gruff.

For more punishment? Or sex? Though her body already pulsed with pain, and her pussy ached, she'd willingly offer her body for whatever he needed to give her. Because she needed it, too. Anything to bring them back into balance —whatever he saw fit.

She crawled up onto the sleepdisk and arranged herself in the middle, on her belly.

"Spread your legs."

She slid her thighs apart, her pussy pulsing in rhythm with the throb of her ass.

Seke climbed over her, hooked both his thumbs at the apex of her thighs, and parted her. She glanced over her shoulder to see him doing nothing more than staring at the vulnerable pink heart of her sex, still wet with his rainbow-colored seed. He moved his thumbs lightly in the slightest caress against her bottom.

"Beautiful girl." His voice sounded gravelly. "Your pussy was made for me, wasn't it?"

She'd loved Johan very much, but yes—in this moment, it seemed her pussy, her body—*veck*, her entire soul—had been made entirely for Seke. "Yes."

Satisfaction flared in the gleam in his eyes, the surge of intent behind his movement evident as he climbed over her, cock stiff for her once more.

He entered easily this time; she'd been made ready by the spanking and their previous coupling. With his weight braced on his hands beside her head, he rocked into her.

She moaned, renewed pleasure spearing through her. He eased in and out, far more gentle this time. She lifted her ass to meet his thrusts, to take him deeper and bring the angle of his cock against the most sensitive part of her inner walls. Her core quaked, tightening around his cock.

"Stars, Leora, the way you squeeze my cock like a tight little glove..."

He shifted to one hand and used the other to pin her down at the nape, imprisoning her for his assault.

As always, his show of dominance made her go limp with submission, wet with arousal. His cock slid in and out gently, lovingly stroking her insides, turning the fire to molten lava.

"I should *veck* you all night as punishment," he growled, but his tempo had increased, breath sounded strangled. He needed to come as badly as she did. "Do you like to see me lose control, little slave? Does it give you power to know I broke a life vow for this?" He slammed in deeper, harder. "Just for this?"

Yes.

It did give her power, but the bitterness and anger in his voice diminished the glow.

"Forgive me," she gasped again.

Again, he didn't answer, except by *vecking* her so deep and hard it seemed he'd split her in two.

The hand at her nape slid around the front of her throat, cradling her neck. Without squeezing or cutting off her breath, he lifted, forcing her upper back into an arch and reminding her how easily he could end her life with just one squeeze or twist of his hand. It produced only excitement—she trusted Seke with her welfare. He wouldn't allow harm to come to her.

"So. *Vecking*. Beautiful." Seke growled the words on each violent thrust then buried himself deep and came a third time.

She mewled and flexed her toes, thighs thrusting out straight beneath him, pussy clamping down in spasms of pleasure. She lost track of time as the room spun and dipped and her body went languid and limp.

Distantly, she registered Seke pulling out of her, dropping beside her on the sleepdisk. His heavy arm curled around her waist and pulled her up onto her side, her back against his front.

His body trembled as much as hers as he held her.

He hadn't forgiven her, but he still took care with her.

Always.

～·～

Because he knew he'd never sleep—perhaps never again—he didn't let his little human sleep, either.

He shouldn't have punished her. It certainly wasn't her fault he'd broken his vow.

She'd never asked to be brought into his chamber, stripped, and given intimate punishments that drove them both mad with desire. Just because she'd wanted satisfaction as badly as he, didn't make her the culprit.

"Tell me about your other masters," he said. He'd voice-commanded the lights off, so they lay in darkness, her small body nested into his larger one, her scent filling him, surrounding him. He didn't want to admit how *right* it felt to hold her. Post-coitally.

He didn't even want to think about the implications of his actions. Couldn't think of them. How would he face himself the following planet rotation, knowing he'd sacrificed all his honor for a rough *veck* with a human female?

A *veck* that had been out of this galaxy. Better than any he'd had with Becka, his one true mate. Why was that?

He didn't want to think about that, either.

So he questioned his little slave, who had stiffened.

"What do you mean?"

"Daneth found you on an agrifarm. Who was your master there?"

"We didn't have one master. There were guards and directors. We were lucky because they mostly left us alone if we did our work."

"And if you didn't?" He didn't know why he needed to know all this. It was like picking a scab—a morbid fascination with what hurt him most—the idea of some other being in charge of his little human.

"Mostly they used shock-sticks for punishments. Occasionally there was flogging, usually on the bare back." Her voice took on a hollow, empty quality that made him want to take back his questions.

"I'm sorry." He stroked a hand down her arm. "What I really want to know..." His sword hand itched. "Give me names—anyone who hurt you. *Ever.* I will avenge you."

She gave a short bark of surprised laughter and turned in his arms. Her human eyes didn't see in the dark as well as his, and she searched for his face with her hand. Her fingertips found his cheek, and she traced the line of his jaw. "The return of my daughter was all I ever longed for."

"You will see her soon." He covered her hand with his, pressing her smooth palm against his cheek. "I'm sorry to have kept her from you, even for a few planet rotations."

Pain flitted across her face, and regret washed over him.

"What if she...doesn't like us?"

He pulled her fingers toward his mouth and kissed them. "How could she not like you? You're her mother, who never stopped longing for her."

"She's so different from us. What if she resents that her life was worse than ours? What if she blames me for not protecting her?"

He pulled her hand to his heart. How he wished he'd let them reunite when Rok had asked. That these worries had remained, even a few extra planet rotations, slayed him. "Stop. You cannot think that. She didn't want to come immediately because her place is with Rok. That doesn't mean she harbors ill will toward you." Leora nodded and snuggled in against his chest. The action touched him. His fragile little human—so trusting, despite his rough treatment.

He pulled her tight against him and buried his face in her hair.

"Do you forgive me, Seke?"

Something lurched and caught in his solar plexus. The tangled bundle of guilt he'd been trying to keep at bay. "You, yes. It's myself I can't forgive."

CHAPTER SIX

Seke dragged his body from the sleepdisk. He'd never felt so heavy in his life. Grief over breaking his vow to Becka brought back the guilt of her death, as strongly as if it had just happened.

He wasn't sure if the fact that *vecking* Leora had been the most satisfying experience of his life made it better or worse.

Worse. Because knowing that having her had been better than Becka— more satisfying on every level—not just the physical one—only increased his guilt.

Worse—because he didn't know how to keep it from happening again. How to get her out of his mind and heart. How to save himself from the crushing shame.

It was early—still dark on Ocretia—but Zandians didn't require as much sleep as humans. He stepped into the washtube to clean up then dressed and left the chamber. Stars knew if he stayed, he'd be waking Leora up to round four. Just sleeping next to her had been torture, even with the many orgasms he'd had.

Somehow she both satisfied him and left him craving more. He'd hoped giving in this one time would get her out of his system, but it seemed that was impossible. He needed her again. In every position. All *vecking* planet rotation.

He found Zander in the Great Hall, pacing along the long table. Though the prince did not turn, he knew Zander had heard him enter.

"Free Leora." Zander's voice sounded scratchy. "She is no longer a slave. She and Lamira may come and go as they please."

In actuality, that was impossible. As humans, they couldn't go free anywhere in Ocretia without being seized. If picked up without a master, they'd certainly be sent to a death pod of their own. Lamira and Leora were stuck with their Zandian masters, whether they called them master or not. But it was the principle that mattered. Zander had seen what Seke had hoped he would see—freedom had to be offered.

"I will tell her, my lord. It is the right decision."

Zander turned and, in the pale light of the Ocretion moons shining through the windows, he appeared blanched with apprehension. "I cannot allow Lamira to take the young, though." His voice sounded choked.

Seke's brows drew together. Did Zander really think Lamira would leave? His beautiful human mate loved him as deeply as he loved her. Not to mention she had no other place to go besides the hijacked death pod.

"She will not leave you, Zander. Is that your fear?"

Zander drew in a long breath. "Yes. But I'm mastering it."

"Good." He left the struggling prince to his thoughts, before his own yanked him under.

Leora, free.

Out of his chamber. Out of his life.

Yes, this was for the best. Why, then, did his chest feel like it would explode? He walked swiftly toward the battle arts studio. He needed to move his body, free his mind. He stepped into the quiet studio and lit a flame behind a Zandian crystal, sending the flicker and glow of amber crystal-amplified light through the room. Pressing his palms together at his forehead, he drew his unruly thoughts into the center of his head and contained them.

Blessed quiet expanded out, matching the silence of the room. He rotated slowly, stretching his toes to grip the floor, grounding him. With a sudden, percussive movement, he drew his palms apart and lunged to the side, one palm flexed.

In a silent solo dance, he continued, moving energy through his body and out into space, aligning his body with his mind and spirit. His muscles relished the familiar movement, especially after the tension they'd been carrying since...no. He called his thoughts back to the center of his head.

No thought. Especially not about her.

Rotating slowly, he jabbed and kicked, breathed and aligned. He stayed for hours, not wanting it to end. Not wanting to think.

But Ocretion sunlight filled the studio, and sounds of full activity in the pod came through the walls.

As he ended his practice, he expected clarity of mind. A clear, easy decision. But he hadn't been able to clear his mind of the presence, the essence of Leora. She filled his senses, even when she wasn't there.

He shook his head, as if the movement might dislodge her from his brain. He was a warrior. Master of arms. He upheld the code of honor Zandian warriors had followed for thousands of solar cycles. When he made a vow, he kept it.

Breaking his vow to Becka's memory had shown a weakness in his psyche

—one he now had the opportunity to correct. With a little space from Leora —some distance, he'd be able to master his weakness.

When he gave Leora her freedom, he'd be free of the constant torment of being near her. He could go to the death pod to train the human troops and not have to suffer seeing her in the corridors or wondering what she was doing.

Resolved, he squared his shoulders and marched back to his chamber.

~.~

Lamira lay curled on the sleepdisk, watching an entertainment hologram. Zander had given her a communication device as a gift after they mated and loaded it with things he thought she'd find interesting—particularly, ancient movies and books from Earth. He'd been delighted when she asked for all the Zandian media he could provide, as well. She wanted to understand the planet and species she'd joined.

The door to their chamber whooshed open, and Zander entered, his muscled warrior's body graceful for someone so large. For the first time since they'd returned to the palatial pod, he gazed directly at her.

Her heart stuttered. She knew that look, and she didn't like it. His eyes were shadowed with grief; the set of his mouth said he was deeply troubled. The last time she'd seen that face had been when he'd moved her out of his chamber, believing she was a danger to him because she'd refused to tell him how she knew his life would be in danger.

She scrambled off the sleepdisk and stood, one hand dropping protectively to her thickened belly. "Zander?"

"Lamira." His voice sounded heavy. Defeated, even.

A tap sounded on the door, and Zander hit the panel to open it, as if expecting visitors. Several pod workers came in carrying tools.

Zander pointed toward the cage he sometimes used to keep her, which hovered a few inches from the ceiling. "Dismantle it and place it in storage."

Panic flapped in her chest.

He was getting rid of her. Setting her aside again.

She skittered to Zander's side and touched his arm. "Zander? What's going on?"

He turned to her and spoke stiffly. "You are no longer my slave. After the birth of my young, you are free to go."

His words struck her, worse than any shock-stick. They nearly knocked her to the floor. She felt the blood drain from her face but managed to raise her hand and slap Zander as hard as she could.

Surprise sprang to his features. Confusion.

If she'd hoped to goad him into his usual domination—force him to grab her wrists or pick her up, or somehow claim her as he often did, the slap failed on every level.

It didn't even make her feel better.

How dare he treat her like nothing more than the breeder he'd purchased?

He'd *vecking mated* her. She wore his crystals on her body. She shared his sleepdisk, carried his young.

She'd thought he loved her.

She sure as hell loved him.

Tears blinded her vision, but she whirled before giving Zander the satisfaction of seeing how he'd wounded her. Dodging one of the workers, she ran out of the chamber and down the hall.

~.~

Leora stretched her body, sliding her legs out over the silky bedding. She'd slept longer than normal, exhausted from Seke's rough and wonderful treatment the night before. She tested her body, slightly disappointed to find she didn't feel the soreness anymore, though her skin heated just remembering all the ways he'd had her.

Ooh, yes—a sore spot on the back of her pelvis from the *vecking* against the wall. She smiled, remembering the intense satisfaction of finally consummating their mutual lust. She wanted him to take her again—had hoped he would that morning, but she'd woken alone.

She wanted to learn to please him in every way imaginable. To drive him to distraction. To suck his thick purple cock hard enough to make him bellow.

The door slid open, and Seke entered. His gaze fell on her, lying on the bed, still naked, save for the collar and cuffs. His eyes darkened as the door closed behind him.

Her nipples pearled up when his heated gaze raked across her body.

He walked to the side of the sleepdisk, but instead of climbing on, he held out his hand. She placed her smaller hand in his and allowed him to help her off and bring her to stand before him.

"Leora." He spoke with reverence, as if this might be a ceremony, of sorts. Reaching behind her, he lifted her hair and unclasped the collar about her throat.

Her belly fluttered with anticipation. Like a fool, she thought he might replace it with something more meaningful, some symbol of his affection, which was evident in the warmth of his gaze, the gentleness of his touch.

He picked up one of her hands, rotated the wrist up and removed the cuff then repeated the action with the other. He lowered her wrist with the same reverential movement then picked up her white robes from the shelf nearby and swung them around her shoulders, fastening the clasp at her throat.

Were they going somewhere? A mating ceremony, perhaps?

Cradling her face in his large hands, he tipped her head forward and kissed the top of it. "Leora, the prince has declared you free. You no longer serve me, except as Master at Arms to your host."

She waited. There had to be more.

He inclined his head in a small bow. "You may return to your own chamber."

That was it? That was all? Wait...*what?*

"You are dismissed."

Dismissed? What the *veck?*

Pride made her smooth the confusion from her face. She dipped into a curtsy and somehow made it out of his chamber on wobbly legs, heart rapping against the inside of her ribcage like knuckles on a door.

She held her head high and walked away, down the corridor, blind to the beings she passed. Thoughts broke apart and came together in different arrangements, like pieces of a puzzle, but none fit.

What had just happened? Was Seke saying good-bye?

Really? After what they'd shared?

Surely not.

And yet, no other answer seemed to fit. She found her way to her chamber, which she hadn't been in for four planet rotations. The once-familiar room seemed so different now.

No, *she* was different.

Seke had changed her.

And...left her? *Vecking* left her? After what they'd been through? The things he'd done to her?

A great trembling started in her core and moved through her body. Like an earthquake, splitting her open, sending cracks and fissures in all directions. She pulled her robes around her more tightly and clamped her teeth together to keep them from chattering.

This couldn't be.

She felt like a *vecking* fool. An idiotic, *vecking* fool.

Falling on the bed, she opened her mouth to wail, but no sound came out. No tears, nothing.

She was broken beyond repair.

CHAPTER SEVEN

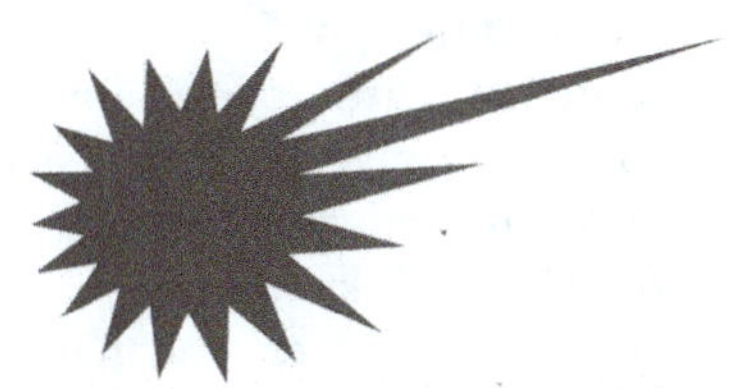

Lamira marched straight to the loading dock and onto one of Zander's airships, which seemed to be in preparation for flight. She marched past the workers and guards, plopped down in a seat in the cockpit, and strapped herself in. Wherever the *vecking* ship was headed, she was going, too. So long as it was away from Zander.

Seke stepped on, stooping to fit his huge body through the frame of the door. He paused when he saw her, then continued, seating himself in the pilot's seat. He spoke in a low voice into the communication device on his cuff. "Are you aware your mate is buckled into my airship?"

She heard Zander swear then nothing more.

Seke didn't turn to look at her, focusing on activating all the screens and controls on his ship for the flight.

A few moments later, Zander stormed onto the ship, followed closely by Daneth, his physician.

Her mate had never looked more crazed. She'd seen him angry, and she'd seen him troubled. Usually, he held himself with great reserve, but the way he dashed onto the ship, eyes wide and barely focusing was entirely new. "What are you doing?"

She folded her arms over her chest. "I'm leaving. Getting *away* from you."

"I cannot allow that," Daneth spoke up immediately. The doctor's main focus was about monitoring her and the young's health.

"Shut up," Zander barked at Daneth. He stomped over to her and unfastened her harness. "You're not going anywhere."

"Oh, really?" She surged to her feet, hands on her hips. "I thought you just gave me my freedom? Or was that all excrement?"

Zander's muscled chest moved with heavy breaths, and he slammed his palm against the ship wall, rattling the entire panel. "Where are you going?" he bellowed.

Obviously, his brain had short-circuited, because she'd already told him that. She had to admit, seeing him so distressed brought a small measure of satisfaction.

"Did you think you could just breed me and set me aside?" she demanded. "Did you think I'd give you your young and just sail happily away? You're a *vecking* idiot, if that's what you thought!" Her voice had risen to near hysterics, and Daneth stepped forward, waving his palms as if to calm her down.

"She's showing signs of severe stress."

"You don't *vecking* say?" Zander snapped.

Seke had stood and joined the little party, and the three males had her surrounded, but she noted they all gave her ample space. Apart from Zander unbuckling her harness, no one had moved closer or touched her.

"I take it you set her free?" Only Seke's manner remained unruffled.

Zander didn't take his eyes from her, and he seemed to be trying to communicate something, but she didn't know what. "Yes." Zander swiped a hand across his face. "I attempted to master my fear." He still stared at her, looking half-mad. "I don't think it worked."

"Something was lost in the communication." Again, Seke's voice was calm, the words slightly dry. He circled behind Zander and nudged Daneth. "We'll leave you two to discuss things in private."

Daneth looked back at her then down at his cuff where the readouts of her vital statistics were displayed. "Calm her down," he warned Zander as he left.

She turned her back on Zander, walking to face the cockpit, though the view was of nothing other than the hangar door.

"Lamira, you are my mate."

She sniffed at the word *mate*, since he hadn't treated her anywhere close to a mate for the past five planet rotations.

"It wasn't right for me to keep you as a slave at the same time I called you mate."

She whirled on him, eyes narrowed. "You said you did so because I..." She choked on her words. *Because I love your domination.*

The chasm between them seemed too wide. She couldn't bring herself to mention their intimate play of master and slave—the punishment and commands that brought her to her knees in ecstasy.

"I justified it that way." His voice was heavy. "But the truth..." He stepped closer but didn't touch her. "The truth is I was afraid to let you go."

She whirled and smacked his chest with her open hand. "Go where? Where in the galaxy could I go? Humans don't roam about on their own in this territory, or hadn't you noticed?"

He made an impatient gesture. "You left with Rok. You're connected with the underground human resistance. You could find places to hide just as your sister did."

"My sister almost *died* because she was found! And I didn't *leave with Rok*—I was goading you into action. Or did you really think I didn't want you to follow?"

He blinked several times. "I *hoped* you wanted me to follow."

"Stupid male! How can you think I could live without you?" She choked on the last words, and the tears she'd held at bay through anger suddenly sprang to her eyes.

Finally, he reached for her. In a flash, he had her crushed against his chest, strong arms wrapping her up tightly. "How could you think I'd ever want you to go?" He sounded choked, as well.

"I'm sorry I left. I shouldn't have put our young in danger like that."

He shoved her away from his body and gave her a tiny shake. "You shouldn't have put *yourself* in danger like that."

She gave a hiccuppy laugh. "I knew you wouldn't let anything happen to me."

He closed his eyes and shook his head. Then his eyes flew open. "Come here." He scooped her up into his arms and carried her off the ship.

Seke and Daneth stood at the loading dock, waiting.

"You're clear for departure," Zander said to Seke as he carried her past them.

"Lamira, let me try again." He walked down the corridor to their chamber. The door slid open, and he carried her inside. "You are my one true mate. I don't ever want you to feel trapped here. Or with me. I would never keep you here against your will. You're free, in my eyes, even if the rest of the galaxy won't recognize it."

Eyes moist, she clung to his neck and buried her face there. "Thank you," she choked. "I love you, Zander."

He sat down on the edge of the sleepdisk and eased her to stand on the floor in front of him. When his fingers began to pull up her skirt, she flushed with the knowledge of his intent.

If it was to make love, she'd be on her back on the mattress. This was punishment. And she couldn't wait. She'd been dying for Zander to punish her and clear the air between them. It always reset them and, as Daneth's monitoring probes had proven when she first arrived, aroused her. Zander had cleared spanking with his hand or a flexible strap with Daneth as safe during pregnancy.

"And despite what I just said"—he pulled her across his lap so her torso rested on the bed, using a pillow to lift her chest so her growing belly wasn't constricted—"I forbid you to ever leave me." His thumbs hooked in the sides of her panties, he tugged them down to her thighs. His hand clapped down on her upturned ass with a resounding crack.

She wiggled, her satisfaction their game had begun warring with the initial shock of pain. She knew from experience it would wear off as soon as the blood rushed to the area—usually around two dozen spanks.

He stopped and rubbed away the sting, obviously in a forgiving mood. He slapped the other side and massaged.

She loved this—his domination. The closeness. The understanding between them of what she liked and how he liked to give it.

He continued with the slow cadence of slap and rub until she arched her bottom into his hand, eager for him to get on with either more punishment or pleasure. He took the hint and started spanking her in earnest, sending a delicious tingle of pain through her buttocks, which translated directly into heat in her core.

"You scared the *vecking* life out of me, Lamira," he said, palm falling in a rapid cadence. "I don't ever want to feel that way again."

She let one of her legs slide open and off his lap, angling his hard knee between her legs to grind against. He lifted the knee and pulled her closer, still alternately spanking one cheek then the other.

"I'm going to be turning this beautiful bottom pink every night."

She sighed in bliss, endorphins kicking in and mingling more pleasure into the mix of pain.

"Every night until I no longer remember the feeling of you leaving."

"I love you!" she blurted.

He stopped spanking with a laugh. "Little Lamira, you make it impossible for me to punish you."

She waggled her bottom in what she hoped was an enticing manner. "Keep going, master."

He slapped her ass. "I'm not your master anymore. Just your mate."

"You'll always be my master. I like it that way. Remember?"

But Zander had had enough spanking. With her pregnancy, it was hard to get him to spank her for long or with anything other than his hand. He lifted her off his lap. "Hands and knees, love."

She obeyed, climbing onto the middle of the sleepdisk with her ass in the air.

Zander growled in approval, following her and stripping off his tunic. He slapped her tingling cheek. "A spanking every night and then a nice long *vecking* to remind you who will always chase you when you run."

"I won't run!" she protested, and yelped when he slapped the back of her thigh. "I'm yours, Zander. Forever."

"Mmm." He stroked a huge hand up her back. The head of his cock nudged her entrance, and she arched and pushed back, desperate to feel him inside her. "You want this cock, my little mate?" He teased her outer lips, rubbing it over her slit.

"Yes," she whined. "Please."

He slid inside her, and she clamped down, muscles clenching with delicious pleasure.

"Ah, *veck*, Lamira," he groaned. "You keep up that squeezing and this will be remarkably...brief."

She laughed, a husky sound that didn't even sound like her.

"You're so *vecking* tight. So wet and swollen. So perfect for your master." He slid out and pushed back in. "And I am still your master."

"Yes," she breathed. "You'll always be my master. Ruler of my universe."

Zander muttered a low curse and gripped her hips, pumping in and out, angling deep inside her to bump the bundle of nerves deep inside that set her on fire.

She mewled, toes curling, fingertips digging into the covers. "Zander, *please*."

"*Veck.* You have to stop squeezing that sweet little...*veeeeeeck.*" Zander buried his cock, holding her hips to keep her ass pressed back against his loins as he came.

She shuddered in a climax, muscles squeezing around his cock, milking it for his rainbow-hued seed. "Zander," she gasped.

He helped her to her side, cock still inside her, and kissed her neck. "I missed you, sweet little human. I'm sorry I handled things so badly." He eased out of her, kissing and sucking along her neck. His teeth grazed her shoulder. "I should've just punished you immediately. But you'd run away from me. And I realized losing you was my biggest fear. I tried to master that fear by facing it —giving you the freedom you deserve."

She rolled to face him, sliding her swollen breasts against his chiseled chest. "Thank you for that freedom." She touched the smooth skin of his cheek. "But I'm not leaving. And I preferred it when I thought you'd never *allow* me to leave."

He ran a fingertip down her bare arm. "You like being owned. I told you so when we mated."

"Only by you," she murmured.

Zander pulled her against his body, tucking her head under his chin. She inhaled his masculine scent, nuzzled his chest, and sighed. Finally, things were right in her world again.

CHAPTER EIGHT

Seke put the battleship in cloaking mode, making it invisible to tracking, before he left the hangar. It would be disastrous if the Ocretions tracked ships flying to and from their training location. Zander had been granted asylum by the Ocretions after he escaped the Finnian takeover of his planet. If the Ocretions discovered he'd interfered with their justice system by intercepting the death pod, he'd have to engage in war with them, too. And that was a battle Seke doubted they'd win.

Even with the cloaking, he flew a roundabout course to get to the death pod, just in case. It lay moored on an uninhabitable planet outside of Ocretian territory. The two hundred humans who'd been destined for death were housed on it, and they'd sent several of Zander's new battleships so Rok could teach the humans to fly.

Before Zander had assigned Leora to him for training, Seke had been eager to get to the death pod, as his skill in training for war would finally be put to good use. But now, he could barely dredge up excitement. Numbness seeped into every pore, weighing him down as if cold stones filled his chest.

Leora.

How had he left her behind? It had been a supremely selfish act—he'd needed to atone for his lapse in willpower—but at what cost? Breaking Leora's heart?

Did his little human suffer over his sudden dismissal? When she'd turned pale and left abruptly, he'd wanted to tear his horns off. But maybe he read too much into it. Maybe he hadn't hurt her.

Except he knew that was wishful thinking. He'd forged a bond with her and then broken it. A master did not abandon his pupil—or slave, as the case may be.

Still, separating from her was the only answer. He couldn't give himself to her. He owed his allegiance to Becka. He would never mate again. And Leora deserved more than a master who used her body without any intention of mating. At least there was one thing he could do for her—send Lily back to visit.

Touching the communications device on his cuff, he called Rok and Lundric. "Seke to Zandian Freedom." He used the new name they'd given the death pod. "I'm coming in for landing on Shooku. Send someone to meet me at the hatch."

"Welcome, Master Seke. I'll be there," Lundric answered.

He landed the ship, putting an oxygen helmet on before disembarking, as the atmosphere on the planet was toxic. Until they recovered Zandia, the occupants of the death pod had to stay on it.

The hatch of the death pod opened, and he stepped into the decompression chamber. Once the opening sealed, a green light blinked, telling him it was safe, and he removed the helmet.

Lundric opened an interior door for him and bowed. "Master Seke, welcome." Lundric briefed Seke on the status of the training, and they walked together to Rok's headquarters.

"And the female?" Seke asked after his questions about the training had been satisfied.

A muscle under Lundric's eye jumped. "What female?"

"The one holding you by the balls—was it Cambry? Have you won her yet?"

Lundric scowled. "Don't ask."

Lily rounded the corner as they arrived in front of the office used as a headquarters, and came to a stop when she saw them. Rok stepped out into the corridor, dropping a hand on her shoulder in a subtle sign of support and protection.

"Master Seke—what's going on with my mother and sister? Are they prisoners?"

Rok folded his arms over his chest, his gaze assessing.

"No." Thank the stars that matter had been cleared up before he arrived. "They await your visit—both are eager to spend time with you. Rok, if you wish to take her to the palatial pod, Lundric and I will oversee things here."

Lily tilted her head to look up at her mate. Her hair slid back to reveal chips of flawless Zandian crystal decorating her ears. Rok, despite his lack of allegiance to Zander or his species, had mated her in Zandian tradition.

Why did that make Seke's chest ache even more? Was it because he missed having a mate? No, the ache for Becka had left long ago, though the guilt had not. This pain came from longing for what he'd never have—Leora pierced and decorated with his crystal.

Bitterness welled up, coated his tongue. But bitterness at what? Returning to his celibate lifestyle had been his own choosing.

"May I fly the ship?" Lily asked Rok. The unguarded eagerness in her expression would have charmed him, except it, too, reminded him of Leora. Lily—though mostly a stranger—looked just like her mother. And he'd seen that same openness in Leora after he'd broken past her reserve. He'd been fortunate enough—honored, even, to catch a glimpse of what she kept hidden inside.

Before he left her.

Rok smiled indulgently. "Of course. How else will you learn?"

Lundric shuddered beside him, and Seke had a feeling it had to do with an innate Zandian instinct to protect their females—which meant keeping them out of the cockpits of battleships. But Rok clearly had a different viewpoint on the matter.

"And land, too?"

"No." Rok spoke with the quick decisiveness of a true leader. Lamira had once had a vision of Rok leading their troops, and it seemed her vision would prove true. "It will be too difficult. You can land when we return to this planet."

"When can we leave?"

"I'm waiting on you."

She flashed a grin and dashed into the office, returning with two oxygen helmets. "Let's go."

Rok inclined his head to Seke. "Lundric knows the status of things here on the death pod. Insert yourself wherever you see fit."

For one charged moment, Seke considered correcting Rok. Seke outranked him, and it wasn't Rok's place to give him instructions. But Lamira had seen Rok leading this troop. For whatever reason, this wasn't Seke's show. Perhaps Seke would be needed elsewhere when they attacked the Finn.

Seke nodded and turned to Lundric. "Take me to the training ground."

Stars knew he needed a long, hard, physical fight. Every hour for the rest of his life. How else would he dull the ache of living without Leora?

~.~

After being shut up for so many planet rotations in Seke's chamber, Leora should have been out in the pod, visiting Barr in his kitchen or tending to her plants.

But she couldn't face any of it.

She couldn't bear to see Seke, or anything that reminded her of him—which meant she'd have to go through the rest of her life with her eyes sealed shut. So she'd holed up in her chamber, curled in a ball, sleeping on and off all planet rotation. Her dreams showed her oldest memories of Johan. Their first kiss. The moment he left her, pregnant with Lamira, to lead the slave uprising.

Some small part of her had resented him for it. It wasn't fair, she knew. He'd been fighting for the freedom of their daughters, of their species. He was noble and brave. But he'd put her life in danger. When the uprising failed—as unorganized and spontaneous acts of defiance often do—she'd been picked up and transferred to the agrifarm. If they'd known she was Johan's mate—carried his child—she'd have been executed.

And now Seke had abandoned her as well. Granted, she was neither pregnant, nor in danger, but he saw a lofty ideal as more worth pursuing. And why shouldn't he? She was just a human slave. A female he'd been attracted to, but to whom he owed nothing.

She moaned and changed positions on the bed. If only she didn't feel as if her very soul had been ripped from her with a serrated knife.

A light tap came on the door.

She didn't move, even though she knew it would be Lamira.

"Mother? Are you in there? Let me in."

She sighed and dragged herself from the bed, feeling as if she weighed as much as three airships put together. She activated the door, and Lamira pushed past her, taking her hands.

"What happened? I heard Seke left for the death pod."

Had he? *Veck.* That didn't make it any better..

"That's all." It felt as if a giant brick had been placed on her chest.

"Zander has declared we're no longer slaves. He told you that?"

She blinked at her daughter, noticing the color back in her cheeks, the brightness of her eyes. "You've mended the rift with Zander?"

"Yes. He made me so angry I tried to leave again first, though."

Relieved to listen to someone else's problems, Leora led her to the hover-seats by the little corner table. "What happened?"

Lamira explained their quarrel, blushing as she arrived at their reconciliation. No doubt she'd just had incredible, ravishing sex. She wondered if all Zandians had the capacity to turn human females into weak-kneed, swooning fools with a simple touch or command. Was it their natural dominance? Their size and stature? Or was it something particular to Zander and Seke?

"So what happened with Seke? He never broke his vow of celibacy, then?"

Her shoulders sagged. "Actually, that's the worst part. He did. But he hated himself and me for it. And when Zander gave him leave to end my training, he took the opportunity and dropped me like a hot coal."

"I suppose you are like a hot coal to him." Lamira tapped her lips with her fingertips.

"Thanks," she said drily.

"I don't mean you would burn him. Only that there's fire between you. He can't touch you without coming away changed."

Lamira's unexpected poetics had tears filling her eyes. "I don't think that's it," she said stiffly.

Thankfully, Lamira changed the subject. "Lily's coming. She's on her way now—Zander just told me. Why don't you wash up so you're ready when she gets here?"

Leora took that to be Lamira's kind way of telling her she looked awful, so she agreed, trudging to the washtube. The idea of seeing Lily did brighten her outlook slightly, as did the shower.

After she dressed, she and Lamira went to the kitchen to let Barr know another human would be arriving, and they'd require extra food.

~.~

A mother's reunion with her long-lost daughter shouldn't include moping over a male. Somehow, though, she'd blurted the whole story. After taking Lily on a tour of the pod, the three women had spent at least five hours sitting at one end of the long dining table, eating, talking, and drinking sweet blueberry wine.

Zander and Rok had left them to it, although the males had checked in a few times to see how they were doing. Lily had filled them in on her torrid love affair with Rok—how she'd stolen his ship, only to have him rescue her and keep her prisoner, punishing her in ways she'd discovered she loved.

Lamira had shared her story of being purchased as Zander's breeder, and what it was like to be the first female the palatial pod had housed. Lily had some fierce questions about their captivity—whether they were still held as slaves or not—which led to telling Leora's short and tumultuous tale with Seke.

"If he didn't bear so much guilt for saving Zander instead of his mate and children, he might be a different being," Lamira said. "But holding himself away from you is how he chooses to punish himself." Sometimes Lamira sounded wiser than her years. "How did Rok escape Zandia?" she asked Lily.

"He said he got lucky. He lived in the palace because his father was a laborer there. A guard helped him and two daughters of an important advisor get out through an underground tunnel. They got to a ship and flew off the planet. They were shot down over Stornig, where he was adopted and raised by locals."

"Two daughters of an important advisor." Lamira's eyes had the unfocused look they took on when she was seeing with her inner eye. "Seke's two daughters."

Leora stiffened, sitting straight up in her hoverseat. "Are you sure?" she asked sharply.

"Remember? I only saw his mate and infant had died in the invasion."

Lily focused on her sister. "Rok told me there was something unusual about you." She glanced over at Leora. "I've always thought I had good gut instincts. Does it run in the family?"

Leora nodded. "Gut instinct is what I rely on as well. Lamira was born with this special knowing. We had to hide it to keep her from being logged as unusual and executed." She turned back to Lamira. "What do you see?"

"The girls were Seke's."

"Did they survive the crash?" Lily asked. "Rok never knew."

Lamira was quiet for a long moment, listening, looking inward. "They're alive. I can't see where. It feels dark to me. Imprisoned, perhaps. Or just unhappy." Her focus returned. "They need our help."

Leora rose to her feet. "You must tell him."

"*I* must tell him? Shouldn't *you*?"

Just the thought of seeing Seke's face sent her heart rate crashing, a tumble of sputtered breath and seizing muscles in her chest. "I—I can't. I don't want to see him. This won't change anything between us."

"Maybe not, but he should know. And you're the one to tell him. You're the one he confided in about his family."

Her heart continued to flip-flop in her chest. "All right. I'll tell him. But I'll wait until he returns and I can do it in person."

Rok ambled in. "Are you three *still* eating?" he teased. "I've never understood how such tiny beings could require so much food. Lily depleted my ship's entire store of food while she was on it."

Lily's laugh rang out. "That's not true." She stood up and sauntered to her mate, whose eyes followed the swing of her hips with an appreciative gaze. "Did you recharge in the crystal room?"

He nodded. "I did." He flexed his biceps. "Can't you tell?"

She laughed again, her pleasure at being near her mate so palpable, Leora thought she could almost see waves of love transferring between the two.

Both her daughters had found their true mates—in an alien species, no less. She couldn't be happier for them.

Sweet Mother Earth.

She wanted her own alien mate. She wanted Seke. But not if he didn't want her. The weariness returned to her limbs. She stood, too, needing to be alone.

At least she had a grandbaby to look forward to. It would give her some purpose in her otherwise empty life.

Seke worked without a break all planet rotation, but nothing distracted him from, nor made a dent in, his misery. Leora filled every thought. He felt her presence with him, as if they were still locked together in his chamber, as if he might turn and find her just a few meters away at any moment.

He'd made Lundric practice hand-to-hand combat with him for two hours after most of the pod had bedded down for the night, hoping to dull his agony, but it was no use.

Now, as he walked through the silent corridors, the unease of the humans seemed to radiate from the very walls. The Zandians had saved them from their death, but the humans still didn't trust them. No one slept in the prison cells that had housed them on the way there, even though Rok had disabled all the locks. They chose, instead, to bed down together on floors in the larger halls. They obeyed orders warily—interested in learning how to defend themselves but not sure they could trust their trainers.

He didn't blame them.

Utilizing the humans to fight their war in exchange for sanctuary once Zandia was won was either a stroke of pure genius, or it would be the downfall of their war plan. Since the vision had come to Lamira, he had to trust it was genius. Still, Prince Zander had been granted sanctuary on Ocretia, and their empress wouldn't take kindly to the siphoning off and freeing of their slaves.

Hopefully by the time they realized they were harboring escaped slaves, the Zandians would have regained enough power to hold their own.

Seke's cuff blinked with an incoming hologram from Zander. He accepted it. "Please tell me you worked everything out with your mate."

"I did. I'm not sure whether to thank you or throttle you for the advice you gave me."

"Come over here and try to throttle me. I could use a challenge."

"Yes." Zander hesitated, and he realized, for once, his pupil might have been trying to give him advice. "A vow of celibacy may have made sense before our species was in danger of extinction."

His brows slammed down. *Veck* this. Zander had no *vecking* idea what his vow was about.

"You saved me instead of them, didn't you?"

Breath whooshed in his lungs before he expected it, and he almost choked.

"I should have known that. I should have guessed. I'm so coddled here, it never occurred to me. I knew you lost them, but I didn't realize you might have had a choice of who to save."

Seke swallowed, hard. His stomach sank like he'd eaten a boulder. "There was no choice." He barely got the words out. Zander had become a son to him, after they escaped. He'd practically raised the boy—he loved him like his own family. "I am Master at Arms. I serve the Zandian throne."

Zander looked stricken. "I'll never be able to repay that debt. Even if I win back Zandia."

It was a heavy task Seke had set on the prince's shoulders from a young age. Seke had forced the same sense of duty on Zander he'd upheld himself. Zander had to study for war, amass enough wealth, and lead a campaign to regain their home. But there was no way he'd let the boy carry the weight of his family's death, too. Seke forced breath into his lungs. Out of them. Memories from the invasion flashed before his eyes. The marble ceiling of the ancient palace crashing down around them, explosions everywhere.

"You were closer," he croaked. "I had a better chance of getting you out than I did going for them. We'd probably all be dead if I'd chosen differently."

He'd forgotten that truth in his daily self-condemnation. He hadn't just chosen for duty. He'd made the only choice there had been—the one that saved two Zandian lives.

Zander rubbed his ear. "If you're honoring your family with this vow out of love, then I bow to you. But if it's out of obligation, or guilt—"

"Don't." He held up his hand. He didn't want Zander's philosophies on the matter. He had enough swirling in his head to keep him up every night for a solar cycle.

Zander raised his arm with the fist bent at a ninety degree angle, as was the traditional Zandian greeting. "I honor your honor." He spoke the benediction in their native tongue.

Seke bowed to his hologram. "I honor your honor." He ended the transmission before he choked up. As he walked slowly back to his chamber, a tenuous peace settled like a mantle over his shoulders. He hadn't chosen honor over family—he'd made the only choice available to him. Saving Zander over his own children had been the result of circumstance, not his orchestration. That adjustment of focus changed things, somehow. It put to bed the largest chunk of guilt he carried.

And it had been so long since he'd lost them, his grief for his family no longer stung. With the layer of guilt removed, their death was like a box he could move within, instead of the coffin he'd chosen. What did that mean for his vow? Did it change things?

He activated the door to his own small sleeping chamber with a numeric code—the death pod was a primitive craft. The room was no more than a cot and washtub. With a groan, he sank to the cot and dropped his face into his hands. His body was weary, but his mind still ran in one hundred directions. And all of them led to Leora.

He hoped her visit with Lily had gone well.

Maybe he'd just check on her. He had access to the security feed from the palatial pod via his wrist cuff. He wouldn't let it become a habit to spy on her, but tonight—just tonight—it might put his mind at ease to see her.

He flicked on the feed and found her chamber.

Oh holy Zandian moons. No.

His female slumped with her back against the door, as if she'd just come in. Tears streaked her beautiful face.

Had things gone badly with Lily? Did she feel guilty over their lost years?

"Seke," she whispered. Her hands came to her throat, and he realized they held the collar he'd used on her. Where had she found it? He'd sent all the equipment to storage. The fact she'd sought it out and stolen the collar for her own keeping made ice flush through him.

Veck.

The tears were over him. The pain he'd caused her. He'd hoped she hadn't grown as attached as he had, but he should have known. She'd given him her heart. And he'd *vecking* handed it back without so much as a kiss.

Without thinking, he found himself on his feet, moving out the door. He didn't stop to give Lundric orders, didn't pause for anything. He put his oxygen helmet on. The hatch opened and closed behind him. He boarded his ship and flicked on the switches. With the ship in cloaking mode, he took off, on the most direct course for the palatial pod.

Veck the vow. *Veck* everything.

Leora was his.

~.~

Leora pushed her damp hair out of her face and swiped at her tears with the back of her hand. She couldn't cry forever. There had been worse things in her life. She'd had her three-year-old taken from her. Had lost her mate. Had survived as a slave for over forty solar cycles.

Life was easy for her now. She'd been offered freedom. She wasn't required to work. She lived in beautiful, luxurious surroundings with servants who tended to her needs. Why, then, did it feel like she couldn't go on?

She voice-commanded the lights off and curled up on her sleepdisk, even though she knew sleep wouldn't come.

The door to her chamber slid open.

She jerked the covers up to her chin and blinked. A huge Zandian male stood silhouetted in the doorway. By the breadth of his shoulders and the tilt of his horns, she knew it must be her Zandian.

"Seke?"

The door shut, enclosing them in darkness.

"Forgive me, Leora."

She flew off the sleepdisk, throwing herself in his direction, unable to see but knowing he'd catch her.

He did.

She wrapped her legs around his waist, arms banding around his neck. He returned the embrace, pulling her tightly against his warm body, one arm hooked under her bottom, the other around her back. He twisted, rocking her from side to side.

"I'm sorry," he murmured into her hair. "I shouldn't have left you. I will never leave you like that again."

"Seke." Her voice choked with emotion. "I'm sorry I pushed you. I shouldn't—"

"Shh. Don't apologize. You did nothing wrong. I alone am to blame."

"No. Stop shouldering the galaxy." In the dark, she sought his face and laid her palm against his smooth cheek. "I will share your burdens."

Seke went still. "I believe you would." His voice was hoarse. "But I would never ask that of you, little one. A Zandian male protects his mate."

A burst of joy exploded in her chest. "Mate?"

"Will you wear my crystals?"

"Yes," she gasped, hardly daring to believe her ears. Happy tears sprang to her eyes and coated her lashes.

His lips found her neck, and he nipped her, lowering her hips until her mouth came flush with his. He claimed it, tongue licking between her lips, lips demanding. She lost herself in the kiss, hardly noticing he'd set her on her feet and was backing her up to the wall.

The sound of fabric tearing made her jump. Seke ripped her robe from her shoulders. He spun her around. "Hands on the wall, little one," he breathed in her ear.

She flattened her palms against the wall, arching and pressing her bottom back at Seke.

She heard the rustle of discarded clothing, and Seke's arms came around hers, forearms planted on the wall just outside her hands.

"Spread your legs, Leora. I need to put my cock in you now or I won't go on breathing."

"I'm ready," she whispered. Her pussy, already moist from their kiss, had turned molten the moment he'd given the order to put her hands against the wall. His dominance triggered instant arousal.

Without needing his hands to guide him, he positioned his cock at her entrance and thrust upward.

She cried out with pleasure as he nearly took her off her feet.

"I'm going to *veck* you so hard you'll go hoarse from screaming." Seke's coarse, growled speech preceded a bite on her ear.

She moaned her assent, offering him full control of her body. He gave her his cock in deep, hard thrusts, wrapping one arm around her waist to hold her steady for the assault.

"This pussy belongs to me, now," he growled. "Doesn't it?"

"Yes, master."

He chuckled. "I am still your master, aren't I?"

Her eyes rolled back in her head as waves of pleasure swept through her. "Yes."

"I'm going to *veck* you like this anytime I like. Anywhere. In every position." It was a good thing he held her up, because her legs had turned to jelly.

"I'm going to give you more pleasure than you know possible. And you'll learn to pleasure me."

"Yes, *yes!*"

"Tell me what you need, sweet Leora."

"You," she panted. "I just need you."

He *vecked* her so hard stars danced behind her eyes.

"You have me."

He grabbed a hoverseat and dropped into it, seating her on his lap, facing away from him. "Ride my cock, love." He gripped her hips and moved her rapidly up and down over his thick cock.

Her head hung forward, breasts bounced, and the need to come made her scream in her throat.

"Who do you belong to?"

"You," she whined. "You, Seke. Please, oh *veck, please.*"

He reached around and found her clit. The moment he rubbed it, she lost control, legs shoving straight out in front of her, feet flexed, her entire body convulsing as her pussy squeezed Seke's huge cock.

"That's it, little human," he growled and slid her up and down a few more times before he, too, went off with a curse and a shout.

~.~

Seke didn't want to ever leave the sleepdisk. Leora lay cradled against his body. Her sweet, citrus scent filled his nostrils, copper hair fanned out behind her on the sheets. He hadn't meant to be rough with her again, but he couldn't help himself. She brought out the beast in him.

But he'd make it up to her. They had a lifetime in which he could learn to take his time and find out exactly what she liked—where she wanted his mouth and fingers. What made her scream. Not that their first attempts hadn't been explosively satisfying for both of them.

Her dark lashes fluttered open, and her green-eyed gaze fell on him. She made a contented sound and tossed one leg over his hips, bringing her small palm to his chest.

He held it there, against his heart.

"Are you at peace with this? With us?" she asked.

"Yes. I believe—" He stopped and cleared his throat, which was closed with emotion. "I believe I made the only decision available to me when the Finn invaded. I couldn't have saved my family—there was no time. Dying with them wouldn't have served Zandia. I've put my guilt to rest and, with it, the vow that served no one."

"Seke, I have something to tell you."

She sounded serious, and he had to work to keep from stiffening. "Tell me."

"When Zandia was invaded, Rok was in the palace, too. He told Lily a guard helped him escape, along with two other children."

Seke didn't move. His breath had stopped as he waited for her to go on.

"Lamira believes they were yours."

His heart jammed up in his throat so tight he couldn't speak. "My daughters? They escaped?"

"They were shot down over Stornig. Rok doesn't know what happened to them, but Lamira believes they're alive."

Seke dropped his head onto the pillow, unable to hold it up. His eyes smarted. "Lamira thinks?" He choked. "My daughters are alive?"

"Yes." She straddled him and found his hand, picking it up with both hers and squeezing it. "We'll find them, Seke."

He opened his arms. "Come here."

She smiled and slid down, draping her delicious little body over his larger one.

He couldn't speak. Couldn't do anything but hold his female tight. Loving her was the best reason for living he had. She was his heart—his life—an extension of his very soul. To think he could have her—and his daughters—seemed like more than he'd ever believed he deserved. More than was possible.

But here she was. Her lithe body wriggled over his, a serene smile playing over those perfect lips as she offered to help him find his daughters.

"Thank you," he whispered, closing his eyes to savor the moment.

She kissed his chest. He kissed her hair. And then he flipped her on her back and pinned her wrists, ready to give her the first *vecking* of the day.

HIS HUMAN REBEL

CHAPTER ONE

Cambry must have a flashing *molest me* sign over her head. She'd been trying to give off the *don't come near me* vibe, but maybe it didn't translate on this forsaken planet.

Sleep on the death pod would be impossible. Even without the constant shuffle and murmur of low voices filling the hall packed with two hundred human refugees, Cambry didn't trust the human male who'd settled his sleep pad next to hers.

What she really needed, more than decent sleep, was a weapon. A laser gun would be amazing, but she'd settle for a piece of piping or a stick. Even a sharp nail.

She'd seen the human chatting up another female at dinnertime. He gave off that creepy vibe she'd learned at an early age to beware. When the female rebuffed him and joined in a close pack with several other beings, he'd changed his focus to Cambry.

Cambry knew the fact she hadn't joined or formed her own little protective grouping made her a target, but bonding with strangers wasn't really her thing. She hadn't survived twenty-three years living in the slave tenements below the factory where she worked without a healthy wariness for all other beings, male or female. She'd never trusted anyone but her only family member, her younger brother, Tal.

The pang in her chest at his loss nearly took her breath.

The squeak of a boot passed nearby, and she lifted her gaze. One of the Zandian guards strolled a few meters away. Nearly seven feet tall, broad-shouldered, and hugely-muscled, the male oozed masculine power and virility. Though he appeared young, she'd seen him giving orders to the other guards.

He must be some kind of supervisor. "Hard to sleep in this animal pen, isn't it?" he murmured, coming closer.

Great, now she'd attracted attention from him, too. That flashing sign must be really bright.

He crouched down, which surprised her. Making her crane her neck up to look at and answer him would be the usual bullshit authoritative thing to do to a human slave. Beings who thought they were superior didn't usually get down on her level.

"Yeah." She made a weak attempt at a smile.

Like all the Zandians who had supposedly "rescued" them from death, he had peachy-purple skin and horns on the top of his head. The intensity in his long-lashed brown eyes made her catch her breath. What did he see? He studied her like he really *saw,* like he really *wanted* to see. It made her itchy, as if all her vulnerabilities might be exposed if she let him keep looking.

"Can I get you something? A blanket or sleeping pad?"

She swallowed down more surprise. Was he actually being friendly? Chivalrous? Did that even exist between prisoners and guards? Slaves and masters? Aliens and humans?

Because that's what they still were. If the Zandians thought Cambry bought their so-called "rescue" of the beings on the death pod, they were sorely mistaken. Yes, they'd prevented her death that day, but anyone with a brain knew they'd only delayed it. Now, they wanted to send them all on a death mission to take back their planet Zandia. Naturally, they wanted humans on the front lines—their deaths didn't matter.

"No thanks."

"You don't dare shut your eyes, do you?"

Perceptive male. Third time he had surprised her. She vowed not to let it happen again. Whatever his game, she needed to figure it out—quick. Before she fell for it. Because the handsome Zandian oozed charisma. That must be how he'd worked his way into a position of power at such a young age.

When her non-answer served as acknowledgement, his gaze turned to a smolder, making flutters cascade in her belly. "I'll keep watch so you don't have to. I promise no one will bother you tonight."

Her heart picked up speed. Not because it was a good line, but because something in the solemn utterance made her actually *believe* him. But why would this male promise her anything? What did he care if she slept well or not?

His promise produced a visceral reaction in her. Heat curled low in her belly as she measured his physical ability to defend her. His arms bulged with solid muscle; pectorals stood out in stark relief beneath the finely woven white uniform tunic. She'd already noticed he moved with a grace and ease belying his large stature. Yes, he probably could effectively handle any threat that came his way. And it shouldn't turn her on so much that he'd offered *her* his protection.

When her nipples stiffened beneath her tunic, she folded her arms across her chest to hide them, fighting off her attraction for the obviously virile male. "Don't bother. I don't trust you more than any other being here."

His lips quirked. "Smart female. Well, I'll watch over you just the same. I don't like seeing you unprotected." He reached for his sword belt and unclipped a slender titanium object about the length of her palm and the width of two fingers. He offered it to her.

She looked at it without moving, then, when she realized what it was, snatched it out of his hand before he changed his mind. Grasping the handle, she unsheathed the small dagger and held it to the dim light, examining the blade. Razor sharp. Gleaming. *Praise our long-lost Mother Earth.*

A shock of warmth traveled through her chest. Another being had understood her well enough to offer the tool she desired most at the moment. It threw her off balance. She was used to males seeing her as an object, looking at what they might take from her. This one—a being in a position of power no less—looked and *gave* her something.

His lips turned up even more at whatever he saw in her face—the shine of appreciation, perhaps. Or maybe awe at his generosity and trust. Because he should've seen she was far from trustworthy. She'd be using the dagger and any other means she could find to escape this rathole as soon as possible.

She wet her lips with her tongue, trying to ignore the way his gaze dropped to her mouth and heated. "Thank you."

"I'm Lundric."

She blinked. Not *Master* Lundric or *Captain* or whatever his title was. Just *Lundric.* She supposed she owed him her name in return, though it went against her personal code of keeping herself closed off.

He waited.

"Cambry."

"Cambry," he repeated in a soft voice, as if savoring the sound of her name on his tongue. He stared at her another moment, like he was drinking her in, then stood and positioned himself against a nearby wall, making his intent clear. *I promise no one will bother you tonight.*

She and her brother had always looked out for one another. They'd been a team, watched each other's backs. But she couldn't trust anyone else to do it. Even so, a chink fell from her shield, jumbling her emotions. Fear and loss warred with the stirring of something warmer. The idea of having Lundric watch over her should *not* make her feel safe. She needed to stay vigilant, look for her opportunity.

She palmed the knife and lay down on her side with her back to the wall and her face toward her creepy neighbor. No, she was on her own until she found and freed Tal.

. . .

Cambry. The name suited the exquisite female. Lundric had been fascinated by the auburn-haired human from the moment he saw her. She held her chin high, walked with an aggressive swagger, and carried herself with ready alertness, like she was prepared to address any threat. She also gave off attitude in waves. He had no doubt she could defend herself with the proper weapon. Which was why he gave her one.

A woman so beautiful would have admirers. And he didn't trust any male here—human or Zandian. He hated thinking of her being vulnerable to attack. The mere idea of it had him clenching his fists, a red haze seeping in and stealing rational thought.

So he leaned up against the wall near her nest on the floor to watch over her. He ought to make the rounds—walk the perimeter of the large hall to make his presence felt, but nothing could tear him away from his vigil.

He'd already decided she belonged to him. *His* little human.

He'd been raised to believe humans were inferior, weak. They were an enslaved species, after all. Yet Zander, the prince of his species, had taken the human slave, Lamira, as his mate. Rok, his superior here, had mated her sister, Lily. He'd heard his mentor, Master Seke, the Zandian Master of Arms, had been given their mother as his slave concubine.

So why shouldn't he have one, too? There were no Zandian females of mating age left—his species was nearly extinct. And rumor had it Daneth, the prince's physician, had determined Lamira to be the best gene match for Zander to breed. If humans were the closest, most beneficial species for them to mate, he would gladly take one. This one.

They were headed to war. His whole life had been spent preparing for it. It only made sense for him to also breed before they left. Daneth had already taken and frozen Lundric's seed as a precaution, but wouldn't leaving an actual child be better? He had to do his part to preserve what little was left of Zandian genetic code.

What a lie. He didn't give a *veck* about preserving his genetic code. He just wanted Cambry. The fierce little rebel with cunning intelligence behind those big brown eyes. The female who snatched a dagger up and looked ready to use it. The beautiful, tough little human. He'd like to tame the wild animal right out of her. Teach her no harm would ever come to her by his hand, but there would be plenty of pleasure.

Teach her not to bolt when he wrapped his fist in that dark auburn mane and pulled her head back while he drove deep from behind. When he pinned her slender wrists above her head and licked and sucked those magnificent little breasts he'd seen shifting beneath her tunic. What color would her nipples be? Pink? Peach?

It wasn't just physical, though his need for her had been immediate and undeniable. No, he also wanted to find out what had hardened the little human and figure out how to win her softness back.

Cambry. His human. He would ask the prince if he could have her.

He kept his post beside her for the rest of the night, satisfied when she finally did slip into a restless sleep, drifting off for an hour at a time before jerking awake and looking around. She glanced over at him each time and he lifted his chest as if to show her it made him proud to be the one who watched over her. From now on, he'd be the *only vecking being* who had the privilege. A duty he took more seriously than death. Because if anyone threatened that little human—his female—he'd crush them.

The center of the pod didn't have windows, so it was hard to tell when dawn came. Living without light would be difficult for the Zandians, who relied on light for energy more than food. They'd have to make frequent trips to Zander's palatial pod for the crystal-amplified light baths. It didn't do much to improve the prisoners'—make that *former* prisoners'—morale, either. The group— mostly humans with a few odd other species mixed in—still wore the down-trodden faces of any refugees. Rok's female, Lily, had been working hard to instill hope, and some seemed to believe her promise of a better life on Zandia, but most braced their shoulders as if ready for another attack on their dignity.

As the beings began to rouse, he turned on the sunlight simulator. A new group of guards came in for next shift, reporting to him for duty and carrying boxes of nutrition packs. He eyed the packs with distaste. They were disgusting compared to the meals he'd enjoyed on the palatial pod, but he was tired, his energy weakened from lack of food and light. He needed rest, but there was no way in hell he was going to let his female sleep another night in this crowded hall.

As the beings filed forward to receive their nutrition packs, he gave orders to his guards. "They need to be given living quarters today."

Rok, his superior, had already mentioned the necessity, so he didn't feel like he was stepping out of line by ordering it done today. "Allow them to self-select who they will house with. Give them housing in the prison cells, offices, closets, anywhere you can find. For those who remain in the prison cells, show them the locks have been disabled. Remove the doors if they're too nervous. They need to settle in because this pod will be our home for many planet rota-tions—maybe even a solar cycle, depending on how quickly we can get them trained."

"Yes, Captain Lundric," his guards murmured.

Cambry stood up, holding herself with the same ever-present wariness he'd seen on her from the beginning. She'd listened to every word, but mistrust still reflected on her face.

"Start with filling the cells. Sten, you and I will scout other possible housing options." He lifted his chin at Cambry as if she were one of his men. "You come with us to help scout."

She clenched her jaw, her hand tightening on the dagger she'd attached to her belt.

Her mistrust shouldn't wound him so much. Her gaze darted from him to his guard, Sten, then over to the human male still pretending to sleep beside her—the one she'd been afraid of the night before. He knew, in her mind, she'd be smarter to stay in the hall. There was safety in numbers.

Hand still on the dagger, chin lifted, she stepped toward him, accepting his order.

It took all his willpower not to throw her over his shoulder and carry her off to his quarters, declaring her won. Stars, how he wanted to claim that lithe little body.

Soon. *Veck*, yes, soon.

He fished a nutrition pack out of the box and tossed it to her. "Come." He resisted the urge to push Cambry in front of him, even though his every instinct screamed to stay at her back where he could protect her. Until she trusted him, it would make her itchy to have him behind her. He led the way down the hall, purpose helping him push through fatigue. There was no way he could sleep until he got his female settled somewhere safe.

"Don't Zandians eat? Or do you hide the decent food somewhere else?"

He looked over his shoulder at her, surprised a slave on a death pod dared used such a surly tone with him. Not that it didn't make him hard as *veck*. He loved the fight in her. It drew him in as much as her hot-as-magma looks.

She had the sense to flinch under his look, her projected confidence flickering. She swallowed. "Sorry, am I supposed to call you *Captain* or something?"

He smirked. "Little female, you can call me anything you like." *Master. Protector. Yours.* "It won't change a thing."

Her confidence slipped a little further, and he could almost see her mind working as she puzzled over his statement.

All the offices had been taken by the Zandians, and his guards slept in the bunkroom used by the Ocretion guards before they took over the pod. Still, there had to be some other place for her. He used his palm to activate the doors on room after room, assessing their potential and giving Sten orders on what to do with each one.

When he found a small storage area, big enough for a bed and even a chair, he stopped looking. "We'll empty this. Stack the supplies neatly in the hallway," he ordered both of them.

Cambry hesitated, obviously not wanting to enter the small space due to the possibility of being trapped in there with them.

"You stay out here. We'll hand you the supplies for stacking." He reached in and grabbed the first box, swiveling to drop it into her arms.

Theirs hands brushed when she took it, and his gaze tangled with hers. She had warm brown eyes, her lashes the same dark auburn of her thick hair. She seemed to be searching his face for something, so he let her look, hoping he showed whatever she needed to see.

She swallowed and took the box, turning away quickly, but not before he saw confusion on her beautiful face.

~.~

Lundric—*Captain Lundric*, she'd learned—actually growled when his guard Sten tried to hand her a box. Lundric snatched it from him, glaring Sten down with an animalistic show of dominance. She wasn't sure whether to slap his face at the audacity or laugh at his territorial act over her. She probably ought to be more afraid.

If she had half a brain, she wouldn't have come on this errand alone with these two. Even with the dagger Lundric had given her, the two could probably overpower her, although she'd give them one helluva fight first.

The image of the two of them shoving her into the storage space and taking turns having their way with her flickered through her mind...and sort of turned her on. No, Sten having a turn didn't excite her, but the crazy image of him holding her down while Lundric shoved his way deep into her—

Sweet Mother Earth! What was wrong with her? Her panties were actually dampening at the idea of being forcibly taken by this huge specimen of masculine power. What had lulled her better instincts into complacency?

It was too much to believe he really saw into her and understood her needs and desires, and yet...he *had*. He'd given her the dagger. Now he was supposedly finding some safer places for them to sleep, although she still didn't know whether to trust his plan. But, if it was a ploy, what did he stand to gain? Someplace to get her alone, maybe?

She stacked boxes neatly outside the closet.

"So what did you do to land yourself on the wrong side of Ocretion law?" His question was deceptively casual. Even though his back was to her, she saw the charge of tension run through him, waiting for her answer.

"I killed three guards."

It was true. But she'd also thrown it out as a threat, and he clearly caught her intent because, when he swiveled with the next carton, the corners of his mouth tugged up. "I have no doubt you did." He looked almost...*proud* of her.

Bizarre.

As he handed her the box, his focus dipped to her lips like they had the night before. What did he want to do to her mouth? Kiss it? Claim it?

A shiver ran through her. She didn't even know what *claim it* meant, but it seemed to fit the hunger flickering behind his gaze. She dropped the carton and immediately looked back, watching Lundric's powerful back ripple when he stooped to pick up another box. Sten caught her looking and hid a smile as he looked away.

To hell with him. What did he think was so funny?

When they'd emptied the little storage room of all its contents, Lundric turned to her. "Let's go get your things."

Her brows shot up. "This is for me?" Her safety meter spun wildly and landed on *no way*. She took a step backward. "I'm not going in there."

Lundric held his palms out, as if to show he had no weapon. "Take it easy. No one is trying to trap you, little female." He drew his fist back and smashed the palm-activated door lock panel beside the door.

She bit back the involuntary shriek of surprise choking her throat. The power behind that fist was dizzying. She made a mental note never to put herself on the receiving end of it.

The panel sparked and flashed and then died out. He shoved the pocket door open and closed. "See? Nothing I can do from the outside now. I'll fashion you some kind of clip you can use from the inside. You control the lights inside, too. See?" He showed her the button just inside the door that turned the lights on and off.

Prickles covered her skin. Had he really done all this...for *her*? To keep her safe? Or—since he already believed he'd protected her the night before—to give her some semblance of control over her own safety? It was too much to believe, and yet, something in the way he watched her, as if her reaction mattered—*really mattered* to him—made her think it was true.

He took a step closer, his expression going soft. When he reached for her face, she jerked away on an inhale. His hand dropped to his side, all the power and hunger she saw there tightly leashed. Once more, the lips turned up. Instead of inspiring anger, it seemed her resistance amused him.

"Go get your bedroll."

She nibbled on her lip, still assessing the danger. She tossed her ponytail and tried opening and closing the door herself. He was right—it didn't lock now. With a single nod, she strode back down the corridor in the direction they'd come.

It would've been a better exit if she'd gone in the right direction.

Lundric waited until her steps slowed before he whistled. When she looked back, he wore a broad grin. Obviously, the warrior thought it funny.

She pursed her lips and marched back, her worn boots clomping on the floor, Lundric's appreciative gaze sending heat creeping over her cheeks. When she reached them, Lundric gave a low chuckle.

"You find me entertaining, Captain?"

"Yes," he drawled. "I find everything about you entertaining, little female." The parts he left unspoken seared her skin, made her breasts grow tight and heavy, her pussy damp. He inhaled sharply. She sensed tension from him, as if he only barely held back from grabbing her and throwing her down to have his way with her.

Like a skittish animal, she darted away, out of his reach, cursing herself for showing fear. Only the fear this time wasn't of physical harm. It was something deeper. Darker. Something that had her body feeling tingly and alive for the first time in ages.

She stomped back to the large hull where they'd slept. Only half the beings remained, huddled in groupings. Her bedding had disappeared, as the entire room had been straightened up, the blankets stacked in a neat pile by the door. One guard led a group of eight past her as she came in. She thought someone might stop her, ask where she'd been, but it seemed a human walking around unattended wasn't cause for alarm.

Interesting.

She picked up two blankets—one to lie on and one to cover herself, and swiftly rolled them into a bundle. She should wait here, in this room, to see what was happening with the rest of the prisoners. She shouldn't be spending time alone with the captain, who had clearly taken an interest in her beyond guard-prisoner.

One of the guards pointed at her. "Who are you camping with?"

She looked around, gut fisting up with dread. None of the groups looked friendly. And she already had her own room.

Which probably came with a whole mess of strings attached.

Somehow, she couldn't muster a great deal of fear of those strings, though, even having seen Lundric's right hook and the dark hunger in his eyes. He'd shown respect for her—hadn't touched her, had given her a weapon, had looked after her safety.

Maybe he didn't have any dark intent.

Or maybe morbid curiosity had her wondering just how it would feel to have those huge arms cage her, that powerful body drag her into submission. He looked like the kind of male who took a female long and hard. Maybe tied her up first and slapped her ass.

She fought back the reaction her body had to those thoughts and cleared her throat. "Captain Lundric has found a closet for me down there," she said, waving toward the hallway.

She expected more interrogation, or demands for proof, but he merely nodded and moved on. Free, she slipped out the door, taking long strides back to her closet. In the hallway outside it, she met Lundric, carrying an entire cot —yes the whole structure—under one arm.

"I found you a bed," he grunted.

She willed her giddy little heart to slow back down. They probably had lots of beds lying around the pod. It wasn't like he was some kind of hero or something. She stepped back to allow him to enter her closet and shove the bed against the far wall, so she'd face the door as she slept. Exactly where she would've placed it. He'd already placed a single chair in, as well.

"There you go. I'll work on a lock before nightfall." He turned and walked away before she could even say thank you.

Not that she was sure she was going to.

But the point was, he didn't wait for any thanks.

She shoved the door closed and leaned her back against it, her mind too full of Lundric.

So far, none of the terrible things she'd thought would happen since she was thrown on this pod had occurred. She hadn't been executed by the Ocretions. She hadn't been raped, or sold to a new slave owner. Each new turn was stranger and stranger. And this one with Lundric was the strangest yet.

CHAPTER TWO

Lundric woke up stiff in more ways than one. After working long past his shift end ensuring the refugees were settled, he'd slept on the floor of the bunkroom, since he'd carried his cot into Cambry's closet. So the aching neck wasn't a surprise.

The stiff cock could be attributed to Cambry, too. His dreams had all featured the fiery human. The pretty braids pulling her hair back into the bushy ponytail. The flip of that thick tail when she tossed her head. The length of her legs and the sway of her ass as she walked in front of him, a haughty grin curling her lips.

She had so much fight in her, his little rebel. How he'd love to wrestle her to the floor, feel her wriggling body beneath his as the struggle heated them both. Because he knew it would. He'd smelled her arousal that morning, known the irresistible pull he felt toward her wasn't just one-sided.

He sat up and checked the time. *Veck.* His shift was about to start, which meant the refugees were bedding down already. He hadn't had a chance to fashion a latch for the inside of Cambry's door. He shoved his feet into his boots and tromped down the corridor.

Cambry's door was shut tight. Was she already sleeping? His cock stirred at the thought of her lying on his bed, just behind the door.

His bed. Exactly where she belonged.

He paused. Should he check on her? No. If he stopped now, he wouldn't want to leave. Better to make the rounds first and come back. He went to Rok's office, which served as their headquarters, to meet his guards and assign their duties for the night shift. Rok and his little human, Lily, were nowhere to be found, no surprise there. The two of them spent a great deal of time locked in their sleeping quarters together. Rok had even pierced her with Zandian crystal, marking her as his permanent mate.

A thrill went through him at the thought of adorning Cambry with his gems. He'd do it that night, if he thought it would bind her to him. But their traditions meant nothing to her. He'd be better off buying her as a slave to make himself her master, much as Zander had done with Lamira.

He knew exactly what orders he'd give her, the moment she was his to command. *Strip. Kneel.* No, maybe not *kneel* because how would he touch her sweet little pussy if she was sucking his dick? Maybe the first thing he'd do would be to tie her arms and legs wide and spend an entire planet rotation exploring what made her scream in pleasure.

No. Tying her up would be too easy. She liked to fight. Better to hold her down with his body. Or to train her to obey. *If you move your hands from this position, I'll have to whip you...*

What he wanted was the assurance she'd be in his bed forever. After his mother's abandonment, he couldn't tolerate fickleness. Or flightiness.

His guards gathered, and he handed out assignments, keeping the corridor with Cambry's closet for himself. Sten hid a smirk, but he immediately quashed it when Lundric stared him down. He counted to twenty-five after the guards dispersed then made his way to Cambry's closet. The light was off inside. At least, when he peered through the crack, it looked dark. He pressed his ear to the door and listened for the sound of her breathing, but the metal was too thick. He couldn't hear it.

If she was asleep, he wouldn't bother her, but if she was awake, she might enjoy a little company. He pried the door open a centimeter then another. He cursed, remembering he'd promised her a lock by bedtime. It was too dark inside to make out her figure on the bed. A flash of movement just behind the door made him throw it wide, but not before his little warrior had buried a dagger deep into the place where shoulder met chest.

He grunted, restraining his instincts demanding he fight back.

"You stabbed me?"

Her eyes were wide, the whites shining in the light from the corridor. She stood in nothing but her loose, untied tunic—no leggings beneath, a fact that had his brain stuttering, despite his injury.

He grasped the handle of the dagger and yanked it out of his flesh, wiping his blood on his shirt. "With my own dagger, no less."

"What were you doing sneaking into my room?" Her words held more bravado than her face, which still wore shock. She took a step back into the room, and he followed, turning on the light and shutting the door behind him.

"I wasn't sure if you were asleep. I didn't want to wake you if you were."

Her eyes narrowed, but they flicked to his wound and her brows puckered.

He pulled off his tunic and undershirt, loving the way her gaze riveted, not on the bloody gash, but on the muscles of his chest.

She swallowed. "Here." She picked up her leggings from the floor, balled them up, and reached toward his wound.

"Wait, don't use your—"

Too late. She pressed the fabric against the gash. He shouldn't complain if her leggings got soaked in blood—leaving her nothing to cover those long sexy legs with.

She held the cloth tight, obviously experienced enough to know it took a lot of pressure to stop bleeding. Her effort caused her to lean into him, her breasts brushing against his ribs.

He covered her hand with his.

Her breath lifted and lowered her chest in short bursts. She licked her lips —*veck*—*those lips.* "I'm sorry. Should you get medical attention?"

He shrugged. "It's a flesh wound. Zandians heal quickly."

Another lick. She was *vecking* killing him with that little pink tongue of hers. "Well, should I—do you want me to clean it and stitch it up? Stop the bleeding?"

He couldn't stop the feral grin spreading across his face. *Veck*, yes, he wanted her little hands touching him. With a rough voice, he managed to mutter, "Yes."

She must have mistaken his raging libido for blood loss because she said, "Is there a med-kit? Are you all right to stand? Maybe you should sit. I'll go for help."

He shook himself. "You're not *vecking* going *anywhere* like that. I'll get it." Before she could protest, he shoved the door back open, exited, and shut it tight behind him, still holding her leggings to his bleeding wound.

He managed to get to the medical treatment room and back without running into any other beings, thank the stars. He sure as hell didn't want to have to explain a knife wound to any of his men or superiors. It would make him look weak and put Cambry in danger of answering to someone else for her actions. Plus, he'd have to explain why he'd given her a dagger in the first place.

He knocked this time, muttering, "It's me," before he opened the door.

Cambry had the audacity to grin. "Afraid I'd stab you a second time?" She had the dagger back in its holster on her hip.

Dearest Zandian star, her smile dazzled. He loved seeing her like that— rebellious, confident. With one hip cocked, her lean muscular legs jutted out beneath the short tunic. Her nipples steepled the fabric, and he doubted she wore any kind of underclothing. *Vecking* stars, did she even have on panties? His heart rate ramped up as desire flamed hotter. "I wouldn't let it happen a second time, little female. But I won't creep up on you again."

Was it strange he was *proud* of her for stabbing him? He was glad his little female could defend herself. He'd glimpsed the warrior in her from the start, and he *vecking* loved it.

He grabbed the chair and pulled it toward him with a scrape then plopped down and removed the blood-soaked fabric. Already, the wound had clotted.

Even so, she sucked in her breath as she came closer to inspect it. "You aimed too high," he observed. "Or were you expecting a Zandian?"

She focused on the wound as she doused it with disinfectant then reached for the needle and spidersilk thread. "I aimed for a human. I meant to stab downward from the nape."

He didn't like the moment of hesitation before she answered, as if she held something back. He tensed. "One in particular?"

"No." She answered too quickly.

"That one who slept next to you last night."

She had to move closer to get the right angle on the wound, and after trying from both his side and standing between his knees, she ended up straddling one of his thighs.

Her delectable scent filled his nostrils. Though she managed not to touch him, her heat radiated through his pants, scorching every place he felt it. He clenched his fists at his sides to keep from grabbing her ass and hoisting it right over his rock-hard cock.

"Yes, that one. Or another. I don't trust any being here."

Though he'd already observed her general mistrust, he took exception. She was locked alone in a room with him, wasn't she?

Her pale slender fingers deft with the needle, she didn't flinch at poking his flesh and pulling the thread through, doing what had to be done. Her immunity to his pain turned him on, though, by nature, he preferred to be the one who inflicted pain. She tied off the knot and leaned in to bite off the thread, giving him the perfect view of her pert little breasts, bare, as he'd suspected, beneath the tunic. When she pulled back, she caught him looking and her eyes narrowed.

"Enjoying yourself?" Her hands went to the swell of her hips.

Veck, does she have panties on?

"Believe me, baby, you'd know if I was enjoying myself." His lids drooped to half-mast. "I'd have you pinned down with those sexy thighs spread wide, and you'd be the recipient of all my joy."

~·~

Cambry drew in a sharp breath, her pussy clenching at the warrior's crass words. She ought to be afraid of him, but she wasn't. Instinctively, she knew he didn't mean her harm. If he hadn't forced her yet, he probably wouldn't, especially after what she'd done to him.

"Does that mean you forgive me for stabbing you?" Her voice sounded foreign to her own ears—husky. Full of sex. She dismounted from his thigh and attempted to move away, but his hands, which she'd watched strain at his sides with tortured restraint while she'd straddled him, settled on her hips and drew her back between his legs.

"Not quite."

Her body—unused to touch—jerked, knees trembled.

His eyes burning with dark intent, he rotated her sideways. "Hands on the wall." He gave her upper body a shove, forcing her compliance before she could decide if she wanted to obey. Her hands flew out to catch herself, and she stood, tipped at the waist, her ass a perfect target for Lundric's right hand. She had no doubt what he intended.

"Don't move those hands from the wall. If you do, I will whip your ass until you scream. Got it?"

She ought to be angry at the thought of receiving abuse from yet another oppressive master, but only flutters of excitement filled her belly.

Lundric's huge palm crashed down on her upturned ass, and she listed to the side. "You *are* wearing panties."

Does he sound gleeful?

He pulled her back into place. "You hold this position for me, baby. This is punishment, and I'm going to make sure you learn something from it."

Again the strange flutters. What did he expect her to—*ack*. She held her breath when his hand crashed down again, then stayed on her ass, rubbing away the sting.

He shoved her tunic up and pulled the back of her panties down until they just bared her ass. "*Vecking* stars, that's pretty." He sounded almost reverent. To her shock, he grasped the front of her panties and yanked them up, pulling and tightening the fabric until it applied pressure to her clit.

She couldn't restrain the gasp of surprise and pleasure rocketing through her. Tipping her hips forward, she leaned into it, hungry for more.

She also made the perfect target for his palm, which smacked her tingling cheek once more. She tucked her tail to dodge the next spank, and he followed through, pulling up on her panties even more, sending a wave of dizzy pleasure through her.

She panted, waiting on her tiptoes, fingers splayed wide against the wall, desperate for more.

"That's where I want you." He spoke more to himself than to her and began spanking her with hard, swift strokes. She danced under the onslaught, leaning into her panties, which pleasured her with every twist and turn as his hand punished, making her ass burn with the intensity.

"Stop, please," she whimpered, but he didn't stop. Instead, he began to jerk her panties up in short bursts, fast and hard, never pausing in his assault on her ass.

She crested the peak and fell over the other side in an eruption of pleasure, her pussy clenching on nothing but a pair of panties, head swimming with visions of Lundric's bare torso, those enormous muscles in all their power.

He spanked and panty-jerked her right through her climax but stopped the moment she collapsed her head against the wall, one of her hands sliding down as she sagged. He surged to his feet, caging her against the wall, his big hand covering the one that had slipped, his body pressed against hers. She registered his cock at her back with an aftershock of pussy-clenching. His lips found her ear, breath came hot against her neck. "What did I tell you about moving these hands?"

Her ass throbbed in response, already hot and tingling from the hand spanking. She sure as stars hoped he wasn't serious about whipping her.

"Please, Lundric." She wanted to kick herself for begging like a helpless female.

He bit her ear, hands coasting down her sides to squeeze her throbbing ass. "*Now* I forgive you," he murmured, pulling up her panties. He continued to massage and squeeze her bottom over the panties, and she helplessly pushed it into his hands, loving the way he made her feel, even if it confused the hell out of her.

"Captain Lundric?" The disembodied voice sounded from somewhere on her floor.

Lundric cursed and jumped back, stooping to search the pile of his tunic and undershirt for his comms unit. "What is it?" he snapped.

"There's a disturbance in cell 8—a fight amongst refugees."

"I'll be right there." He turned to her. She'd already taken the interruption as an opportunity to yank her head back to reality. To steel herself against whatever this bizarre interaction had been.

But the apology on his face sank her. Like he owed *her* something more. When he hadn't even taken pleasure. Had only given it—along with punishment.

Confusion swirled with post-orgasmic languor and lack of sleep. She watched, blankly, as he pulled his clothes back on over his beautiful chest. She wondered how he'd explain the blood on his clothes. Picking up her bloodied leggings, he said, "I'll wash these tonight so they're dry by morning. Push the chair against the door. It won't keep it from opening, but it will serve as an extra barrier in the dark until I install a latch. I'll drop your leggings on the chair when they're done."

She nodded.

"I'll keep watch over your room, baby. You can rest." Without warning, his arm reached out and snaked around her waist, and he yanked her body against his. His cock still stood rigid, and she experienced a stab of guilt he hadn't found release. Not that she'd been ready to offer it to him. "Thank you," he murmured.

She pulled away, and he let her go. "For what?"

A roguish grin split his face. "For stabbing me. How else would I get my hands on that tight little ass of yours?"

Dearest Mother Earth, he'd made her blush. *Nothing* made her blush.

He grasped her nape and pulled her head forward to drop a kiss on her hair. Then he winked and left, pulling the door shut tight behind him.

She waited, listening for the sound of his boots as he walked away, but there was only silence.

He was waiting for her. "The chair?"

"This chair isn't going to be a barrier to anyone getting in," she grumbled, but a goofy smile stretched her lips as she dragged it into position. He cared about her safety.

"Thank you." *Stars*, she loved his deep, gruff voice.

Her clit throbbed in time with her ass as she walked the two steps to her cot. She sank down onto it with a sigh of pleasure. She hadn't slept on anything even semi-cushioned in a hundred planet rotations. Not since she'd killed the guards and been caught escaping the factory housing.

She hooked her thumbs in her panties and slid them off, bringing her knees up to her chest to get them over her feet. Her hands slid over her heated ass, exploring the sensation.

She'd been beaten as a child by the Ocretion factory foremen, and when she was grown, they'd used shock-sticks for punishment. Nothing compared to this sensation of heat and tingling and pain, more exciting than unpleasant because of the context. Her fingers found her pussy, and she shivered with pleasure at her own touch. Her folds were swollen and slick, and a little raw, but in the best possible way. She worked her sex and pictured her giant Zandian warrior—how he had to duck to fit through the doorway, his beautiful muscled chest and arms, the way his lids had drooped with desire for her, the sense of tightly leashed lust. What else could he do to her body?

I'd have you pinned down with those sexy thighs spread wide...

Her hips snapped up with another climax, her internal walls contracting once more on nothing. For the first time in at least four years, she wanted to have sex. Wanted to know what that powerful body felt like over hers, under hers, behind hers.

She slowly lowered her hips back to the cot, stroking all the aftershocks out of her pussy. She'd probably regret all of it tomorrow, but, for now, it felt like in a lifetime of oppression, one small thing had gone right. She had a cot, her own closet, and two orgasms. It wasn't freedom. It wasn't finding Tal, but it was a start.

CHAPTER THREE

Cambry took a front row seat for the first training session. Or she would have if there were seats to be had. While the Zandians had sent supplies and battleships, they still didn't have chairs, or beds or changes of clothing, so they'd all sat on the floor of the large hall where she'd slept—or actually hadn't slept—the first night.

Rok, the young Zandian warrior who appeared to be in charge, had sorted them into groups based on their interests. Some would learn to fly the battleships, others would practice navigation and communication skills to serve as co-pilots, and most of them would learn hand-to-hand combat. Those too sick or wounded had been taken to a sick bay where beings interested in learning medical care and assisting with battle wounds would nurse them.

She'd volunteered for pilot training. It didn't take a genius to figure out the only way off the uninhabitable planet they'd crashed into was in an airship, so she intended to learn how to fly one. First chance she got, she'd fly herself straight out of the galaxy. No way she was waiting around to fight a war on Zandia she had no stake in.

Rok stood in front with his crew of non-Zandians. An unkempt old Venusian, two Stornigians, and a huge being of a species she didn't recognize.

Rok's human girlfriend came in and dropped to the floor near Cambry. "Hi, I'm Lily," she said, holding out her hand in the ancient human gesture of greeting.

If she weren't hoping to ingratiate herself with the trainers enough to get into an airship, she would have rebuffed the girl's overtures. This was the female who'd been singing the song of human freedom on Zandia, trying to get them all to believe in some kind of "promised land."

She reluctantly put forth her hand. "Cambry." She supposed she shouldn't begrudge Lily her misplaced faith in the Zandians. And maybe, for Lily, the promised land would be true. After all, she had captivated her Zandian warrior so well, he'd been willing to take down this entire death pod to save her.

Now Rok and his warriors were stuck with the two hundred other beings who had come with Lily. Of course, they couldn't just set them free. If word got back to the Ocretions they didn't all perish, Lily and Rok would have a price on their heads. So, they'd decided to make soldiers out of them for their own purposes.

Most of the beings there were just content to have had their death sentences cleared. Nothing much changed for them. They'd traded one master for another; Work and obedience were still required of them with the penalty death if they didn't give it.

But Cambry had decided back at the factory, when her brother was taken from her, it was time to get herself free. She had a rare opportunity to learn a skill that would facilitate her goal.

Rok whistled and brought the room to attention. There were about one hundred beings there, and all their attention went to the large warrior. His gaze traveled over the group, resting on Lily, where Cambry had the feeling he'd wanted to focus all along. His face went soft, as if she had the power to bring him to bliss simply with her presence in the room.

Cambry stole a glance at Lily, who appeared equally riveted, cheeks turning a soft shade of pink. "How'd you meet?" she found herself asking.

Lily smiled, not dragging her focus from her male. "I stole his ship."

Cambry choked on a laugh, her opinion of the young woman rising. "Is that so?"

"Yeah." Their eyes were still locked. "But then he caught me and kept me prisoner." She said it like it was the sexiest, most romantic thing in the galaxy, and after what happened with Lundric last night, she almost understood.

How would she like to be Lundric's prisoner? Tied up and available for his use. Or bent over his knee and punished for disobedience.

I will whip your ass until you scream.

Why did she almost want to push him into delivering such a consequence?

As if conjured by her lustful thoughts, Lundric strode in. He appeared tired and a little pale but still panty-dropping gorgeous. She hoped the pallor wasn't from blood loss. If he'd been a human, that wound she'd inflicted could've been deadly. She shuddered to think how horrible she'd feel if Lundric were lying in the sick bay now, fighting for his life because of her. Sweet Mother Earth, how she prayed he hadn't been downplaying it for her sake.

Rok launched into some kind of introduction, but she only had attention for Lundric. He stood at attention behind Rok, but his gaze immediately fell on her, as if he'd known where she sat from the moment he walked in the door. His eyes blazed with heat and a promise. A tingle of warmth swept through her, the memory of what they'd done the night before barreling into her mind and making her belly flutter. *Veck*, was she blushing?

"Looks like you've found a Zandian admirer, too," Lily murmured.

"I stabbed him last night with his own dagger."

Lily stifled a giggle, finally tearing her attention away from her mate to look at Cambry. "Well, I guess that's the key. Maybe you have to significantly offend them to win their undying love."

Undying love.

Her stomach clenched. That wasn't what she and Lundric were about. Shared lust, yes. Mutual pleasure, absolutely. She'd already decided she wanted more. But she wasn't looking for a mate. She had one boot out the door. As soon as she found her chance, she was escaping. And yeah, stealing one of their ships, just like Lily had. Heh.

Maybe Lundric would take her prisoner. Except she couldn't be caught, and she wasn't playing around. She needed to find and free her brother. Only then could she consider any kind of future with any species of being. Who knew? Maybe the Zandians would win their planet back, and she could return the ship and waltz back into Lundric's life.

But no, her gut said he'd never forgive her for deserting.

She considered the intensity with which he'd treated her—watching over her, securing her safety, washing her leggings and returning them neatly folded in the middle of the night. He might not think this thing between them was as casual as she did.

Even that niggling worry couldn't dissuade her from wanting more of Lundric, though. And soon.

~.~

Lundric couldn't stop watching Cambry, his beautiful female. She'd blushed when he first saw her, her porcelain skin turning an enchanting shade of pink beneath the smattering of freckles. He wondered how she'd look with that mane of hair flowing free over her shoulders and around her face. Like a *vecking* goddess. He wanted to bury his fingers in it, wrap it up in his fist, tickle her breasts with the ends.

Rok gave the refugees the rundown on how training was going to go. Lundric had to admire Rok—he wasn't one to hear himself talk. He kept it brief then ordered them to break into groups of twelve and assigned a Zandian warrior to each group.

"Take them to a ship. Let each one sit in the cockpit and handle the controls. There's no better way to learn than doing. Test them until they have it down."

He marched over to take Cambry's group, which also happened to contain Rok's female. Rok squared off with him. "I've got this one."

He willed his jaw to relax. "You'll need to make the rounds and supervise. I'll take this group after you're finished demonstrating."

Rok's mouth flattened into a thin line. Lily slipped her hand through his arm, and his shoulders relaxed by a fraction. She murmured something only he could hear, and Rok's expression turned musing as he contemplated Lundric. When he turned to give Cambry the same look, though, Lundric growled.

Rok's lips twitched. "I see. All right, Captain. We'll go to the ship together, then."

Lundric fell in beside Cambry as they walked to the hatch, where they each took an oxygen helmet for the short walk from the pod to the battleship. He resisted the urge to double-check Cambry's to be sure she had it on correctly. Not only was she an intelligent, capable female, but she wouldn't appreciate his treating her like a child. He'd seen the way she'd sat front and center for the meeting. She was there to learn. The best thing he could do was stay out of her way.

Once everyone had suited up, they stepped into the interim chamber then out onto the barren land of Shooku, the uninhabitable planet where the pod had crashed. Waterless and made of red dust, the planet's landscape looked the same in every direction. Its air didn't have enough oxygen content for their lungs, and the temperature was hot enough to make his clothes stick to his body within moments. They quickly boarded an airship and closed the hatch, crowding into the small cockpit.

"The only way to learn to fly is by practicing," Rok announced, guiding Lily into the pilot's seat. "That's how I learned. It's how you will learn, too. By the time we enter a real battle, you will know how to fly the hell out of these things." He then explained every button switch and control on the panel.

One of the human males cleared his throat. "So, how exactly will this battle look?"

Rok flicked a glance at Lundric. A smuggler who had been raised away from Zandians, Rok wasn't really one of them. He'd earned his position by being the best pilot of their species. "I'm not sure yet. My job is to ready pilots for the fleet. But Prince Zander and others like Captain Lundric have spent most of their lives preparing for this. Isn't that right?"

He couldn't deny the flare of satisfaction at the curiosity in Cambry's gaze. "That's true, yes."

"How old were you when Zandia was invaded?" Rok asked.

He cringed. It was odd to have this bonding moment in front of every riveted being on the battleship. "Seven solar cycles. You?"

"Eight. How'd you survive?"

He swallowed hard. The memory wasn't a pleasant one—not in the least. "I got lucky. I was off-planet at the time with my grandparents."

Rok leaned past Lily and flicked on the engine then dropped into the copilot's seat. "I escaped with a guard who was able to fly an ancient airship we found, no bigger than this one. If he hadn't known how to fly, we would've died. It's a skill every being should have. So, let's get started."

He instructed Lily and allowed her to take off and fly a few hundred meters before helping her land. "Lundric, take my seat. Let each student practice takeoff and landing—three times each, until they get the feel of it."

"Yes, Captain." He didn't know what Rok's exact title was, but since he answered to him, he thought he ought to give him one.

Rok's lips twisted into a lopsided grin. "Am I a captain, now, too?" He bent his arm at a ninety degree angle in the traditional formal Zandian greeting but then threw it away with a cavalier, "Thanks, friend."

Lundric lifted his chin at Cambry, inviting her into the pilot's chair. He slid in beside her. She'd paid attention to Rok and was quick to execute the steps necessary for takeoff, as if trying to do them all before he prompted. He closed his mouth and let her do her thing, waiting until she had a question.

"So—like this?" She pushed on the controller.

He covered her hand with his, mostly because he couldn't stand being near her and not touching that smooth pale skin again. He bumped the level to a higher speed. "Now, push it away from you, gently."

The ship lifted, wobbled, and touched back down with a sickening jolt. All the beings groaned and shouted in protest as heads bumped and bodies jostled. Yeah, Rok's method of training probably wasn't the safest. They didn't even have seats and harnesses for all the beings crowded on the ship. But who was he to complain? He got to tutor Cambry, which was all he really cared about.

"Let's try again." He hadn't taken his hand off hers. "Don't think of the ship as separate from you. Become the ship. Close your lids and just feel—no, really—there's nothing out here to hit. That's it, shut your eyes and pay attention to how it feels. When is the right time to lift off?"

She accelerated, this time pressing down to launch the craft at exactly the right moment. It wobbled but immediately stabilized.

"You did it!"

Her lids flew open, and she beamed. "I did it!"

Stars, he loved that smile on her. It transformed her taut, serious features into divine radiance.

"Now, land. Eyes open, this time, but imagine you're a bird alighting on the ground. You don't want to stumble or trip as you come down. Adjust your speed—*slower!*—that's it. Pull up now."

She pulled up too hard, and he applied pressure to the back of her hand to level the craft out. It bumped and skidded to a stop, and the whole group laughed with exhilaration.

He grinned, reluctantly removing his palm from Cambry's slender hand. "Next."

~.~

Cambry would give anything for a shower.

With no water source on Shooku, the Zandians had ordered water on the pod be rationed. It could only be used as fast as the pod could recycle it, which was teeth-gnashingly slow. Captain Rok had announced while he understood every being wanted to bathe, they would only receive the privilege once a week, and they would not be permitted a shower or tub, just one small basin-full. Enough to dunk her head, not her body.

Cambry received her wash-card, and it was for five planet rotations from that day. After their flying lesson, which had been a thrill beyond what she'd hoped, there'd been more housekeeping. They were each assigned chores as the Zandians worked to establish routines and order from the chaos.

Lundric had disappeared—she presumed to sleep. At some point, he'd installed a simple but effective latch on the inside of her door, so even if she wanted him to, he couldn't sneak into her room that night.

She perched on the edge of her cot, loneliness gnawing at her. Not the ache of missing Tal, which was still there, but a fresher sort of emptiness that could be caused only by the enormous horned warrior who'd taken an interest in her.

A tap sounded at her door, and she leaped up, forcing the grin from her face. She'd known he'd come. "It's me," he said softly.

It's me.

Were they already at that stage? Shouldn't she play hard to get, still?

But she already had the door unlatched, and he shoved it open.

"Take me to a shower, and I'll let you take me."

She hadn't seen the cocky young warrior lose composure before, but he did now. Lundric's jaw dropped then snapped shut with a frown. "What the *veck?*" he spluttered, clearly angry at her request.

Why? Because she'd propositioned him? Hadn't that been what he was after?

She didn't play the sexual card—not ever, but it felt easy with him. It felt safe. She leaned in and let the tips of her breasts brush against the hard ridged muscles of his stomach. "I don't want you to touch me until I'm clean. It's been a really long time since I've had a chance to bathe. Please, Lundric?"

The muscles in his jaw eased, somewhat, but he grasped her wrists and pressed her back against the door, wrists pinned beside her head. He was seven feet of solid, aggressive male giving off a threatening vibe, but she wasn't scared. A low, persistent hum had started up between her legs.

"Do you make bargains like that often?" he snarled.

Ah. Jealousy. She could handle that. In fact, she rather relished it.

"No, Captain. Never." It wasn't a lie.

His eyes narrowed as he studied her face as if to determine culpability. "Sex is not a commodity between us, little female," he growled. "It's not something you trade or use to manipulate. You already belong to me." He knocked her feet apart, shoving one hard thigh between her legs and pulling his knee up until he lifted her to her toes, suspended by her crotch. She rocked her pelvis forward, grinding her clit against the solid muscle.

"If you get my cock, it's because I decide you deserve it. Understand?"

She sucked in a breath, too shocked to speak. White-hot anger flooded through her, along with a trace of fear, but behind it came fully charged lust, which overpowered her indignation.

He doesn't mean it, she chanted to herself. This was the way he approached sex. She'd seen last night how he liked to dominate.

And still her hips undulated over his knee, as if he'd been offering her sex instead of threatening to deny it.

She moistened her lips, knowing it would catch his attention, loving the hungry way he stared at them. "Wh-what do I deserve tonight?"

His cock lengthened against her belly. When his mouth descended on hers, flames erupted behind her eyes, turning her vision to a lustful haze of sparking lights. He dragged his open mouth over hers, sucked her lower lip, nipped it. Magically, he had both her wrists pinned with one hand as the other cupped her throat, squeezing only enough for her to register the threat, not enough to hurt or actually block her windpipe.

Her pussy clenched as she neared orgasm from a kiss, alone.

She'd thought she knew what sex was all about. Had practiced with a few partners—other slaves at the factory. But this—what Lundric did to her—proved she'd never left the training ground. She knew nothing about blind pleasure, bone-melting desire, a willingness to give herself over to a male who wasn't even remotely safe. He bit her lower lip again as he pulled away and stared down with a heavy-lidded gaze.

She'd been wrong. His irises weren't brown—they were violet. And his horns had thickened and leaned toward her, as if they, too, wanted to dominate.

"Oh I definitely think you deserve a *vecking*," he rumbled. With his body flattened against hers, his deep voice reverberated through her, sending shock waves down her inner thighs to her curling toes. He nipped her earlobe. "Long, hard and from behind. *While* you shower. Come on." Abruptly, he released her, and she registered the loss of his body with acute disappointment.

He picked up her hand and led her out of the room, pulling the door shut tight, as if she had something in there worth stealing. Her palm felt small engulfed in his larger one, and she marveled at the gesture. It seemed like it ought to feel far more foreign to her than it did. She couldn't recall anyone ever holding her hand before, and yet Lundric's grip felt so right, so easy and normal and perfect. She followed him through the corridors, not caring about the curious glances they received from Zandians as they passed.

He took her to a small washroom and locked the door. His tunic and undershirt came off in one fluid motion over his head, during which time he bored a hole in her with his hot gaze. She gasped when she saw how much his stab wound had healed. It appeared weeks old instead of one planet rotation.

Lundric frowned. "Clothes off by the count of three. One..." His pants came off, and she stalled in her stripping as she stared at his gigantic cock. "Two." His voice held a distinct note of warning.

She fumbled with the tie of her tunic and wrestled it off.

"Three."

She shoved her leggings down off her legs.

"Too slow, baby. Next time I tell you to strip you'd better move faster or there will be consequences."

Her pussy and anus clenched at the same time. Even her butt cheeks gave a little squeeze at the threat of punishment, the memory of his spanking the previous planet rotation making her breath quicken.

He strode to the shower, his huge cock bobbing as he walked. She joined him when he turned on the water, but he held her back with a hand on her forearm. "Wait, it's too cold."

Thoughtful warrior.

"Now." He dragged her in.

She turned in the spray of warm water, not sure how long she'd have and wanting to get every part of her wet. Lundric turned it off and accepted a dollop of soap from the automatic dispenser. He rubbed a lather between two palms. She moved to get her own soap, but he spun her around and shoved her up against the wall, his soapy hands coasting up and down her sides, over her backside, down her thighs. He lathered her inner thighs, stopping agonizingly close to her pussy but never touching it. He gave breasts the full treatment, however, kneading and squeezing them until they grew tight and heavy, pinching her nipples until her pussy spasmed.

"Spread your legs, Cambry." Lundric's voice sounded rough and gravelly.

She obeyed.

"How do you think I should *veck* you?"

"H-hard. From behind." Wasn't that what he'd promised?

His hand smoothed down her hip. "Good girl," he murmured thickly just before he speared her with his erection.

She shouted at his girth, her body stretching to accommodate his enormous size.

"Good girl," he repeated, moving with the most miniscule and maddening pulse inside her as she got used to being filled by him.

The words fell like jewels, glittering between them. No one had ever praised her, nor had she wanted anyone's approval. But hearing his satisfaction made her belly flutter with excitement. She pushed her hips back to take him deeper.

He groaned. "You feel so good, Cambry. *So. Vecking. Tight.* He started to rock with more movement, filling her and easing back. He brought his mouth close to her ear, one hand sneaking around the front of her to stroke her clit. "You're lucky I'm back on shift soon, or I'd *veck* you all night."

She made a humming sound in her throat.

"Tell me something. Do you like having my cock inside you, pretty girl?"

"Yes, Captain."

"Who does this tight little pussy belong to?"

She balked at his possessiveness, but her hesitation only made him slam into her harder, lifting her to her toes and making her scream with pleasure. "You!" she shrieked. "It belongs to you, Lundric."

He gentled his movements again, scything in and out in maddening thrusts. "That's right, baby." He traced a light circle over her clit. "My pussy. *Mine.*"

"Yours," she whispered. "Please..."

"Take it, baby. You don't have to beg tonight. Not when you're being such a good girl."

He pinched one nipple and her clit, and she climaxed, loving the way it felt to have his huge cock buried deep this time when she came.

Nothing had ever felt so right as the way he filled her, the way he played her body like a master musician plays an instrument, the way he thrust upward in sharp movements the moment she'd finished until he, too, orgasmed, his shout echoing off the walls, entering her body through her ears, her pores, her breath.

Before he pulled out, he turned on the warm water, enveloping her in the soothing spray as she suffered the loss of his body.

~.~

Cambry's offer to trade sex for a shower had offended him. If all he'd been interested in was sex, he would've pushed it the night before. He *vecking* hated the thought of her treating it like some smarmy deal they made, in which they traded favors for favors. No.

She was his *vecking* female. He'd known it from the moment he saw her. And it was about far more than sex. He wanted her forever—as his mate, his slave—whatever it took to bind her to him. The thought of losing her made him sick.

He took another dollop of soap and sudsed her hair, ignoring how the surprise in those big eyes warmed the center of his chest. She shoved his hands away, trying to take control, and he smacked her ass, hard, her wet skin and the walls of the washtube making the slap loud.

She yelped and immediately went still. Submission was out of character for her, and so, like the night before, he treasured that she gave it to him willingly. He knew it was solely based on trust, not weakness.

He pushed her into the spray, and she rinsed off. When he turned off the water, the automatic dryer came on with a hard blast of not-quite-warm-enough air. These sure weren't the luxury washtubes he'd grown accustomed to on Zander's palatial pod. He slipped out and handed Cambry her clothing then quickly dressed in his white uniform.

When they emerged they met Lily in the corridor. Her lips curved into a knowing smile when she took in their damp hair and the chamber they'd exited. She passed them then turned back and called, "Cambry."

He picked up Cambry's hand as they stopped, making it clear she was with him.

"My sister sent some supplies today. Why don't you come and take some for yourself."

Cambry's expression turned uncertain. From what he'd seen of her behavior since he arrived on the pod, she didn't form friendships or bonds quickly or easily, mistrust being her first reaction to others.

Lily glanced at him. "They sent a crystal for the Zandians, too. You look like you could use it. Have you been eating here?"

He frowned, *vecking* hating any being thinking him weak. The wound from the night before had healed rapidly, but the blood loss and being away from crystal and light made his body slower to repair than usual.

Lily rolled her eyes. "No, I'm not calling your malehood into question. Rok says Zandians have to eat more when they're away from the crystals. That's how he survived as a child away from Zandia."

Lundric gnawed on that. It would've been nice to know he needed to eat more often upon arrival, but he supposed he should have. He just hadn't spent much time away from the palatial pod.

"Come on, both of you. Stop acting like I'm trying to poison you or something." Lily beckoned them in her direction and starting walking away.

He raised his brows at Cambry, who shrugged, and they followed.

Rok and Lily's chamber was not grand or large. Several travel crates stood along one wall, and from these, Lily started pulling things out. "Here, these should fit you." She tossed a pair of leggings and an undershirt on the small bed.

Cambry picked them up. "Yeah, thanks. I could use a change of clothing."

"I know. Every being can. I have placed a standing supply requisition list out to the palatial pod, ordered from most important to least. These things weren't on the list, but my mother sent them. I don't even know what all of them are, but they sure as hell 'aren't anything I ever had as a slave." She pulled out large bottles of soap and gel and oil.

Lundric recognized them as the products found in washrooms on the palatial pod. His need to take care of and provide for his female made him stride forward and gather a few of them. "Thank you." He caught the wink of sparkle on her earlobes and sucked in a breath, an ingrained sense of reverence rippling through him at the recognition of their traditional mating.

He bowed to Lily. "Congratulations on your mating."

Lily touched the crystal studs and beamed, blushing a little. "Prince Zander sent them to Rok so he could mate me in the Zandian tradition."

Desire swept through Lundric like wildfire. *Mate Cambry.* The urgency to bind Cambry to him forever in this and every other way possible nearly blinded him. He wanted the union recognized by Prince Zander, by his fellow species and pod mates. By every human on the pod.

And, most importantly, by Cambry.

But how? How did this Zandian-human mating occur? Prince Zander had bought his mate. Rok had rescued his, although Lundric had heard through some grumbling by Rok's Stornigian foster brothers he'd bartered weapons for her.

"Here." Lily held out a fist-sized raw Zandian crystal, and a shudder of energy went through him. No wonder he'd felt stronger just being in the room. He took it into his palm and wrapped his fingers around it, closing his lids to savor the spike of energy.

"Rok is trying to come up with some kind of light-bathing room here, like you have on Prince Zander's pod, but it's hard when we're so limited on space," Lily explained. "Of course, if necessary, you can just fly back and forth to use Prince Zander's, but Rok doesn't want to attract Ocretion attention with too much traffic."

He held the crystal up to the stab wound and swore he could feel the blood beneath it heating, energy shifting and rearranging to bring his flesh back to its normal, unmarred appearance. "Mind if I take it?" he asked. "I have an idea where it might be installed for all of us to use."

"For all of you purple-skinned giants. Sure."

"Thank you." Lundric bowed and led Cambry out of the room, clutching both the bath products for his female and the crystal.

In the hall, Cambry eyed the crystal. "So, what's with the rock?"

Even though she was human and wouldn't understand, his need to provide for his female made him offer the gem to her. She took it, examining the different facets and whistling. "This must be worth a fortune."

"It is. Zandian crystal is the reason our planet was taken over by the Finn. They are valuable throughout the galaxy because they have wide applications in laser and light-bending technologies."

Cambry tossed it in the air as if testing its weight, and he winced, snatching it before it landed in her palm again.

"It's sacred to us."

"Oops."

"King Zander and his queen refused to sell the crystals for technology. So the Finn invaded and committed mass genocide, killing off every member of my species they found on the planet. Only those who managed to escape or were off-planet at the time survived."

They'd arrived in front of Cambry's door again, and Lundric shoved it open, bringing in the bottles of luxury products and arranging them in a neat row along the wall.

She took over and shoved them under her cot.

"I can build you a shelf in here, if you like."

She stared at him as if he had two heads. "Yes...maybe. Thank you. But back to your story. Why were you off-planet when they invaded?"

The familiar deadness swept through his chest. He hated this part of his life story. The worthlessness he'd felt as a boy, before Master Seke had given him purpose.

As if sensing his darkness, she stepped forward and laid her slender palm on his chest.

He looped an arm around her waist and pulled her snug against his body, letting her feel how quickly his need for her regenerated. "My mother didn't want me. She'd sent me away to live with her grandparents on Aurelia. My grandfather was the Zandian ambassador to the United Galaxies." Aurelia was a neutral, peaceful planet, near Ocretion territory, that housed the United Galaxies.

To Cambry's credit, she quickly hid the flash of pity that sprang to her face. "I'm sorry."

He shrugged. "I'm not. I wouldn't be alive if she hadn't been a selfish beast. I would never have been trained by Master Seke, who is an incredible master of battle arts. I wouldn't be Prince Zander's chief of security, or a captain of the royal guard who protect and serves the prince. So being unwanted was the best thing that ever happened to me." He heard the touch of bitterness in his voice and hated the weakness in him the wound still bore.

"Are they still alive? Your grandparents?"

He shook his head. "No. They died of old age within one planet rotation of each other about ten solar cycles ago. They couldn't live without each other. Theirs was truly a love match." He smiled, despite the tug of sadness still echoing through him at their loss. They'd been good to him, doing their best to raise him, despite their old age. When Master Seke had invited him to move into the palatial pod to train with the prince himself, they'd been so proud. When he pictured winning Zandia back for their species, it was for them—to honor their love of the planet from which he personally didn't bear any happy memories.

"Why are the crystals sacred? And what bath was Lily talking about?"

"To Zandians, the crystals have life-giving properties." He lifted the gem to his wound once more and smiled faintly as he felt its hum. "They bring a sense of peace and calm to those who touch them, and when used in windows or skylights, amplify the sun, which we require as energy to survive."

Cambry's smile turned teasing. "You just showed me your weak spot, warrior."

He shook his head. "No, my weak spot is this," he gripped her ass possessively, pulling her even tighter against his body.

"Are you going to make me the recipient of your joy again?" she purred.

His cock surged painfully against his pants, and he groaned. "Soon," he choked against her damp hair. "Right now, I have to work." It took all the self-control in the galaxy to release her and step away, but he did it.

Soon he would bind her to him so she and all the pod recognized what he knew to the depths of his marrow.

She belonged to him.

CHAPTER FOUR

After the incredibly satisfying—in more ways than one—shower, Cambry ought to have been ready to retire to her room, but a restless energy had her loathe to stay holed up in her tiny closet until dinner. Odd. When had she ever preferred the company of strangers—or beings in general—to solitude? It had always been she and Tal with plenty of alone time in between.

Maybe she'd just take a walk around the pod. It was strange to feel so free. While she still considered herself and all the other "refugees" to be essentially prisoners, they hadn't been treated that way. There were no curfews or restricted movements. The first time she'd walked the hall alone, yesterday, she'd been certain one of the guards would stop her, haul her back, or punish her. But none of those things had happened.

She just didn't like leaving her little chamber unlocked. Since Lundric had smashed his fist into the control panel, there was no way to lock it from the outside. Not that she regretted the loss of the control panel in the least. She never would've let him lure her in there if it had still been active. It wasn't so much she had anything to steal—although she'd guess most every refugee there would love the skin products—it was more that she'd hate to return and find someone waiting in there to ambush her. Thank the stars—and Lundric—she still had the dagger he'd given her.

She closed her door tightly and set off through the corridors. Although she had no purpose, she affected the walk of a being who did not want anyone to hail her or try to engage her. Except she wasn't even sure that was true anymore. The beings she'd engaged with—namely Lundric and Lily—had not yet harmed her. In fact, they'd both given her gifts. A dagger and skin products might not seem like much to a Zandian, but they were the most valuable things she'd ever owned.

She walked through the row of prison cells, taking in the way they'd turned into nests. Though little had changed in architecture or even furnishings, there was a settled feel to them now. Beings talked or rested. Faces and shoulders were relaxed; chatter was easy. Like hers, their defenses had started to come down. At the end of the row, she took a right and looped back through a second row of cells.

If she'd been in one of these cells, her guard would not be down. There were too many beings, too many variables for staying safe. Lundric had truly done her a favor by providing her with her own space. But had it come at too high a cost? What were the huge alien's expectations of her now?

Who does this tight little pussy belong to?

Did he really believe that? Or was it his form of dirty-talk during sex? Because she belonged to no male, no matter how considerate. No matter how much he made her knees weak and her core turn to molten lava.

She almost wished she hadn't learned about his past. Seeing him as a fully dimensional being instead of just a virile young prison guard changed things. *Veck*, she had to see all the Zandians with a little more sympathy after hearing about the genocide of their species. Although, at least those who escaped death were free and, from the looks of it, rich. Her species was still enslaved on most planets.

She came out of the second row of cells and turned left down a corridor she didn't know. When it dead-ended, she reversed direction and headed back. She wondered if she'd run into Lundric.

As she rounded the bend, a fist smashed into her temple, and her vision went black.

~.~

"Wake up, red."

Her face stung with a slap. Her head screamed as she cracked her eyes and tried to make sense of her surroundings. The creepy male who'd slept near her the planet rotation she met Lundric swam into her vision.

His lips stretched into a chilling smile. "That's right. I waited until you woke up. I prefer you awake for this."

Her adrenaline kicked into high gear, clearing her head. She struggled to move but found herself pinned below the male. One of his hands squeezed her throat, and he straddled her waist. Her clothes were still on, thank Mother Earth.

He closed the fist around her throat enough to cut off her breath.

She struggled harder, vision turning red. *Don't panic—fight.* She clawed at his hands, scraping his skin under her nails, drawing blood.

"Get...the hell off me," she wheezed and bucked her hips, trying to dislodge him, but he weighed too much. His grin grew wider.

"Keep fighting, red. I love the struggle." He eased his grip on her throat, and her vision returned as he let her draw a few ragged breaths.

So—a torture game.

To hell with this. She wasn't about to let this asshole win.

Think, think! Where was she? A dark corner somewhere. Not a chamber—just a corridor.

The dagger.

Why had it taken her this long to remember her weapon? She kept up the struggle with one hand as her other swept down, searching her pocket.

Gone.

Where in the hell had it gone?

The creep choked her again, his fingers crushing her throat in a bruising grasp. She swept her hand from side to side, searching for the knife on the floor. It must have fallen out, had to be somewhere. *Lundric.* She found herself calling his name in her head. Her vision darkened again, lights bursting at the edges.

Hoping he didn't plan on killing her yet, she forced her body to go prematurely limp, but before she could act, her vision went dark, and she lost consciousness again.

When she returned, a roar filled her ears, along with a horrible crunching sound. A figure loomed over her—shadows sweeping across her vision. She coughed for air and forced her body to move. It obeyed, no longer weighed down or pinned.

As she struggled to sit, she saw Lundric's powerful back, heard his ferocious growl. He held the human male by a broken neck and swung with unbelievable might, crushing his skull against the wall.

Shock at the gruesome violence made her croak, "Lundric...*stars*."

He dropped what was left of the male to the floor in a shapeless puddle and whirled. "*Cambry.* You're alive! No, don't look." He moved his body to block her view of the dead man.

The anguish in his expression moored her. The brittle reality of her attack and Lundric's violence eased its choke hold. She drew a ragged breath as Lundric lunged across the distance between them to scoop her into his arms. "Holy Zandian star, Cambry," he choked, blinking rapidly. "I thought you were *vecking* dead for a moment there."

The movement of his walking made her head and neck hurt. "Slow down," she rasped, and he immediately stopped.

"*Veck.* Tell me what's wrong. Where does it hurt?"

Her hand went to her throat. "I'm all right," she managed to say. "Bruised...that's all."

His walk turned slow and careful as he watched her with an intensity that warmed some of the numbness from her chest. She'd thought of Lundric in those moments of the attack—but hadn't allowed herself to believe he'd rescue her. But he had. As he'd promised from the night they'd met, Lundric was her protector. For the first time since Tal was taken from her, she didn't feel so horribly alone in the universe.

She touched his face. She didn't want to speak, nor would she know what to say if she did.

He leaned into her touch, lids drooping. "Cambry." He spoke it like a prayer, a lament, and an invocation all at once.

"Cambry."

~.~

He'd like to kill that human a million times over. But thank the stars—*thank the stars*—Cambry was alive. When he'd arrived to find her lifeless on the floor beneath the male, his vision had turned red. No thoughts ran through his mind, only the blind instinct to kill.

Veck, he'd known that human male was trouble. Or, rather, Cambry had known. He'd seen her size up and assess the danger that night the male had casually put his sleeping pad beside hers. The death pod had been filled with humans headed for their execution. While there were many innocent, there were probably just as many dangerous criminals. Lundric should have protected his female. He had himself to blame for this incident.

They didn't have a doctor on the pod, and he didn't want to bring her to the sick bay where she'd be ogled by others, so he took her directly to Rok and Lily's chamber. Lily had been acting as the de facto nurse for the pod.

He knocked on the door.

Cambry lifted her head from his shoulder, and, realizing where they were, kicked in protest.

"Who is it?" Rok bellowed.

"Lundric. I've killed a human, and Cambry requires assistance."

A curse sounded behind the door and a few moments later, the panel swished open, with both Rok and Lily appearing as if they'd dressed in a hurry.

"Set her on the bed," Lily said immediately.

"Who did you kill? What happened?"

"I left the body in the north corridor." He laid Cambry down as gently as possible.

"I'm all right." Her voice still had a terrible raspy quality from being choked. Angry red welts on her neck would soon turn to bruises. Another lump swelled at her temple. Seeing those marks on her made his fists clench all over again. "Go." She waved him off.

He hesitated, but Rok propelled him out the door. He explained what happened briefly to Rok as he led him to the mess, which—thank the stars—hadn't been found by any being.

"You should have called for backup immediately. You can't just leave a corpse like this," Rok snapped, hauling the body off the floor. "Do you know what this is going to do to refugee relations?"

"I'll report to Prince Zander and Master Seke now."

Rok scowled. "Do it. And call in one of your guards to clean up the mess, for stars' sake!" He stalked away with the body.

"Yes, Captain," he muttered. Lundric hit his communicator to call both Master Seke and Prince Zander.

Prince Zander's device answered, but both males' heads sprang up. They'd been together when he called. "What is it?" Seke asked sharply.

"I killed one of the humans," he admitted. Guilt at the trouble he'd caused his superiors warred with the remaining anger at the threat on his female.

"What happened?" the prince demanded.

He swiped his hand across his cheek, sensing the human's blood there. "He forced himself on C—one of the females. I ended it."

Seke raised his brows. "By killing him?"

His nostrils flared. "Their necks break easily."

"And the female?" Zander asked.

"Cambry. I want her." There. He'd said it. He needed to secure the female as his. If he'd done that sooner, she might not have been threatened.

"Excuse me?"

Veck. That had come out all wrong. He cleared his throat, marshaling his manners. "May I take a female slave, as you both have done?"

They stared at him.

"Please, my lord?" he added.

"You are not in a position to beg any favors of me, Lundric," the prince snapped. "We need the strongest allegiance possible from these humans or they'll never serve as an army for us. Right now, you'd better be thinking about how to control the damage you've done to Zandian-human relations on that pod."

Veck, of course the prince was right. He'd failed his ruler and Cambry both, this planet rotation. He bowed. "Yes, my lord."

Zander moved to end the hologram transmission, but desperation made Lundric try again. He *needed* to secure Cambry as his own—for his sanity and her safety. "What about the female? What about Cambry?"

"I've granted you nothing. If you want the human female, cultivate a bond."

Did he mean to court her like he would a Zandian female—if any of mating age were still alive? Relief poured through him. That meant the prince granted Cambry her own sovereignty to choose. No one else, presumably Prince Zander included, would have the right to take her from Lundric. He need only convince Cambry. He squared his shoulders and nodded, once. "Thank you, my lord."

~.~

Cambry sat up too fast, forgetting the bruise on her temple. It throbbed, making her wait until her vision cleared to stand up. She'd refused any analgesic from Lily the previous planet rotation but had accepted a cold pack before locking herself in her room to sleep.

Her dreams had been a twisted mix of all the scenes in her life where she'd been in grave danger, except Lundric always showed up, protecting her with the fierceness of an animal. The memory of what he'd done to the male who'd attacked her should make her sick. The level of violence was greater than she'd seen before. And yet it didn't.

It made her feel safe.

Thoughts of Lundric made her reach for the bottles of cosmetics Lily had given her. She uncapped a lightly fragranced oil for the skin. It smelled of fruit, citrus, perhaps, not that she'd ever had the pleasure of eating the Earth-based food the Ocretions cultivated on agrifarms. She undressed and rubbed it over her body, imagining Lundric's hands massaging her instead.

Hearing the breakfast bell, she quickly redressed and unlatched the door. It wouldn't budge.

"What gives?" she muttered and tried again. It stuck, then abruptly slid open, and she immediately saw the reason. Lundric had been leaning against it. He whirled, drinking her in like a starved man.

"Did you stand here all night?"

His eyes traveled to her temple then the bruises at her throat, and he clenched his fists, scowling.

"If you keep glaring at me like that, I'll have to stay away from you until my bruises heal," she said lightly, trying to brush past him.

He lunged, caging her against the door without touching her. "You won't stay away from me," he growled, brows dipped low on his forehead. His irises had turned purple, the way they did when he was turned on, but this time she thought it was more out of anger.

It was odd how she wasn't the least bit afraid of the giant, angry warrior. The one she'd seen crush a man's skull as if it were a cracker. Her body reacted to his aggression like it was a come on, nipples steepling her tunic, a steady thrum starting up between her legs.

"How would I keep you safe?"

Her laugh sounded husky. She reached up and gripped the lapel of his white uniform. "What would you do if I...*ran?*" She ducked under his arm, laughing as she bolted, not surprised when he caught her around the waist and hauled her back against his front. His hot breath feathered across her ear.

"You don't *vecking* run from me." He bit her ear then inhaled deeply. "What is that scent?" He dragged his open mouth down her neck, jerking away when he touched her bruises.

"*Veck.* I'm so afraid I'll hurt you," he choked.

To hear the fearsome warrior say he was afraid—*of hurting her*—made every bone in her body go soft.

"M-maybe you'd better punish me for running." She thought she sounded breathless. Excited.

A growl rocketed from his throat, and he dragged her backward into her chamber, slamming the door shut and locking it. "Clothes off," he commanded, but before she could obey, his hands tore at her tunic, helping her strip. He sat on the cot and pulled her over one knee, her torso lying on the cot.

"Why do you smell so good?" Already she heard the urgency in his voice, the notes of desperation, as if her scent drove him so wild, he couldn't control himself.

"It's the oil Lily gave me." She could hardly make her tongue form sounds because his huge palm was stroking her bare ass and it felt... So. Incredibly. Good.

The palm retreated and then fell, harder than she expected. She jerked and bit her lip, humming a little in her throat as the pain bloomed across her skin, heat racing over her buttocks and pooling at her core where her clit pulsed with a persistent throb.

He slapped her again.

"Ow. Not so hard," she gasped.

Lundric gave a dark chuckle. "Oh, no, little female. You don't get to tell me how you get spanked. You asked for this. Now I'm in charge. I'm going to turn this pretty little ass of yours bright red. Do you want to know why?"

Her belly twisted with mingled fear and excitement. She pushed her tiptoes against the floor to lift her ass.

Another hard slap.

"Why?" she gasped.

"For scaring the *vecking* daylights out of me last night. For driving me mad at all times with those beautiful long legs, this juicy ass." He slapped said anatomy again, hard. He worked his other hand under her hips and stroked a finger along her dewy slit. She pushed into it, forcing the tip of his thick digit inside her entrance, but he pulled it out and spanked her even harder.

"Who's in charge, Cambry?"

"I am?" She laughed, surprising herself. When was the last time she'd laughed?

A flurry of spanks rained down on her burning ass and the backs of her thighs at the same time his finger rubbed her clit. "You are not, my little rebel.

And I'm not going to stop spanking you until I'm sure you'll remember who you belong to as you sit through flight lessons all morning."

The combination of sting and his possessiveness stole her breath. She wriggled under the onslaught. "Lundric...*Lundric*!"

He stopped spanking her, and flipped her over onto the cot before he dropped to his knees on the floor to cup her heated cheeks in his hands. "Open for your male, Cambry."

She let her knees drop open, her breath going still at the reverent way Lundric drank in her pussy. He parted her nether lips with his thumbs, still doing nothing but staring.

"Lundric," she protested.

He lowered his head and dragged his tongue from anus to clit, sending her into spasms of pleasure. "Where do you want my tongue, little female? Show me."

Her inner thighs trembled, her chest rose and fell in short pants as she reached down between her legs and tapped her clit "Here," she gasped.

His eyes gleamed. "Yes, that's a good place to start." He flicked his tongue over the sensitive bud.

He suctioned his lips over it and sucked as his thumb pushed into her pussy, his middle finger tapped her anus. Her hips jerked into the air. She grasped both the horns on his head and squeezed.

He shouted, eyes flying wide, and the horns thickened and pulsed in her palms. "*Vecking* stars, Cambry."

She released his horns like hot coals. Had she hurt him?

"If you touch my horns again, I'm going to lose it before I ever get my cock inside you." His irises were pure violet now.

Her mouth widened in a naughty grin. "Is that so?" She stroked the horns, hooking them in the crook of her thumbs and forefingers and circling their bases.

Lundric groaned. "That's it, beautiful female. Now you're getting my cock." He stood up and shoved his uniform pants down, letting his impressive length spring free.

She licked her lips, leaning up on her elbows to watch him climb over her. The moment his head was in reach again, she went for his horns.

"*Veck*..." He dragged the head of his cock through her dripping pussy.

She moaned with pleasure. "Yes, Lundric. Please."

He plunged into her tight channel, and she bit her lip on a gasp, squeezing his thick horns with a pulsing grip. "You must want to be *vecked* hard, little female," he growled, but she could hear his loss of composure in his voice, sense it in the jerky plunge of his cock in and out of her. He drew in shuddering breaths.

She arched into him, rubbing her nipples against his skin, hooking her ankles behind his back.

He stopped moving and shook his head. "Feet down, baby. You don't get to control."

She whimpered but released her legs, dropping her feet back to the cot. His grin was wicked as he braced one palm against the wall behind her head to shove in balls deep. "I'm going to *veck* you so hard, you won't walk straight for the rest of the planet rotation, pretty female."

"Take me, Lundric," she moaned.

He pulled out, flipped her onto her belly, and lifted her up to her hands and knees. He entered her again, holding her hips steady for his hard pumps, flesh slapping flesh as he pounded in and out. Apparently still not satisfied, he picked her up by the waist and walked forward on his knees until they reached the wall. "Hands on the wall, sweet female."

She obeyed.

He braced his hands beside hers.

Oh veck, *yes.*

This was their position. The head of his glorious cock hit the sensitive tissue on the front wall of her channel with each thrust.

Lundric dropped one hand between her legs and slapped her clit.

She screamed and tumbled over the edge into orgasmic explosion. Her muscles tightened around his cock, squeezing in quick bursts.

Lundric roared his approval and *vecked* her even harder, slamming in another four, five times until he came, filling her with his hot seed.

When they both had finished, her body turned to rubber, and she fell against the wall. Lundric scooped her into his arms and sat on the cot. His lips found hers, the most gentle of probing.

She answered it, kissing and nibbling, opening her mouth to his tongue. When they parted, he looked down at her with something akin to wonder.

"I'd better go," she murmured. "I don't want to miss breakfast."

Lundric immediately stood and set her gently on her feet. "I would *never* allow you to go hungry," he said with the solemnity of an oath. He used the corner of his tunic to clean her of his seed, which was...*rainbow hued.* Whoa. Well, alien sex delivered, that was all she knew.

She grinned. "Thank you, warrior." Her legs wobbled as she attempted to dress herself. Lundric didn't help, cupping and rubbing her ass with a satisfied growl.

She twisted to look. "Yes, you left your marks on me. Feel better?"

His grin was all satisfied male. "Much."

CHAPTER FIVE

Lundric finished installing the metalwork he'd bent to hold the Zandian crystal up against the window in his bunkroom. There weren't many windows in the pod, and apart from the cockpit, this room had the biggest. Plus it held the greatest number of beings, so they could all benefit.

Since Lily had given it to him, his wound had completely healed, and his energy had returned. He was relieved he wouldn't need to return to Zander's palatial pod—he didn't want to leave Cambry. In the last few planet rotations, he'd grown to admire her even more. She'd picked up flying faster than any other being, and every time he was with her, she let down her guard a little more.

Still, despite his constant assertions she belonged to him, he could see she didn't take him seriously. He headed now to the big meeting room, where they were practicing hand-to-hand combat. He *vecking hated t*hat Cambry was there. The thought of her in a fight made him want to crush another skull. Yet, he had to admit the need for the practice. They were training the humans to be warriors, after all—male and female alike. And despite the fact it made him want to rip beings limb from limb, she would probably see combat. They all would.

He entered the room, scanning quickly for the flash of red hair that made Cambry easy to spot. *There.* Rok had them paired off with partners, and they were practicing with long staffs, swinging and blocking each other. Cambry moved with grace, a natural at battle arts, striking out as she circled her older male opponent.

Brilliant female.

He didn't move, not wanting to miss a single moment of watching Cambry. "She is fond of you."

He startled at the voice just below his elbow and looked down to see Mierna, Rok's elderly Venusian crewmember. Venusians were known for mind reading and intuition, but every time Lundric had seen Mierna, she'd been drunk on brownbeer. He looked down at her big watery eyes and unkempt hair with a mixture of pity and annoyance.

"You wish to possess her, but you don't know the secrets of her heart."

He barely restrained the urge to roll his eyes. Fortune-telling wasn't an art he had any appreciation for. He managed a noncommittal grunt as a reply.

"Do you know what she seeks?"

"No," he said, barely keeping the exasperation from his voice.

She touched the side of her nose in a gesture meaningless to him. "You cannot keep her until you learn."

Her words were meaningless, too.

He forced a smile that probably looked more like a grimace and stalked away, not toward Cambry, though every cell in his body pointed in her direction, but to Rok, to receive his orders.

Rok tossed him a staff and swung his in an arc, lowering into a ready stance. Though Rok had no formal training like Lundric and Zander had received from Master Seke, he was a natural warrior who clearly had spent a lifetime fighting. His other crewmates—the two Stornigians who were Rok's foster brothers—tumbled and wrestled each other in a gleeful tussle.

Rok came at him quickly, swinging the staff at Lundric's head. He ducked and swung for Rok's feet. Rok had swung for the place where Lundric held the staff, and he had to drop it to avoid getting his hands smashed. He stopped it with his foot and flicked it back into the air, catching it and swinging it toward Rok's exposed middle.

Rok grunted with approval, dropping into a backward hinge to avoid the strike. He grinned. "You and me. Before your shift tonight."

Lundric shook his head. "No offense, but I'd rather be wrestling with a different being when I'm off-duty."

Rok smirked, glancing in Cambry's direction. "Who could blame you?"

Lundric growled, and Rok chuckled. "Easy, warrior. I have my own human to contend with. Just don't let your practice slip."

"I won't, Captain."

~·~

Cambry tossed the staff back into the box, exhilaration from the fighting racing through her. She'd seen Lundric and Rok go at it briefly. Holy star, it had been a beautiful sight! The two males were evenly matched, though Lundric had far more grace while Rok looked more like a street fighter. They both moved with surprising lightness for such massive warriors, and they clearly loved the battle arts. She was learning to love them, too. It almost made her want to stay—just to learn more. But she couldn't.

She had learned how to fly. She'd known how to navigate. They hadn't taught her how to engage the weaponry on the battleships, yet, but she'd manage. Every day she spent on this pod was a day she could be looking for Tal, and, yet, she'd been postponing her departure. She'd told herself she was waiting for the right opportunity—the perfect chance to slip away undetected.

But that was a lie.

Her reasons for dragging her feet were only about one particularly possessive and dominant male. She also should acknowledge every planet rotation she stayed with Lundric would make it harder to leave.

The next opportunity she got, she needed to take. Or she needed to create her own opportunity. Tal had been sold by the factory owners where they both worked. She needed to go to Ocretia and find a way to access their slave database to locate him. It wasn't much of a plan, but it was better than sitting around and accepting the fate some other being shoved at her.

Still, the thought of leaving Lundric felt like shards of glass being driven through her chest. She liked to think maybe they'd meet again, after she found Tal. But she knew, even if they did—which was highly unlikely, considering he was part of the suicide mission to take back Zandia—he'd never forgive her. She could no longer pretend his interest was just about scratching a sexual itch.

Lundric waited for her at the door, his gaze heating the closer she drew to him. "You enjoyed yourself," he observed, a look of fascinated amusement dancing over his features.

She shrugged. "Why shouldn't I?"

"Fight all you like, little rebel, just know this: I will rip out the throat of anyone who leaves a mark on you."

Laughter bubbled up in her—as it had with more frequency lately. His overprotectiveness should bother her, but all she could do was marvel at the fact someone besides Tal cared about her well-being. She wrote it off as hyperbole, like she did with all his absurdly possessive declarations. She breezed past him. "You leave marks on me every planet rotation," she tossed over her shoulder.

His huge hand collided with her ass, and this time she giggled out loud.

Dearest Mother Earth, she'd never giggled before in her life. Particularly not with a male. Lundric made her feel...*lighter.* His intensity, his protection and care allowed her to relax some of the tight control, the overriding anxiety and fear she'd always lived with.

He closed his large hand around hers, and she was surprised at how comfortable it felt. How right. "What now, little female? Are you hungry again?" Lundric thought it amusing how often and how much she ate. Once he'd realized she worried about missing meals, he'd started asking every few hours if she was hungry. She hadn't seen him eat yet. Apparently, the Zandians only ate once a week, so long as they had access to their crystals.

"No, not yet. But I have to do my chores." She'd been assigned laundry duty. It was menial work compared to the tasks she'd done at the factory—building complex circuit boards and programming the software for robots—but she didn't mind.

"I'll help."

She peered up at him, taking in the sturdy line of his jaw, the long lashes framing his brown-purple irises. "Isn't it time for you to sleep?"

"I don't need sleep. Are you trying to get rid of me?" He spoke lightly, but a shadow had fallen across his face.

"No, stupid, I just—"

"Stupid?" His brows shot up, and the world tilted as he scooped her over his shoulder, smacking her ass with his huge, paddle-like hand. "Are you sure you want to call me that?"

She shrieked and laughed, kicking her feet as he clomped down the corridor, spanking her as he went. They passed a Zandian guard, who looked amused, but the clump of humans they passed stared with what appeared to be dislike. Whether it was of her or Lundric, she couldn't be sure. Maybe they resented her for cultivating special favors with their guards. Maybe they'd heard he'd killed a human.

"I'm sorry—*sorry*! Please put me down." Her face was surely as red as her hair.

Lundric lowered her to her feet but held her close, the heat of his huge, hard body radiating through her clothing. He gripped her nape and tilted her head up for a kiss. Though she wanted to be somewhere more private, especially with the group of humans looking on, her body melted into his, pussy turning to liquid heat.

His kiss was just enough to leave her wobbly-kneed, and he seemed to know it because the smug warrior smirked as he released her. "Let's go, little female." He walked with her, through all the cells, where she collected laundry from the bins—blankets and sheets, mostly. Some towels. No being had thrown clothing in, probably because they didn't have much extra clothing to wear.

Lundric insisted on pushing the large wheeled cart. When she tried to force him to let her—because she cringed to think what the other humans would say when they saw she'd convinced a guard to help her do her chores—he tossed her into the cart, too, running to drive it at top speed through the corridors.

She laughed and stood up in the cart, balancing without holding on, surfing the careening cart.

They reached the laundry room, and Lundric caught her up as she climbed out, lifting her the rest of the way and settling her with her legs wrapped around his waist.

"Mm," he growled against her neck and walked her backward. He pinned her back against the wall and ground his hips against hers. "This is how I've been wanting you."

Her pussy dampened her panties at the pressure from his cock. "Not here, Lundric," she protested, even as she rubbed herself over his hardened bulge.

"You think you have a choice?"

She brought her fist down on his massive shoulder without real effort. "Yes."

"I *veck* you wherever I like, and you say *thank you*."

She rolled her eyes. "Get off me, you arrogant lug." Her words might have meant something if she hadn't been undulating her hips against his in the lewdest possible manner.

"Naughty girl. I can feel how much you want my cock."

Her gaze flicked to the open door.

Lundric bit her ear. "Don't worry, little rebel. I'll shut the door. Do you really think I'd allow any other being to see you?" He eased her to the floor and shook his head with a dark look. "Never."

She sucked on her lip and watched his broad back as he walked to the door and shut it. It was hard not to feel like royalty around Lundric. Every day she fell further under his spell. The one that made her forget her miserable past, the loss and loneliness. The need to be ready to defend her life at every moment. Even though she knew it was a false sense of security, an illusion she'd soon be horribly divested of, Lundric was like the magnet that kept drawing her closer.

~.~

Lundric turned back to his aroused female, the need to satisfy her making his blood hum. He relished the way she'd softened to him over the past week. His little rebel was beginning to trust him, beginning to receive everything he wanted to give her. Pleasure. Satisfaction. Protection. He wanted to provide for her, to make her life easier, even though she was the toughest, most capable female on the pod.

Even though he still scented her arousal, he saw he'd half lost her in the moment he left. Her face clouded with some inner conflict. What was she thinking? It had something to do with him, he'd bet his last crystal. He didn't believe she feared him, despite her play at resistance.

He stalked back to her, taking his time, predator approaching his beautiful prey. When he reached her, he picked her up by her narrow waist and plopped her on top of the long, industrial-sized washing machine.

"There's no getting away from me now, little female."

She kicked up her chin. "Is that a challenge?"

A surprised burst of laughter erupted from him, echoing off the walls of the small room. He touched her cheek with the backs of his fingers. "It was not so long ago you refused to be closed in a room with me," he said softly. He brushed her lower lip with his thumb. "The old Venusian said I need to know the secrets of your heart."

Her smile fell away, wariness returning.

A chill washed over him from his neck down to his boots. What was his little female hiding? What didn't she want to show him? He *vecking hated* uncertainty. He needed to know Cambry belonged to him. Forever. He couldn't stand a repetition of his mother's fickle love. He'd recovered from maternal abandonment, but he wouldn't recover from losing Cambry. He *refused* to ever accept her leaving.

His fear had already morphed to aggression, his masculine pride demanding he claim her here, now, but he drew a deep breath and willed himself to calm down. The prince said he had to win her. Force was not an option, not that he'd ever allow Cambry to be hurt or unhappy on his watch.

He pushed her knees open and curled his hands under her thighs, yanking her hips forward on the machine.

She gasped and fell back on her hands behind her.

Without waiting a moment, he thrust his head between her legs, biting at her pussy through her leggings. Her wanton moan made his cock turn harder than stone. "Do you want me to lick your pussy, beautiful female?"

"Y-yes," she breathed, her inner thighs trembling against his ears.

He rubbed his knuckle over the seam of her pants, stimulating her clitoris. "Tell me three secrets."

She stilled. "What?"

He continued the slow knuckle treatment. Her pussy dampened her panties and pants, and the scent made it hard for him to maintain control. "You heard me. Three secrets."

She rocked her hips to meet his knuckle, and he smirked. "You want my mouth there, don't you, pretty girl?"

"What kind of secret?"

Again, foreboding twisted in his gut. He cocked his head to the side and locked gazes with her. "I don't know. What are you hiding from me, Cambry?"

Her face went pale, confirming his worst fears. Now she played at sounding casual. She tossed her long ponytail back over her shoulder. "I'm not hiding anything. I'll answer three questions. You ask them."

He reached for the thread holding her hair back and broke it with his fingers. The thick mane fell down in riotous waves. Gorgeous locks of brown, red, and copper wove in and out in soft curls. He wanted to see it all the way down—the little braids around her face unwound, as well. He wanted to make rules for her about her hair—that she must always take it down for him, or that he'd be the only male to see it unbound. But he wasn't in a position to make demands like that. Yet. Stars, he needed to be.

He pushed the fingers of one hand into the braids, bunching them up to gently tug her head back. With the other hand, he continued to massage her pussy. He struggled to think what her secrets could be. What were his worst fears? "Have you already been mated, Cambry?"

Her lips fell open with pleasure, lids drooped. He couldn't wait to bring her to orgasm, to watch that beautiful face contort as she toppled over the peak. But not until he had answers.

"Mated? I wasn't a virgin, is that what you mean?"

He removed his touch from her pussy as punishment for not answering his question. "No, that's not what I meant. Bound to another male. Do humans not mate?"

Her cheeks turned pink. He always found it enchanting when she blushed, because she was normally so composed, so fierce. "We once called it marriage, yes."

A dark shadow loomed over him.

"I mean, no. I've never married or mated. No."

He let out a rough breath and returned the pad of his thumb to her pussy, stroking lightly up and down the seam of her outer lips.

"Do you love another male?"

She hesitated for a beat before she shook her head. "No." The answer sounded definitive, yet the pause had ice prickling through his veins. *Veck.* Who was this other male? Was he dead? Or alive? Did she pine for him? Was she waiting for him? He wanted to slam a fist through the wall and demand to know everything.

But scaring his female would be disastrous.

What else could he ask? What other secret might she carry in her heart? Or was there nothing? The old Venusian was probably just speaking in riddles. But no, Cambry had appeared to be hiding something. He *had* to ask the hardest question of all, even though it was too soon. He had to know what was in her heart.

"Do you wish...would you like...tobematedtome?" He said the last words in a rush, forcing them from his mouth. Breath held, he forced himself to watch her face.

Her eyes flew open, but not with pleasure. She, too, stopped breathing. Her throat worked. "Lundric, I—"

He covered her mouth with his hand, too much of a coward to hear what she would say. "Don't answer. It was too soon, I know. I haven't won you yet. I'll keep working."

For some reason he couldn't fathom, her eyes filled with tears.

Not wanting to slog through the awkward moment and determined to *vecking* prove he could offer her something she couldn't live without, he yanked her pants and panties down and tossed them to the side. "Give me this pussy," he growled as he palmed her ass and lifted it to meet his mouth.

She'd done her part and answered his questions. She deserved her reward. He couldn't *vecking wait* to show her pleasure. His tongue parted her lips, tracing the swelling inner petals of her sex. He circled her clit then suctioned his lips over it and sucked hard on the tiny bud.

Cambry cried out. Her torso fell back, and she wrapped her fists around his horns, bringing him painfully close to the brink of orgasm, without a single touch of his cock. His horns stiffened and pulsed in time with his cock as he *vecked* her with his tongue, making it into a hard point. He replaced it with two fingers, which he curled inside her to stroke her inner wall as he sucked and nipped at her labia then reattached his mouth to her clit. With his free hand, he thumbed her asshole. The moment he pressed there, she came, closing her mouth on her scream so it reverberated in her throat, still echoing off the walls.

Her hips bucked up and down, but he kept his fingers and mouth working her through the spasms of her climax, following her frantic movements with a satisfaction so much deeper than achieving his own pleasure would have brought.

She finally went limp, a soft moan sighing from her lips. "Lundric."

He wished to always hear his name on her lips with that hoarse, wrung-out sound of contentment. "That's right, little female. Lundric makes you scream." He eased his fingers from her and planted one last kiss on the apex of her pussy, which sent it into another paroxysm of quakes.

She sat up and slid her butt off the washer, turning to present it to him. "Do you want to spank me?" Her voice was little more than a ragged whisper. Despite the way his cock surged with excitement, the question also caused his heart to compress.

His little female felt guilty. She wanted his punishment to atone for not accepting him as her mate. Well, he'd *vecking* give it to her, then. He loved spanking that pretty little ass, leaving his marks for her to remember where he'd been. He gripped her hair and tugged her head all the way back. "You like feeling my hand on your ass."

"Yes," she admitted.

"Because you know I'm safe? Or because you like the danger?" He wasn't going to ask why she needed this punishment. Wasn't going to mention mating again. Not until things were clearer between them.

"Both." Her husky voice made him squeeze his cock through his pants.

He let his hand fall, hard.

She choked on a breath and rose to her tiptoes.

He slapped again, abusing the under part of her buttocks, the enchanting place where ass met thigh. As he continued, her breath grew ragged and she jerked with each smack but always returned to position, offering her sweet little ass for his chastisement.

"I like punishing you, sweet female."

"Why?" she croaked, gasping as he struck her again.

"I *vecking* love everything about it. The sounds you make. The way your ass looks when it's painted red by my hand. The way it feels under my palm." He shoved her tunic up her back and licked a long line from the base of her spine to her shoulder blades. "The trust you show me when you submit." He took his cock out and dragged the head through her moistened lips. "*Vecking* you afterward."

She arched back, pushing her hips against the head of his cock to encourage his entry.

He rocked slowly into her, shaking with the effort of holding back. "Showing you my strength even though we both know ultimately—when it comes down to it—you're in charge."

"Lundric...please," she whined.

"That's right, little rebel. You're already begging—just the way I want you." He braced one hand on the washer beside hers and gripped the side of her hip with the other. "You give it to Lundric, now. Tell me who owns you." He *beat* into her with his cock, pumping hard, slapping his loins against her ass, shoving deep and nearly lifting her from her toes with each instroke.

"Yes," she gasped. "You own me."

He knew she meant *in this moment*. In this moment, he owned her, not forever. But he would take what he could get while he figured out how to wrest the promise of forever from her.

Control slipped, and his vision tunneled. All he knew was the sweetest pleasure of Cambry's pussy squeezing his cock. All he saw was her thick mane of hair sprawling down her back. All he heard were her panting breaths, the little grunts and cries she made as he pummeled her pussy with his cock, imagining he was marking it like his hand marked her ass, giving her something to remember him by, to keep the sensation of him with her when he went to sleep and she stayed up.

"Cambry." He didn't recognize the guttural sound from his own mouth.

"*Take me. Take me*, Lundric."

*Zandian sta*r, he needed her with such desperation. He wanted to consume her, to rid the separation of their bodies until they became one. Inseparable. Being. He roared and heard Cambry echo with a scream.

His orgasm shook his entire body, limbs quaking as his ass squeezed and he shot his pleasure into the deepest reaches of her tight channel. Her muscles squeezed his cock, milking it for his seed, making his eyes roll back in his head.

He dropped his forearms to the washing machine, caging her against him as he caught his breath. "I should have asked before—" he started gruffly, then cleared his throat. "You didn't say anything, so I'm assuming—"

"They gave all female slaves at the factory a shot to prevent pregnancy. It lasts at least another two years." He didn't miss the bitterness in her tone. Did she want a baby? *Veck*, he wanted to give her one with a desperation that stunned him.

"Yes, all right." He kissed the back of her neck. "I'm clean of any disease."

"So am I."

"I'm sorry I didn't ask the first time."

She turned in his arms, peering up at him quizzically. Her eyes turned liquid again, and she reached for his face. "I keep thinking there must be a trick, here," she croaked.

He covered her hand with his own, pressing it against his cheek. "What trick?"

Her throat moved. "No one's ever been good to me without demanding something in return. Except for—"

"Who?" he demanded, unable to keep the sharpness from his tone. Was this the other male she'd loved?

"Family," she mumbled, dropping her gaze.

Later, he would wish he'd pressed for more information about her family. But the moment was so raw, so perfect; he didn't want to mar it with something that seemed to make her sad.

He kept his tone light. "Oh, I'm demanding, little female. I demand everything in return." *I want your* vecking *soul.*

She smiled and lifted her face for a kiss, which he delivered with as much gusto as he knew how.

CHAPTER SIX

Cambry landed the battleship on the rocky terrain, only skidding a few yards this time. A surge of satisfaction ran through her. She was ready. Maybe not to fly defensively, but to fly. To fly away.

"Nice work, Cambry," her Zandian trainer, Vokart, said. He'd taken her and three others out for practice that planet rotation, much to Lundric's fury. Lundric's superior, an older Zandian named Master Seke, had arrived and had demanded Lundric's attention in the sparring room. "Charl, your turn."

Cambry climbed out of the pilot's seat and swapped places with Charl, a young, dark-skinned human who said little but handled the ship like he'd been flying all his life. She missed flying with Lily, who had left with Rok to visit her mother and sister on the pod the Zandians considered home. Lily had confessed to being nervous before she left. Like Cambry, she'd been taken from her parents as a toddler, and so she had no memory of her mother and had never known of the existence of her sister, Lamira, until Lamira arrived with Rok to rescue her from the Ocretion Death Pod.

Lily said their reunion had been awkward, since they were strangers, and unlike Lamira, she hadn't spent a lifetime looking for a sister. She'd chosen to remain on the training pod with Rok, rather than accept the invitation from Prince Zander, her sister's mate, to stay at his pod. As the planet rotations passed, though, she'd felt guilty over shunning a relationship with her newly discovered sister and the mother she barely remembered, so Rok had arranged a visit.

It had been on the tip of Cambry's tongue to confess her own family situation to Lily. Their stories weren't the same, but she might understand the pain Cambry experienced at being separated from her own sibling, the need to find him, as Lamira had needed to find Lily.

But then she remembered Lundric. *Would you like to be mated to me?*

He'd been jealous of her love for another. She'd seen the spark of possessiveness when she hesitated answering his question about whether she loved another. If she told him about her brother, would he suspect her plans to find him? He read her so well.

Precious Mother Earth, she felt like her insides had been torn apart. Nothing made sense to her anymore. She didn't know if her judgment could be trusted when it came to Lundric. This mission of fighting for Zandia was still a death mission. Just because she'd found solace in a wonderfully attentive Zandian warrior didn't mean she should give her life for his cause.

Or did it?

No, it couldn't. Because she had to find Tal. He needed her. She was his older sister. She'd held him in her arms as a child and promised they'd always have each other, no matter what the factory foremen did to them. And if she gave her life for this hopeless Zandian cause, Tal would be alone. And she would've broken her promise to find him.

She needed to get away at the first possible chance. She was becoming too attached to the Zandians and her pod mates. Far too attached to Lundric, her incredible warrior. The longer she allowed him to believe she would mate him, the more he would hate her when she left. She needed to go before both their hearts broke at what she had to do.

Unfortunately, her heartbreak was already a foregone conclusion.

She finished flight training, and they exited the battleship and went back to the training pod. Lundric was waiting for her at the entrance, his face tense. The tension drained away when he saw her, and his fists unclenched.

For fun, and to challenge him, she ran and launched herself at him, full speed.

He grunted as he caught her, his forearm hooking under her ass to hold her straddled around his waist. "I should get *you* into the sparring room," he growled against her neck. "You could use a sound thrashing, couldn't you, pet? Instead, I've spent all afternoon helping my master exorcise his demons."

"What demons?"

"A female, I believe. Lily's mother. I've never seen him like this."

She nibbled on her lip. She'd had very few examples of loving relationships in her life. People in the factory used one another for sex, or clung together out of necessity—shoring up against weakness, the way she and her brother had. But after exploring amorous relations with Lundric, watching Rok and Lily, and now hearing of another Zandian who cared deeply about a human female, she wondered what she really knew about relationships. Nothing, it seemed.

"How did your training go, little female?"

"Wonderfully." She was surprised to hear how cheerful she sounded. And the truth that anything had been great in her life surprised her. But she felt exhilarated by what she'd learned and accomplished in a short time. She ran a fingertip over one of Lundric's horns.

He groaned. "Be careful, little rebel. You're about to get yourself *vecked* in short order, and I was going to see if you wanted to fly some more."

"You were?"

He lowered her to the ground and adjusted his swollen cock. "I wanted to murder Vokart for taking you out when it should have been me. Do you want more practice?" He smiled at what must be the goofiest grin on her face. "Yes?"

"I'd love that."

Lundric changed their direction, leading her back the way she'd come. He put a helmet on her, adjusting the strap under her chin with care that made her belly flutter. They exited the pod, but when Cambry boarded the battleship Lundric indicated, he didn't follow her on. "I think you're ready to solo, little rebel."

She stopped breathing.

"Can you handle it? I'll be right here on communications if you have any questions or problems." He tapped the comms unit attached to the helmet.

"U-um. Yes. I'm ready. Let's do it." Her heart thundered, hacking its way right out of her chest. Oh stars. This was her chance. She could shut the hatch on this battleship and fly away. Get back to Ocretia and find her brother.

Lundric gripped her helmet and pulled it forward to tap his in a forehead kiss of sorts. He must have misunderstood the conflict raging inside her as nerves because he said, "You'll be fine."

"Yeah." Despite the oxygen pumping through her helmet, she couldn't drag enough air into her lungs. "Thank you, Lundric. Thank you so much." She didn't want this to be their goodbye, but how else could it be? If she acted strange, she'd lose this chance. Even so, she wished she'd left him a gift or a message, or somehow been able to show him how much he'd meant to her.

He grinned like she was being silly and gave her a little shove. "I'll see you when you land." He slapped her ass. "You know what you're doing."

It *vecking* broke her heart that he stood there cheering her on while she was about to betray his trust and fly away. She didn't want to leave this way, but a window of opportunity had appeared, and she had to take it. They didn't come around often enough.

The hatch closed, and she settled into the pilot's seat, still struggling to breathe.

"Communication check." Lundric's deep, calm voice spoken directly in her ear made her jump. She adjusted the helmet and touched her comms unit. "Loud and clear, Captain."

"You're clear to take off whenever you're ready."

She forced herself to take deep, steadying breaths as she flicked on the control board and started the engine.

Goodbye, Lundric. I love you.

. . .

He was surprised at how nervous Cambry seemed. His little rebel was always so self-possessed, so brave. It made his heart squeeze to see her unnerved. His instinct to fight her monsters, to shield her from anything frightening her made it hard to shove her in the ship and send her off alone. But he'd seen her exhilaration every time she flew. His rebel was born to fly, to fight. His need to protect couldn't hold her back.

He sat in the loading dock to watch her flight from the viewing screen.

"Battleship 3 taking off." She used the proper communication protocol they'd taught the trainees. The battleship lifted into a hover then ascended gently.

"Beautiful takeoff, Cambry. Now fly in a circle around the planet."

"Copy that, Captain." Her voice sounded choked.

Alarm bells started sounding in his head. Something was off with his female. He should have read it sooner.

"Thank you...for everything." Her voice cracked, and the communication went dead.

"Cambry, what the stars—?" *No.*

Battleship 3 shot out of the atmosphere and into hyperdrive, vanishing from his sight. *Oh veck no.* He ran for hatch, not bothering to finish putting his helmet on before he barreled out into the toxic atmosphere of Shooku. What the *veck? No, no, no.*

Cambry left me.

As he ran for a battleship, fear zinged through him, ricocheting off his ribs and chest, plowing through his gut, tearing his insides to shreds. She couldn't have run off. And yet he knew with absolute certainty she had.

That *thank you* had really been *goodbye.* She'd been choked up. He'd given her an opportunity to run, and she'd taken it. She'd probably been planning this from the start. She'd been using him to her advantage while she bided her time, waiting to escape.

A horrible metallic taste coated his tongue. It tasted of betrayal. Abandonment. Like his mother, Cambry hadn't found him worth staying for. But he had no time to wallow in his own emotional issues. He fired up a battleship and launched it into space. Because the battleships were part of the same fleet, Battleship 3's coordinates showed up on his screen. He programmed her location as his flight path and punched the hyperdrive, following her out of the atmosphere of Shooku, toward Ocretia.

Why in the stars was she running back there? It wasn't safe for his female.

If any being scanned her barcode and identified her, she'd immediately be put to death.

And that was only half the crisis. His stomach churned. Even if he wanted to, he couldn't allow Cambry to leave. In addition to putting her life at risk, her presence in Ocretion territory would also put the Zandians' entire mission in grave danger. If any being discovered her, it would be known their death pod had not crashed into a smuggler's ship, as they'd circulated. Prince Zander would have to run or fight Ocretia, which would divert all his resources from the real fight of winning back Zandia.

No, Cambry couldn't go free, and since he was the fool she'd played, it was his responsibility to bring her back. What an idiot he'd been—believing she cared about him. She'd been just another treacherous human in a difficult position, and she'd used him to get out of it.

He had to bring her back. Prince Zander would be furious. The thought of anyone imprisoning or harming her made his knuckles turn white on the controls. No, there was no way in the galaxy he'd allow any being to touch her. He would take responsibility for her, whether she liked it or not.

He emerged from the hyperthrust right behind Cambry. She swerved and dipped, the ship only wobbling marginally before she righted it.

Good girl.

Even now, he couldn't stop feeling proud for how *vecking brilliant* his human was. And she was still *his* human, even after what she'd done. He chased her, needing to get close enough to use the magnetic ray on her ship. She dropped down and halted, sending him flying past her. He cut to the right to make a tight circle. She hadn't fired on him. She'd had a perfect shot and had failed to take it. Although his treacherous heart squeezed, certain it meant she cared for him, he chased those thoughts back. She'd used him and left. He meant nothing to her.

And her hesitation to fire was her downfall, because now he had her. He flew low over the top of her ship and dropped down, sending the magnetic beam of energy to capture her ship. It slowed the velocity of both ships, his engine whining with the effort of dragging double its weight through space. Even so, he used hyperdrive because the risk of being seen in Ocretion territory greatly outweighed the danger of blowing out his engine. It worked; the short burst of extreme speed flung them back to just outside Shooku's atmosphere. Shooku, the uninhabitable planet where Rok and Prince Zander had forced the Death Pod down, lay just outside Ocretion territory, where few travelers would ever stray.

He steadied the controls as they broke through, and managed to land her ship without crushing it beneath his own or dropping it from too high an altitude.

He should request backup. The moment he released the magnetic ray to land his own craft, she could simply take off again. But he didn't want any other being involved. Thankfully, she didn't run, and he didn't even want to begin puzzling over why. He dropped his battleship to the ground and pulled on his helmet before charging out to catch his wayward rebel.

~.~

Cambry couldn't move. Her limbs had turned to ice, heart frozen in her chest. She tried to rally her courage, to take off and make another run at freedom, but she didn't have it in her. She'd used up all the will to leave Lundric once. She didn't have any left. Besides, he'd only catch her again. He'd just shown her how easy it was. She didn't know enough about cloaking or navigating to avoid recapture.

Now, what?

She saw Lundric stomping toward her battleship, fury evident in every determined swing of his arms and the set of his shoulders. What was the Zandian punishment for stealing a ship and deserting? Would they throw her in a prison cell? Execute her?

That outcome mattered less to her than Lundric's reaction. Did he hate her?

The hatch opened, letting the toxic air from Shooku flood in. Lundric stormed on. Even behind his face shield, she saw the angry slash of his brows, the bitter shape of his mouth.

She didn't move, still frozen to her chair, holding her breath against the poisonous air.

As always, Lundric moved swiftly and efficiently, palming the top of a helmet and dropping it on her head.

She drew a breath of the oxygen, even though it felt like her lungs had been crushed by a huge weight.

He lifted her by her nape to stand and guided her out the hatch. His touch was firm, but he hadn't hurt her.

She didn't fight—didn't even look for a weapon. Now, like in space, she couldn't bring herself to harm Lundric, which would be the only way she'd escape him. She could have shot his ship down. She'd had the chance, but her thumb wouldn't move to do it. Self-preservation had failed in the face of damaging him.

"Lundric—"

"Not a word." His voice snapped like a whip. He propelled her through the airlock and into the pod, where he pulled off her helmet and hung it beside his own without looking at her.

His edict not to speak was almost a blessing because she didn't know what she would say anyway. What words would heal this wound she'd inflicted?

He led her down the corridor, past the office serving as Zandian headquarters. Master Seke flew out of it.

"What in the *veck* happened out there?" Seke demanded.

She opened her mouth to say something, to shift any responsibility for her actions from Lundric. She could handle whatever punishment they issued her—even death—but she wouldn't stand by and let Lundric lose his position for showing her kindness.

His kindnesses. Veck. There'd been so many. Her heart wrenched over what she'd done to him. To them. Unrecoverable damage to a male who hadn't deserved her betrayal.

"Training exercise." Lundric spoke before she could, his words as stiff as his stance, his face hardened into stone. He'd receded into himself, leaving only some outer shell she hardly recognized.

She'd done that to him.

And he'd just lied for her. The shock of wonder made her head spin.

Seke's eyes narrowed, and he folded his arms over his chest, looking from Cambry to Lundric. "You have thirty minutes to make a full report on the *exercise*." The steel in Master Seke's voice couldn't be missed.

"Yes, master." Lundric bowed and pushed on.

The fact he'd protected her after what she'd done, considering his obvious agony over her actions, made it so much worse. And infinitely better. Lundric was still on her side, after what she'd done to shatter his trust.

How could that be?

Or did he simply wish to be the one to squeeze her life out? No, he could have already done it. A tiny speck of hope kindled in her solar plexus. He stilled cared about her. Maybe he could find a way to forgive.

Lundric kicked the door to her tiny chamber open and shoved her inside, latching the door. He grasped her wrists and pinned them behind her back, tying them together with a handkerchief. In deafening silence, he yanked down her pants and panties.

Though she faced a furious alien warrior, her instinct to fight in the face of danger was absent. All she experienced was a loose-limbed surrender. She stepped docilely out of her pant legs, breath rising and falling in shortened bursts. She waited to see what Lundric would do next.

He hadn't looked at her once since he'd come for her, but his agony, his devastation came through in waves. He paced to the cot and picked up her blanket, flicking it open then doubling it and rolling it into a cylinder. He set it in the center of the cot and pointed at it. "Lie down," he barked.

Oh. She lost her breath.

His intention suddenly became crystal clear. Even more so when he stripped the leather sword belt from his waist.

A starstorm of flutters kindled in her belly, and her palms turned clammy and cold. But still no alarms went off spurring her to fight or flee. A whipping from a giant, angry alien was endurable. Because he was an angry, giant alien who cared about her. One who had lied to his superior in order to handle her punishment on his own.

She'd accept whatever he had to give her.

Acceptance didn't stop her legs from shaking as she walked to the cot and lay over the rolled blanket, which lifted and tilted her bare ass up for Lundric's punishment.

He wound the buckle end of the belt around his fist in what seemed like an agonizing delay. The entire time, the skin on her buttocks twitched in anticipation of the whipping.

When the first stroke landed like a line of pure fire, she flung a leg off the cot, lurching to get away. Lundric stopped her with nothing more than a stern point of his finger. She froze, halfway off the cot.

"Get back in position and stay there until I say you can get up." The tightness in his voice gutted her.

"Yes, Captain," she whispered, her throat hoarse. She obeyed despite the agony of the first welt. If he needed this to make them whole again, she'd give it. What she feared most, though, was that it wouldn't. That nothing would repair the rift she'd put between them.

He whipped her with his belt, over and over again, striking the lower part of her buttocks. Each stroke seared her bare skin, marking it and leaving her raw. The strokes fell too quickly for her to cry. Ten. Twenty. Thirty strokes. Her legs writhed on the cot, but she stayed where he'd commanded, absorbing his anger, his retribution. He stopped at forty.

She panted into the cot, struggling to catch her sobbing breath. Her bottom throbbed in time with her pulse. She imagined it must be swollen and raw.

Lundric hadn't moved. She didn't have the courage to look at him but sensed him still standing at her side, towering over her with dark bitterness.

Because she had no excuse, because any apology she gave would fall flat, she offered the one thing her position allowed. She spread her legs.

Lundric's breath audibly caught. He neither spoke nor breathed for what seemed like a long moment. Finally, he asked, "You think you deserve my cock?" There was a sneer to his voice, but underneath she heard layers of hurt.

"No," she croaked. Now the tears that hadn't come during the whipping smarted. His punishment she could take, but his rejection? She'd rather go through ten Ocretion executions than endure the pain of losing Lundric.

"The only place you'll be taking my cock is in your ass."

It *vecking* gutted her that he left off the *little human,* or one of the other endearments he had for her, but she celebrated the fact he still wanted her.

"Do you want to take it there?"

Sweet Mother Earth, even in his anger, he still respected her agency. Was he giving her a choice?

"Yes, please." She almost didn't recognize her voice, which sounded tiny.

Lundric uttered a harsh curse, the first outward sign he'd given of his turmoil. He picked up her hips and shifted her onto her knees, perpendicular to the bed, her ass in the air, facing him. With her hands tied behind, her face rested on the mattress. She heard a rustle of movement and the sweet-smelling citrus oil Lily had given her dribbled down her crack.

She nearly wept at the kindness because there was no way Lundric's huge cock would fit in her tight ass otherwise. "Lundric, I—"

His palm crashed down on her welted ass, and her words broke off on a yelp. "Don't speak unless spoken to." His harsh edict made her nose burn.

She whimpered as the well-oiled head of his cock nudged her back entrance, and he applied steady pressure. She forced herself to breathe, willed her muscles to relax and accept his plunder. "I'm sorry," she whispered.

"*Quiet.*" He breached her entrance. The sensation was half-pleasure, half-shame, and it had her pussy clenching with need. She wished she had use of her hands to touch herself there. But this wasn't for her. It was an offering to Lundric, and while she couldn't do much in her position to satisfy him, she could hold still and relax into the riot of sensation he caused.

"*Veck*, Cambry," he spat as he braced her hips. "It doesn't matter what you do, I'll never be cured of the need to possess you."

She sobbed, heat and desire and residual pain from her whipping turning her delirious.

"Tear out my *vecking* heart. Use me. Manipulate me with that body. That smile. I'll still want to mark you forever as mine."

"Lundric, please—"

"Did you think I used you back?" he cut her off, harshly. "Do you think all I wanted was this? To *veck* this pretty little body as much as I wanted? I *never vecking* used you. I could've taken you any way I liked. No. My part was real. I *killed* for you. I would *die* for you. You are *my vecking female*. I love you."

He loved her. That incredible revelation seemed tragic considering the pain and anger in his words.

"I would have cared for and protected you every *vecking* planet rotation for the rest of our lives."

Would have.

Those words confirmed her worst fears. Even as he swore he needed her, he'd spoken in the past tense, like they were through. Over. Done. At the same time he declared his love for her. The last pieces of her heart splintered and fell away. He may not be able to resist this last *veck,* but he was done with her, emotionally.

Tears dampened the mattress, but she held her sobs in, not wanting him to hear. Wanting him to finish, to take his bitter pleasure out on her in the way he'd chosen.

He reached around and cupped her mound, one finger sinking into her wetness as he continued to pump into her ass, stretching and filling her beyond what she thought was possible. "Did you think it was all a transaction, little female? You'd win everything you needed from me in exchange for offering this?"

"No!" she wailed. "It was real!"

He pounded into her harder and the intensity of the sensations made stars dance in her vision. "Don't. *Lie,*" he growled behind clenched teeth and shoved in, balls deep, sending his anger, his rejection, right into her with his seed.

She wept.

~.~

Veck. Hearing Cambry cry cut his insides like he'd eaten glass. He eased out of her tight back hole and untied her wrists then used the handkerchief to clean them both.

He had to bite back the urge to apologize, to hold her and rock her until her tears dried. He'd taken it upon himself to punish her on behalf of Prince Zander or his officers. He couldn't show weakness now.

Though he'd freed her wrists, Cambry hadn't moved from the kneeling position he'd placed her in. Her surrender was the only thing that made this scene bearable. If she'd fought him—if he'd had to put a knee in her back to whip her into submission, he would have done it as his duty, but it would have slain him.

He plucked her from the bed and sat on the chair, holding her on his lap. He thumbed away a tear lingering on her cheek.

She hadn't climaxed, and she didn't deserve to, but his pride demanded he show her he still had command over her body. She may not care about him, but he sure as stars would ensure she needed him to bring her to satisfaction. He hiked one of her knees up to her shoulder, spreading her wide.

"You don't get pleasure here today." He slapped his fingers down over her pussy.

She shrieked, her anus and pussy contracting.

He slapped again, harder.

She squirmed in his arms, gasping. "I didn't use you, Lundric." Her voice had a pleading tone.

It flayed him to hear his name on her lips. He wanted to believe her but he wouldn't be made a fool twice. He slapped again.

"I didn't ask for your favors." She writhed, her hips jerking, legs fighting to close.

He spanked her pussy, hard. *"Lies."* She'd bargained her body for a shower, hadn't she? He should have known then none of it was real.

"The shower, yes," she gasped, realizing her mistake. "But not us—*ooh!*" Her wet pussy made the most enticing sound every time he slapped it. Her squirming had his cock hardening again. He slapped faster, recognizing the frantic note of her gasps. "Lundric. *Ah-oh! Please.*"

Holy Zandian Star, her approaching climax brought his need right back to the edge.

"Lundric, I swear! I'm not some sex slave who—*oh Mother Earth!*—offers up her body to any male in authority." Her pants became cries. "It wasn't a trick." Words tumbled from her mouth. "It was *you.* Only you," she babbled.

He ignored the words, listening instead to the sound of her need, brought to the brink by his hand. It was the only thing he could trust about her. *This was no lie.*

I've never—*never* used sex to—"

"Shut. *Up.*" He pitched forward and pivoted her to her back on the cot, her knee still drawn up to her chest. Following her down, he speared her with his erection.

She cried out with pleasure, her fingernails digging into his shoulders, chin lifting to the ceiling. The way her pussy clenched around his cock sent a tremor through his thighs, his balls tightening, ready to explode once more.

He *vecked* her hard, the position unforgiving, her sex splayed open, spread for him as he angled deep into her channel.

How could anything that felt this good be wrong? No, he'd made no mistake about Cambry. She was his female. Whether she accepted him or not.

"You *left,*" he growled, punishing her with his cock, their flesh slapping together like a third spanking. "You *vecking* left."

Her mouth opened, and he saw horror there. He didn't understand it, but even if he had, there was no stopping now. He had to *veck* her within an inch of her life. Holding back was not an option. It was like his life depended on this moment, on forever branding her with his rainbow-hued cum.

"I had to—I had to find my brother."

He froze, dick mostly withdrawn, hovering above her.

"They separated us. I've been trying to get to him ever since. That's why I ran away from the factory. Why I was sentenced to the death pod."

He impaled her with his cock again, shoving deep. "Why didn't you just tell me?" *Slap.* "You think I can't locate a slave in the Ocretion kingdom?" He drove into her.

"Ung." She cried out each time he plowed into her.

"You think I wouldn't do that for you?"

Tears swam in her big beautiful eyes. "I—I never considered—" She sought his gaze, but he *vecked* her so hard hers rolled back in her head.

"No, don't pretend you had no choices here. If you wanted to stay and be with me, you would have."

He steeled himself against her shock and sorrow, driving himself to his finish.

"I'm sorry. Lundric, I'm so sorry."

He roared, bruising his thighs on the edge of the cot as he thrust so deep and hard, the cot collapsed beneath them. Cambry screamed, wrapping her legs behind his back and holding him in tight as her muscles spasmed around his cock, drawing his seed deep inside of her.

As the deafening thunder in his ears faded, he became aware of pounding on the door, and Cambry's arrested posture as she listened to the shouting male voice behind the door.

"*Lundric!* Do you hear me?"

Excrement. Master Seke.

Still in battle mode, he disentangled himself from Cambry and leaped to his feet, yanking the cot, with her on it, back up and snapping the legs in place. He shoved his cock back in his flight pants.

Cambry scrambled up and hopped as she pulled on her pants.

He put his palm on the door handle. "Coming." To Cambry, he growled, "Lock this behind me. Do not open it for anyone but me."

Her face paled and pupils narrowed, but she nodded and obeyed.

Outside her door, Seke gripped his tunic and slammed him up against the wall. "Don't you ever *vecking* lie to me again. Zandians don't lie. Your deceit lacks honor." Seke placed his forearm over Lundric's windpipe, allowing him breath in measured doses.

Lundric didn't fight back. His mentor was right—he lacked honor.

"Say it. Tell me what happened."

"She ran away. I brought her back." He hated speaking the words, even though Seke already knew. They stung like salt in a fresh wound.

"I know you're in love with her, but you don't forsake your training, your species, your friends. You don't put everyone at risk."

"I couldn't—" He struggled to draw enough breath to defend himself. "I couldn't let anyone else punish her. I would *vecking* kill any being who touched her."

"You think we don't know that? No being's going to hurt your female. But that doesn't mean you compromise the safety of everyone on this pod and the security of our mission."

"Zandia and honor before love, right Seke?" It was a low blow. A terrible blow Lundric should not have taken. When Zandia had been invaded, Seke had made a fateful choice—saving Prince Zander over finding his own female and children. Though he never spoke of it, Lundric knew his master suffered for his choice.

The color drained from Seke's face before he slammed Lundric's head back against the wall. "Don't you *vecking* throw that in my face."

Lundric regretted his words immediately. "I'm sorry—I'm sorry. I don't judge you. I never have. Forgive me. I know you suffer every day."

A haunted shadow fell over Seke. "You don't know anything," he rasped.

"No," Lundric agreed.

"I don't know anything, either." The heaviness in Seke's tone matched his own. Lundric got the sense Seke wasn't thinking only about his lost family, but also about Leora, the human female he'd fallen for.

"Listen," Seke said heavily, easing back on the pressure on Lundric's throat. "Your female has an agenda that doesn't align with ours. If you don't find a way to make them come together, you're going to be faced with a choice—your female or the fight for the survival of our species."

Lundric scrubbed a hand over his face. "That's a bit dramatic, isn't it?"

"Is it?" Seke finished releasing him and walked away without waiting for an answer.

He sagged against the wall, sorrow weaving through the shards of pain in his chest, leaving him battered. Was a female who didn't even care for him worth endangering his species?

Stars, he wished he knew the answers.

-.-

Cambry waited after Lundric's conversation with Master Seke ended, expecting—hoping—Lundric would come back, but he hadn't. She'd stood at her door and listened to every word, every thud of bodies crashing against the other side of her wall.

She swam in guilt for the position she'd put him in with his superiors. She didn't want him to have to choose between her and Zandia. Despite her dislike of the Zandians' choice to use the humans as their army, she'd developed some sympathy for their cause. She didn't want their species to die out any more than she wanted humans to remain enslaved.

Lily claimed Zandia would be some kind of Shangri-La. A beautiful place where the humans who fought for her would be free. She still didn't buy that story. What guarantee did they have that, even if they survived the takeover of Zandia and it was successful, they would be offered freedom?

But she didn't care anymore. Because after hearing the way Lundric and Seke had spoken about her, something had changed.

I would vecking kill any being who touched her. Lundric had punished her himself so no one else would. That part didn't surprise her. She'd come to believe the sincerity of Lundric's attachment.

It was Seke's response that made her believe all the Zandians might be as honorable as Lundric.

You think we don't know that? No being's going to hurt your female.

He made it sound like they recognized Lundric's bond to her. As if it was something real and sacred. As if Lundric's claim on her took precedence over any form of justice they might want to see served.

She wasn't even sure how to process that, but it changed things. Everything had changed since Lundric had marched her back into the pod. As she'd flown away, she'd thought her heart would never repair from the break of leaving him. It was worse, even, than when Tal had been taken from her, sold to some other factory master. So, on some level, she'd wanted to be caught and dragged back by her giant warrior. But she'd hurt him. Badly. The Lundric she knew had retreated, and what was left was just a hull of his normal self.

At first, she hadn't been sure which part angered him—that she'd violated his trust, or stolen the ship, or tricked him. But when he was *vecking* her—in his uniquely dominant way—it became clear she'd reopened the wound inflicted by his mother. She'd left.

And now he didn't believe her feelings for him were real.

Her heart ached as if physically bruised. It was so much worse than her throbbing ass, or her well-used anus and pussy, or all the other small bruises Lundric had left from the rough *vecking*, which she wouldn't trade for anything. While Lundric may have shut her out emotionally, he had been painfully direct with her physically, and she loved his honesty.

She would have to find a way to prove to him she hadn't been faking anything with him, either—that all her responses to him were as honest as his expressions of love.

Lundric had told her not to open the door for any being but him. He didn't say whether she could leave of her own accord. Though her stomach growled with hunger, she skipped dinner and stayed in her chamber, too raw emotionally and physically to face any being. Exhaustion, both emotional and physical, soon crept over her, and she pulled off her pants and crawled into bed to sleep.

In the middle of the night, she woke to the scrape of a knife through the door, lifting the latch. She fumbled under the mattress for the dagger Lundric had given her and swung up to sit, holding her breath as the huge outline of a Zandian appeared silhouetted in the doorway.

"It's me," her warrior muttered, shutting the door behind him. "I didn't want to wake you."

Her chest tightened. Despite his anger, he still showed such consideration of her.

I love you.

The realization of the depth of her attachment to him shouldn't surprise her, but she'd spent her whole life believing only Tal could be trusted. Only Tal deserved her love.

"Lie down."

Still sleep-fogged, she sank back on the cot. Lundric slid onto the narrow bed beside her, making the legs groan with his added weight. He draped an arm around her waist and pulled her tight against him.

"Lundric?" she'd whispered.

"Shh. Go back to sleep."

He'd come to sleep with her? They never slept together because his shift spanned the night. But he'd come back just to hold her. Tears closed her throat.

His hand slid down her side and covered her ass, fingertips gently exploring the welts on the backs of her bare legs. "We'll find forgiveness, you and I." He sounded uncertain.

She wanted to assure him she bore him no grudge for his treatment that day, but her fear he may never forgive her made the words stick in her throat. Tears slipped down her nose.

Somehow, though she'd been silent and it was pitch-black in her room, Lundric knew, because his thumb mopped them up.

"Don't cry, Cambry. Go to sleep." His voice sounded heavy, tired.

Because she didn't want to cause him more stress, she obeyed, letting her lids close and matching her breath to his until she slid back into sleep, nestled against his massive chest.

CHAPTER SEVEN

Cambry walked toward the guard's sleeping quarters. She hadn't seen Lundric anywhere, all planet rotation.

He'd left before she woke that morning. She didn't even know how that was possible—she always slept with one foot on the floor, alert to any danger, so she should have felt or heard him move. But she hadn't. Maybe she felt that safe in his presence.

She didn't know how long he'd stayed or why he'd felt the need to come in and hold her. Had it been to comfort her? Or himself? She wanted to ask, but she couldn't find him. He'd been absent in her flight training.

She drew a breath, mustering the courage to knock on his bunkroom door.

Sten answered. He rubbed his face with one hand, looking groggy. Light poured out of their room, amplified by what appeared to be the crystal Lily had given Lundric for his healing.

"I'm sorry. I didn't mean to wake you." She tried to peer past him into the room, but he shifted subtly to block her view. "Is Lundric here?"

Sten shook his head. He didn't smile or offer anything more. She'd sworn Vokart and the other flight instructors were less friendly to her than usual that planet rotation, but she might just be paranoid. No being had said anything to her about what had happened the planet rotation before. She'd half expected to be kept from flying that day or even thrown in a cell or locked in her chamber. She'd certainly expected to be called up to Master Seke or Rok or even taken to the palatial pod to answer to Prince Zander for what she'd done.

But nothing had happened. She'd woken to find Lundric gone. Had dared to leave her chamber for breakfast and attended training as if nothing had happened. She'd been allowed to fly, although she suspected her trainers watched her far more closely than usual. But Lundric was missing.

"He's not here," Sten said.

Disappointment wilted her like a balloon losing air. "Do you know where I might find him?"

Sten shook his head. "If he didn't tell you where he was going, I'm not going to."

No, she hadn't imagined the animosity. It was real.

She sank against the doorframe, needing it to hold her up. "Listen, I know I'm probably not your favorite human right now, but I—"

"I can't help you, and I was trying to sleep." Sten shut the door in her face.

She stuck her boot in the door before it shut.

The huge warrior looked down at the boot then at her, lifting a brow.

She swallowed down the fear his challenging look inspired. "Please."

"No. Move your foot."

"Sten, who's at the door?" a sleep-disgruntled voice called from inside the bunkroom,

"Would you shut the *veck* up?" another one called.

She withdrew her foot. Sten shut the door, leaving her standing there, staring at the gray metal door, her stomach heavy as a stone.

Where had Lundric gone? Was he in trouble because of her? Maybe he'd been summoned to the Zandian palatial pod to see Prince Zander.

She lifted her chin and marched to their headquarters. A Zandian warrior stood in the office.

"Is Master Seke here? Or Rok?"

"Seke went back to the palatial pod and Rok hasn't returned. Lundric's also gone. I'm next in command after Lundric. What do you need?" He studied her. "Ah. You're Lundric's female."

She flushed but forced herself inside the office and stuck out her hand in a human-style greeting. "I'm Cambry."

He looked at her hand like he didn't know what to do with it and raised his fist at a ninety degree angle. "Samsen."

"Where has Lundric gone? When will he be back?"

Samsen folded his arms across his chest. "I don't know, and if he didn't tell you himself, no one else around here will."

"What is that? Some part of your code of honor?"

"Yes."

She meant to be strong, but the fear Lundric wanted to put distance between them, or that he was in trouble because of her made her heart thump too hard against her sternum. "Will he be back?" Her voice was an octave higher than normal.

Samsen shrugged. "I cannot say." He studied her for a moment. "You are safe here."

Annoyance flashed through her. Did he think she was afraid without Lundric? Stars, these Zandian warriors truly were so chivalrous. Grudging appreciation melted away her irritation.

"I'm not concerned for my safety. I need to speak with Lundric. If you hear from him, will you relay the message?"

He bowed. "I will."

She dipped into a curtsy—the first she'd offered any of the Zandians. "Thank you."

As she walked away, she chewed on her lip, her stomach churning. She needed her male back. They had things to discuss. She'd hurt him, and she wanted to fix the rift she'd caused. The trouble was, even if she knew where he was, she wasn't sure how to fix things.

~.~

It took Lundric three planet rotations to locate the twenty-year-old slave named Tal, the only living relative linked to Cambry in Ocretion slave records. He found the young man working as a slave in a factory not far from the one Cambry had escaped from.

He used his life savings to purchase the human, though he had to buy three other males with him, to avoid raising suspicion. The four of them all sat in his battleship now, their wrists in manacles, their faces masks of wariness.

He faced them. "Humans, you have a choice. I only need one of you—the young one." He lifted his chin toward Tal. The boy's hair was brown, not auburn, but he had the same pale coloring as Cambry, with the light dusting of auburn freckles over his nose and identical brown eyes. He also had the same intelligent mistrust in his gaze. They narrowed when Lundric indicated him.

"The rest of you can come with me, or I can sell you back to other Ocretions. If you come with me, you will no longer be slaves, but you'll serve the same master I do, follow the rules I follow, and will have to fight the battles I fight to win a better life. The choice is yours."

"Who is your master? Where are we going?"

"I cannot tell you where, and if you decide to go with me, you cannot change your mind. Once you've seen our headquarters, you cannot leave. My master is Prince Zander, the rightful ruler of the planet Zandia."

From their blank faces, he would bet they'd never heard of Zandia or Zander.

"What about me? Why do you need me?" Tal demanded.

"I will tell you after they've made their decisions." He didn't want to mention Cambry in front of the humans if they were not coming along. Any hint to Ocretions his female was still alive would put her, his species, and his mission at risk. "So, humans? Make your decisions, quickly. I don't have time to waste."

The oldest one, a tiny man with white-streaked hair, shrugged. "I'll go with you."

The wiry male in the middle slouched lower in the chair. "What is the work?"

"Battle." Maybe when they won Zandia there'd be more, but it was all he had ever known.

The wiry man grinned a broken-toothed smile and sat up straighter, flexing his fingers in the manacles. "Battle, eh? Count me in."

The third man, nervous and missing one eye, ducked his head, as if Lundric might not notice him.

"What about you?" Lundric demanded.

The male muttered something softly under his breath, but Lundric couldn't make sense of it. He appeared to be a bit simple.

"Quin is in, aren't you, Quin?" the wiry male asked.

Quin bobbed his head. "Quin is in, yes, Quin is in."

"Good."

"So? Will you tell me now? What do you need me for?" Tal asked again.

"Cambry wants you." His voice roughened just speaking her name.

Tal's face transformed as well. It went from brazen defiance to a mixture of hope and anxiety. "You have Cambry?" His voice raised in pitch.

He nodded.

"She's alive? Because I'd heard—"

"She's alive. So you will come with me. Agreed?"

The boy swallowed and nodded.

Lundric unlocked each human's manacles even though there was a chance they could overpower him and take the ship. "Buckle up. We'll be there soon." He dropped into the pilot's seat and started up the engines.

Back to the pod. To Cambry. He rubbed his sternum, which had ached since the moment she'd left him. Maybe now that she had her brother, she would no longer run. He couldn't make her love him, but he could, at least, provide what she needed to be content. Because he wasn't letting her go—not ever again.

~.~

Cambry swooped around Shooku, pushing the battleship to go faster, diving in and out of the rock formations to practice her skills. Vokart gripped the edges of the copilot's chair with white knuckles, but he didn't say a word.

"Captain Lundric requesting permission to land." The deep sound of her warrior's voice crackled over the comms unit.

Her heart bounded. Lundric had returned! She swung the craft around, searching the skies for him. *There.* He had just entered the planet's atmosphere.

"There's one student flight in the air, Captain, but otherwise you're clear," someone spoke from the landing dock.

Without asking permission, she positioned her craft and executed her best landing yet.

She'd already unsnapped her harness before she turned to Vokart.

He pursed his lips, appearing half-annoyed, half-amused. She'd asked him a dozen times for information on Lundric's disappearance and return. "Permission granted," he rumbled. "If you were going to ask."

"Yes, I was," she said, already halfway out of the craft. "Thank you."

She grabbed a helmet and shoved it over her head, running the distance to the pod. Lundric and four other beings had gone in ahead of her. She entered through the hatch and waited for the atmosphere to clear before opening the interior door.

"Lundric!" she shouted as soon as she entered, ripping her helmet off and hanging it on a hook on the wall.

Lundric and another warrior stood with four human males. One of them snapped his head in her direction.

"Cambry!" The voice that answered wasn't Lundric's.

"Tal!" Her heart flew up to her throat. She ran for her younger brother, and he met her halfway, grabbing her and squeezing so tightly, he picked her up from the ground.

"You've grown," she laughed, tears leaking from the corners of her eyes. "At least two more inches since I saw you last."

"Have I?" he asked gruffly, his voice choked. "They told me you were dead. That you killed three guards escaping and they sentenced you to death. What happened?"

She tore her focus from her brother to look at the broad-shouldered warrior standing several feet off, watching with eyes still shadowed in pain. A Zandian was leading the three other humans away.

When Lundric saw her looking, he nodded once and strode off down the corridor.

"Lundric!" She bolted after him. "Lundric, wait!"

He turned just in time for her leap, catching her as she hurtled at him.

She strangled him in a hug, burying her face in his neck. "Thank you." She dropped little kisses behind his ear. "Thank you, Lundric."

"Stop."

Her heart twisted.

He pried her from his massive body, lowering her to the floor. "I like the show of appreciation, but that's not why I did it."

The emptiness of his tone slapped her. Blood drained from her face as she realized her warrior was still just as withdrawn as he'd been before he left to find her brother. Her eyes watered. "I *know* that. You did it because you're Lundric and it's what you do. Because I'm your female."

He went very still, watching her warily. "Yes."

Tal had joined them, and he cleared his throat. "So—?"

She drew back from Lundric to include her brother. "So, you've met Lundric?"

Tal nodded and extended his hand.

She reached over and folded his fingers into a fist bending his elbow to form the ninety degree angle of the Zandian greeting. "This is how they do it."

Lundric's gaze lighted on her face with the curious, appreciative glint they usually held, but then it dimmed again. "I'll let you two catch up." He turned and walked away.

"Wait—Lundric?"

He didn't turn or acknowledge her, his broad shoulders stiff as he disappeared around the corridor.

Her nose and throat burned.

Tal squeezed her shoulder. "You want to tell me what's going on?"

She blinked rapidly and forced a smile. "Come on. Are you hungry? Let's get some lunch." She brought him to the main meeting room where the food packs were being distributed and picked up two.

They settled on the floor with their backs against a wall to eat.

"So, what is this place? How did you get here?"

"It's a bizarre story." She tried to push back the thoughts tangling around Lundric, the irrepressible urge to keep running to him, to keep leaping until he kept her.

"This originally was the death pod the Ocretions put me on. But I got lucky. They also put an escaped human slave named Lily on here. She happens to be the sister of the Zandian prince's mate. Her boyfriend, a Zandian captain named Rok, orchestrated her rescue and pulled this pod down. So now, all the beings on the pod have been conscripted into the Zandian army, and we're being trained for battle, because they want to take their planet back. Are you following?"

Tal grinned. "I'm trying. So who's Lundric?"

"My mate. Except he's still angry with me for stealing a ship and trying to leave to find you."

"Who flew the ship?"

Her lips curved into a self-satisfied smile. "I did. They'll train you, too, if you want."

She didn't really have to ask. Her brother was a born warrior, like her. "*Veck*, yes. When can I start?"

An alarm went off, screeching through the pod and echoing off the metal walls. "Ocretion police ships have entered the atmosphere. All pilots report to the loading dock. Repeat, Ocretion police ships have entered the atmosphere. Every pilot report to the loading dock. This is not a drill."

She scrambled to her feet. "Come on, let's go."

Tal raced behind her as they ran to the loading dock.

She didn't wait for instructions like the rest of the humans gathered, but grabbed two helmets and followed the Zandian warriors out of the pod, running over the rocky ground for a battleship, her brother right behind her.

"Cambry!" Lundric's anguished roar came over the comms unit. She stopped in her tracks, looking around for him. He'd halted in the hatch of a battleship when he'd caught sight of her.

He thought she was running again. She'd just have to prove to him she planned to stay.

Battleships lifted off the ground around them and, above, the first shots were fired.

"Fire at will, repeat, fire at will!"

"Get back in the pod," Lundric roared, jumping into his ship.

Veck that. She was a trained pilot, and they needed her. She resumed running toward the next available battleship and jumped on, waiting until Tal joined her before closing the hatch. "Buckle up," she shouted as she jumped into the pilot's seat. "You're on weapons because I don't know how to work them."

Tal whooped and slid behind the controls. "Whoa," he breathed with appreciation, lighting up as he took in the state-of-the-art craft. "Where did they get all these ships?"

"They're rich. But almost extinct."

"Hence their interest in human females?"

"I suppose," she mumbled, slightly offended at having her relationship with Lundric reduced to the economics of available females. That must have been how Lundric felt thinking she'd only been interested in him for the ways he could help her.

But she knew Lundric's interest in her wasn't just because she was female. He'd seen her. Been attracted to her. She had to show him she felt the same.

She lifted off and entered the fray. She saw at least four Ocretion police ships, all firing on them. "Hang on," she yelled and made a tight turn, swinging the craft around to get behind one of the police ships. "Fire, Tal!"

Tal shot the laser. It went wide, and the police ship dropped down, out of range. "Give me another chance—I'm still figuring out how these work," he yelled.

Below them, the pod lifted from the ground, the battleships circling around, protecting it as it made an escape. Where was it going? She hoped the Zandians had a plan. And she sure as hell wished she'd been privy to it, because she had no idea where to rendezvous if they survived this battle.

"On the right, on the right!" she shouted as one of the police ships appeared in their range.

Both ships fired on each other. She held tight when the ship sustained damage to the wing, but Tal nailed them with laser fire, and the police ship exploded.

"I did it!" he yelled. "Give me another one."

"We might not have a chance!" She gripped the controls with all her might, trying to direct the craft as it fell into a spin.

Her mind raced, trying to remember what Rok had said about recovering from a spin. *Cut the power, turn away from the spin and push down.*

The ground came hurtling toward them, and her fingers flew over the controls, cutting power and pushing down and left, away from the spin. Nothing happened. Ten more seconds and they'd hit ground and they wouldn't survive a fall from the height they'd been hit.

The craft wobbled. She pushed harder on the controls, encouraged she'd made any kind of change in the spin.

"Cambry!" Lundric's cry rang in her helmet's comm unit.

"I've got it!" The craft wobbled harder, then banked hard to the left, out of the spin. *Thank sweet Mother Earth.*

A second fleet of police ships appeared in the atmosphere, dozens of them.

"Retreat, retreat!" The command blared in her ears but three ships were chasing Lundric, at least she thought it was Lundric.

She joined the chase, Tal firing on the police ships from behind. He hit one, two. The third spun around them and fired directly on them. The windshield exploded in a ball of fire. Not willing to go down easily, she gunned the ship forward and rammed it into the police ship. Both ships hurtled toward the ground.

"Cambry, *Cambry, no!*"

Their descent slowed. The magnaray. Lundric must be above them. But her ship was on fire, which meant a fireball could travel through the magnaray and blow up Lundric's ship.

"Leave us," she screamed. "Release the ship!"

"Never." His growl conveyed 100 percent determination.

Their ship lifted away from the ground. Five police ships surrounded them.

Tal unbuckled, racing to the rear of the craft. "Is there more firepower back here?" he shouted.

"I don't know!" She hadn't been trained in the weaponry part yet, just flying, but since the craft was unflyable and the forward part of the ship was on fire, she followed Tal.

"Here they are." Tal climbed a ladder toward an upper deck.

She ascended behind him, only able to squeeze her torso into the small area made for one being. They both took controls, firing as rapidly as they could, causing the police ships to dodge and fall away, out of their range.

"Nice work, Cambry and Tal." Lundric's deep voice rang in her ear. "Hang on, I'm going to get you out of there."

A lurch indicated Lundric had entered hyperdrive. She squeezed her eyes closed and held her breath, waiting for the explosion that ended them all.

A second passed. Then another.

Still alive.

She opened her lids. They were in space, hovering near the pod. Other Zandian battleships circled it. And the giant hangar-ship, an open craft that had housed all the smaller battleships, hung beside it.

"You are not cleared for landing in the hangar, Captain Lundric. Your cargo is on fire. Repeat, your cargo is on fire." The lack of oxygen in space should have extinguished all the flames, but the cabin pressure kept the fires burning inside.

"Then get the fire spray ready, because I'm landing," her warrior growled.

"No, Lundric, don't," she cried. She didn't want to be responsible for setting the entire hangar on fire and wiping out all of Zandia's battleships in one fell swoop.

Her mind racing, she ran for the container of fire spray located below on her craft. "Tal, help me with this," she shouted.

Her brother scrambled down and the two of them attacked the fire on their ship. She needed to get it out before Lundric dropped them onto the hangar.

~.~

The only thing keeping Lundric from a total implosion was the fact that Cambry's voice still registered on his comms unit. She was alive. Stars, she was still alive.

Twice back there, he'd been sure he'd lost her. What in the name of Zandia's true star had she been thinking? At first, he'd feared she planned to run away again—to take her brother and leave. But she hadn't. She'd stayed to fight, and he was so *vecking* proud of her courage and prowess as a pilot.

His little rebel—so brave. Such a fighter.

The moment he docked her ship and then his own, he leaped out. A crew already had the fire under control and had helped Cambry and Tal to evacuate the destroyed craft.

"Cambry!" He sprinted toward her.

She ran for him.

He opened his arms wide and caught her when she launched, squeezing the breath right out of her. "What in the *veck* were you thinking? I told you to go back to the pod."

She scrambled out of his arms and stood facing him, chin lifted, her small fingers wrapped in the front of his uniform. "I'm a Zandian pilot," she said, the determination in the set of her mouth daring him to disagree. "I fight for Zandia."

He staggered a bit under the weight of her declaration. Truly? Had she taken his cause on as her own now? What had changed her mind?

He grasped the back of her head and pulled it against his chest, lowering his lips to her hair. "I guess I'll have to get used to your being in danger, then," he said gruffly, emotion closing his throat. He didn't want to. He wanted to forbid his female from ever putting herself in danger again, but it would go against her nature. Cambry was a warrior like him. So was her brother, if the way he'd been shooting back there had been any indication.

He pulled her head back and cradled her face. "You were brilliant back there—both of you." He lifted his gaze to include Tal, who hovered awkwardly nearby. "Thank you for serving Zandia. The prince will be pleased with your service."

She probably didn't give a *veck* what the prince thought, but he did. He needed Zander's approval to mate her, to keep her, and with the stunt she'd pulled stealing the ship earlier, it might have been difficult. This act of service would go a long way toward mending things.

"Captain Lundric, Master Seke is demanding an immediate report," one of his guards informed him.

He nodded. There was too much work to do. Holding Cambry would have to come later. He kissed her forehead and released her. "Get yourself to medical. That's an order." He threw in a stern glance to be sure she understood the meaning of the word *order*.

She merely smiled. "Yes, Captain." Something in her voice made him think she enjoyed taking his orders.

She'd better. He had a hundred more in mind just as soon as he settled the chaos at hand.

CHAPTER EIGHT

Cambry hissed as she climbed off the cot, her fresh laser tattoo still raw.

"Are you sure that's how his name looks in Zandian? Because if I just wrote *idiot* on your back, you're going to look pretty stupid." Tal wiped off the laser ink gun Lily had managed to procure and put it back in its box. Lily and Rok had arrived immediately before the battle began with Ocretion police. They believed they had unwittingly attracted attention and led them there.

"I verified it with three different Zandians. They all told me it said *Lundric.*"

"You're really serious about this male, aren't you?" Her brother folded his arms across his chest and narrowed his eyes at her. "I have to admit, I'm shocked."

"Why are you shocked?" A spike of defensiveness rose up, and she prepared to defend Lundric's worthiness.

He shrugged. "I've just never seen you this way. You're like a different person."

"In a bad way or a good way?" she asked warily.

He grinned. "A good way. Definitely. Are you fishing for my approval here? Because you have it. Lundric won it the minute he came to that factory for me. But even without that, I knew he was the one by how you are with him. You're different. Happier. More open. And he obviously would do anything for you. So, yes. A good way."

A knock sounded on her door.

"He's here." Nerves made her stomach flutter. "Get out, quick."

"I'm leaving, I'm leaving. Stars, you'd think you'd want to spend a little more time with me after how long we've been apart. *Kidding!*" He dodged her slap as he opened the door. "Good afternoon, Captain." He made the Zandian greeting with his fist in the air. "She's been waiting for you." Tal slipped past a frowning Lundric and disappeared.

Lundric had dark circles under his eyes. She doubted he'd slept for the past two planet rotations since the battle with Ocretion police, and she'd hardly seen him. The Zandians hadn't found a place to dock the pod or hangar, so they'd continued to float through space just on the outskirts of Ocretion territory. They were in an area Rok knew from his smuggling days, staying off the radar while they worked on a new plan. From what their intelligence had gathered, the Ocretions did not know it was Prince Zander who had taken possession of their death pod and launched battleships against their police, but it may only be a matter of time before they did. The Zandians were trying to move up their timeline for recovering Zandia, hoping to do it *before* they had to wage battle against the Ocretions.

The good news was the battle had won further allegiance from the beings on the pod. Now that they'd seen the Zandians wage a second battle against their former tormentors, their eagerness to join the fight had increased. Trust between Zandians and the refugees on the pod had improved.

Lundric shut the door behind him and dropped the latch into place, but he made no move toward her. The haunted quality to his gaze that had been there since her betrayal hadn't left. He looked at her like a starved man who knew he'd never get enough to eat.

She had to dispel him of that myth. Holding his violet gaze, she peeled off her panties and leggings, then her tunic, and stood before him, nude.

He leaned his head back against the door, fingers opening and closing into fists at his sides. "Cambry, you don't have to—"

"I know. I never thought I did." She took a step toward him. "I wasn't using you, Lundric. I *never* used you. I just..." She knotted her fingers in front of her, suddenly wishing she'd waited to strip until after they'd had this conversation. She didn't want to touch him until she'd said everything, either. Didn't want him to think she was using sex to mend things.

"Trust doesn't come naturally for me. I'm sorry I didn't ask for your help in finding Tal. I should have. And I'm so sorry I violated the bond between us. Most of all I'm sorry I left you."

He flinched at the last one. Yes, that was the crux of the issue for him, she was sure of it. His mother had left him, and she'd done the same.

"It was a mistake, and I was relieved when you caught me. If you'll still have me, I swear I won't leave again." That was the honest truth. It was why she'd had Tal brand her flesh with his name. She needed to prove her commitment. She drew a breath. It was odd how facing her imminent death in a flaming battleship was easier than what she had to ask next. "Am I still your female?"

Lundric's irises turned violet, and something in his shoulders relaxed. "Always," he growled, reaching for her.

"Wait, wait." She skittered back out of his reach. "I want to show you something."

He frowned. "What is it?"

She rotated slowly, giving him the view of his name tattooed at the base of her spine between the two dimples on the back of her pelvis.

Lundric said nothing, and she waited, legs trembling, breath rasping in her chest. She dared to look over her shoulder. Her warrior had his fist stuffed in his mouth, and his face had flushed a deep purple.

"Do you like it? I know this isn't the way Zandians show ownership, but it's the way humans are marked by their masters." She touched the barcode at her nape, put there at birth by her first Ocretion master.

"I have this, too, if you want to mark me in the Zandian way." Her hand shook as she drew out the piercing gun Lily had lent her. "But I understand if you don't want to mate me anymore. Or yet. Or whatever."

Zander dropped his fist away from his mouth and scrubbed a hand across his face. "Take down your hair."

The deep command surprised her, but her nipples stiffened. She heard the promise of retribution and sex in the roughness of his tone. She pulled her hair from the thread gathering it behind her.

"The braids, too."

She unwound the small braids holding the hair back from her face, letting it all cascade to her shoulders in thick waves.

"This is how you'll come to me, always." Lundric advanced, a predatory tension to his prowl. "I'm glad you've become inured to the idea of mating me, because I never intended to let you go, Cambry."

His words should have offended her, but instead they made her heart sing, her pulse race with anticipation of his touch. She wanted to launch herself at him but forced herself to remain still. To allow him to claim her in whatever way he chose.

"Do you know where a Zandian pierces his female?" Lundric's horns were stiff and thick, tilting toward her. She longed to suck one deep into her mouth.

"N-not exactly. Her ears?" Her breathy voice sounded over the scrape of his exhale above her. She'd seen the glint of crystals in Lily's ears.

He pinched both her nipples and pulled. "Anywhere he likes," he said darkly. "The ears show all others she is mated. But he marks her nipples and clit to claim the most intimate parts belonging to only him."

A thrum of energy pulsed between her legs. Would he really pierce her there?

"Interlace your fingers on the top of your head."

She obeyed. He picked up the piercing gun and shook out the tiny bag filled with Zandian crystal jewels that had come from Prince Zander, himself. They were meant for Rok and Lily, but Lily promised their mating ceremony was complete and she and Lundric were welcome to use anything that was left.

Lundric fit a stud into the gun. His lids drooped as he slid one nipple between the jaws. "Don't move, Cambry."

She held her breath.

Lundric pulled the trigger, and the stud punched through her nipple, causing her to cry out. Lundric swallowed her cry with a kiss, the gun clattering to the floor as his arm circled her waist and his hand cradled the back of her head.

He kissed her with an open mouth, tongue sweeping against the seam of her lips, mimicking the motion of his hips against her belly as he plunged it in and out of her mouth. When he pulled away, his expression was soft. He cupped her chin. "Good girl," he murmured. "Are you all right?"

She nodded.

He screwed the cap onto the open end of the stud then picked up the gun and loaded it with a second stud. "You're taking a lot of pain for me tonight, little female." There was pride in his tone.

"Anything you ask of me," she whispered, legs still trembling.

He fitted the gun over her other nipple and shot the stud through. She bit her lip against the cry it drew from her and tasted a drop of blood.

Lundric's nostrils flared as if he smelled it. He attached the end crystal onto the stud then sucked her lower lip into his mouth in another long kiss. "Hold your hair up," he rasped when he pulled away.

She lifted her hair back from her face, and he pierced her earlobes, sucking each into his mouth first.

"One more. Lie on the bed and spread your legs."

Her heart thumped. He'd been serious about piercing her clit. She bit back the protests and questions that sprang to the tip of her tongue. She had to show Lundric her trust. This ritual held meaning to his species, and she wished to honor it.

~.~

Lundric's cock was ready to explode. Nothing could be more beautiful than the sight of Cambry lying back on the cot with her knees open. Her breath came in quick pants, lifting and lowering her beautiful peach-tipped breasts.

He fit another stud in the piercing gun and dropped to his knees in front of the cot, unable to resist giving her a bit of pleasure first. He parted her labia and drank in the sight of her pretty little flower. "Who does this pussy belong to?"

"You, Lundric." She didn't even hesitate.

"That's right," he growled and lowered his head between her knees. He traced his tongue along the inside of her innermost lips, making her jerk and gasp. The fresh tattoo on her back must be rasping against the cot, but she didn't complain. She grasped his horns, and he groaned, cock swelling painfully against his uniform pants.

He suctioned his lips over her clit, sucking hard. She squeezed both his horns, rubbing her thumbs over the tips as she pumped.

Somehow, he mustered enough willpower to pull away. He picked up the piercing gun. "I'm going to pierce the hood, not the actual clitoris." He pinched the flesh between two fingers.

She jerked and moaned at his handling of her most sensitive bundle of nerves.

He inserted the flesh between the jaws of the gun and pulled the trigger, sending a horizontal bar through the hood. He affixed the end crystal and sat back to admire his handiwork. "Beautiful," he murmured. "You're a Zandian now."

"Yes," she murmured, looking half-drunk. Her cheeks had flushed a charming shade of pink.

"No sex until it heals," he announced, chuckling at the shocked outrage on her face. "Don't worry, little human, I can still *veck* your ass."

A wariness crept back into her demeanor, but she sat up and arranged herself on her hands and knees on the cot.

Her willingness to give herself any way he demanded moved him. The power she'd given him affected him more than any drug, more than any crystal, more than sunlight itself.

He stood and plucked her from her place on the cot, sitting and arranging her over his knees. "A spanking first. For scaring the *veck* out of me in that battle."

Again, no protest from his female, although she'd always enjoyed her spankings. He ran his hand over her smooth skin, noting the faint marks still there from the whipping he'd given her the week before. "Does this still hurt?"

"No. My skin marks easily because I'm a redhead, that's all." She struck a reassuring tone, like she was afraid he might hold back.

"Good. Because I love spanking this ass, especially now that it has my name tattooed above it." He began a steady pace of slaps, watching her ivory skin turn light pink then dusky rose. He spanked until she squirmed and her breath quickened, then he leaned over and planted a kiss on each cheek. "Sweet little human."

He reached for the bottle of oil and rubbed it all over her reddened ass, giving it a few more slaps to show her how much more it could sting. "On your knees, beautiful," he murmured, helping her into position on the bed.

He coated his cock with the oil and massaged a generous amount into her anus. "Open for me." He pushed the head of his dick against her back entrance and held a steady pressure until she relaxed for him. "Good girl." He wedged his cock into her tight hole and gripped her nape as he eased in.

Her back bowed, and she panted, the tiny mewls on her exhales driving him mad. "You look so *vecking* beautiful like this."

Her laugh came out in a sob, and his cock drove deeper, prying her open.

"Do you like having my cock in your ass, Cambry?" He eased back and slid in once more, going slowly because he recognized how challenging the position was for her, felt the tremble of her body, and heard the whoosh of her breaths as she worked to accommodate him.

He gave a low laugh as he repeated the slow pump. "You don't know whether to say *yes* or *no*, do you, little female? You know I'll give you pleasure, but I'm also going to work you hard for it, aren't I?"

She gave a long, wavering moan.

"Am I right?"

"Yes," she whispered.

"You're a good girl to take my cock like this. I won't ask for it every time. Maybe I'll reserve it for when you require punishment."

"Lundric."

He heard the tremor in her voice, the terrified need. He reached around and plunged two fingers into her pussy, careful not to hit the fresh piercing with the heel of his hand. "Is that better, baby?"

"Oh stars, yes. Lundric, please?"

He bumped her ass in short thrusts that sent her farther onto his thrusting fingers.

"Lundric, oh please, oh please, oh please? *Lundric!*"

"I *vecking* love it when you beg, beautiful girl." He gripped her hair with his free hand and pulled her head back. "Who gives you pleasure, baby?"

"Lundric! Lundric does!"

His thighs flexed and control fled. "Who do you belong to?"

"You! I belong to you! Oh please, Lundric, I have to come!"

He closed his eyes and allowed his climax to sweep through him, thrusting deeper into her ass and staying as he continued to pump his fingers. "Come, little human. Come now."

Her orgasm shook her entire body, and she collapsed forward onto her belly on the cot. He followed her down, his cock still buried in her ass, fingers coated in her juices as her muscles clamped down on them.

He hovered over her trembling body, drinking in her scent, savoring the rightness of their position. He had his female. Cambry was his—forever.

"Lundric," she murmured as he eased out. Her blissed-out voice sounded far away.

"Yes, baby?"

"I don't know how I got so lucky to be your mate."

He kissed her neck, bit the shell of her ear. "I love you, little female. I'm going to take care of you. Provide for you. Protect you. Make you happy. I swear it on all the crystals of Zandia."

She rolled to her side to gaze up at him, cupping his cheek with her hand. "What does a Zandian female promise to her mate?"

His heart filled in a rush of warmth. "Never to leave," he choked.

Her big brown eyes were liquid pools of warmth as she lifted her lips for a kiss. "I love you," she murmured, just before he claimed her mouth for what he intended to make the most thorough kiss of her life.

CHAPTER NINE

Cambry fidgeted with the white Zandian guard's uniform she'd opted to wear instead of her usual tunic and leggings.

"You look beautiful." Lundric's voice was gruff.

She'd worn her hair down for him because she loved the way he stared at her when she did—as if he never wanted to look away.

He took her hand in his larger palm and led her off the battleship into a cool, climate-controlled dock that was part of Prince Zander's palatial pod.

She drew in a breath, throwing back her shoulders and lifting her chin, determined not to embarrass Lundric, who had brought her to meet his ruler, Prince Zander.

Guards stood inside the door, but they merely nodded as Lundric strode past them.

Her jaw dropped. The palatial pod was exquisite. The walls were made of some kind of natural plaster, each in its own beautiful color. Periwinkle blue, pale yellow, crimson. Even the corridor walls glowed with color. Natural light streamed in everywhere—from windows and skylights, amplified with the Zandian crystals like the one Lundric had installed on their pod. Opulent, woven rugs covered the floors, and everything seemed to be made of natural substances—hard marble, stone, wood. She wondered if it had all come from Zandia.

If so, then Zandia really *was* the promised land Lily had described to the refugees.

"This is the Great Hall," Lundric murmured, bringing her into a huge room with vaulted ceilings. A young man dressed in white sat on a raised chair —no, a throne—and a line of Zandians queued up to speak to him.

Lundric led her to the line. "Once a week, Prince Zander's pod is open to any Zandian. They may come and use the crystal light bath and eat the weekly meal with him. He sits in here to hear their requests or complaints. To resolve any disputes, we do not rely on the Ocretion justice system but employ one of our own."

She swallowed. "Does Prince Zander know about...what I did?"

Lundric nodded. "Yes. He knows you stole a ship and tried to escape. He also knows you fought with his warriors to defend the pod."

"Am I here to answer for it?"

Lundric's hesitation didn't put her mind at ease. "We all answer to Prince Zander. He knows you have been punished and that my trust in you has been restored."

Her hand grew clammy in Lundric's palm. He squeezed it. "I'll be right here beside you."

She drew on the strength from Lundric. For the first time, she faced a form of authority she didn't hate. Didn't wish to rebel against or hold herself separate from. It was a new feeling, the desire to impress, to be accepted.

The line moved up, each Zandian having his or her allotted time with the ruler. From what she could tell, they were mostly older beings. She wondered how many young Zandians were left in the galaxy.

When their turn came, Lundric led her forward and bowed low.

She curtsied.

"My lord, may I present my mate, Cambry?"

She dragged her gaze up to rest on the neckline of his finely woven tunic, not sure if looking him in the face was allowed.

He appeared to be around the same age as Lundric and was handsome in his own way. "Cambry. The female who stole my best guard's heart."

"I prefer to think I earned it, my lord." As soon as the words left her mouth, she regretted them. Would he think her too sassy?

The corners of his lips twitched. "Stealing is part of your repertoire, though, is it not?"

Her face heated. "My lord, I deeply regret stealing your battleship. I promise it will never happen again." She dared another glance at his face.

He studied her with a penetrating gaze. "I understand you are a capable pilot, Cambry, and that you are willing to serve in my army."

"Yes, my lord."

"Your service is welcome, as is your union with Lundric. I trust your bond with him will keep you loyal."

A rush of relief made her blink rapidly. She dropped another curtsy. "Thank you, my lord."

"My mate is looking forward to meeting you. There aren't many females around here. Lundric will introduce you before the evening meal."

She curtsied once more, sensing the dismissal, and Lundric led her out of the Great Hall. They didn't make it far, though. He pushed her up against the wall in the corridor, grinding a sizeable erection against her belly.

"Do you know how hard it makes me to present you as my mate here?"

She laughed, low and husky, and squeezed his erection through his pants. "I'm getting a hint."

Footsteps sounded down the hallway, and Lundric pulled back just before a large Zandian passed them, an unconscious dark-haired human female draped over his shoulder.

She tensed, fingers automatically seeking the dagger Lundric had given her.

Lundric dropped a restraining hand on her shoulder. "Daneth, who is that?"

The Zandian didn't stop, but he shifted the female on his shoulder. "A human. For breeding."

Lundric winced. "Daneth is our resident physician, charged with the restoration of our species," he explained as the doctor passed them with his inert cargo. To Daneth, Lundric said, "You're not breeding her against her will, though, *right*?"

The Zandian seemed to catch Lundric's warning tone because he finally stopped walking and turned back, looking from Lundric to her, understanding dawning on his expression. "Oh. Welcome to the pod, Cambry. No, not against the female's will. Prince Zander has recently forbidden Zandian owner-ship of slaves of any species. If she chooses not to participate in my experi-ment, I will find another place for her. But my program selected this particular female as the best possible surrogate for the frozen Zandian eggs I plan to fertilize *in vitro*."

Lundric winced again. "Uh, glad to hear it. Thank you, Daneth. Good luck."

"Thank you. And congratulations on your recent mating. If you'd like, I can run both your genes through my program to—"

"No thanks," Lundric cut him off, pulling her hand to lead her in the oppo-site direction. As soon as they were alone again, he stopped and leaned his forehead against hers. "Oh stars. Please tell me that didn't worry you."

She giggled. "Only a little. Do you really think that female will be all right?"

"Zandians have honor. Daneth's crazy program is what brought Prince Zander to Lamira, his human mate, so it can't be too far off."

"Well, he did seem crazy, but I believe a Zandian master would be far better than an Ocretion one, no matter the circumstances. Look how much better off all the refugees are now."

"You really do believe that now?"

"Yes."

"You haven't just joined the fight for me?"

She sucked on her lower lip. "I go where you go. I fight where you fight. I'm your female. So, yes, I joined the fight for you. But I also think Zandia is worth fighting for. And I've come to trust in Zandian leadership. Aligning with Zandians is a good choice for any human. For my brother. For the others on the pod. Probably for that female, too."

Lundric's shoulders relaxed, tension dissolving from his face. He scooped her up to straddle his waist. "I'm going to go practice my own Zandian breeding study with a human right now," he growled. His hands cupped her ass, squeezing.

She giggled and tightened her thighs around his waist, her pussy moistening. "Yes, we'd better start practicing."

He carried her down the corridor and put his hand against a panel, which caused a door to swish open. "I will need every available hour to study this little human body." He tossed her onto a floating oval sleepdisk draped in blue spidersilk. "I'd better get started right away."

Her lids lowered as she watched her handsome warrior crawl up over her, horns erect, irises turning violet.

She spread her arms wide. "Here I am. Yours to study."

He pounced over her and pinned her wrists above her head. "Yes, mine." He rubbed his horns across her neck. "Mine to pleasure."

She arched into her warrior's touch, a purr of contentment in her throat, her heart full to the brim with Lundric. "Thank you, Lundric," she whispered as he sucked her neck.

"For what?" he murmured against her skin, his hands roaming under her uniform top.

"For making me yours."

"You've always been mine." He cupped her mound, rubbing the piercing with the heel of his hand. "It just took you a while to recognize it."

Her eyes watered with love. "Well, thank you for showing me the way."

He moved between her legs, drawing down her pants and spreading her thighs. "Was this the way?" He lowered his head and licked into her.

She reached for his horns, already breathless. "Yes," she panted. "I believe it was…"

THE END

Thank you for reading *His Human Rebel!* The books seems to be alternating between heavy non-con and lighter D/s (through no design on my part—it's just what the characters dictate). If you missed the non-con in this one, stay tuned for *His Human Vessel,* which will be heavy on the breeding and medical BDSM themes! Some of you are wondering how I can make Daneth sympathetic as a hero. Read **His Human Vessel** to see if I succeed (turn the page for an excerpt)!

If you're not on my newsletter list, please sign up! You'll get free books, bonus scenes, discounts, and my thoughts on D/s in books and the bedroom. <u>You can sign up here.</u>

FROM THE AUTHOR

Thank you for reading *The Zandian Masters books 1-4*! If you enjoyed this anthology, I would really appreciate it if you would leave a review. Your reviews are invaluable to indie authors in marketing books so we can keep book prices down.

HIS HUMAN VESSEL - EXCERPT

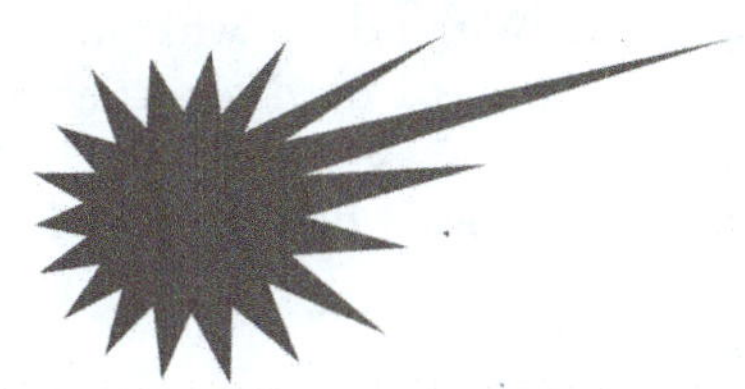

The restraints around Bayla's wrists kept her from rubbing her nose.

In dim awareness, she tried to move her hand again to relieve the itch, but it caught, yanked against an unyielding strap.

With a sharp inhale, she jerked fully awake as the memory of the huge horned alien with an injector gun rushed back. He'd shown up at the fertility farm where she and sixty other human females had been enslaved and bought her following a brief inspection. Then, without a word to her, he'd pressed the device to her neck, and everything had gone black.

She blinked at the light and took in her situation. She was naked, strapped down to an examination table by leather cuffs. The alien, who was not an Ocretion, the species who'd taken over Earth and enslaved all humans, wore a white lab coat and stood near a window with his back to her. This being was taller than humans or Ocretions, and he had purple-hued skin and eyes. He spared a glance over his shoulder at her sudden movement then turned back to what he was doing.

His silent treatment irritated the hell out of her. Did he not speak Ocretion? No, he must. She'd heard him speaking to the fertility farm slave masters when he'd bought her.

She licked her dry lips. "What are you doing with me?" Her voice cracked from lack of use.

The alien turned and walked to her side, a needle in his hand.

She flinched when he approached, but, with the restraints, couldn't move. "Did you hear me? Can you tell me what's going on?"

He ignored her and pinched the skin at the crease of her elbow, inserting the needle then drawing a vial of blood.

She looked away, her stomach queasy. Although she'd been bred and raised for nothing more than this purpose—to have her body poked and prodded, inseminated and vacated over and over again, she still hadn't grown used to it.

She attempted to distract her mind as he fit a second vial to the tube. The lab room was small but bright. The window was unusual—she wasn't sure she'd ever seen one like it. It didn't let in much light, but a skylight in the ceiling somehow magnified sunlight through a crystalline structure, casting beams throughout the room. In fact, there didn't appear to be any artificial light in use at all.

Having spent most of her life in a metal box with no natural light, she found it a profound improvement. It would be almost cheerful if she weren't naked and strapped to a table. With no clue what was going to happen to her.

"Where are we? How long was I out?" she tried again, but still the alien ignored her.

He walked away, and she allowed herself to look at her arm, now neatly bandaged.

"Hello? Can you hear me?"

He turned. Despite the alien features, she found him exceptionally handsome, but that was probably the fertility drugs talking. He was tall and broad-shouldered. His skin was purple-ish peach and smooth, his hairless jaw square. The horns on the top of his head gave him a rugged appearance.

"Is it customary where you came from for a slave to speak before she is spoken to?" He sounded more curious than angry.

A flush of something foreign rippled through her at his rebuke. She couldn't be embarrassed, could she? Did she really care what this horned alien thought?

She kicked up her chin. "Normally, I am informed immediately what is expected of me," she said primly, as if she lived to serve her masters.

"Ah. I see. Very well. I shall inform you. I am Daneth, master physician for the Prince of Zandia. You will call me *Master.* You will maintain silence unless I speak directly to you, especially if others are in our midst."

She feigned remorse and lowered her eyes. "Yes, Master. What will Master use me for?"

"Our species lacks females of breeding age. I purchased you as a vessel to implant and grow a Zandian young."

The familiar wave of nausea and dread filled her. *Not another pregnancy.* She couldn't bear to have another baby taken from her arms. Of course, this one would be an alien, so maybe it wouldn't hurt so much. She hoped conception would be a long and difficult process. She needed time to steel herself for another loss.

"In addition to your silence, I expect your complete obedience and respect. Any defiance will be immediately punished."

It wasn't anything new. Every slave master demanded the same, and yet, from him, it sounded halfway exciting. Perhaps that was only because she was naked and immobilized when he gave the pronouncement. What orders would she have to obey?

"Will I be sexually serving you?"

The doctor's brows flew up, and he dropped the test tube he'd been shaking. It rolled under her bed.

Had she flustered him?

He bent to pick it up, and, when he stood, he'd composed his face. "That won't be nec—" His eyes fell on her mouth and stayed there. She swore his horns stiffened and tilted in her direction. He cleared his throat. "No." His voice sounded thick.

Her gaze dropped to his crotch, where the bulge of his cock seemed to grow for her.

When he noticed her focus, annoyance flashed over his face and his shoulders stiffened. He turned back to the counter, where he appeared to be running tests on her blood samples.

So. Her hot alien master found her attractive. To her surprise, that pleased her. Was it because he didn't seem to welcome the attraction? For the first time, she had a bit of leverage on a master. He may not want to act on his attraction, but, as a breeder, she'd been trained to satisfy, and she had no doubt she'd get him to cave.

Based on the way her nipples stood up as she contemplated her seduction, she doubted pleasing him would be much of a hardship.

He muttered to himself in what sounded like a voice log of her test results. "Estrodial, 25 to 75 picograms per milliliter, progesterone..."

"Will I sleep in your bed?" She began her cock-tease.

He whirled, his skin turning a darker purple. When his gaze fell on her erect nipples, he blinked rapidly. He referenced the cuff he wore on his arm, which had some kind of readout. "That idea arouses you?"

What did that cuff tell him? She hated having her game turned back on her. She shrugged, affecting cool indifference. "Not particularly."

He tilted his head, studying her. She didn't love his attention, this time, though, because it was definitely more curious scientist than interested male. "I understand humans have a different sense of truth than my species, but this is your first and only warning. I will punish every lie."

Something tightened in her belly and loosened between her legs. Heat uncoiled there, swirling and pulsing.

READ HIS HUMAN VESSEL
READ ZANDIAN MASTERS BOOKS 5-8

READ THE ENTIRE ZANDIAN MASTERS SERIES

His Human Slave (Book 1)

COLLARED AND CAGED, HIS HUMAN SLAVE AWAITS HER TRAINING.

Zander, the alien warrior prince intent on recovering his planet, needs a mate. While he would never choose a human of his own accord, his physician's gene-matching program selected Lamira's DNA as the best possible match with his own. Now he must teach the beautiful slave to yield to his will, accept his discipline and learn to serve him as her one true master.

Lamira has hidden her claircognizance from the Ocretions, as aberrant traits in human slaves are punished by death. When she's bought by a Zandian prince for breeding and kept by his side at all times, she finds it increasingly harder to hide. His humiliating punishments and dominance awake a powerful lust in her, which he tracks with a monitoring device on her arousal rate. But when she begins to care for the huge, demanding alien, she must choose between preserving her own life and revealing her secret to save his.

His Human Prisoner (Book 2)

HE DIDN'T BELIEVE IN DESTINY—UNTIL HE MET HER.

When a beautiful human slave steals Rok's ship and leaves him stranded on an abandoned planet, he's furious. Discovering her sister is the mate to the prince of his species only makes him more determined to find her and punish her thoroughly for her crimes. Yet when he captures her, he finds her impossible to resist. Punishment becomes exquisite pleasure as he teaches her to submit.

Lily's attraction to the huge Zandian warrior unnerves her. She's never been moved by a male, nor interested in sex before, but Rok coaxes every bit of emotion out of her as he demands her complete surrender. But he intends to turn her over to the authorities, which will mean her certain death. She must find a way to escape the handsome alien before she loses her life—or worse—her heart.

Training His Human

"YOUR OBEDIENCE TRAINING BEGINS TODAY."

Seke has no interest in owning or training a slave. Not even Leora, the beautiful human who had captivated his thoughts and fantasies since her arrival on their pod. As the Zandian Master of Arms, he has a war to plan and new troops to train. He can't be tempted by the breathtaking human slave, who, according to Prince Zander, grows aroused by punishment. Yet he can't allow another male to bring her to heel either. Not his Leora.

In all her lifetime as a slave, Leora might have submitted in body, but never in mind. But the prince has given her to the huge, scarred warrior, Seke, for punishment and she finds he has unexpected ways of bending her to his will. Ways that leave her trembling and half-mad with desire. But her new master is unwilling to take a new mate, and she fears that once he deems her training complete, he will set her aside, leaving her heart in pieces.

His Human Rebel

CONSCRIPTED BY AN ALIEN ARMY, SHE PLOTS HER ESCAPE...

Cambry doesn't believe the aliens' propaganda for one minute. The Zandians may have saved her from one death, but they planned to send her to another. She bides her time, waiting for her chance to get away and find her brother, enslaved by a different species. The only thing she didn't count on was Lundric, the tempting Zandian warrior who, for some reason, decided she was his female.

Lundric knew the fierce little rebel Cambry belonged to him the moment he saw her toss that auburn hair in defiance. He knows she hasn't accepted him or the Zandian's cause, but he vows to win her, no matter what it takes. But when Cambry steals a ship and attempts to escape, even his harshest punishment may not restore the trust between them.

His Human Vessel

HE PURCHASED HER TO BEAR A CHILD...HE WILL ALSO OWN HER SUBMISSION.

Bayla's destiny had been set from the beginning. Her body would be used for sex and breeding. Nothing changed when the sexy Zandian doctor purchased her from the baby farm and brought her to his examination room.

Nothing. And *everything.*

Daneth has always lived in his head, letting science govern his thoughts and choices. Having Bayla in his lab shouldn't change that, but somehow the submissive human female gets under his skin. No matter how harshly he punishes her, she responds to his touch with passion, sparking a lust that threatens to distract him from his plans.

When Bayla learns Daneth has a weakness for her, she presses her advantage, but she has no desire to bear yet another child and have it taken from her arms. If only she could figure out how to stay with the dominant alien doctor but avoid the pregnancy...

Her Mate and Master

"I'm your master. When I give you an order, you obey."

Talia didn't escape her slave master only to be shackled again. Not even by a sexy male built of solid muscle who does wicked things with his fingers and tongue. Not even one of her own species who says he knows her father—the father she doesn't remember.

No, she isn't about to trust Tomis, the Zandian warrior who rescues her from the Finn, especially after he sets her body on fire with a series of humiliating punishments. But it's breeding season on Zandia and the crystals activate her hormones, making her desperate for satisfaction, even at the hands of the arrogant warrior bent on saving both her and his species.

Zandian Pet

"ON YOUR KNEES, PET."

Taramina could survive slavery, even as a pet in Prium's Intergalactic Emporium. She always knew she'd escape.

She just didn't know escape would come in the form of a powerful handsome male of her own species. Especially one whose rough handling incites a fever in her she hasn't felt before.

But she intends to make a fresh start, which means severing ties with the dominant Zandian who once held her collar and a leash. The male who knows just how to master her.

No, she can't be his pet. Not after what she's been through.

So why does she keep coming back for more?

His Human Possession (Book 8)
He doesn't want her to offer.

He prefers to take. Demand. Conquer.

Leti only intended to seduce the alien warrior. Because the game was to survive.

Ingratiate herself to a new master.

She never thought she'd fall for the giant horned warrior who rescued her from slavery.

But it's easy to make him lose control. All she has to do is tempt him, and his need to master her takes over.

Paal's species battle to take back their planet.

All of their futures dangle by a thread.

Leti and Paal should cling together as they fight for freedom, but her every seduction drives a wedge between them. And when he learns her secret, it just may be the end.

Their Zandian Mate

Three Zandian warriors. One female assigned for reconditioning.
They'll punish.
Demand.
Claim.
Teach.